MARY WOLLSTONECRAFT SHELLEY

FRANKENSTEIN
OR
THE MODERN PROMETHEUS

WITH ESSAYS IN CRITICISM

Annotated with Critical Introduction

by Kim Il-Yeong

Shinasa

CONTENTS

CRITICAL INTRODUCTION

◉ 작품의 에디션 ·· 7
I. 매리 셸리(Mary Shelley)의 생애 ······················ 8
II. 작품의 배경 ·· 13
  ◉ 시대적 배경 ··· 13
  ◉ 창작 배경 ·· 14
III. 작품 분석 ·· 16
  ◉ 영향을 미친 문학 작품 ································· 16
  ◉ 작품 구조 ·· 18
  ◉ 작품의 주제 ··· 19

Preface ··· 27

TEXT OF *FRANKENSTEIN OR THE MODERN PROMETHEUS*

Letter I ·· 33
Letter II ··· 38
Letter III ·· 43
Letter IV ··· 44
Chapter I ·· 55
Chapter II ··· 61
Chapter III ·· 70
Chapter IV ·· 79
Chapter V ·· 89
Chapter VI ·· 97

Chapter VII 107

Chapter VIII 119

Chapter IX 130

Chapter X 138

Chapter XI 147

Chapter XII 157

Chapter XIII 164

Chapter XIV 172

Chapter XV 179

Chapter XVI 189

Chapter XVII 200

Chapter XVIII 207

Chapter XIX 219

Chapter XX 230

Chapter XXI 242

Chapter XXII 255

Chapter XXIII 268

Chapter XXIV 277

ESSAYS IN CRITICISM 313

CRITICAL INTRODUCTION

◉ 작품의 에디션

이 작품은 3개의 권(Volume)으로 나뉘어져 익명으로 런던의 한 출판
사에 의해 1818년에 처음으로 출판되었다. 하지만 이 작품의 집필을 적
극 권장한 남편 퍼시 셸리(Percy Shelley)가 1822년 세상을 떠나자, 매리 셸
리(Mary Shelley)는 이 소설이 탄생하게 된 배경을 설명하는 introduction과
함께 작품의 내용의 일부분을 수정하여 1831년 1권(volume)으로 구성된
새로운 에디션을 내놓는다.

1818년 에디션과 새 에디션의 차이는 크게 보아 주인공 프랑켄스타인
(Frankenstein)과 관련된 것들이다. 새 에디션에서 매리는 남편 셸리의 모
습을 연상시키는 프랑켄스타인을 보다 이상주의자로 그림으로써, 그에
게 내려졌던 도덕적 비난을 완화하고자
하였으며, 자신의 외모를 많이 닮은 프랑
켄스타인의 아내 엘리자베스(Elizabeth)에
게는 좀 더 유순하고 배려 깊은 집안의
천사 이미지를 부여하였다.

또한 1818년 에디션에는 엘리자베스가
프랑켄스타인의 고모의 딸, 즉 그의 고
종 사촌 동생으로 설정되어 있었지만, 근
친상간에 대한 대중의 비난을 피하기 위
해서인지, 1831년 에디션에서 엘리자베스
는 전쟁 중에 목숨을 잃은 밀라노 귀족
의 고아가 된 딸(밀라노 귀족의 아내이
자 엘리자베스의 어머니는 엘리자베스
를 낳다가 목숨을 잃은 것으로 되어있어,

『프랑켄스타인』 1831년 판 표지그림

매리를 낳고 곧이어 세상을 떠난 매리의 어머니 울스톤크라프트((Mary Wollstonecraft)를 떠올리게 한다)로 그려지고 있다. 또한 새 에디션에는 사회 약자에 대한 동정심이나 배려하는 마음의 중요성을 좀 더 강조하였으며, 결국은 모든 것이 신의 섭리에 따라 결정된다는 기독교적인 신념을 담아내었다.

    * 본 주석본은 1831년 에디션을 사용하고 있다.

I. 매리 셸리(Mary Shelley)의 생애

    매리 셸리는 1797년 8월 30일 영국의 수도 런던에서 태어났다. 그녀의 아버지는 무정부주의자이자 당시 영국의 급진주의자들의 중심역할을 하며, 영국 낭만주의의 사상적 토대를 마련한 고드윈(William Godwin)이었으며, 그녀의 어머니는 여성 스스로가 독자적으로 사고하고 행동하기를 촉구하는 『여성의 권리에 대한 옹호』(A Vindication of the Rights of Woman, 1798)라는 저서를 남긴, 가히 영국 최초의 본격적인 여성주의자라고 불릴 수 있는 울스톤크라프트였다. 하지만 매리의 삶은 처음부터 순탄하지만은 않았다. 그녀의 어머니 울스톤크라프트는 매리를 낳은 지 열흘 후, 산욕열로 세상을 떠났기 때문이다.

    가정부이자 유모였던 루이자 존스(Louisa Jones)의 손에 자랐던 매리의 어린 시절은 그리 만족스럽지 못하였다.

Wollstonecraft(1759–1797)

어머니의 사랑 없이 살아가야만 하였던 매
리는 아버지의 사랑을 받으면서도 고독한
삶을 피할 수 없었던 것이다. 그러다 그녀
의 아버지 고드윈이 1801년 전 남편에게서
얻은 두 명의 자식을 데리고 살던 크레어몽
(Mary Jane Clairmont)과 결혼을 하게 되자,
매리의 상황은 더욱 나빠지게 되었다. 새
아내를 얻은 고드윈의 부부사이는 좋았지
만 상대적으로 매리는 아버지의 사랑을 덜
누리게 되었기 때문이다.

William Godwin(1756–1836)

　결혼 후 고드윈은 출판사를 운영하면
서 수입을 더 늘리고자 어린이용 책과 문
구류 등을 팔았다. 하지만 그의 기대와는 달리 별다른 소득을 얻을 수 없
었고, 오히려 많은 빚을 지게 되는 상황에 처하게 되었다. 이런 가운데서
도 고드윈은 자식들의 교육에는 상당한 열의를 보였던 것 같다. 매리에
게 정식 교육을 많이 시키지는 않았지만 고드윈은 광범위한 분야를 직접
가르쳤고, 경우에 따라서는 가정교사를 두
어 그녀의 공부를 지도하게 하였다. 심지어
고드윈은 자신의 집을 수시로 방문하던 당
시 사상가들이나 시인들, 가령 당시 영국의
대표적인 낭만주의 시인인 코울리지(Samuel
Taylor Coleridge)와 같은 시인을 만날 수 있는
기회를 자식들에게 주었던 것이다. 특히 매
리에 대한 교육은 고드윈의 다른 아이들의
교육과는 사뭇 달랐다. 매리는 어렸을 때부
터 고드윈이 직접 쓴 수많은 아동용 도서를
접할 수 있었으며, 1812년에는 고드윈처럼 급

Samuel T. Coleridge(1772–1834)

Percy Bysshe Shelley (1792–1822)

진주의자였던 백스터(William Baxter)의 집에 매리를 보내 매리의 사상의 폭을 넓혀주었기 때문이다.

그녀의 생애에 있어 획기적인 사건은 영국의 대표적인 낭만주의 시인 셸리(Percy Bysshe Shelley)와의 만남이었다. 그녀의 아버지의 사상을 흠모하여 고드윈의 집을 자주 찾았던 시인 셸리는 자연스럽게 고드윈의 딸 매리를 접할 수 있었으며, 이내 곧 이들 사이에는 사랑의 불꽃이 일어났다. 하지만 이들의 사랑의 행로는 순탄하지, 아니 순탄할 수가 없었다. 고드윈은 자신의 딸 매리가 시인 셸리와 만나는 것을 탐탁지 않게 여겼고, 셸리 자신은 1811년 해리엇 웨스트브룩 (Harriet Westbrook)와 이미 혼인한 몸이었기 때문이었다. 그러나 매리와 셸리는 자신들만의 사랑을 키워가며, 1814년 7월 프랑스로 사랑의 도피 여행을 떠나게 된다. 이곳에서 이들은 당나귀와 마차를 이용해서 스위스, 독일에까지 가나, 결국 자금 부족으로 다시 영국으로 귀환하게 된다.

영국으로 돌아왔을 때 이들의 상황은 녹녹치 않았다. 이때 셸리의 아이를 임신하고 있었던 매리는 자신과 셸리와의 관계를 인정하지 않으려는 아버지 고드윈을 피해 다른 곳에 거처를 정해 경제적 어려움 속에서 생활할 수밖에 없었기 때문이다. 그러다 1815년 3월 매리는 예정일 보다 두 달이나 먼저 태어난 아기의 죽음을 맞이하게 된다. 프랑켄스타인이 만든 괴물처럼 이름조차 지어주지 못한 아기의 죽음으로 한동안 매리는 우울증에 시달렸으며, 시신이 되어 차가워진 아이의 몸을 불 앞에서 비벼 도로 살려내는 꿈을 꾸곤 하였다고한다 (죽은 이를 살려내고 싶은 그녀의 욕망이 바로 시체에게 생명을 불어넣는 시도를 한 프랑켄스타인을 연상시킨다). 하지만 매리는 곧 다시 임신을 하게 되었고, 조부의 임종으로 상당한 유산을 물려받게 된 셸리와 함께 좀 더 나은 환경으로 이주하여, 그곳에서 자신의 아버지의 이름을 딴 둘째 아이 윌리엄을 1816년 1월에 출산하게 된다.

1816년은 매리의 이름을 온 세상에 알리는 획기적인 일이 벌어지던 해였다. 이해 5월 시인 셸리와 매리는 제네바(Geneva) 호수 근처에 있는 빌라를 임대해 같이 시간을 보내게 되는데, 이때 같이 있던 시인 바이런의 제안에 따라 초자연적인 소재의 이야기를 각자 지어내 보기로 한 결과, 매리는 자신의 걸작 『프랑켄스타인』(frankenstein)을 구상하게 되었기 때문이다.

스위스에서 이렇게 지낸 후 다시 영국으로 돌아온 매리와 셸리는 충격적인 사건을 맞이하게 된다. 1816년 12월 셸리의 처 헤리엣이 하이드 파크(Hyde Park)에 있는 호수에 투신하여 자살한 것이다. 이에 헤리엣과 셸리 사이에서 난 두 아이의 양육권을 얻어내기 위해 매리와 셸리는 변호사의 권고에 따라 그해 12월 30일 정식 결혼식을 올리지만, 이들의 예상과는 달리 그 다음해인 1817년 3월 법정은 셸리에게 아이에 대한 양육권을 주지 않았다.

1818년 1월 『프랑켄스타인』을 익명으로 출판한 후, 매리는 그해 3월 건강 악화와 채무에 시달려 이태리로 떠나게 된다. 하지만 매리에게 이태리에서의 삶은 평탄치 않았다. 그녀는 자신의 두 아이를 모두 잃었기 때문이다. 1818년 9월에는 클라라(Clara)를, 1819년에는 윌리엄을 잃어, 매리는 심한 우울증에 빠지게 되었는데, 1819년 11월 매리의 4번째 아이인 플로렌스(Percy Florence)의 탄생으로 어느 정도 힘을 얻긴 하였지만, 아이들의 죽음은 매리에게는 평생의 후유증으로 남게 되었다.

이런 개인적인 불운에도 불구하고 이태리에서 매리는 왕성한 창작 활동을 보였다. 매리는 『프로세르피나』(Proserpine)와 『마이다스』(Midas) 등과 같은 드라마를 썼을 뿐 아니라, 『마틸다』(Matilda)나 『발퍼가』(Valperga) 등을 저술하였기 때문이다. 하지만 매리의 불운은 다시 이어지기 시작했다. 매리는 또 다시 아이를 유산하였고, 1822년 7월에는 집으로 귀환하려고 셸리가 탄 배가 투스카니(Tuscany) 연안에서 폭풍을 만나 뒤집혀 셸리가 익사하고 말았기 때문이다.

남편의 죽음 후, 매리는 저술활동을 통해 생계를 이어가기로 결심을 하고, 1823년 영국으로 돌아와 자신의 부친의 집 근처에 거처를 잡는다. 이때부터 그녀는 남편 셸리의 시 세계를 올바르게 알리고자 셸리의 시를 편집하기 시작하여, 1824년에는 셸리의『유고시선집』(Posthumous Poems)을, 1839년에는 셸리의 『시작』(Poetical Works)을 각각 출판하였고, 뒤이어 셸리가 쓴 에세이, 편지 등을 포함한 셸리의 산문집을 출판하여 급진주의자로서 혹은 위험한 사상을 지닌 인물로서 당대 평판이 좋지 않았던 남편 셸리가 사실은 이상주의자이며 아름다움을 추구하는 낭만적인 시인임을 널리 알려, 남편의 명예를 회복하는데 상당한 일조를 하게 되었다.

이외에도 매리는 바이런과 셸리의 비망록을 쓰는 사람들의 집필을 도와주면서도 소설 창작에도 몰두하여 1826년에는 『최후의 인간』(The Last Man)의 출판을 기화로 『퍼킨 워벡의 행운』(Perkin Warbeck, 1830), 『로도어』(Lodore, 1835), 『포크너』(Falkner, 1837)와 같은 소설을 집필하였고, 1830년에는 첫 에디션과 내용이 다소 다른 『프랑켄스타인』의 새 에디션(New edition)의 판권을 팔았다.

1839년부터 매리는 뇌종양으로 몸에 마비가 오고 극심한 두통에 시달렸다. 이로 인해 매리는 더 이상 아무런 저술활동을 하지 못하게 되었고, 1851년 2월 53세의 나이로 체스터 스퀘어(Chester Square)에서 숨을 거두게 된다.

II. 작품의 배경

◉ 시대적 배경

매리가 태어나던 1797년은 프랑스 대혁명(1789년)이 일어난 지 얼마 되지 않은 해였다. 따라서 이 시기의 영국에서는 프랑스 대혁명과 유사한 사회변화가 일어날까 두려워하는 보수적 집단과 프랑스 대혁명과 같은 사건이 군주제를 종식시키고 민주주의의 도래를 가능하게 한다고 생각했던 급진주의자들 간의 팽팽한 긴장이 존재하고 있었는데, 이런 첨예한 대립의 중심에는 매리의 부친이자 급진주의자들의 리더로서 역할을 하였던 윌리엄 고드윈이 있었다.

이런 아버지뿐만 아니라 자신의 남편이 된 시인 셸리(셸리도 고드윈의 사상을 흠모하였으며 그에게 지대한 영향을 받았다)의 영향을 받은 매리는 자연 그들이 신봉하였던 자유와 평등의 이념을 지고의 가치로 받아들였고, 이를 통해 보다 나은 국가 혹은 사회를 건설할 수 있다고 믿었다. 이런 매리의 생각은 자연 『프랑켄스타인』의 작품 배경으로 제네바(Geneva)를 선택하게 하였다. 공화정을 펼치고 있었던 제네바는 여전히 "타락한" 군주제의 지배하에 놓였던 유럽 국가들에게 있어서는 자유를 구가하는 국가의 표본이었으며, 사회제도가 인간을 타락시키고 인간의 선한 본성을 왜곡시킨다고 주장한, 따라서 고드윈의 무정부주의적인 사상과 프랑스 대혁명의 사상적 밑거름을 형성하였던 루소(Rousseau)의 탄생지이기도 하기 때문이다.

프랑켄스타인이 학업을 시작하였던 인골스타트(Ingolstadt)도 이런 맥락에서 그 의미가 있다. 계몽주의를 신봉하던 자유사상가로 구성된 소위 일루미나티(Illuminati)라고 불리던 비밀 혁명 그룹이 — 프랑스 대혁명의 배후 세력으로 간주되기도 하였던 이 단체는 기존의 유럽사회 체제의 전복을 그 목적으로 삼고 있었기 때문에, 고드윈의 사회 철학과도 그 맥을

같이 한다고 볼 여지가 있었다 — 바로 인골스타트 대학의 법학 교수인
아담 바이스하우프트(Adam Weishaupt)에 의해 1776년 5월 1일에 창설되
었기 때문이다.

◉ 창작 배경

John William Polidori(1795-1821)

1816년 5월 매리는 새 어머니가 데려온 딸
인 클레어 클레어몽(Claire Clairmont), 그리
고 시인 셸리와 함께 제네바로 여행을 떠나
게 된다. 이곳에서 이들은 당대의 대표적인
낭만주의 시인이자 셸리와 절친한 관계에
있던 바이런(Lord Byron)을 만나 같이 여름
을 보내기로 하였기 때문이었다. 먼저 제네
바 호수 (Lake Geneva: 당시에는 레만 호로
불렸다) 근방에 도착한 매리와 셸리 일행의
뒤를 이어 바이런(Lord Byron)도 그의 주치
의인 폴리도리(John William Polidori)와 함께

제네바 호수

제네바에 도착하여 숙소를 정하였다. 이들
은 이곳에서 글을 쓰기도 하고, 호수에서 같
이 보트를 젓기도 하며, 밤새 이야기를 나누
기도 하는 등 많은 생활을 공유하였다.

그러던 어느 날 며칠 동안 내리는 비로
바깥 외출을 하기 힘들어 집안에 머물며 한
가로이 이야기를 나누며 시간을 보내던 중,
이들의 화제는 18세기 과학자들의 실험과
죽은 생물을 살리고 시체에 생명을 불어 넣
었다고 전해지는 에라스무스 다윈(Erasmus
Darwin)에 대한 이야기를 바꿨었다고 한다.

Erasmus Darwin(1731-1802)

또한 불어로 번역된 독일의 유령이야기를
같이 읽었던 이들은 유령이야기를 누가 가장 잘 쓰는지 시합을 하자는
바이런의 제안에 따라 각자 이야기를 지어내기로 하였다. 하지만 이 제
안을 하였던 바이런은 흡혈귀에 관한 이야기를 구상하다가 중도에 포기
하였고 (후에 바이런의 주치의인 폴리도리가 이 흡혈귀 이야기를 확장하
고 새로이 구상하여 영국의 최초의 흡혈귀 소설인 「뱀파이어」(Vampyre)
를 출판한다), 셸리는 자신의 어린 시절을 소재로 이야기를 하려다 곧 포
기하였다고 한다. 하지만 바이런과 셸리가 나누던 생명의 원리에 대한 대
화를 떠올리며 삶과 죽음의 경계에 대해 골똘히 생각하던 매리는 신체
부위를 조합해서 거기에 생명을 불어넣은 내용의 이야기를 쓰기로 결심
하게 된다 (후에 매리는 이 작품을 구상하게 된 그날을 "어린 시절에서
인생으로 처음 발 걸음한 순간"이라고 회상하였다). 처음 매리는 이 내용
을 소재로 단편소설을 쓰려하였지만, 남편 셸리의 제안에 따라 이야기를
확장하여 그녀의 최초 장편소설인 『프랑켄스타인』을 집필하게 되었던
것이다.

Ⅲ. 작품 분석

◉ 영향을 미친 문학 작품

　어린 시절 당대의 유명 작가나 과학자, 사상가들이 고드윈의 집을 자주 찾았던 탓에 매리는 직·간접적으로 이들을 접할 기회가 여러 번 있었다. 고드윈의 집을 자주 찾았던 작가로는 그녀의 미래의 남편이 된 시인 셸리이외에도 영국의 수필가 찰스 램(Charles Lamb), 비평가이자 수필가인 윌리엄 해즐릿(William Hazlitt), 낭만주의 시인 코울리지 등이 있었다. 이들 중 매리에게 특히 문학적인 영향을 주었던 작가는 코울리지인데, 특히 매리가 소파 뒤에 숨어서 그가 낭송하던 것을 들었다고 전해지는 코울리지의 「노수부의 노래」(Rime of the Ancient Mariner)는 매리의 『프랑켄스타인』에 많은 문학적 영감을 주었다. "위험한 바다의 신비에 대한 열정"을 갖고 있는 노수부처럼 "안개와 눈의 땅"에 대한 열망으로 위험한 북극항해를 시도한 『프랑켄스타인』의 프레임 화자인 월튼(Walton) 선장은 누이동생에게 보내는 편지에서, 자신은 노수부처럼 앨버트로스(Albatross: 노수부는 배 위를 맴돌던 앨버트로스를 죽였는데 이 죽은 앨버트로스는 저주가 풀리기 전까지 노수부의 목에서 떨어지지 않게 된다)를 죽이지 않을 거라고 말함으로써 「노수부의 노래」에 나오는 내용을 직접 언급조차 할 정도이니 말이다.

　이 작품에 영향을 미친 또 다른 작가로는 18세기 영국소설가 리처드슨(Samuel Richardson)을 들 수 있을 것이다. 매리는 이 작품을 집필하기 전 리처드슨이 쓴 『파멜라』(Pamela)와 『클라리사』(Clarissa)를 읽었다고 하는데, 이 두 작품은 『프랑켄스타인』의 시작 부분과 끝 부분에서처럼 편지 형식으로 진행되고 있다. 즉 매리 셸리가 이 작품에 편지를 주고받음으로써 전개되는 서신 형태를 부여한 것은 리처드슨의 소설에서 그 영향을 받아서 인듯하다.

　　내용면에서 이 작품에 많은 영향을 미친 작가는 매리의 아버지 고드윈
이다. 고드윈은 자신의 무정부주의에 대한 옹호를 『정치적 정의』(Political
Justice)라는 저서에서 뿐만 아니라, 『캐럽 윌리엄스』(Caleb Williams)라는
소설을 통해서도 제시하고 있는데, 『캐럽 윌리엄스』에 담긴 진보적 개혁
사상이 프랑켄스타인의 이상주의를 통해 제시되면서 동시에 진실을 쫓
는 일이 결코 사회를 위해 좋은 것은 아니라는 사실도 제시되고 있기 때
문이다. 포클랜드(Falkland)라는 귀족의 살인 행각을 밝혀내려는 캐럽 윌
리엄스는 자신의 "지식에 대한 잘못된 갈구"가 자신을 포함해 많은 선량
한 사람들을 불행에 빠트리게 되었다는 사실을 깨닫게 되기 때문이다.

　　『프랑켄스타인』에 내용상 가장 많은 영향을 끼친 작품은 17세기 영국
시인인 밀튼(John Milton)의 『실낙원』(Paradise Lost)이다. 매리는 이 작품을
집필하기 몇 년 전 밀튼의 『실낙원』을 몇 번 읽었으며, 그녀가 『프랑켄스
타인』을 구상하게 된 제네바에는 밀튼이 실제로 머물렀던 저택이 있었기
때문에, 매리는 자연 이 작품 집필에 인류 창조의 이야기를 담고 있는 밀
튼의 『실낙원』을 염두에 두었을 것이다.

　　이러한 사실은 프랑켄스타인의 괴물이 『실낙원』의 신은 아담(Adam)
과 이브(Eve)를 아름답게 만들었지만 프랑켄스타인은 자신을 흉측한 모
습으로 만든 것에 대해 통탄하는 장면을 통해서도 엿보인다. 여기서 더
나아가 괴물은 자신이 『실낙원』의 아담이 아니라, 아담을 타락시킨 사탄
과도 같은 존재라고 생각한다. 그는 자신은 "대 악마[사탄]처럼 그 안에
지옥을 품고 있다"라고 말함으로써 『실낙원』에서 사탄이 하는 말을 떠
올리게 하기 때문이다. 하지만 괴물은 여기서 더 나아가 자신은 『실낙원』
의 사탄보다도 못한 존재라고 생각한다. 혼자 고립되어 있는 프랑켄스
타인의 괴물은 "사탄은 자신을 존경하고 자신에게 용기를 북돋아주는
동료 혹은 동료 악마들이 있지만 나는 혼자이며 미움만 받는다"라고 말
하기 때문이다.

◉ 작품 구조

이 작품에는 19세기 작품으로는 보기 드물게 여러 명의 화자가 등장한다. 프레임 화자인 선장 월튼(Walton)이 자기 누이에게 보내는 편지로 시작하는 이 작품은 K. 월튼이 자기 누이에게 보내는 편지로 끝난다. 즉 이 작품은 월튼 선장이 프랑켄스타인과 그의 피조물인 "괴물"(monster)과 대면하고 이들의 이야기를 누이에게 전하는 구조를 갖고 있는 것이다. 따라서 우리는 프랑켄스타인의 시각과 괴물의 관점에서 본 이야기와 이들의 이야기를 전해들은 월튼 선장의 관점에서 이들의 이야기를 접하는 것이다. 하지만 이들 이외에도 이 작품에는 여러 인물들의 소리가 여러 사람을 통해 전달되기도 한다.

프랑켄스타인의 말과 괴물의 이야기는 그를 직접 만난 월튼을 통해 독자에게 전달되지만, 괴물의 이야기는 오로지 프랑켄스타인을 통해 전달되기도 하기 때문이다. 재미있는 것은 괴물도 다른 사람의 이야기를 전달하는 위치에 있다는 것이다. 헛간에 숨어서 프랑스 망명인들의 삶을 훔쳐보았던 관계로 괴물은 그들이 나눈 이야기와 대화를 우리에게 전해주기도 하기 때문이다(이것은 다시 프랑켄스타인을 거쳐 월튼에게 전달되는 내용이다). 따라서 여러 층으로 형성된 서사를 접하게 되는 독자들은 여러 시각에서 이 작품을 볼 수밖에 없게 되는 것이다. 재미있는 사실은 이처럼 여러 층으로 형성된 서사를 통해 우리는 각각의 작중인물의 성격과 세계관을 접할 수 있으며, 같은 상황을 놓고 다르게 보는 이들의 (특히 프랑켄스타인과 괴물의) 시각을 통해, 진실이 얼마나 상대적인지 혹은 타자를 이해하는 것이 얼마나 어려운지 깨닫게 되는 것이다.

예를 들어 맨 먼저 월튼 선장에게 자신의 이야기를 들려주는 프랑켄스타인은 괴물을 사악하고 무자비하며 잔인하고 악마적인 존재로 인식하는 반면, 괴물은 자신이 얼마나 섬세한 감정을 지녔으며 자신에게 조금이라도 관심과 애정만 사람들이 보였더라면 그리고 자신의 추한 모습을 보고 사람들이 경멸하고 돌을 던지지만 않았다면, 선량한 존재로 살았을 거란 이야기를 하여 독자들의 공감을 산다. 즉 프랑켄스타인의 입장에서 보면 괴물은 자신의 형제와 아내를 죽인 사악한 악마와 같은 존재이지만, 괴물의 관점에서 보면, 자신을 버려둔 채 도망간 프랑켄스타인과 자신의 도움을 받고서도 자신에게 총을 겨누고 또 돌을 던진 사람들에 대해 원망하고 거기에 대해 보복하고자 하는 마음이 생긴 것은 매우당연한 것이다.

⊙ 작품의 주제

A. 절대적 타자(Other)로서의 "괴물"(monster)

프랑켄스타인은 자신이 창조한 존재에게 이름은 붙여주지 않고 단지 "괴물"(monster)이라고 명명하며 심지어는 철전지 원수처럼 적대시하기까지 한다. 프랑켄스타인은 자신이 만든 피조물에 대해 왜 이런 적대적인 감정을 갖고 있는 것일까? 그 이유는 그가 만든 피조물이 갖고 있는 흉측한 혹은 보통 인간과 다른 모습에서 찾을 수 있을 것이다. 프랑켄스타인은 사람의 시체의 여러 부위를 뜯어내 조합을 하여 그를 만들어 냈기 때문이다. 그가 자신의 피조물을 괴물이라고 칭한 것도, 이 "괴물"이 아무런 잘못도 저지르지 않았는데도 불구하고 사람들에게 따돌림을 당하고 박해를 당해만 했던 것도 바로 이 흉측한 혹은 부자연스런 모습 때문이었다. 이런 점에서 "괴물"이라는 호칭은 남과 다르다는 이유에서 붙여졌던 것이고 그가 남들에게 적대시되는 것도 그가 바로 타자(Other) 혹은타자의 상징이기 때문인 것이다.

프랑켄스타인이 만든 괴물이 상징하는 타자(성)는 여러 측면에서 살펴볼 수 있다. 막시즘의 시각에서 이 작품을 보는 주요 비평가 중 하나인 프랑코 모레티(Franco Moretti)는 이 괴물을 19세기 산업사회에 확산되

Edmund Burke(1723–1792)

기 시작하던 프롤레타리아 계급의 상징으로 혹은 자신들의 권리를 주장하고자 사회적 소요를 일으키는 노동자나 하층민으로 보며, 기득권 층 혹은 자본가 계급이 프롤레타리아 노동자 계급에 대한 혐오감을 이런 식으로 표현하고 있다고 주장하였다. 괴물을 자본가에 의해 모든 것을 빼앗긴 하층민의 상징으로 보는 이런 시각은 괴물이 쉴 곳도 없어 숲이나 버려진 남의 집 헛간에서 기숙할 수밖에 없었다는 사실이나, 먹을 것 입을 것 하나 제대로 없어 열매나 견과류 등을 먹고 살아갈 수밖에 없었던 사실을 고려해 보면 어느 정도 타당성을 지닌다.

이렇듯 타자의 상징으로서의 괴물은 당대 영국의 보수적인 시각에서 보면 기존 사회체제를 위협하는 정치적 급진주의자들의 상징으로도 볼 수 있다. 1830년대에 급격하게 일어났던 민주주의로의 개혁 혹은 노동자의 권리를 주장하는 움직임에 대해 당시 언론매체들이 "프랑켄스타인의 괴물"이라고 칭했던 것은 바로 이런 맥락에서였던 것이다. 하지만 누구보다도 사회 개혁가로서 보수진영으로부터 괴물처럼 취급되어 왔던 사람은 바로 매리의 부친 윌리엄 고드윈이다. 『프랑스 혁명에 관한 고찰』(Reflections on the Revolution in Framce, 1790)에서 1789년 프랑스에서 일어났던 프랑스 대혁명의 여파에 대해 우려를 표방하며, 프랑스인의 봉기를 괴물로 묘사하였던 에드먼드 버크(Edmund Burke)의 관점에서 보면 고드윈은 분명 괴물과도 같은 존재였는데, 이런 시각은 버크이외에도 여러 보수진영 인사들에게서도 발견되기 때문이다. 당시 보수적 시각을 대변하였던 『반 자코뱅 리뷰』(Anti-Jacobin Review)와 같은 잡지는 고드윈의 사상을 "괴물이 낳은 산물"로 보았고 토마스 드 퀸시(Thomas de Quincey)는 고드윈을 프랑켄스타인에 의해 창조된 괴물과도 같다고 말하였기 때문이다.

타자로서의 괴물은 인종적인 관점에서도 살펴볼 수 있다. 자신들의 치부를 위해 아프리카에서 강제로 데려온 흑인 노예들의 낯선 모습은 당대 영국인에게는 흉측하게 보여져, 그들에게는 괴물처럼 보일 수 있었을 것이다. 더구나 이들 흑인 노예가 점점 증가하게 되자 영국인들은 이들로부터 값싸게 얻어낸 노동력은 생각지 않고, 이들의 수가 늘어나는 것을 점차 두려워하기 시작하여 이들의 증가를 막고 싶어 하기 까지 하였다. 프랑켄스타인이 여자 "괴물"을 만들어 달라는 괴물의 요청을 결국에는 거부하고 거의 완성단계에 있던 여자 괴물을 파괴한 것은 바로 이 때문이다. 프랑켄스타인은 괴물에게 배우자가 생기면 결국 이들이 자손을 낳고, 그 자손들의 숫자가 점차 늘어나 인간사회를 위협하는 존재가 될 까봐 두려웠던 것이다.

이렇듯 프랑켄스타인의 괴물은 사회 약자로서 사회 변방에 있는 존재 혹은 외부세계에서 당시 영국사회에 진입한 외부인으로서 타자의 상징이다. 그 타자가 누구의 타자인지는 보는 시각마다 다르겠지만 여전히 공포와 두려움의 대상으로서의 타자인 것만은 분명하다. 이런 점에서 프랑켄스타인이 만든 괴물은 당대 영국인들 더 나아가 모든 인간이 갖고 있는 두려움의 대상으로서의 타자성을 상징하는 것이다.

B. 프랑켄스타인 또 다른 자아(Alter Ego)로서의 괴물과 월튼

겉으로 보기에 프랑켄스타인과 괴물은 화합할 수 없는 서로 이질적인 존재처럼 보인다. 하지만 가장 혐오스럽고 이질적인 존재로 프랑켄스타인이 인간 사회에서 사라지기를 원하는 괴물만큼 그와 닮은 존재는 없다. 우선 둘 다 자연의 아름다움과 숭엄함에 전율을 느낀다. 프랑켄스타인은 막내 동생 윌리엄(William)이 죽었을 때와 억울한 누명을 쓰고 저스틴(Justine)이 교수형 당했을 때 산으로 향한다. 자연세계는 감정을 순화하고 정신적 치유를 가져다 줄 수 있다는 생각에서였는데, 실제로 프랑켄스타인은 자연에서 위로를 받는다.

이는 19세기 낭만주의 시인들이 자연 속에서의 경외감과 희망을 노래하는 것과 일맥상통한다. 낭만주의 시인들에게 자연은 인간 본연의 모습을 되찾아 주고 인간의 정서를 고양시키는 숭엄한 장소이기 때문이다. 자연 속에서 이러한 위안을 받는 것은 프랑켄스타인뿐만이 아니다. 봄이 되어 기온이 오르고 얼음이 녹자, 괴물은 푸른 잎과 꽃을 보며 위안을 받는다. 더 나아가 그는 신이 창조한 삼라만상이 다 아름답다고 느끼며 자신의 추한 모습을 잠시나마 잊고는 행복감에 빠지게 되기 때문이다. 즉 괴물은 봄의 숲에서 나는 향기와 다채로운 색깔의 꽃과 나무들을 바라보며 기쁨에 도취되어 자신이 혼자라는 사실, 또한 자신은 인간들과 같이 할 수 없는 존재라는 사실을 잊게 될 정도로 자연 속에서 행복한 삶을 잠시나마 누리는 것이다.

하지만 프랑켄스타인이 절친한 친구 클러밸(Clerval)과 동생 윌리엄 그리고 아내 엘리자베스를 괴물에 의해 잃자, 괴물에 대한 그의 분노는 극에 달하였고 괴물에 대해선 복수심을 갖게 된다. 그런 고통에 시달리는 프랑켄스타인은 스스로를 "지옥"에 비유하면서 "나는 악마의 저주를 받아, 내 안에 영원한 지옥을 갖고 다닌다"라고 말하는데, 흥미로운 사실은 존 밀턴의 『실낙원』에 나오는 이 대사를 『실낙원』을 통해 말을 배운 프랑켄스타인의 괴물 자신도 했다는 점이다. 그도 인간들에게서 뿐만 아니라 자신을 만든 프랑켄스타인에게서 조차 배척당하자, 프랑켄스타인처럼 증오심에 불타 "나는 대 악마처럼 내 안에 지옥을 품고 있다"고 말하였기 때문이다. 이처럼 이 둘은 서로에 대한 증오감으로 서로 대척점에 서 있는 것 같지만 사실상 여러 면에서 너무도 흡사하여 한 인간의 양면처럼 보인다. 즉 프랑켄스타인이 적대시하며 싸우고자 하였던 괴물은 바로 그 자신으로, 괴물은 프랑켄스타인의 또 다른 자아인 것이다.

프랑켄스타인과 또 다른 자아는 괴물만이 아니다. 이 작품의 프레임 화자이자 프랑켄스타인에 관한 이야기를 우리에게 전하는 월튼 선장도 프랑켄스타인의 또 다른 자아다. 우선 월튼 선장과 프랑켄스타인의 공통점은 작품이 시작할 때부터 분명하게 드러난다. 월튼은 누이에게 보내는 편지에서 자신은 남들이 가지 않았던 미지의 세계에 대한 열망을 갖고 있으며, 위험을 무릅쓰고라도 북극으로 가는 최단 항로를 개척하고 나침반의 바늘을 움직이는 신비로운 힘의 비밀을 밝혀 인류에게 공헌하겠다는 자신의 이상을 밝힌다.

하지만 그도, 생명 창조의 위업을 달성하여 인류에 공헌하겠다고 생각은 하지만 막상 이를 그 누구에게도 알릴 수 없는 프랑켄스타인과 마찬가지로, 자신의 생각을 공유하고 이해할 친구가 없다. 또한 둘은 다 어머니가 일찍 세상을 떠나 외로움을 느끼는 존재다. 월튼의 어머니가 일찍 사망했다는 사실은 작품에 명확히 제시되지는 않지만, 그가 자신의 가족 관계에 대해 언급하지 않고, 누이 마가렛과 거의 어린 시절부터 고아처럼 지냈다는 암시를 하며, 어머니가 아니라 누이에게 자신의 근황을 알리고 자신의 외로움을 토로한다는 사실은 그가 일찍이 부모를 여의었음을 시사한다. 이는 프랑켄스타인의 경우도 마찬가지다. 그의 어머니는 엘리자베스를 간호하다 병이 전염되어 일찍이 사망하여 프랑켄스타인은 어머니의 정을 그리워하며 외롭게 살아갔기 때문이다.

또한 둘이 인류를 위한 일에 매진하려 하였지만 부친의 반대에 부딪힌다는 것도 공통점이다. 월튼은 항해가 혹은 탐험가로서의 꿈을 가졌지만 아버지의 반대에 부딪혔고, 프랑켄스타인은 연금술을 공부하고 싶었지만 연금술을 "슬픈 쓰레기"(sad trash)로 간주하는 부친으로부터 별 다른 지지를 받지 못했기 때문이다. 이와 관련하여 둘 다 낭만적인 기질을 갖고 있다는 사실이 이들의 최대 공통점이다. "나는 탐험되지 않은 영역을 갈 것이다"라는 월튼의 말은 삶과 죽음의 경계를 허무는 작업, 즉 죽은 자를 살리는 일에 매진하겠다는 프랑켄스타인의 야망과 일맥상통하기 때문이다. 이러한 야망은 매리 셸리의 남편이자 낭만주의 시인인 셸리의 철학과도 통한다. 인류에 대한 공헌을 꿈꾸며 시를 그 이상의 실천방법으로 생각한 낭만주의 시인 셸리처럼 월튼도 젊은 시절에 낭만주의 시인이 되기를 꿈꾸어 왔기 때문이다.

하지만 무엇보다도 또 다른 자아로서의 두 사람의 관계를 짐작할 수 있게 하는 것은 프랑켄스타인을 대하는 월튼 선장의 말이다. 항해 도중 항상 자신을 이해할 수 있는 사람이 없다며 외로움을 느끼던 월튼 선장은 프랑켄스타인을 만난 이후로 마음을 터놓을 수 있는 친구를 만났다며, 그에 대한 "애정이 매일매일 자라난다"고 고백하였기 때문이다. 이에 프랑켄스타인도 월튼 선장이 자신과 같이 지식에 대한 열정을 가지고 있다는 사실을 알고는 그도 자신과 같이 불행해지기를 원하지 않는다면 자신의 이야기를 들어보라고 그간 괴물 창조와 관련된 자신의 비극적 삶을 말하는 것이다.

이렇듯 이 작품에는 자신을 이해하고 알아줄 수 있는, 다시 말하면 자신의 또 다른 자아에 대한 그리움이 드러나 있다. 이런 의미에서 월턴 선장의 프랑켄스타인에 대한 마음은 괴물의 프랑켄스타인에 대한 마음과 유사하며, 이들은 각각 서로에 대한 또 다른 자아인 것이다. 작품 말미에 프랑켄스타인이 죽자 괴물이 그의 죽음을 슬퍼하면서 자신도 프랑켄스타인을 따라 죽음의 세계로 들어가겠다는 암시를 하고 떠나는 것은 바로 자신의 존재를 가능케 했던 또 다른 자아가 사라졌기 때문이다. 이런 점에서 프랑켄스타인과 괴물과의 관계는 창조자로서의 아버지와 피조물로서의 아들의 관계를 넘어 도플갱어(Doppelganger)와도 같은 관계인 것이다.

C. 위험한 과학과 지식

19세기는 과학이 급속도로 발전한 시기였다. 특히 화학에 대한 관심이 고조된 시기였는데, 1808년 산화칼슘과 산화수은의 전기분해를 통해 칼

슘을 발견한 당대 유명 화학자였던 험프리 데이비 경(Sir Humphrey Davy)의 잇단 방문에 화학에 관해 많은 관심을 갖게 된 매리는 데이비 경의 화학에 관한 저서를 탐독하여 그 저서에 담긴 내용을 이 작품에 등장하는 화학 교수를 통해서 전하기까지 하였다.

　시인 셸리의 과학에 관한 관심도 이에 뒤지지 않았다. 셸리는 대학시절 마법에 관한 저서도 탐독했지만 전기와 동전기학(galvanism)에 관한 저서도 탐독할 정도로 과학에 관심이 많았고, 1816년에는 매리를 데리고 서로 손을 잡은 사람들 사이에 전기가 흐르도록 한 프랑스 과학자 가르느랭(Garnerin)의 실험을 보러가기도 하였다.

　또한 당시에는 전기 자극을 통해 죽은 사람을 살리고자 하는 실험도 있었다. 이러한 실험을 실시한 사람 중 이탈리아 과학자 조반니 알디니(Giovanni Aldini)가 특히 유명한데 그는 사형이 집행된 지 얼마 지나지 않은 사람들을 소생시키는 일에 몰두하며, 물에 빠져 죽거나 숨이 막혀 죽은 사람을 되살릴 수 있는 가능성에 대한 연구를 하여 영국의 과학기구인 왕립학술원(Royal Society)의 찬사를 받기도 하였다.

　셸리가 18세기 말부터 급속도로 발전하기 시작한 과학 테크놀로지에 대해 관심을 가지고 있었던 것은 분명하다. 하지만 그녀의 시각은 급격한 과학이 가져다주는 혜택뿐만 아니라 그 부작용에 대해서도 생각했던 것 같다. 그녀는 과학이 인간에게 자유와 혜택을 가져다 줄 수 있다는 생각에 대해 회의를 품고 있음을, 인류를 위한다는 명분하에 과학적 지식을 추구하였던 프랑켄스타인의 행위가 그에게 가장 소중한 가족과의 단절, 더 나아가 가족들을 죽음으로 몰았다는 사실을 통해, 또한 과학적 진리의 추구가 인류를 위한 것이 아니라 타인에게 해가 될 수 있음을 프랑켄스타인의 또 다른 자아이기도 한 월튼 선장을 통해 제시한다. 나침반의 바늘을 움직이는 힘의 비밀을 밝혀내어 인류에게 빛을 전하겠다는 포부에 북극을 탐험하였던 월튼은 결국 배를 얼음에 끼게 함으로써 동료 선원들의 목숨을 위태롭게 만들었기 때문이다.

매리는 과학적 지식의 추구가 인간 사회에 재앙이 될 수 있다는 사실을 바로 그런 지식의 피해자인 프랑켄스타인의 입을 통해서 자신과 같은 이상주의자인 월튼에게 전달한다. "내[프랑켄스타인]가 일찍이 그랬던 것처럼 당신[월튼]도 지식과 지혜를 쫓고 있구려. 당신의 소망을 이루는 것이, 내 경우에서처럼, 당신을 무는 뱀이 되지 않기를 간절히 바라오." 여기서 더 나아가 프랑켄스타인은 월튼에게 자신의 이야기에서 교훈을 얻으라고 촉구하며, "내 고통에 대해 배워, 당신의 고통을 더 배가 하지 마시요"라는 말로 월튼의 과학적 지식의 추구가 결국은 고통으로 이어질 것이란 예언을 한다.

결국 월튼은 프랑켄스타인의 설득으로 그렇게 목마르게 추구하였던 과학적 지식을 포기하고 고향으로 배를 돌려, 동료 선원과 자신의 목숨을 구하는데 바로 이것이 매리 셸리가 이 작품을 통해서 전하고 싶은 주요 메시지 중 하나다. 과학이 설령 인류를 위한 것일지라도 동료 혹은 가족과의 고립을 수반하는 과학적 지식의 추구는 재앙이라는 것 말이다. 허나 재미있는 사실은 매리 셸리의 이런 메시지가 자신의 남편인 셸리에 대한 비판으로도 읽힐 여지가 있다는 점이다. 프랑켄스타인의 이름인 빅토(Victor)가 셸리가 어린 시절 자신의 이름으로 자주 삼았던 빅터(Victory)라는 이름을 떠올리게 한다는 점에서도 짐작할 수 있듯이, 프랑켄스타인의 모델은 바로 매리의 남편 셸리이기 때문이다. 셸리는 프랑켄스타인처럼 세상을 개혁하는데 지대한 관심을 보였으며 과학을 추구하고 자연을 예찬하는 시인이기도 하였으니 말이다. 게다가 셸리 자신도 프랑켄스타인과 자신의 연관성을 알고 있어서였는지 이 작품의 초판에 자신의 생각을 끼어 넣고 매리가 쓴 내용을 바꾸기까지 하였다고 한다. 즉 셸리는 매리가 자신의 이상주의에 대해 부정적인 시각을 갖고 있다는 사실을, 그리고 과학적 이상주의가 폐해를 가져 올 수 있다는 사실을 인식하고 있었던 것으로 그 문제점에 대한 지적을 수용하였던 것이다.

Preface[1]

THE EVENT ON which this fiction is founded has been supposed, by Dr. Darwin[1], and some of the physiological[2] writers of Germany, as not of impossible occurrence. I shall not be supposed as according[3] the remotest degree of serious faith to such an imagination; yet, in assuming it as the basis of a work of fancy, I have not considered myself as merely weaving a series of supernatural terrors. The event on which the interest of the story depends is exempt from the disadvantages of a mere tale of spectres or enchantment. It was recommended[4] by the novelty of the situations which it developes; and, however impossible as a physical fact, affords a point of view to the imagination of the delineating[5] of human passions more comprehensive and commanding[6] than any which the ordinary relations of existing events can yield.

I have thus endeavoured to preserve the truth of the elementary principles of human nature, while I have not scrupled[7] to innovate upon their combinations. The Iliad,[8] the tragic poetry of Greece — Shakespeare, in the *Tempest* and *Midsummer Night's Dream* — and most especially, Milton,[9] in *Paradise Lost*, conform to this rule; and the most humble novelist, who seeks to confer or re-

---

1 Darwin: 에라스무스 다윈(Erasmus Darwin, 1731-1802)을 지칭; 그는 『종의 기원』(On the Origin of Species)을 쓴 찰스 다윈(Charles Darwin)의 조부로 18세기 말 당시 가장 널리 알려진 과학자 중 하나다. 고드윈의 친구로서 고드윈의 집을 자주 방문하였던 그는 매리에게 많은 영향을 주었다.
2 physiological: 생리학적.
3 according: '부여하다'(accord).
4 recommended: 추천될 만한. 매력적인.
5 delineating: 묘사하다.
6 commanding: 권위를 지닌.
7 scrupled: 주저하다. 망설이다.
8 Iliad: 『일리아드』 고대 그리스의 시인 호메로스가 쓴 트로이 전쟁을 다룬 서사시.
9 Milton: 17세기 영국의 서사시인(John Milton)을 지칭하는 것으로 창세기를 소재로 쓴 그의 대표작 『실낙원』(Paradise Lost)은 이 작품에 많은 영감을 주었다.

ceive amusement from his labours, may, without presumption, apply to prose fiction a licence, or rather a rule, from the adoption of which many exquisite[1] combinations of human feeling have resulted in the highest specimens of poetry.

The circumstance on which my story rests was suggested in casual conversation. It was commenced partly as a source of amusement, and partly as an expedient[2] for exercising any untried resources of mind. Other motives were mingled with these as the work proceeded. I am by no means indifferent to the manner in which whatever moral tendencies exists in the sentiments or characters it contains shall affect the reader; yet my chief concern in this respect has been limited to the avoiding the enervating[3] effects of the novels of the present day and to the exhibition of the amiableness of domestic affection, and the excellence of universal virtue. The opinions which naturally spring from the character and situation of the hero are by no means to be conceived as existing always in my own conviction; nor is any inference[4] justly to be drawn from the following pages as prejudicing[5] any philosophical doctrine of whatever kind.

It is a subject also of additional interest to the author that this story was begun in the majestic region where the scene is principally laid, and in society which cannot cease to be regretted. I passed the summer of 1816 in the environs[6] of Geneva. The season was cold and rainy, and in the evenings we crowded around a blazing wood fire, and occasionally amused ourselves with some German stories of ghosts,[7] which

---

1 exquisite: 절묘한. 매우 훌륭한.
2 expedient: 방책. 술책.
3 enervating: 힘 빠지게 하다. 약화시키다.
4 inference: 추측. 추론.
5 prejudicing: 손상시키다. 피해를 끼치다.
6 environs: 주변 지역. 교외(郊外).
7 German stories of ghosts: 독일의 콩트집 『팡타스마고리아니』(Fantasmagoriana; or Collected Stories of Apparitions of Specters. Ghosts, Phantoms, etc.)를 지칭하는데, 이들은 이 독일 콩트집의 불어 번역본을 읽었다고 한다.

happened to fall into our hands.[1] These tales excited in us a playful desire of imitation. Two other friends[2] (a tale from the pen of one of whom would be far more acceptable to the public than anything I can ever hope to produce) and myself agreed to write each story founded on some supernatural occurrence.

The weather, however, suddenly became serene; and my two friends left me on a journey among the Alps, and lost, in the magnificent scenes which they present, all the memory of their ghostly visions. The following tale is the only one which has been completed.

MARLOW, September 1817.

---

1 fall into our hands: 우리 수중에 들어가다.
2 Two other friends: 뱀파이어에 관한 이야기를 조금 진행하다가 포기한 바이런 경 (Lord Byron)과 자신의 어린 시절을 소재로 이야기를 구상하던 시인 셸리를 지칭한다.

Text of

Frankenstein;
or,
The Modern Prometheus

Volume I

Letter I

To Mrs. Saville, England.

St. Petersburgh[1], Dec. 11th, 17 — .

YOU WILL REJOICE to hear that no disaster has accompanied the commencement of an enterprise which you have regarded with such evil forebodings.[2] I arrived here yesterday; and my first task is to assure my dear sister of my welfare, and increasing confidence in the success of my undertaking.

I am already far north of London; and as I walk in the streets of Petersburgh, I feel a cold northern breeze play upon my cheeks, which braces[3] my nerves, and fills me with delight. Do you understand this feeling? This breeze, which has travelled from the regions towards which I am advancing, gives me a foretaste of those icy climes.[4] Inspirited[5] by this wind of promise, my day dreams become more fervent and vivid. I try in vain to be persuaded[6] that the pole is the seat of frost and desolation; it ever presents itself to my imagination as the region of beauty and delight. There, Margaret, the sun is forever visible, its broad disk just skirting[7] the horizon, and diffusing[8] a perpetual splendour. There — for with your leave, my sister, I will put some

---

1 Petersburgh: 러시아의 수도이자 주요 항구도시.
2 forebodding: 불길한 징조(예감).
3 braces: 긴장시키다. 정신들게 하다.
4 climes: 기후.
5 inspirited: 원기를 북돋우다. 고무하다.
6 persuaded: 확신하는.
7 skirting: …의 가[변두리]를 지나다.
8 diffusing: 흩뜨리다. (빛) 발산하다.

trust in preceding navigators — there snow and frost are banished; and, sailing over a calm sea, we may be wafted[1] to a land surpassing in wonders and in beauty every region hitherto discovered on the habitable[2] globe. Its productions and features may be without example, as the phenomena of the heavenly bodies undoubtedly are in those undiscovered solitudes. What may not be expected in a country of eternal light? I may there discover the wondrous power which attracts the needle[3]; and may regulate a thousand celestial observations that require only this voyage to render their seeming eccentricities[4] consistent for ever. I shall satiate[5] my ardent curiosity with the sight of a part of the world never before visited, and may tread a land never before imprinted by the foot of man. These are my enticements,[6] and they are sufficient to conquer all fear of danger or death, and to induce me to commence this laborious voyage with the joy a child feels when he embarks in a little boat, with his holiday mates, on an expedition of discovery up his native river. But, supposing all these conjectures to be false, you cannot contest[7] the inestimable benefit which I shall confer on all mankind, to the last generation, by discovering a passage near the pole to those countries, to reach which at present so many months are requisite[8]; or by ascertaining the secret of the magnet,[9] which, if at all possible, can only be effected by an undertaking such as mine.

These reflections have dispelled the agitation with which I began

---

1 wafted: (바람에 실려 가듯) 가볍게 이동하다.

2 habitable: 거주할 만한.

3 needle: '나침반의 바늘'을 지칭.

4 eccentricities: 기묘함,

5 satiate: 충족시키다.

6 enticements: 유혹. 마음을 끄는 것.

7 contest: 이의를 제기하다. 의문시 하다.

8 requisite: 절대적으로 필요한.

9 secret of the magnet: 자력이 어떻게 발생하고 어떻게 작용하는 지에 관한 과학적 정보는 이 작품이 출판될 당시에는 존재하지 않았고, 1821년에 가서야 '전기학의 아버지'라고 불린 영국의 물리학자 마이클 패러데이(1791 - 1867)에 의해 정립되었다.

my letter, and I feel my heart glow with an enthusiasm which elevates me to heaven; for nothing contributes so much to tranquillise the mind as a steady purpose[1] — a point on which the soul may fix its intellectual eye. This expedition has been the favourite dream of my early years. I have read with ardour the accounts of the various voyages which have been made in the prospect of arriving at the North Pacific Ocean through the seas which surround the pole.[2] You may remember that a history of all the voyages made for purposes of discovery composed the whole of our good Uncle Thomas's library. My education was neglected, yet I was passionately fond of reading. These volumes were my study day and night, and my familiarity with them increased that regret which I had felt, as a child, on learning that my father's dying injunction[3] had forbidden my uncle to allow me to embark in a seafaring life.

These visions faded when I perused, for the first time, those poets whose effusions[4] entranced my soul and lifted it to heaven. I also became a poet[5], and for one year lived in a Paradise of my own creation; I imagined that I also might obtain a niche[6] in the temple where the names of Homer and Shakespeare are consecrated. You are well acquainted with my failure, and how heavily I bore the disappointment. But just at that time I inherited the fortune of my cousin, and my thoughts were turned into the channel of their earlier bent.[7]

---

1 steady purpose: 확고한 목적.
2 North Pacific Ocean … pole: 당시 탐험가들은 동양에 더 빨리 가는 항로로 남아메리카나 아프리카를 지나지 않고 북극해를 관통하여 가는 방법이 있을 거라고 생각하여 그 항로를 개척하고자 열망하였는데, 이 항로는 소위 "북서 항로"(Northwest Passage)로 불리웠다.
3 injunction: '명령'. '지시'; 월튼 선장의 아버지는 아들의 과학적인 지식의 추구를 달갑지 않게 여겼다.
4 effusions: (감정을 있는 그대로 드러낸) 표현(문구).
5 I also became a poet: 월튼 선장은 정서가 풍부하고 자연을 사랑하는 시인 셸리를 여러 면에서 닮았는데, 프랑켄스타인도 이런 속성을 갖고 있다.
6 niche: (조각품 등을 놓는) 벽감(壁龕).
7 bent: 좋아함. 성향.

Six years have passed since I resolved on my present undertaking. I can, even now, remember the hour from which I dedicated myself to this great enterprise. I commenced by inuring[1] my body to hardship. I accompanied the whale-fishers on several expeditions to the North Sea; I voluntarily endured cold, famine, thirst, and want of sleep; I often worked harder than the common sailors during the day and devoted my nights to the study of mathematics, the theory of medicine,[2] and those branches of physical science from which a naval adventurer might derive the greatest practical advantage. Twice I actually hired myself as an under-mate[3] in a Greenland whaler,[4] and acquitted myself to admiration.[5] I must own I felt a little proud when my captain offered me the second dignity[6] in the vessel, and entreated me to remain with the greatest earnestness; so valuable did he consider my services.

And now, dear Margaret, do I not deserve to accomplish some great purpose? My life might have been passed in ease and luxury; but I preferred glory to every enticement[7] that wealth placed in my path. Oh, that some encouraging voice would answer in the affirmative! My courage and my resolution is firm; but my hopes fluctuate, and my spirits are often depressed. I am about to proceed on a long and difficult voyage, the emergencies of which will demand all my fortitude: I am required not only to raise the spirits of others, but sometimes to sustain my own, when theirs are failing.

This is the most favourable period for travelling in Russia. They fly quickly over the snow in their sledges; the motion is pleasant, and, in

---

1 inuring: 익숙하게 하다. 단련되게 하다.

2 medicine: 의학.

3 under-mate: (상선의) 하급 항해사.

4 whaler: 포경선.

5 acquitted myself to admiration: acquitted myself는 '행동하다', '처신하다'; to admiration은 '탄복할 정도로'; 즉 탄복할 정도로 일을 잘 해 나갔다는 의미.

6 dignity: 지위. 계급.

7 enticement: 유혹. 마음을 끄는 것.

my opinion, far more agreeable than that of an English stage-coach.[1] The cold is not excessive, if you are wrapped in furs—a dress which I have already adopted; for there is a great difference between walking the deck and remaining seated motionless for hours, when no exercise prevents the blood from actually freezing in your veins. I have no ambition to lose my life on the post-road[2] between St. Petersburgh and Archangel.[3]

I shall depart for the latter town in a fortnight or three weeks; and my intention is to hire a ship there, which can easily be done by paying the insurance for the owner, and to engage as many sailors as I think necessary among those who are accustomed to the whale-fishing. I do not intend to sail until the month of June; and when shall I return? Ah, dear sister, how can I answer this question? If I succeed, many, many months, perhaps years, will pass before you and I may meet. If I fail, you will see me again soon, or never.

Farewell, my dear, excellent Margaret. Heaven shower down blessings on you, and save me, that I may again and again testify my gratitude for all your love and kindness.

Your affectionate brother,
R. WALTON

---

1 stage-coach: (여러 사람이 함께 타는) 역마차.

2 post-road: 역로. 우편물 운송도로.

3 Archangel: 러시아의 항구 이름; 백해(White Sea)에 있는 주요 항구로 미카엘 대천사 (Archangel Michael) 수도원이 있어서 이런 이름이 붙여졌다.

LETTER II

To Mrs. Saville, England

Archangel, March 28th, 17 — .

HOW SLOWLY THE time passes here, encompassed[1] as I am by frost and snow! yet a second step is taken towards my enterprise. I have hired a vessel, and am occupied in collecting my sailors; those whom I have already engaged appear to be men on whom I can depend and are certainly possessed of dauntless[2] courage.

But I have one want which I have never yet been able to satisfy; and the absence of the object of which I now feel as a most severe evil. I have no friend,[3] Margaret: when I am glowing with the enthusiasm of success, there will be none to participate my joy; if I am assailed by disappointment, no one will endeavour to sustain[4] me in dejection. I shall commit my thoughts to paper,[5] it is true; but that is a poor medium for the communication of feeling. I desire the company of a man who could sympathise with me[6]; whose eyes would reply to mine. You may deem me romantic, my dear sister, but I bitterly feel the want of a friend. I have no one near me, gentle yet courageous, possessed of a cultivated as well as of a capacious mind, whose tastes

---

1 encompassed: 둘러싸인(surrounded).

2 dauntless: 불굴의. 용감한(brave).

3 I have no friend: 월튼 선장처럼 사회로부터의 고립은 이 작품의 주요 모티브 중 하나다. 프랑켄스타인이나 그가 만든 괴물(monster)도 사회로 부터의 고립감을 강하게 느끼기 때문이다.

4 sustain: 격려하다. 힘내게 하다(support).

5 commit my thoughts to paper: 내 생각을 종이에 적다.

6 company of a man who could sympathise with me: 고립이 이 작품의 주요 모티브인 것처럼 자신과 공감할 수 있는 사람을 찾는 것도 이 작품의 주요 모티브 중 하나다. 따라서 월튼 선장은 자신의 누이에게 자신의 이야기를 들어달라고 편지를 쓰고, 프랑켄스타인은 자신의 이야기를 월튼 선장에게 하며, 프랑켄스타인이 만든 괴물은 자신을 만든 프랑켄스타인에게 자신의 이야기를 들어달라고 청하는 것이다.

are like my own, to approve or amend my plans. How would such a friend repair[1] the faults of your poor brother! I am too ardent in execution, and too impatient of difficulties. But it is a still greater evil to me that I am self-educated: for the first fourteen years of my life I ran wild on a common,[2] and read nothing but our Uncle Thomas's books of voyages. At that age I became acquainted with the celebrated poets of our own country; but it was only when it had ceased to be in my power to derive its most important benefits from such a conviction that I perceived the necessity of becoming acquainted with more languages than that of my native country. Now I am twenty-eight, and am in reality more illiterate than many schoolboys of fifteen. It is true that I have thought more, and that my day dreams are more extended and magnificent; but they want (as the painters call it) keeping[3]; and I greatly need a friend who would have sense enough not to despise me as romantic,[4] and affection enough for me to endeavour to regulate my mind.

Well, these are useless complaints; I shall certainly find no friend on the wide ocean, nor even here in Archangel, among merchants and seamen. Yet some feelings, unallied to the dross of human nature[5], beat even in these rugged[6] bosoms. My lieutenant, for instance, is a man of wonderful courage and enterprise; he is madly desirous of glory: or rather, to word[7] my phrase more characteristically, of advancement in his profession. He is an Englishman, and in the midst of national and professional prejudices, unsoftened by cultivation, retains some of the

---

1 repair: 정정하다. 바로잡다.

2 common: (도시 가운데에 있는) 공원.

3 keeping: (회화에서) 먼 곳에 있는 것과 가까운 곳에 있는 것과의 적절한 관계를 유지하는 것을 지칭; 여기서는 '조화'를 의미한다.

4 romantic: '낭만적'이란 이 용어는 19세기 초에 과도한 상상을 하는 비현실주의자를 지칭하는 용어로 부정적으로 사용되기도 하였다.

5 dross of human nature: dross는 '불순물', '정제되고 남은 찌꺼기'; 따라서 인간의 본성 중 좋지 않은 부분을 지칭한다.

6 rugged: 소박한.

7 word: 말로 나타내다.

noblest endowments[1] of humanity. I first became acquainted with him
on board a whale vessel: finding that he was unemployed in this city, I
easily engaged him to assist in my enterprise.

The master is a person of an excellent disposition and is remarkable in the ship for his gentleness and the mildness of his discipline[2].
This circumstance, added to his well-known integrity and dauntless courage, made me very desirous to engage him. A youth passed
in solitude, my best years spent under your gentle and feminine
fosterage,[3] has so refined the groundwork[4] of my character that I cannot overcome an intense distaste to the usual brutality exercised on
board ship: I have never believed it to be necessary; and when I heard
of a mariner equally noted for his kindliness of heart, and the respect
and obedience paid to him by his crew, I felt myself peculiarly fortunate in being able to secure his services. I heard of him first in rather
a romantic manner, from a lady who owes to him the happiness of
her life. This, briefly, is his story. Some years ago he loved a young
Russian lady of moderate[5] fortune; and having amassed a considerable
sum in prize-money,[6] the father of the girl consented to the match.
He saw his mistress once before the destined ceremony; but she was
bathed in tears, and, throwing herself at his feet, entreated him to
spare her, confessing at the same time that she loved another, but that
he was poor, and that her father would never consent to the union.
My generous friend reassured the suppliant,[7] and on being informed
of the name of her lover, instantly abandoned his pursuit. He had
already bought a farm with his money, on which he had designed to

---

1 endowments: 타고난 재질(특성).
2 discipline: 징계. 처벌.
3 fosterage: 양육. 육성.
4 groundwork: 토대. 기반.
5 moderate: 보통의.
6 prize-money: 포획한 적군의 배에서 얻은 금품.
7 suppliant: 탄원자.

pass the remainder of his life; but he bestowed the whole on his rival, together with the remains of his prize-money to purchase stock,[1] and then himself solicited the young woman's father to consent to her marriage with her lover. But the old man decidedly refused, thinking himself bound in honour[2] to my friend; who, when he found the father inexorable,[3] quitted his country, nor returned until he heard that his former mistress was married according to her inclinations. "What a noble fellow!" you will exclaim. He is so; but then he is wholly uneducated: he is as silent as a Turk, and a kind of ignorant carelessness attends him, which, while it renders his conduct the more astonishing, detracts[4] from the interest and sympathy which otherwise he would command.

But do not suppose, because I complain a little or because I can conceive a consolation for my toils which I may never know, that I am wavering[5] in my resolutions. Those are as fixed as fate; and my voyage is only now delayed until the weather shall permit my embarkation.[6] The winter has been dreadfully severe; but the spring promises well, and it is considered as a remarkably early season; so that perhaps I may sail sooner than I expected. I shall do nothing rashly: you know me sufficiently to confide in my prudence and considerateness whenever the safety of others is committed to my care.[7]

I cannot describe to you my sensations on the near prospect of my undertaking. It is impossible to communicate to you a conception of the trembling sensation, half pleasurable and half fearful, with which I am preparing to depart. I am going to unexplored regions, to "the

---

1 stock: 가축(livestock).
2 in honour: 도의상.
3 inexorable: (결심이) 변함없는. 움직일 수 없는.
4 detracts: (명성 따위를) 떨어뜨리다(손상시키다).
5 wavering: 흔들리는.
6 embarkation: 출항.
7 committed to my care: 나에게 맡겨진.

land of mist and snow;"[1] but I shall kill no albatross[2]; therefore do not be alarmed for my safety or if I should come back to you as worn[3] and woeful as the "Ancient Mariner." You will smile at my allusion; but I will disclose a secret. I have often attributed my attachment to, my passionate enthusiasm for, the dangerous mysteries of ocean, to that production of the most imaginative of modern poets. There is something at work in my soul which I do not understand. I am practically industrious — painstaking; — a workman to execute with perseverance and labour: — but besides this, there is a love for the marvellous, a belief in the marvellous, intertwined in all my projects, which hurries me out of the common pathways of men, even to the wild sea and unvisited regions I am about to explore.

But to return to dearer considerations.[4] Shall I meet you again, after having traversed immense seas, and returned by the most southern cape of Africa[5] or America? I dare not expect such success, yet I cannot bear to look on the reverse of the picture[6]. Continue for the present to write to me by every opportunity[7]: I may receive your letters on some occasions when I need them most to support my spirits. I love you very tenderly. Remember me with affection, should you never hear from me again.

Your affectionate brother,
ROBERT WALTON.

---

1 land of mist and snow: 19세기 영국의 낭만주의 시인 코울리지(S. T. Coleridge)가 쓴 「노수부의 노래」(The Rime of the Ancient Mariner)에 나오는 노수부는 "안개와 눈의 땅"을 갈망한다고 말하고 있다.

2 I shall kill no albatross: 「노수부의 노래」의 수부는 바다 위를 나는 알바트로스(albatross)를 죽임으로써 저주를 받게 된다.

3 worn: 야윈. 초췌한.

4 to return to dearer considerations: To return은 '본론으로 돌아가서'; considerations은 '중요한 문제'; 즉 좀 더 중요한 본론으로 돌아가 이야기하자면.

5 the most southern cape of Africa: 아프리카 대륙 최남단에 있는 '희망봉'(Cape of Good Hope)을 지칭.

6 reverse of the picture: 정반대의 상황(사태).

7 by every opportunity: 기회가 닿는 대로.

Letter III

To Mrs. Saville, England.

July 7th, 17 —.

MY DEAR SISTER,

I write a few lines in haste to say that I am safe and well advanced on my voyage. This letter will reach England by a merchantman[1] now on its homeward voyage from Archangel; more fortunate than I, who may not see my native land, perhaps, for many years. I am, however, in good spirits[2]: my men are bold, and apparently firm of purpose[3]; nor do the floating sheets of ice that continually pass us, indicating the dangers of the region towards which we are advancing, appear to dismay[4] them. We have already reached a very high latitude; but it is the height of summer,[5] and although not so warm as in England, the southern gales, which blow us speedily towards those shores which I so ardently desire to attain, breathe a degree of renovating[6] warmth which I had not expected.

No incidents have hitherto befallen us that would make a figure in a letter.[7] One or two stiff[8] gales, and the springing of a leak[9] are accidents which experienced navigators scarcely remember to record,; and I shall be well content if nothing worse happen to us during our

---

1 merchantman: 상선.
2 in good spirits: 기분이 좋은.
3 firm of purpose: 의지가 굳은.
4 dismay: 당황케 하다. 낙담시키다.
5 height of summer: 한 여름.
6 renovating: 힘나게 하는.
7 make a figure in a letter: '글자의 형태로 쓰다'; 즉 글로 옮겨 적다.
8 stiff: 강한. 세찬.
9 springing of a leak: (배에 물이) 새는 곳이 생김; 즉 배가 새어 물이 들어오기 시작함.

voyage.

Adieu, my dear Margaret. Be assured that[1] for my own sake, as well as yours, I will not rashly encounter danger. I will be cool, persevering, and prudent.

But success shall crown[2] my endeavours. Wherefore not? Thus far I have gone, tracing a secure way over the pathless seas: the very stars themselves being witnesses and testimonies of my triumph. Why not still proceed over the untamed yet obedient element[3]? What can stop the determined heart and resolved will of man?

My swelling heart involuntarily pours itself out thus. But I must finish. Heaven bless my beloved sister!

R. W.

LETTER IV

To Mrs. Saville, England

August 5th, 17 — .

SO strange an accident has happened to us that I cannot forbear recording it, although it is very probable that you will see me before these papers can come into your possession.

Last Monday (July 31st) we were nearly surrounded by ice, which closed in[4] the ship on all sides, scarcely leaving her the sea room[5] in which she floated. Our situation was somewhat dangerous, especially as we were compassed[6] round by a very thick fog. We accordingly lay

---

1 Be assured that: ⋯하겠다고 분명히 약속하다.
2 crown: 최후를 장식하다; 즉 내 노력이 성공을 거둘 것이란 의미.
3 element: 자연.
4 closed in: 포위하다.
5 sea-room: 조선(操船) 여지(餘地); 즉 배를 조종하기에 넉넉한 해면.
6 compassed: 에워싸다(encompass).

to,[1] hoping that some change would take place in the atmosphere and weather.

About two o'clock the mist cleared away, and we beheld, stretched out in every direction, vast and irregular plains of ice, which seemed to have no end. Some of my comrades groaned, and my own mind began to grow watchful with anxious thoughts, when a strange sight suddenly attracted our attention and diverted our solicitude[2] from our own situation. We perceived a low carriage, fixed on a sledge and drawn by dogs, pass on towards the north, at the distance of half a mile; a being which had the shape of a man, but apparently of gigantic stature, sat in the sledge and guided the dogs. We watched the rapid progress of the traveller with our telescopes, until he was lost[3] among the distant inequalities[4] of the ice.

This appearance excited our unqualified[5] wonder. We were, as we believed, many hundred miles from any land; but this apparition[6] seemed to denote that it was not, in reality, so distant as we had supposed. Shut in, however, by ice, it was impossible to follow his track, which we had observed with the greatest attention.

About two hours after this occurrence, we heard the ground sea[7]; and before night the ice broke, and freed our ship. We, however, lay to until the morning, fearing to encounter in the dark those large loose masses[8] which float about after the breaking up of the ice. I profited of this time to rest for a few hours.

In the morning, however, as soon as it was light, I went upon deck

---

1 lay to: [항해] (이물을 바람 부는 쪽으로 돌리고) 정선(停船)하다.
2 solicitude: 걱정. 근심.
3 lost: (시야에서) 사라진.
4 inequalities: 고르지 않음(크기나 형태가 일정하지 않고 들쑥날쑥함).
5 unqualified: 엄청난.
6 apparition: 갑자기 등장한 인물. 유령.
7 ground sea: 큰 놀(파도).
8 large loose masses: '(빙하에서) 떨어져나간 큰 얼음덩이'를 지칭.

and found all the sailors busy on one side of the vessel, apparently talking to some one in the sea. It was, in fact, a sledge, like that we had seen before, which had drifted towards us in the night, on a large fragment of ice. Only one dog remained alive; but there was a human being within it whom the sailors were persuading to enter the vessel. He was not, as the other traveller seemed to be, a savage inhabitant of some undiscovered island, but an European. When I appeared on deck, the master said, "Here is our captain, and he will not allow you to perish on the open sea.[1]"

On perceiving me, the stranger addressed me in English, although with a foreign accent. "Before I come on board your vessel," said he, "will you have the kindness to inform me whither you are bound?"

You may conceive my astonishment on hearing such a question addressed to me from a man on the brink of destruction,[2] and to whom I should have supposed that my vessel would have been a resource[3] which he would not have exchanged for the most precious wealth the earth can afford. I replied, however, that we were on a voyage of discovery towards the northern pole.

Upon hearing this he appeared satisfied, and consented to come on board. Good God! Margaret, if you had seen the man who thus capitulated[4] for his safety, your surprise would have been boundless. His limbs were nearly frozen, and his body dreadfully emaciated[5] by fatigue and suffering. I never saw a man in so wretched a condition. We attempted to carry him into the cabin; but as soon as he had quitted the fresh air he fainted. We accordingly brought him back to the deck, and restored him to animation[6] by rubbing him with brandy,

---

1 open sea: 망망대해.
2 on the brink of destruction: 죽기 직전에 있는.
3 resource: 수단. 방책.
4 capitulated: 협상하다.
5 emaciated: 야윈.
6 restored him to animation: 그를 정신 차리게 하다. 그의 의식을 되돌려 놓다.

and forcing him to swallow a small quantity. As soon as he showed signs of life we wrapped him up in blankets, and placed him near the chimney of the kitchen stove. By slow degrees he recovered, and ate a little soup, which restored him wonderfully.

Two days passed in this manner before he was able to speak; and I often feared that his sufferings had deprived him of understanding.[1] When he had in some measure recovered, I removed him to my own cabin, and attended on him as much as my duty would permit. I never saw a more interesting creature: his eyes have generally an expression of wildness, and even madness; but there are moments when, if any one performs an act of kindness towards him, or does him the most trifling[2] service, his whole countenance is lighted up, as it were, with a beam of benevolence and sweetness that I never saw equalled. But he is generally melancholy and despairing, and sometimes he gnashes his teeth, as if impatient of[3] the weight of woes[4] that oppresses him.

When my guest was a little recovered I had great trouble to keep off the men, who wished to ask him a thousand questions; but I would not allow him to be tormented by their idle curiosity, in a state of body and mind whose restoration evidently depended upon entire repose. Once, however, the lieutenant asked, Why he had come so far upon the ice in so strange a vehicle?

His countenance instantly assumed an aspect of the deepest gloom; and he replied, "To seek one who fled from me."

"And did the man whom you pursued travel in the same fashion?"

"Yes."

"Then I fancy we have seen him; for the day before we picked you

---

1 understanding: 지적 능력. 식별력.
2 trifling: 작은. 사소한.
3 impatient of: …을 참지 못하여.
4 woes: 고뇌.

up we saw some dogs drawing a sledge, with a man in it, across the ice."

This aroused the stranger's attention; and he asked a multitude of questions concerning the route which the dæmon[1], as he called him, had pursued. Soon after, when he was alone with me, he said, — "I have, doubtless, excited your curiosity, as well as that of these good people; but you are too considerate to make inquiries."

"Certainly; it would indeed be very impertinent[2] and inhuman in me to trouble you with any inquisitiveness of mine."

"And yet you rescued me from a strange and perilous situation; you have benevolently restored me to life."

Soon after this he inquired if I thought that the breaking up of the ice had destroyed the other sledge? I replied that I could not answer with any degree of certainty; for the ice had not broken until near midnight, and the traveller might have arrived at a place of safety before that time; but of this I could not judge.

From this time a new spirit of life animated the decaying frame[3] of the stranger. He manifested the greatest eagerness to be upon deck, to watch for the sledge which had before appeared; but I have persuaded him to remain in the cabin, for he is far too weak to sustain the rawness[4] of the atmosphere. I have promised that some one should watch for him, and give him instant notice if any new object should appear in sight.[5]

Such is my journal of what relates to this strange occurrence up to the present day. The stranger has gradually improved in health, but is very silent, and appears uneasy when any one except myself enters his

---

1 dæmon: 그리스 신화에서 이 단어는 신과 인간 중간 정도의 초자연적인 존재를 지칭하는 용어나 여기서 메리 셸리는 악마(demon)의 의미로 사용하고 있다.
2 impertinent: 무뢰한.
3 decaying frame: 쇠약해지는 신체(몸).
4 rawness: 추위.
5 appear in sight: 시야에 나타나다.

cabin. Yet his manners are so conciliating[1] and gentle that the sailors are all interested in him, although they have had very little communication with him. For my own part, I begin to love him as a brother; and his constant and deep grief fills me with sympathy and compassion. He must have been a noble creature in his better days, being even now in wreck[2] so attractive and amiable.

I said in one of my letters, my dear Margaret, that I should find no friend on the wide ocean; yet I have found a man who, before his spirit had been broken by misery, I should have been happy to have possessed as the brother of my heart.

I shall continue my journal concerning the stranger at intervals, should I have any fresh[3] incidents to record.

August 13th, 17 —

My affection for my guest increases every day. He excites at once my admiration[4] and my pity to an astonishing degree. How can I see so noble a creature destroyed by misery without feeling the most poignant[5] grief? He is so gentle, yet so wise; his mind is so cultivated; and when he speaks, although his words are culled[6] with the choicest art, yet they flow with rapidity and unparalleled eloquence.

He is now much recovered from his illness, and is continually on the deck, apparently watching for the sledge that preceded his own. Yet, although unhappy, he is not so utterly occupied by his own misery but that he interests himself deeply in the projects of others. He has frequently conversed with me on mine, which I have communicated to him without disguise. He entered attentively into all my

---

1 conciliating: 친절한. 조용한.
2 in wreck: 조락한. 몸이 쇠퇴한.
3 fresh: 새로운.
4 admiration: 감탄. 탄복.
5 poignant: 통렬한. 통절한.
6 culled: 취사선택한.

arguments in favour of[1] my eventual success, and into every minute detail of the measures I had taken to secure it. I was easily led by the sympathy which he evinced[2] to use the language of my heart; to give utterance to the burning ardour of my soul; and to say, with all the fervour that warmed me, how gladly I would sacrifice my fortune, my existence, my every hope, to the furtherance[3] of my enterprise. One man's life or death were but a small price to pay for the acquirement of the knowledge which I sought[4]; for the dominion I should acquire and transmit over the elemental foes of our race.[5] As I spoke, a dark gloom spread over my listener's countenance. At first I perceived that he tried to suppress his emotion; he placed his hands before his eyes; and my voice quivered and failed[6] me, as I beheld tears trickle fast from between his fingers — a groan burst from his heaving breast. I paused; — at length he spoke, in broken accents: — "Unhappy man! Do you share my madness? Have you drunk also of the intoxicating draught?[7] Hear me — let me reveal my tale, and you will dash the cup from your lips!"

Such words, you may imagine, strongly excited my curiosity; but the paroxysm[8] of grief that had seized the stranger overcame his weakened powers, and many hours of repose and tranquil conversation were necessary to restore his composure.

Having conquered the violence of his feelings, he appeared to

---

1 in favour of: …에 찬동하며.
2 evinced: 드러내다.
3 furtherance: 진전. 촉진.
4 One man's life or death were … acquirement of the knowledge which I sought: 지식의 추구를 위해 모든 것을 희생할 수 있다는 월튼 선장의 말은 생과 사의 비밀을 풀기위해 자신을 포함하여 가족 모두를 희생시킨 프랑켄스타인을 연상시킨다.
5 elemental foes of our race: 인간의 장애물인 자연의 힘(본질)을 의미한다.
6 failed: 말을 할 수 없었다는 의미.
7 draught: 술의 의미지만 여기서는 상징적으로 자신의 운명을 결정하는 '운명의 술잔'을 의미한다.
8 paroxysm: (감정의) 격발.

despise himself for being the slave of passion; and quelling the dark tyranny of despair, he led me again to converse concerning myself personally. He asked me the history of my earlier years. The tale was quickly told; but it awakened various trains[1] of reflection. I spoke of my desire of finding a friend — of my thirst for a more intimate sympathy with a fellow mind than had ever fallen to my lot;[2] and expressed my conviction that a man could boast of little happiness, who did not enjoy this blessing.

"I agree with you," replied the stranger; "we are unfashioned[3] creatures, but half made up, if one wiser, better, dearer than ourselves — such a friend ought to be — do not lend his aid to perfectionate[4] our weak and faulty natures. I once had a friend, the most noble of human creatures, and am entitled, therefore, to judge respecting friendship. You have hope, and the world before you,[5] and have no cause for despair. But I — I have lost everything and cannot begin life anew."

As he said this, his countenance became expressive of a calm, settled[6] grief that touched me to the heart. But he was silent, and presently retired to his cabin.

Even broken in spirit as he is, no one can feel more deeply than he does the beauties of nature.[7] The starry sky, the sea, and every sight afforded by these wonderful regions seem still to have the power of elevating his soul from earth. Such a man has a double existence: he

---

1 trains of: 일련의 ….

2 fallen to my lot: 내 운명에 닥친.

3 unfashioned: 완전히 만들어지지 않은; 즉 인간은 완벽한 존재가 아니라는 뜻.

4 perfectionate: 완전하게 만들다.

5 the world before you: 밀튼의 「실낙원」의 마지막 부분에서 에덴동산에서 쫓겨나 드넓은 세상에 던져진 아담의 상태를 묘사하는 구절을 연상시킨다.

6 settled: 뿌리 깊은.

7 no one can feel more deeply than he does the beauties of nature: 월튼 선장, 프랑켄스타인, 괴물은 모두 낭만적 성향을 지니고 있으면서 동시에 낭만주의 시인들처럼 자연의 아름다움을 예찬한다.

may suffer misery, and be overwhelmed by disappointments, yet when he has retired into himself, he will be like a celestial spirit that has a halo[1] around him, within whose circle no grief or folly ventures.

Will you smile at the enthusiasm I express concerning this divine wanderer? You would not if you saw him. You have been tutored and refined[2] by books and retirement from the world, and you are, therefore, somewhat fastidious;[3] but this only renders you the more fit to appreciate the extraordinary merits of this wonderful man. Sometimes I have endeavoured to discover what quality it is which he possesses that elevates him so immeasurably above any other person I ever knew. I believe it to be an intuitive discernment;[4] a quick but never-failing power of judgment; a penetration into the causes of things, unequalled for clearness and precision; add to this a facility of expression,[5] and a voice whose varied intonations are soul-subduing[6] music.

August 19th, 17 — .

Yesterday the stranger said to me, "You may easily perceive, Captain Walton that I have suffered great and unparalleled[7] misfortunes. I had determined, at one time, that the memory of these evils should die with me; but you have won[8] me to alter my determination. You seek for knowledge and wisdom, as I once did; and I ardently hope that the gratification[9] of your wishes may not be a serpent to sting

---

1 halo: 후광.
2 refined: 고상한. 순수해진.
3 fastidious: 까다로운.
4 discernment: 통찰력.
5 facility of expression: 뛰어난 표현 능력.
6 soul-subduing: 마음을 가라앉히는.
7 unparalleled: 남과 비교되지 않을 정도의.
8 won: 설득시키다.
9 gratification: 욕구 충족. 만족시킴.

you,[1] as mine has been. I do not know that the relation[2] of my disasters will be useful to you; yet, when I reflect that you are pursuing the same course, exposing yourself to the same dangers which have rendered me what I am, I imagine that you may deduce[3] an apt moral[4] from my tale; one that may direct you if you succeed in your undertaking, and console you in case of failure. Prepare to hear of occurrences which are usually deemed marvellous. Were we among the tamer scenes of nature,[5] I might fear to encounter your unbelief, perhaps your ridicule; but many things will appear possible in these wild and mysterious regions which would provoke the laughter of those unacquainted with the ever-varied powers of nature; nor can I doubt but that my tale conveys in its series internal evidence of the truth of the events of which it is composed."

You may easily imagine that I was much gratified by the offered communication; yet I could not endure that he should renew his grief by a recital of his misfortunes. I felt the greatest eagerness to hear the promised narrative, partly from curiosity, and partly from a strong desire to ameliorate[6] his fate, if it were in my power. I expressed these feelings in my answer.

"I thank you," he replied, "for your sympathy, but it is useless; my fate is nearly fulfilled. I wait but for one event, and then I shall repose in peace. I understand your feeling," continued he, perceiving that I wished to interrupt him; "but you are mistaken, my friend, if thus you will allow me to name you; nothing can alter my destiny: listen to

---

1 may not be a serpent to sting you: '당신을 무는 뱀이 되지 않기 바란다'는 이 구절의 의미는 유혹의 상징인 뱀의 꼬임에 넘어가 파멸되지 않기 바란다는 뜻으로 무모한 과학적 지식의 위험성에 대한 프랑켄스타인의 경고다.

2 relation: 진술.

3 deduce: 추론하다.

4 moral: 교훈.

5 tamer scenes of nature: 사람에 의해 가꾸어지거나 개발된 곳을 지칭.

6 ameliorate: 개선하다. 좋아지게 하다.

my history, and you will perceive how irrevocably[1] it is determined."

He then told me that he would commence his narrative the next day when I should be at leisure. This promise drew from me the warmest thanks. I have resolved every night, when I am not imperatively[2] occupied by my duties, to record, as nearly as possible in his own words, what he has related during the day. If I should be engaged, I will at least make notes. This manuscript will doubtless afford you the greatest pleasure; but to me, who know him, and who hear it from his own lips, with what interest and sympathy shall I read it in some future day! Even now, as I commence my task, his full-toned voice swells in my ears; his lustrous[3] eyes dwell on[4] me with all their melancholy sweetness; I see his thin hand raised in animation, while the lineaments[5] of his face are irradiated by the soul within. Strange and harrowing[6] must be his story, frightful the storm which embraced[7] the gallant vessel[8] on its course and wrecked it — thus!

---

1 irrevocably: '돌이킬 수 없게'. '변경 불가능하게'; 프랑켄스타인은 자신의 운명이 신의 섭리에 의해 결정된 것임을 암시하고 있다.

2 imperatively: 긴급하게,

3 lustrous: 빛나는.

4 dwell on: …에 머무르다.

5 lineaments: 용모. 얼굴 생김새.

6 harrowing: 마음 아픈. 비참한.

7 embraced: 에워싸다.

8 gallant vessel: '당당한 배'; 하지만 이 용어는 '용감하고 멋진(gallant) 사람(vessel)'이란 의미로도 해석될 수 있다. 즉 월튼 선장은 프랑켄스타인을 '멋진 배'에 비유하면서, 폭풍에 배가 난파당하듯이 시련을 통해 프랑켄스타인이 현재와 같은 조락한 상태에 처하게 되었다고 생각하고 있는 것이다.

CHAPTER I

I am by birth a Genevese[1]; and my family is one of the most distinguished of that republic. My ancestors had been for many years counsellors and syndics[2]; and my father had filled several public situations with honour and reputation. He was respected by all who knew him for his integrity and indefatigable[3] attention to public business. He passed his younger days perpetually occupied by the affairs of his country; a variety of circumstances had prevented his marrying early, nor was it until the decline of life[4] that he became a husband and the father of a family.

As the circumstances of his marriage illustrate his character, I cannot refrain from relating them. One of his most intimate friends was a merchant who, from a flourishing state, fell, through numerous mischances,[5] into poverty. This man, whose name was Beaufort, was of a proud and unbending[6] disposition, and could not bear to live in poverty and oblivion in the same country where he had formerly been distinguished for his rank and magnificence. Having paid his debts, therefore, in the most honourable manner, he retreated with his daughter to the town of Lucerne,[7] where he lived unknown and in wretchedness. My father loved Beaufort with the truest friendship, and was deeply grieved by his retreat in these unfortunate circumstances. He bitterly deplored the false pride which led his friend to a conduct so little worthy of the affection that united them. He lost no time in endeavouring to seek him out, with the hope of persuading

---

1 Genevese: '제네바 사람'; 루소(Rousseau)의 출생지이자 프랑스 사상가 볼테르(Voltaire)가 은신처로 삼았던 제네바는 당시 자유의 도시로 그 상징성을 갖고 있었다.
2 syndics: 재판관. (지방) 행정관.
3 indefatigable: 지치지 않는.
4 decline of life: 만년.
5 mischances: 불운.
6 unbending: 불굴의(정신 등). 완고한.
7 Lucerne: 스위스에 위치한 대도시.

him to begin the world again through his credit and assistance.

Beaufort had taken effectual measures to conceal himself, and it was ten months before my father discovered his abode. Overjoyed at this discovery, he hastened to the house, which was situated in a mean[1] street near the Reuss.[2] But when he entered, misery and despair alone welcomed him. Beaufort had saved but a very small sum of money from the wreck of his fortunes; but it was sufficient to provide him with sustenance[3] for some months, and in the meantime he hoped to procure some respectable employment in a merchant's house. The interval was, consequently, spent in inaction; his grief only became more deep and rankling[4] when he had leisure for reflection; and at length it took so fast hold of his mind[5] that at the end of three months he lay on a bed of sickness, incapable of any exertion.

His daughter attended him with the greatest tenderness; but she saw with despair that their little fund was rapidly decreasing, and that there was no other prospect of support. But Caroline Beaufort possessed a mind of an uncommon mould[6]; and her courage rose to support her in her adversity. She procured plain work; she plaited[7] straw; and by various means contrived to earn a pittance[8] scarcely sufficient to support life.

Several months passed in this manner. Her father grew worse; her time was more entirely occupied in attending him; her means of subsistence[9] decreased; and in the tenth month her father died in her arms, leaving her an orphan and a beggar. This last blow overcame

---

1 mean: 가난한.
2 Reuss: 독일의 중심부의 한 지역.
3 sustenance: 생계수단. 생명을 유지하게 해주는 물질.
4 rankling: 악화되다.
5 took so fast hold of his mind: 그의 마음을 강하게 사로잡았다.
6 mould: 특성. 성격(character).
7 plaited: (짚을) 짜다.
8 pittance: 약간의 수입.
9 means of subsistence: 호구지책. 생계수단.

her; and she knelt by Beaufort's coffin weeping bitterly, when my father entered the chamber. He came like a protecting spirit to the poor girl, who committed herself to his care; and after the interment[1] of his friend, he conducted her to Geneva and placed her under the protection of a relation[2]. Two years after this event Caroline became his wife.

There was a considerable difference between the ages of my parents, but this circumstance seemed to unite them only closer in bonds of devoted affection. There was a sense of justice in my father's upright mind, which rendered it necessary that he should approve highly to love strongly. Perhaps during former years he had suffered from the late-discovered unworthiness of one beloved, and so was disposed to set a greater value on tried worth. There was a show[3] of gratitude and worship in his attachment to my mother, differing wholly from the doting[4] fondness of age, for it was inspired by reverence for her virtues, and a desire to be the means of, in some degree, recompensing her for the sorrows she had endured, but which gave inexpressible grace to his behaviour to her. Everything was made to yield to her wishes and her convenience. He strove to shelter her, as a fair exotic[5] is sheltered by the gardener, from every rougher wind, and to surround her with all that could tend[6] to excite pleasurable emotion in her soft and benevolent mind. Her health, and even the tranquillity of her hitherto constant spirit, had been shaken by what she had gone through. During the two years that had elapsed previous to their marriage my father had gradually relinquished all his public functions; and immediately after their union they sought the pleasant climate of Italy, and the change of

---

1 interment: 매장.
2 relation: 친척.
3 show: 징후. 흔적. 겉으로 드러남.
4 doting: (나이가 들어서) 지나칠 정도로 사랑하는.
5 exotic: 외래식물.
6 tend: 이바지하다. 도움이 되다.

scene and interest attendant on[1] a tour through that land of wonders, as a restorative[2] for her weakened frame.

From Italy they visited Germany and France. I, their eldest child, was born in Naples, and as an infant accompanied them in their rambles. I remained for several years their only child. Much as they were attached to each other, they seemed to draw inexhaustible stores of affection from a very mine[3] of love to bestow them upon me. My mother's tender caresses and my father's smile of benevolent pleasure while regarding me, are my first recollections. I was their plaything and their idol, and something better — their child, the innocent and helpless creature bestowed on them by Heaven, whom to bring up to good,[4] and whose future lot it was in their hands to direct to happiness or misery, according as they fulfilled their duties towards me. With this deep consciousness of what they owed towards the being to which they had given life, added to the active spirit of tenderness that animated both, it may be imagined that while during every hour of my infant life I received a lesson of patience, of charity, and of self-control, I was so guided by a silken cord that all seemed but one train of enjoyment to me.

For a long time I was their only care. My mother had much desired to have a daughter, but I continued their single offspring. When I was about five years old, while making an excursion[5] beyond the frontiers of Italy, they passed a week on the shores of the Lake of Como.[6] Their benevolent disposition often made them enter the cottages of the poor. This, to my mother, was more than a duty; it was a necessity, a passion — remembering what she had suffered, and how she had been relieved — for her to act in her turn the guardian angel to

---

1 attendant on: …에 수반되는(부수적으로 따라오는).
2 restorative: 건강을 회복시키는 방법. 치유책.
3 mine: 풍부한 자원. 보고.
4 bring up to good: 잘 키워 좋은 결과를 낳도록 하다.
5 excursion: 여행. 유람.
6 Lake of Como: (북부 이탈리아에 위치한) 코모 호.

the afflicted. During one of their walks a poor cot[1] in the foldings of a vale[2] attracted their notice as being singularly disconsolate,[3] while the number of half-clothed children gathered about it spoke of penury in its worst shape.[4] One day, when my father had gone by himself to Milan,[5] my mother, accompanied by me, visited this abode. She found a peasant and his wife, hard working, bent down[6] by care and labour, distributing a scanty meal to five hungry babes. Among these there was one which attracted my mother far above all the rest. She appeared of a different stock.[7] The four others were dark-eyed, hardy[8] little vagrants; this child was thin and very fair. Her hair was the brightest living gold, and despite the poverty of her clothing, seemed to set a crown of distinction on her head. Her brow was clear and ample, her blue eyes cloudless, and her lips and the moulding of her face so expressive of sensibility and sweetness, that none could behold her without looking on her as of a distinct species, a being heaven-sent, and bearing a celestial stamp[9] in all her features.[10]

The peasant woman, perceiving that my mother fixed eyes of wonder and admiration on this lovely girl, eagerly communicated her history. She was not her child, but the daughter of a Milanese nobleman. Her mother was a German, and had died on giving her birth.[11] The

---

1 cot: 작고 허름한 집. 오두막집.

2 vale: 골짜기. 계곡.

3 disconsolate: 절망적인.

4 penury in its worst shape: 최악의 빈곤.

5 Milan: 밀라노(이탈리아 북부 롬바르디(Lombardy)에 있는 도시).

6 bent down: 기가 꺾인.

7 stock: 혈통. 가계(家系).

8 hardy: 튼튼한. 강건한.

9 stamp: 흔적. 특징.

10 features: 용모. 이목구비.

11 Her mother was a German, and had died on giving her birth: 1818년의 초판에서 엘리자베스는 프랑켄스타인의 고종 사촌으로 되어있으나, 1831년 판에서는 밀라노 귀족의 고아가 된 딸로 설정되어 있다. 또한 엘리자베스의 어머니가 그녀를 낳다가 죽었다는 사실은 메리의 모친인 울스톤크라프트가 메리를 낳은 지 얼마 되지 않아 임종한 사

infant had been placed with these good people to nurse: they were better off then. They had not been long married, and their eldest child was but just born. The father of their charge[1] was one of those Italians nursed in the memory of the antique glory of Italy — one among the schiavi ognor frementi,[2] who exerted himself to obtain the liberty of his country. He became the victim of its weakness. Whether he had died, or still lingered in the dungeons of Austria, was not known. His property was confiscated,[3] his child became an orphan and a beggar. She continued with her foster parents, and bloomed in their rude[4] abode, fairer than a garden rose among dark-leaved brambles.[5]

When my father returned from Milan, he found playing with me in the hall of our villa a child fairer than pictured cherub[6] — a creature who seemed to shed radiance from her looks, and whose form and motions were lighter than the chamois[7] of the hills. The apparition was soon explained. With his permission my mother prevailed on her rustic guardians to yield their charge to her. They were fond of the sweet orphan. Her presence had seemed a blessing to them; but it would be unfair to her to keep her in poverty and want,[8] when Providence afforded her such powerful protection. They consulted their village priest, and the result was that Elizabeth Lavenza became the inmate[9] of my parents' house — my more than sister — the beautiful and adored companion of all my occupations and my pleasures.

Every one loved Elizabeth. The passionate and almost reverential

---

실을 떠올리게 한다.

1 charge: 맡아서 키우고 있는 아이를 지칭.

2 schiavi ognor frementi: 이태리어로 '영원히 분노하고 있는 노예들'이란 의미.

3 confiscated: 몰수되다.

4 rude: 조잡하게 지어진.

5 brambles: 가시나무.

6 cherub: 지품천사(智品天使)로 날개달린 아이의 모습을 하고 있는 것으로 묘사된다.

7 chamois: 샤무아(남유럽·서남 아시아산의 영양류(類)).

8 want: 곤궁.

9 inmate: 같은 곳에 기거하는 사람.

attachment with which all regarded her became, while I shared it, my pride and my delight. On the evening previous to her being brought to my home, my mother had said playfully, — "I have a pretty present for my Victor — tomorrow he shall have it." And when, on the morrow,[1] she presented Elizabeth to me as her promised gift, I, with childish seriousness, interpreted her words literally, and looked upon Elizabeth as mine — mine to protect, love, and cherish. All praises bestowed on her I, received as made to a possession of my own. We called each other familiarly by the name of cousin. No word, no expression could body forth[2] the kind of relation in which she stood to me — my more than sister, since till death she was to be mine only.

CHAPTER II

We were brought up together; there was not quite a year difference in our ages. I need not say that we were strangers to any species of disunion[3] or dispute. Harmony was the soul[4] of our companionship, and the diversity and contrast that subsisted in our characters drew us nearer together. Elizabeth was of a calmer and more concentrated disposition; but, with all my ardour, I was capable of a more intense application[5] and was more deeply smitten with[6] the thirst for knowledge. She busied herself with following the aerial[7] creations of the poets; and in the majestic and wondrous scenes which surrounded our Swiss home — the sublime[8] shapes of the mountains; the changes of the

---

1 morrow: 아침.
2 body forth: 구체적으로 나타내다. 상징하다.
3 disunion: 불화. 갈등.
4 soul: 정수. 핵심.
5 application: 전념. 몰두. 열중.
6 smitten with: …에 사로잡힌.
7 aerial: 영묘한. 환상적인. 꿈같은.
8 sublime: '숭고한(함)'이란 의미의 이 단어는 이 작품 속에서 아주 여러 번 등장한다.

seasons; tempest and calm; the silence of winter, and the life and turbulence[1] of our Alpine summers — she found ample scope[2] for admiration and delight. While my companion contemplated with a serious
and satisfied spirit the magnificent appearances of things, I delighted
in investigating their causes. The world was to me a secret which I
desired to divine.[3] Curiosity, earnest research to learn the hidden laws
of nature, gladness akin to rapture,[4] as they were unfolded to me, are
among the earliest sensations I can remember.

On the birth of a second son, my junior by seven years, my parents gave up entirely their wandering life and fixed themselves in their
native country. We possessed a house in Geneva, and a campagne[5] on
Belrive, the eastern shore of the lake, at the distance of rather more
than a league from the city. We resided principally in the latter, and
the lives of my parents were passed in considerable seclusion. It was
my temper to avoid a crowd and to attach myself fervently to a few. I
was indifferent, therefore, to my schoolfellows in general; but I united
myself in the bonds of the closest friendship to one among them.
Henry Clerval was the son of a merchant of Geneva. He was a boy
of singular talent and fancy. He loved enterprise, hardship, and even
danger, for its own sake. He was deeply read[6] in books of chivalry
and romance. He composed heroic songs, and began to write many a
tale of enchantment and knightly adventure. He tried to make us act
plays, and to enter into masquerades, in which the characters were
drawn from the heroes of Roncesvalles,[7] of the Round Table of King

---

   낭만주의 시인들의 특징 중 하나는 자연에서 이런 숭고함을 찾고자 하는 것이기 때문이
   다.
1 turbulence: 거칠게 몰아치는 바람.
2 scope: (능력 등을 발휘할) 여지. 배출구.
3 divine: 알아내다. 간파하다.
4 gladness akin to rapture: 환희에 가까운 기쁨.
5 campagne: (불어) 시골집.
6 read: 정통한. 조예가 깊은. 잘 알고 있는.
7 Roncesvalles: 에스파냐 북부에 있는 마을로 프랑스에서는 롱스보(Roncevaux)라고

Arthur,[1] and the chivalrous train[2] who shed their blood to redeem[3] the holy sepulchre[4] from the hands of the infidels.

No human being could have passed a happier childhood than myself. My parents were possessed by the very spirit of kindness and indulgence.[5] We felt that they were not the tyrants to rule our lot according to their caprice, but the agents and creators of all the many delights which we enjoyed. When I mingled with other families, I distinctly discerned how peculiarly fortunate my lot was, and gratitude assisted the development of filial love.

My temper was sometimes violent, and my passions vehement; but by some law in my temperature[6] they were turned not towards childish pursuits, but to an eager desire to learn, and not to learn all things indiscriminately.[7] I confess that neither the structure of languages, nor the code of governments, nor the politics of various states possessed attractions for me. It was the secrets of heaven and earth that I desired to learn; and whether it was the outward substance of things, or the inner spirit of nature and the mysterious soul of man that occupied me, still my inquiries were directed to the metaphysical, or, in its highest sense, the physical secrets of the world.

Meanwhile Clerval occupied himself, so to speak, with the moral relations of things. The busy stage of life, the virtues of heroes, and the actions of men were his theme; and his hope and his dream was

---

한다. 778년 카를 대제가 에스파냐를 원정했을 때 매복하고 있던 사라센군에게 패배한 곳으로, 이 전투에서의 영웅 롤랑에 관해서 읊은 서정시 「롤랑의 노래」(La Chanson de Roland)가 유명하다.

1 Round Table of King Arthur: 영국의 전설상의 왕 아더와 그의 원탁의 기사에 관한 이야기를 지칭.

2 train: (사람·동물·차 따위의) 열. 행렬. 일행.

3 redeem: 되찾다.

4 holy sepulchre: 예루살렘의 그리스도 수난지로 그의 묘지였다는 장소에 세워진 여러 건축물을 지칭.

5 indulgence: 관대함.

6 temperature: 'temperament'(기질)의 의미로 사용되었다.

7 indiscriminately: 무차별적으로.

to become one among those whose names are recorded in story as the gallant and adventurous benefactors of our species. The saintly soul of Elizabeth shone like a shrine-dedicated lamp in our peaceful home. Her sympathy was ours; her smile, her soft voice, the sweet glance of her celestial eyes, were ever there to bless and animate us. She was the living spirit of love to soften and attract: I might have become sullen in my study, rough through the ardour of my nature, but that she was there to subdue me to a semblance of her own gentleness.[1] And Clerval — could aught ill entrench[2] on the noble spirit of Clerval? — yet he might not have been so perfectly humane, so thoughtful in his generosity, — so full of kindness and tenderness amidst his passion for adventurous exploit,[3] had she not unfolded to him the real loveliness of beneficence, and made the doing good the end and aim of his soaring ambition.[4]

I feel exquisite pleasure in dwelling on[5] the recollections of childhood, before misfortune had tainted my mind, and changed its bright visions of extensive usefulness into gloomy and narrow reflections upon self. Besides, in drawing the picture of my early days, I also record those events which led, by insensible steps, to my after tale of misery: for when I would account to myself for the birth of that passion, which afterwards ruled my destiny, I find it arise, like a mountain river, from ignoble[6] and almost forgotten sources; but, swelling as it proceeded, it became the torrent which, in its course, has swept away all my hopes and joys.

Natural philosophy[7] is the genius[8] that has regulated my fate; I de-

---

1 subdue me to a semblance of her own gentleness: semblance은 '유사'. '닮음'; 즉 나로 하여금 그녀의 부드러운 모습을 띄게 하였다는 의미.

2 entrench: 침해하다(on, upon).

3 exploit: 업적. 공훈.

4 soaring ambition: 점점 커져가는 야망.

5 dwelling on: …을 길게 논하다.

6 ignoble: 하찮은.

7 Natural philosophy: 자연 철학(지금의 과학, 특히 물리학을 지칭).

8 genius: 따라다니는 신.

sire, therefore, in this narration, to state those facts which led to my predilection[1] for that science. When I was thirteen years of age, we all went on a party of pleasure to the baths near Thonon:[2] the inclemency[3] of the weather obliged us to remain a day confined to the inn. In this house I chanced to find a volume of the works of Cornelius Agrippa.[4] I opened it with apathy; the theory which he attempts to demonstrate, and the wonderful facts which he relates, soon changed this feeling into enthusiasm. A new light seemed to dawn upon my mind; and, bounding with joy,[5] I communicated my discovery to my father. My father looked carelessly at the title page of my book, and said, "Ah! Cornelius Agrippa! My dear Victor, do not waste your time upon this; it is sad trash."

If, instead of this remark, my father had taken the pains to explain to me that the principles of Agrippa had been entirely exploded,[6] and that a modern system of science had been introduced, which possessed much greater powers than the ancient, because the powers of the latter were chimerical,[7] while those of the former were real and practical; under such circumstances, I should certainly have thrown Agrippa aside, and have contented my imagination, warmed as it was, by returning with greater ardour to my former studies. It is even possible that the train of my ideas would never have received the fatal impulse that led to my ruin. But the cursory[8] glance my father had taken of my volume by no means assured me that he was acquainted with its contents; and I continued to read with the greatest avidity.

---

1 predilection: 좋아함.
2 Thonon: 또농(제네바호 남단에 위치한 프랑스의 스파 타운).
3 inclemency: (날씨의) 험악함.
4 Cornelius Agrippa: 아그리파(독일의 천문학자, 마술사, 과학자(1486-1535)).
5 bounding with joy: 기뻐서 뛰며.
6 exploded: 타파되다. 뒤엎어지다.
7 chimerical: 터무니없는.
8 cursory: 대강의. 슬쩍 지나가는 듯한.

When I returned home, my first care was to procure[1] the whole works of this author, and afterwards of Paracelsus[2] and Albertus Magnus.[3] I read and studied the wild fancies of these writers with delight; they appeared to me treasures known to few beside myself. I have described myself as always having been embued[4] with a fervent[5] longing to penetrate the secrets of nature. In spite of the intense labour and wonderful discoveries of modern philosophers, I always came from my studies discontented and unsatisfied. Sir Isaac Newton[6] is said to have avowed that he felt like a child picking up shells beside the great and unexplored ocean of truth. Those of his successors in each branch of natural philosophy with whom I was acquainted appeared, even to my boy's apprehensions,[7] as tyros[8] engaged in the same pursuit.

The untaught peasant beheld the elements[9] around him, and was acquainted with their practical uses. The most learned philosopher knew little more. He had partially unveiled the face of Nature, but her immortal lineaments[10] were still a wonder and a mystery. He might dissect, anatomise,[11] and give names; but, not to speak of a final cause,[12]

---

1 procure: 구하다. 구매하다.

2 Paracelsus: 필리푸스 파라셀수스(Philippus Aureolus Paracelsus, 1493-1541); 스위스의 과학자로 물리학, 화학, 의학교수이기도 하며 수은과 아편을 의술에 도입하기도 하였다.

3 Albertus Magnus: 알베르투스 마그누스; 많은 낭만주의 시인들이 좋아하던 독일의 철학자이자 신학자, 과학자(1193-1280)로 자연과학에 대한 저서를 남겼다.

4 embued: 가득 찬.

5 fervent: 강렬한. 열정적인.

6 Sir Isaac Newton: 뉴턴(1642-1727); 영국의 물리학자이자 수학자, 천문학자로 우주에 대한 비밀은 엄격한 과학적 관찰에 근거하여야 한다고 주장하였다.

7 even to my boy's apprehensions: 소년인 내가 이해하기에도(보기에도).

8 tyros: 아마추어. 초보자.

9 element: 이 세계(우주)를 구성한다고 중세 사람들이 생각하였던 4원소(흙·물·불·바람).

10 lineaments: 윤곽. 모습. 특징.

11 anatomise: 상세히 분석하다.

12 not to speak of a final cause: not to speak of는 '…은 말할 것도 없고'; final cause는 '목적인(因)', '궁극인(因)'의 의미: 즉 궁극인은 말할 것도 없고.

causes in their secondary and tertiary[1] grades were utterly unknown to him. I had gazed upon the fortifications and impedi- ments[2] that seemed to keep human beings from entering the citadel of nature, and rashly and ignorantly I had repined.[3]

But here were books, and here were men who had penetrated deeper and knew more. I took their word for all that they averred,[4] and I became their disciple. It may appear strange that such should arise in the eighteenth century; but while I followed the routine of education in the schools of Geneva, I was, to a great degree, self taught with regard to my favourite studies. My father was not scientific, and I was left to struggle with a child's blindness, added to a student's thirst for knowledge. Under the guidance of my new preceptors,[5] I entered with the greatest diligence into the search of the philosopher's stone[6] and the elixir[7] of life; but the latter soon obtained my undivided attention. Wealth was an inferior object; but what glory would attend the discovery, if I could banish disease from the human frame, and render man invulnerable to any but a violent death!

Nor were these my only visions. The raising of ghosts or devils was a promise liberally accorded by my favourite authors, the fulfillment of which I most eagerly sought; and if my incantations[8] were always unsuccessful, I attributed the failure rather to my own inexperience and mistake than to a want of skill or fidelity[9] in my

---

1 tertiary: 제 3의. 제 3위의.

2 impediments: 방해물. 장애물.

3 repined: 불평하였다.

4 I took their word for all that they averred: take the word for는 '…을 믿다'; 즉 난 그들이 주장하는 바를 모두 믿었다는 의미.

5 preceptors: 선생. 스승.

6 philosopher's stone: '현자의 돌'; 중세의 연금술사들이 모든 금속을 황금으로 만들고 영생을 가져다준다고 믿었던 상상의 물질.

7 elixir: 늙지 않고 영원한 생명을 줄 수 있다고 믿었던 음료의 일종.

8 incantations: 마술. 마법.

9 fidelity: 사실(신빙)성.

instructors. And thus for a time I was occupied by exploded systems, mingling, like an unadept,[1] a thousand contradictory theories, and floundering[2] desperately in a very slough[3] of multifarious[4] knowledge, guided by an ardent imagination and childish reasoning, till an accident again changed the current of my ideas.

When I was about fifteen years old we had retired to our house near Belrive[5], when we witnessed a most violent and terrible thunderstorm. It advanced from behind the mountains of Jura;[6] and the thunder burst at once with frightful loudness from various quarters[7] of the heavens. I remained, while the storm lasted, watching its progress with curiosity and delight. As I stood at the door, on a sudden I beheld a stream of fire issue from an old and beautiful oak which stood about twenty yards from our house; and so soon as the dazzling light vanished, the oak had disappeared, and nothing remained but a blasted stump. When we visited it the next morning, we found the tree shattered in a singular manner. It was not splintered by the shock, but entirely reduced to thin ribands[8] of wood. I never beheld anything so utterly destroyed.

Before this I was not unacquainted with the more obvious laws of electricity. On this occasion a man of great research in natural philosophy was with us, and, excited by this catastrophe, he entered on the explanation of a theory which he had formed on the subject of electricity and galvanism,[9] which was at once new and astonishing to

---

1 unadept: 비숙련자.
2 floundering: 허우적거리다.
3 slough: 구렁텅이. 늪.
4 multifarious: 가지가지의. 다양한.
5 Belrive: '아들다운 해안'이란 의미로, 제네바에서 4마일 정도 떨어진 곳에 위치해 있다.
6 mountains of Jura: 알프스의 북쪽에 위치한 작은 산맥.
7 quarters: 지역.
8 ribands: 가늘고 긴 조각. (pl.) 갈기갈기 (찢어진 상태).
9 galvanism: 화학반응을 통해 발생되는 전기; 이태리 출신의 과학자 루이지 갈바니 (Luigi Galvani, 1737-1798)가 이 전기를 발견하였는데, 그는 죽은 개구리에 이 전기를 쏘고 개구리의 근육이 어떻게 수축하는지 관찰하였는데, 프랑켄스타인 자신도 이와

me. All that he said threw greatly into the shade[1] Cornelius Agrippa, Albertus Magnus, and Paracelsus, the lords of my imagination; but by some fatality the overthrow of these men disinclined me to pursue my accustomed studies. It seemed to me as if nothing would or could ever be known. All that had so long engaged my attention suddenly grew despicable. By one of those caprices of the mind which we are perhaps most subject to in early youth, I at once gave up my former occupations; set down[2] natural history and all its progeny[3] as a deformed and abortive creation; and entertained the greatest disdain for a would-be science, which could never even step within the threshold of real knowledge. In this mood of mind I betook myself to[4] the mathematics, and the branches of study appertaining to[5] that science, as being built upon secure foundations, and so worthy of my consideration.

Thus strangely are our souls constructed, and by such slight ligaments[6] are we bound to prosperity or ruin. When I look back, it seems to me as if this almost miraculous change of inclination and will was the immediate suggestion of the guardian angel of my life — the last effort made by the spirit of preservation[7] to avert the storm that was even then hanging in the stars,[8] and ready to envelope me. Her victory was announced by an unusual tranquillity and gladness of soul, which followed the relinquishing[9] of my ancient and latterly tormenting studies. It was thus that I was to be taught to associate evil with

---

비슷한 실험을 나중에 한다.

1 threw greatly into the shade: … 으로 하여금 빛을 잃게(무색케) 하다.
2 set down: 간주하다(규정하다).
3 progeny: 비슷한 유형의 학문을 지칭.
4 betook myself to: …에 온 노력을 기울이다.
5 appertaining to: …에 관련된(속하는).
6 ligaments: 줄. 끈.
7 spirit of preservation: 날 보호해주는 수호신을 지칭.
8 hanging in the stars: 하늘에 머물고 있는.
9 relinquishing: 포기.

their prosecution,[1] happiness with their disregard.

It was a strong effort of the spirit of good; but it was ineffectual. Destiny was too potent, and her immutable laws had decreed[2] my utter and terrible destruction.

Chapter III

When I had attained the age of seventeen, my parents resolved that I should become a student at the university of Ingolstadt[3]. I had hitherto attended the schools of Geneva; but my father thought it necessary, for the completion of my education, that I should be made acquainted with other customs than those of my native country. My departure was therefore fixed at an early date; but before the day resolved upon could arrive, the first misfortune of my life occurred — an omen, as it were, of my future misery.

Elizabeth had caught the scarlet fever[4]; her illness was severe, and she was in the greatest danger. During her illness, many arguments had been urged to persuade my mother to refrain from attending upon her. She had, at first, yielded to our entreaties; but when she heard that the life of her favourite was menaced, she could no longer control her anxiety. She attended her sick bed — her watchful attentions triumphed over the malignity[5] of the distemper — Elizabeth was saved, but the consequences of this imprudence were fatal to her preserver. On the third day my mother sickened; her fever was

---

1 prosecution: 실행.
2 decreed: 운명으로 정하다.
3 Ingolstadt: 바바리아(Bavaria)의 한 도시에 위치한 대학으로 이곳에서 법학교수였던 아담 바이스하우프트(Adam Weishaupt)는 1776년 일루미나티(Illuminati)라고 불리던 비밀 단체를 창설하였는데, 이 단체는 프랑스 혁명을 배후에서 조장한 세력으로도 간주되고 있었다.
4 scarlet fever: '성홍렬'로 전염성이 매우 강하다.
5 malignity: 치명성.

accompanied by the most alarming symptoms, and the looks of her medical attendants prognosticated[1] the worst event. On her death-bed the fortitude[2] and benignity of this best of women did not desert her. She joined the hands of Elizabeth and myself: — "My children," she said, "my firmest hopes of future happiness were placed on the prospect of your union. This expectation will now be the consolation of your father. Elizabeth, my love, you must supply my place to my younger children. Alas! I regret that I am taken from you; and, happy and beloved as I have been, is it not hard to quit you all? But these are not thoughts befitting me; I will endeavour to resign myself cheerfully to death, and will indulge a hope of meeting you in another world."

She died calmly; and her countenance expressed affection even in death. I need not describe the feelings of those whose dearest ties are rent by that most irreparable[3] evil; the void that presents itself to the soul; and the despair that is exhibited on the countenance. It is so long before the mind can persuade itself that she, whom we saw every day, and whose very existence appeared a part of our own, can have departed for ever — that the brightness of a beloved eye can have been extinguished, and the sound of a voice so familiar, and dear to the ear, can be hushed, never more to be heard. These are the reflections of the first days; but when the lapse[4] of time proves the reality of the evil, then the actual bitterness of grief commences. Yet from whom has not that rude hand rent away some dear connection? and why should I describe a sorrow which all have felt, and must feel? The time at length arrives, when grief is rather an indulgence than a necessity[5]; and the smile that plays upon the lips, although it may be

---

1 prognosticated: 예지하다. 징후를 나타내다.
2 fortitude: 용기.
3 irreparable: 돌이킬 수 없는.
4 lapse: (시간의) 흐름.
5 indulgence than a necessity: 슬퍼하는 것이 꼭 해야 하는 것이라기보다는 감정의 탐

deemed a sacrilege,[1] is not banished. My mother was dead, but we had still duties which we ought to perform; we must continue our course with the rest, and learn to think ourselves fortunate, whilst one remains whom the spoiler[2] has not seized.

My departure for Ingolstadt, which had been deferred by these events, was now again determined upon. I obtained from my father a respite[3] of some weeks. It appeared to me sacrilege so soon to leave the repose, akin to death, of the house of mourning,[4] and to rush into the thick of life.[5] I was new to sorrow, but it did not the less alarm me. I was unwilling to quit the sight of those that remained to me; and above all, I desired to see my sweet Elizabeth in some degree consoled.

She indeed veiled[6] her grief, and strove to act the comforter[7] to us all. She looked steadily on life,[8] and assumed its duties with courage and zeal. She devoted herself to those whom she had been taught to call her uncle and cousins. Never was she so enchanting as at this time when she recalled the sunshine of her smiles and spent them upon us. She forgot even her own regret[9] in her endeavours to make us forget.

The day of my departure at length arrived. Clerval spent the last evening with us. He had endeavoured to persuade his father to permit him to accompany me, and to become my fellow student; but in vain. His father was a narrow-minded trader, and saw idleness and ruin in the aspirations and ambition of his son. Henry deeply felt the misfor-

---

닉 차원 하에서 하는 것이란 의미

1　sacrilege: 신성모독.
2　spoiler: 원래는 '약탈자'란 의미지만 여기서는 사람의 목숨을 앗아가는 '죽음의 사신'을 의인화한 것이다.
3　respite: 연기. 유예.
4　house of mourning: 상중인 집안.
5　thick of life: (활발한) 생의 한가운데.
6　veiled: 숨기다.
7　act the comforter: 위로자로서의 역할을 하다.
8　looked steadily on life: 삶을 직시하다.
9　regret: 슬픔.

tune of being debarred[1] from a liberal education.[2] He said little; but when he spoke, I read in his kindling eye and in his animated glance a restrained but firm resolve not to be chained to the miserable details of commerce.

We sat late. We could not tear ourselves away from each other, nor persuade ourselves to say the word "Farewell!" It was said; and we retired under the pretence of seeking repose, each fancying that the other was deceived: but when at morning's dawn I descended to the carriage[3] which was to convey me away, they were all there — my father again to bless me, Clerval to press my hand once more, my Elizabeth to renew her entreaties that I would write often, and to bestow the last feminine attentions on her playmate and friend.

I threw myself into the chaise[4] that was to convey me away, and indulged in the most melancholy reflections. I, who had ever been surrounded by amiable companions, continually engaged in endeavouring to bestow mutual pleasure, I was now alone. In the university, whither I was going, I must form my own friends, and be my own protector. My life had hitherto been remarkably secluded and domestic; and this had given me invincible repugnance[5] to new countenances. I loved my brothers, Elizabeth, and Clerval; these were "old familiar faces;" but I believed myself totally unfitted for the company of strangers. Such were my reflections as I commenced my journey; but as I proceeded my spirits and hopes rose. I ardently desired the acquisition of knowledge. I had often, when at home, thought it hard to remain during my youth cooped up[6] in one place, and had longed to enter the world, and take my station among other human beings.

---

1 debarred: 배제되다.

2 liberal education: 실리적인 지식보다는 교양(생각)을 넓히기 위한 교육.

3 carriage: 탈것. 마차.

4 chaise: 마차.

5 invincible repugnance: 어찌할 수 없을 정도로 강한 혐오감.

6 cooped up: (좁은 곳에) 갇혀있는.

Now my desires were complied with, and it would, indeed, have been folly to repent.

I had sufficient leisure for these and many other reflections during my journey to Ingolstadt, which was long and fatiguing. At length the high white steeple of the town met my eyes. I alighted,[1] and was conducted to my solitary apartment, to spend the evening as I pleased.

The next morning I delivered my letters of introduction and paid a visit to some of the principal professors. Chance — or rather the evil influence, the Angel of Destruction,[2] which asserted omnipotent sway[3] over me from the moment I turned my reluctant steps from my father's door — led me first to M.[4] Krempe, professor of natural philosophy. He was an uncouth[5] man, but deeply embued in[6] the secrets of his science. He asked me several questions concerning my progress in the different branches of science appertaining to natural philosophy. I replied carelessly; and, partly in contempt, mentioned the names of my alchymists as the principal authors I had studied. The professor stared: "Have you," he said, "really spent your time in studying such nonsense?"

I replied in the affirmative. "Every minute," continued M. Krempe with warmth, "every instant[7] that you have wasted on those books is utterly and entirely lost. You have burdened your memory with exploded systems and useless names. Good God! in what desert land have you lived, where no one was kind enough to inform you that these fancies,[8] which you have so greedily imbibed,[9] are a thousand years old,

---

1   alighted: (마차에서) 내리다.
2   Angel of Destruction: '파멸의 신'; 즉 '죽음의 신'을 지칭.
3   sway: 지배력. 영향력.
4   M.: 'Monsieur'의 약자. 영어의 'Mr'.에 해당.
5   uncouth: 거친. 세련되지 않은
6   embued in: …에 심취한.
7   instant: 순간.
8   fancies: 여기서는 '황당한 이론'이란 의미.
9   imbibed: 받아들이다.

and as musty[1] as they are ancient? I little expected, in this enlightened and scientific age, to find a disciple of Albertus Magnus and Paracelsus. My dear sir, you must begin your studies entirely anew."

So saying, he stepped aside, and wrote down a list of several books treating of natural philosophy, which he desired me to procure; and dismissed me, after mentioning that in the beginning of the following week he intended to commence a course of lectures upon natural philosophy in its general relations, and that M. Waldman, fellow-professor, would lecture upon chemistry the alternate days that he omitted.

I returned home, not disappointed, for I have said that I had long considered those authors useless whom the professor reprobated;[2] but I returned, not at all the more inclined to recur[3] to these studies in any shape. M. Krempe was a little squat[4] man, with a gruff[5] voice and a repulsive countenance; the teacher, therefore, did not prepossess[6] me in favour of his pursuits. In rather a too philosophical and connected a strain, perhaps, I have given an account of the conclusions I had come to concerning them in my early years. As a child, I had not been content with the results promised by the modern professors of natural science. With a confusion of ideas only to be accounted for by my extreme youth, and my want of a guide on such matters, I had retrod the steps of knowledge along the paths of time, and exchanged the discoveries of recent inquirers for the dreams of forgotten alchymists. Besides, I had a contempt for the uses of modern natural philosophy. It was very different when the masters of the science sought immortality and power; such views, although futile, were grand: but now the scene was changed. The ambition of the inquirer seemed to limit itself

---

1 musty: 쓸모없는. 곰팡내 나는.
2 reprobated: 비난하다.
3 recur: 되돌아가다(to). 다시 시작하다.
4 squat: 땅딸막한.
5 gruff: (소리·목소리가) 굵고 탁한. 몹시 거친.
6 prepossess: 영향을 미치다.

to the annihilation[1] of those visions on which my interest in science was chiefly founded. I was required to exchange chimeras[2] of boundless grandeur for realities of little worth.

Such were my reflections during the first two or three days of my residence at Ingolstadt, which were chiefly spent in becoming acquainted with the localities, and the principal residents in my new abode. But as the ensuing week commenced, I thought of the information which M. Krempe had given me concerning the lectures. And although I could not consent to go and hear that little conceited[3] fellow deliver sentences out of a pulpit, I recollected what he had said of M. Waldman, whom I had never seen, as he had hitherto been out of town.

Partly from curiosity, and partly from idleness, I went into the lecturing room, which M. Waldman entered shortly after. This professor was very unlike his colleague. He appeared about fifty years of age, but with an aspect[4] expressive of the greatest benevolence; a few grey hairs covered his temples, but those at the back of his head were nearly black. His person[5] was short, but remarkably erect; and his voice the sweetest I had ever heard. He began his lecture by a recapitulation[6] of the history of chemistry, and the various improvements made by different men of learning, pronouncing with fervour[7] the names of the most distinguished discoverers. He then took a cursory[8] view of the present state of the science, and explained many of its elementary terms. After having made a few preparatory experiments, he con-

---

1 annihilation: 무효화.
2 chimeras: 망상(wild fancy). 황당한 생각.
3 conceited: 우쭐해하는.
4 aspect: 얼굴 생김새.
5 person: 신체. 몸.
6 recapitulation: 개괄. 요약.
7 fervour: 열정.
8 cursory: 대강의. 대략의.

cluded with a panegyric[1] upon modern chemistry, the terms of which I shall never forget: —

"The ancient teachers of this science," said he, "promised impossibilities and performed nothing. The modern masters promise very little; they know that metals cannot be transmuted,[2] and that the elixir of life is a chimera. But these philosophers, whose hands seem only made to dabble in dirt,[3] and their eyes to pore over[4] the microscope or crucible,[5] have indeed performed miracles. They penetrate into the recesses[6] of nature and show how she works in her hiding places. They ascend into the heavens: they have discovered how the blood circulates, and the nature of the air we breathe. They have acquired new and almost unlimited powers; they can command the thunders of heaven, mimic the earthquake, and even mock the invisible world with its own shadows."

Such were the professor's words — rather let me say such the words of the fate, enounced[7] to destroy me. As he went on, I felt as if my soul were grappling with a palpable enemy; one by one the various keys were touched which formed the mechanism of my being: chord after chord was sounded, and soon my mind was filled with one thought, one conception, one purpose. So much has been done, exclaimed the soul of Frankenstein — more, far more, will I achieve: treading in the steps already marked, I will pioneer a new way, explore unknown powers, and unfold to the world the deepest mysteries of creation.

I closed not my eyes that night. My internal being was in a state

---

1 panegyric: 칭송. 찬가.
2 transmuted: 변형(변화)되다.
3 dabble in dirt: 흙장난하다. 장난삼아 흙을 만지작거리다.
4 pore over: 주시하다.
5 crucible: 도가니. 용기.
6 recesses: 후미진 곳.
7 enounced: 선언하다.

of insurrection[1] and turmoil; I felt that order would thence arise, but I had no power to produce it. By degrees, after the morning's dawn, sleep came. I awoke, and my yesternight's thoughts were as a dream. There only remained a resolution to return to my ancient studies, and to devote myself to a science for which I believed myself to possess a natural talent. On the same day, I paid M. Waldman a visit. His manners in private were even more mild and attractive than in public; for there was a certain dignity in his mien[2] during his lecture, which in his own house was replaced by the greatest affability[3] and kindness. I gave him pretty nearly the same account of my former pursuits as I had given to his fellow-professor. He heard with attention the little narration concerning my studies, and smiled at the names of Cornelius Agrippa and Paracelsus, but without the contempt that M. Krempe had exhibited. He said, that "these were men to whose indefatigable[4] zeal modern philosophers were indebted for most of the foundations of their knowledge. They had left to us, as an easier task, to give new names, and arrange in connected classifications, the facts which they in a great degree had been the instruments of bringing to light. The labours of men of genius, however erroneously directed, scarcely ever fail in ultimately turning to the solid advantage of mankind.[5]" I listened to his statement, which was delivered without any presumption[6] or affectation; and then added, that his lecture had removed my prejudices against modern chemists; I expressed myself in measured terms,[7] with the modesty and deference[8] due from a youth

---

1 insurrection: 혼란. 대 격변.

2 mien: 태도. 거동.

3 affability: 친절함. 상냥함.

4 indefatigable: 지칠 줄 모르는.

5 turning to the solid advantage of mankind: 인류에게 실질적으로 유용하게 되다.

6 presumption: 주제넘음,

7 measured terms: 신중히 고려한 말.

8 deference: 존경심.

to his instructor, without letting escape (inexperience in life would have made me ashamed) any of the enthusiasm which stimulated my intended labours. I requested his advice concerning the books I ought to procure.

"I am happy," said M. Waldman, "to have gained a disciple; and if your application[1] equals your ability, I have no doubt of your success. Chemistry is that branch of natural philosophy in which the greatest improvements have been and may be made: it is on that account that I have made it my peculiar study; but at the same time I have not neglected the other branches of science. A man would make but a very sorry chemist if he attended to that department of human knowledge alone. If your wish is to become really a man of science, and not merely a petty experimentalist, I should advise you to apply to every branch of natural philosophy, including mathematics."

He then took me into his laboratory, and explained to me the uses of his various machines; instructing me as to what I ought to procure and promising me the use of his own when I should have advanced far enough in the science not to derange[2] their mechanism. He also gave me the list of books which I had requested; and I took my leave.

Thus ended a day memorable to me: it decided my future destiny.

CHAPTER IV

From this day natural philosophy, and particularly chemistry, in the most comprehensive[3] sense of the term, became nearly my sole occupation. I read with ardour those works, so full of genius and discrimination,[4] which modern inquirers have written on these sub-

---

1 application: 근면함.
2 derange: 교란시키다.
3 comprehensive: 포괄적인.
4 discrimination: 판별력.

jects. I attended the lectures, and cultivated[1] the acquaintance, of the men of science of the university; and I found even in M. Krempe a great deal of sound sense and real information, combined, it is true, with a repulsive physiognomy[2] and manners, but not on that account the less valuable. In M. Waldman I found a true friend. His gentleness was never tinged by[3] dogmatism; and his instructions were given with an air[4] of frankness and good nature that banished every idea of pedantry.[5] In a thousand ways he smoothed for me the path of knowledge, and made the most abstruse[6] inquiries clear and facile to my apprehension. My application was at first fluctuating[7] and uncertain; it gained strength as I proceeded, and soon became so ardent and eager that the stars often disappeared in the light of morning whilst I was yet engaged in my laboratory.

As I applied so closely, it may be easily conceived that my progress was rapid. My ardour was indeed the astonishment of the students, and my proficiency[8] that of the masters. Professor Krempe often asked me, with a sly smile, how Cornelius Agrippa went on? whilst M. Waldman expressed the most heartfelt exultation[9] in my progress. Two years passed in this manner, during which I paid no visit to Geneva, but was engaged, heart and soul, in the pursuit of some discoveries, which I hoped to make. None but those who have experienced them can conceive of the enticements[10] of science. In other studies you go as far as others have gone before you, and there is nothing

---

1 cultivated the acquaintance: 교제하다. 안면을 트다.
2 physiognomy: 인상.
3 tinged by: …이 가미된.
4 air: 태도.
5 pedantry: 현학적인 태도.
6 abstruse: 어려운. 난해한.
7 fluctuating: 변동이 심한.
8 proficiency: 능통함.
9 exultation: 큰 기쁨. 환희.
10 enticements: 유혹. 마음을 끄는 것. 매력적인 것.

more to know; but in a scientific pursuit there is continual food[1] for
discovery and wonder. A mind of moderate capacity, which closely
pursues one study, must infallibly[2] arrive at great proficiency in that
study; and I, who continually sought the attainment of one object of
pursuit, and was solely wrapt up in[3] this, improved so rapidly that, at
the end of two years, I made some discoveries in the improvement
of some chemical instruments which procured me great esteem[4] and
admiration at the university. When I had arrived at this point, and
had become as well acquainted with the theory and practice of natural philosophy as depended on the lessons of any of the professors at
Ingolstadt, my residence there being no longer conducive[5] to my improvement, I thought of returning to my friends and my native town,
when an incident happened that protracted[6] my stay.

   One of the phenomena which had peculiarly attracted my attention was the structure of the human frame, and, indeed, any animal
endued with life. Whence, I often asked myself, did the principle of
life proceed? It was a bold question, and one which has ever been
considered as a mystery; yet with how many things are we upon the
brink of becoming acquainted, if cowardice or carelessness did not restrain our inquiries. I revolved[7] these circumstances in my mind, and
determined thenceforth to apply myself more particularly to those
branches of natural philosophy which relate to physiology.[8] Unless I
had been animated by an almost supernatural enthusiasm, my application to this study would have been irksome, and almost intolerable.

---

1 food: 자료.
2 infallibly: 틀림없이.
3 wrapt up in: …에 몰두해 있는.
4 esteem: 존경. 경의.
5 conducive: 도움이 되는.
6 protracted: 연장시키다.
7 revolved: 곰곰이 생각하다.
8 physiology: 생리학(살아있는 생명체를 연구하는 학문 분야).

To examine the causes of life, we must first have recourse[1] to death. I became acquainted with the science of anatomy: but this was not sufficient; I must also observe the natural decay and corruption of the human body. In my education my father had taken the greatest precautions that my mind should be impressed with no supernatural horrors. I do not ever remember to have trembled at a tale of super-stition, or to have feared the apparition[2] of a spirit. Darkness had no effect upon my fancy; and a churchyard[3] was to me merely the recep-tacle[4] of bodies deprived of life, which, from being the seat[5] of beauty and strength, had become food for the worm. Now I was led to ex-amine the cause and progress of this decay, and forced to spend days and nights in vaults[6] and charnel-houses[7]. My attention was fixed upon every object the most insupportable to the delicacy of the human feelings. I saw how the fine form of man was degraded[8] and wasted; I beheld the corruption of death succeed to the blooming cheek of life; I saw how the worm inherited the wonders of the eye and brain. I paused, examining and analysing all the minutiæ[9] of causation,[10] as exemplified in the change from life to death, and death to life, until from the midst of this darkness a sudden light broke in upon[11] me — a light so brilliant and wondrous, yet so simple, that while I became dizzy with the immensity of the prospect which it illustrated, I was surprised that among so many men of genius who had directed their

---

1   recourse: 접근.
2   apparition: (유령 따위의) 출현.
3   churchyard: (교회 부속의) 묘지.
4   receptacle: 두는 곳. 보관하는 곳.
5   seat: 소재지. 있는 곳.
6   vaults: 지하 납골소.
7   charnel-houses: 납골당.
8   degraded: 부패한.
9   minutiæ: 세세한 점.
10   causation: 인과관계.
11   broke in upon: …에 언뜻 다가오다.

inquiries towards the same science, that I alone should be reserved to discover so astonishing a secret.

Remember, I am not recording the vision of a madman. The sun does not more certainly shine in the heavens, than that which I now affirm is true. Some miracle might have produced it, yet the stages of the discovery were distinct and probable. After days and nights of incredible labour and fatigue, I succeeded in discovering the cause of generation[1] and life; nay,[2] more, I became myself capable of bestowing animation upon lifeless matter.

The astonishment which I had at first experienced on this discovery soon gave place to[3] delight and rapture. After so much time spent in painful labour, to arrive at once at the summit of my desires was the most gratifying consummation[4] of my toils. But this discovery was so great and overwhelming that all the steps by which I had been progressively led to it were obliterated,[5] and I beheld only the result. What had been the study and desire of the wisest men since the creation of the world was now within my grasp. Not that, like a magic scene, it all opened upon me at once: the information I had obtained was of a nature rather to direct my endeavours so soon as I should point them towards the object of my search, than to exhibit that object already accomplished. I was like the Arabian who had been buried with the dead, and found a passage to life, aided only by one glimmering, and seemingly ineffectual, light.[6]

I see by your eagerness, and the wonder and hope which your eyes express, my friend, that you expect to be informed of the secret with

---

1 generation: 발생. 생식.
2 nay: 뿐만 아니라.
3 gave place to: …으로 바뀌다.
4 consummation: 완성. 성취.
5 obliterated: 망각되다.
6 Arabian who had been buried with the dead … ineffectual, light: 『천일야화』(Arabian Nights)에 나오는 신바드(Sinbad)는 자기 아내의 시신과 함께 땅에 묻히게 되는데, 그때 그는 멀리서 비추는 불빛을 따라 그곳을 빠져나온다.

which I am acquainted; that cannot be: listen patiently until the end of my story, and you will easily perceive why I am reserved[1] upon that subject. I will not lead you on, unguarded and ardent as I then was, to your destruction and infallible[2] misery. Learn from me, if not by my precepts,[3] at least by my example, how dangerous is the acquirement of knowledge, and how much happier that man is who believes his native town to be the world, than he who aspires to become greater than his nature will allow.

When I found so astonishing a power placed within my hands, I hesitated a long time concerning the manner in which I should employ[4] it. Although I possessed the capacity of bestowing animation, yet to prepare a frame for the reception of it, with all its intricacies[5] of fibres, muscles, and veins, still remained a work of inconceivable difficulty and labour. I doubted at first whether I should attempt the creation of a being like myself, or one of simpler organisation; but my imagination was too much exalted[6] by my first success to permit me to doubt of my ability to give life to an animal as complex and wonderful as man. The materials at present within my command[7] hardly appeared adequate to so arduous[8] an undertaking; but I doubted not that I should ultimately succeed. I prepared myself for a multitude of reverses[9]; my operations might be incessantly baffled, and at last my work be imperfect: yet, when I considered the improvement which every day takes place in science and mechanics, I was encouraged to hope my present attempts would at least lay the foundations of future

---

1 reserved: 말을 삼가는.
2 infallible: 반드시 일어나는.
3 precepts: 가르침.
4 employ: 사용하다.
5 intricacies: 복잡한 사물.
6 exalted: 의기양양한.
7 within my command: 내 마음대로 (사용)할 수 있는.
8 arduous: 힘든.
9 reverses: 불운. 실패.

success. Nor could I consider the magnitude[1] and complexity of my plan as any argument[2] of its impracticability. It was with these feelings that I began the creation of a human being. As the minuteness of the parts formed a great hindrance to my speed, I resolved, contrary to my first intention, to make the being of a gigantic stature; that is to say, about eight feet in height, and proportionably[3] large. After having formed this determination, and having spent some months in success-fully collecting and arranging my materials, I began.

No one can conceive the variety of feelings which bore me on-wards, like a hurricane, in the first enthusiasm of success. Life and death appeared to me ideal[4] bounds, which I should first break through, and pour a torrent[5] of light into our dark world. A new spe-cies would bless me as its creator and source; many happy and excel-lent natures would owe their being to me. No father could claim the gratitude of his child so completely as I should deserve theirs. Pursu-ing these reflections, I thought, that if I could bestow animation upon lifeless matter, I might in process of time (although I now found it impossible) renew life where death had apparently devoted the body to corruption.

These thoughts supported my spirits, while I pursued my under-taking with unremitting[6] ardour. My cheek had grown pale with study, and my person had become emaciated with confinement. Sometimes, on the very brink of certainty, I failed; yet still I clung to the hope which the next day or the next hour might realise. One secret which I alone possessed was the hope to which I had dedicated myself; and the moon gazed on my midnight labours, while, with unrelaxed and

---

1 magnitude: 중요성.
2 argument: 논거. 이유.
3 proportionably: 비례해서.
4 ideal: 관념적인.
5 torrent: 분출.
6 unremitting: 멈추지 않는.

breathless eagerness, I pursued nature to her hiding-places. Who shall conceive the horrors of my secret toil, as I dabbled among the unhallowed damps[1] of the grave, or tortured the living animal to animate the lifeless clay? My limbs now tremble and my eyes swim[2] with the remembrance; but then a resistless, and almost frantic, impulse urged me forward; I seemed to have lost all soul or sensation but for this one pursuit. It was indeed but a passing trance[3] that only made me feel with renewed acuteness[4] so soon as, the unnatural stimulus ceasing to operate, I had returned to my old habits. I collected bones from charnel-houses; and disturbed, with profane fingers, the tremendous secrets of the human frame. In a solitary chamber, or rather cell,[5] at the top of the house, and separated from all the other apartments by a gallery and staircase, I kept my workshop of filthy creation: my eyeballs were starting from their sockets in attending to the details of my employment. The dissecting room[6] and the slaughter-house[7] furnished many of my materials; and often did my human nature turn with loathing from my occupation, whilst, still urged on by an eagerness which perpetually increased, I brought my work near to a conclusion.

The summer months passed while I was thus engaged, heart and soul, in one pursuit. It was a most beautiful season; never did the fields bestow a more plentiful harvest, or the vines yield a more luxuriant vintage: but my eyes were insensible to the charms of nature. And the same feelings which made me neglect the scenes around me caused me also to forget those friends who were so many miles absent, and whom I had not seen for so long a time. I knew my silence

---

1   unhallowed damps: 신성모독이 저질러진 (무덤의) 축축한 곳.
2   my eyes swim: 내 눈에 눈물이 고였다는 의미).
3   passing trance: 잠시 왔다가 사라지는 몽환상태.
4   acuteness: 강렬함.
5   cell: 작은 방.
6   dissecting room: 해부실.
7   slaughter-house: 도살장.

disquieted[1] them; and I well remembered the words of my father: "I know that while you are pleased with yourself, you will think of us with affection, and we shall hear regularly from you. You must pardon me if I regard any interruption in your correspondence as a proof that your other duties are equally neglected."

I knew well, therefore, what would be my father's feelings; but I could not tear my thoughts from my employment, loathsome in itself, but which had taken an irresistible hold of my imagination. I wished, as it were, to procrastinate[2] all that related to my feelings of affection until the great object, which swallowed up[3] every habit of my nature, should be completed.

I then thought that my father would be unjust if he ascribed[4] my neglect to vice, or faultiness on my part; but I am now convinced that he was justified in conceiving that I should not be altogether free from blame. A human being in perfection ought always to preserve a calm and peaceful mind, and never to allow passion or a transitory[5] desire to disturb his tranquillity. I do not think that the pursuit of knowledge is an exception to this rule. If the study to which you apply yourself has a tendency to weaken your affections, and to destroy your taste for those simple pleasures in which no alloy[6] can possibly mix, then that study is certainly unlawful, that is to say, not befitting the human mind. If this rule were always observed; if no man allowed any pursuit whatsoever to interfere with the tranquillity of his domestic affections, Greece had not been enslaved, Cæsar[7] would have spared his country; America would have been discovered more gradu-

---

1 disquieted: 불안하게 하다.
2 procrastinate: 지연시키다.
3 swallowed up: 없애다. 말살시키다.
4 ascribed: …탓으로 돌리다.
5 transitory: 일시적인.
6 alloy: 혼합물.
7 Cæsar: 로마의 황제 'Julius Cæsar'를 지칭.

ally; and the empires of Mexico and Peru had not been destroyed.[1]

But I forget that I am moralising[2] in the most interesting part of my tale; and your looks remind me to proceed.

My father made no reproach[3] in his letters, and only took notice of my silence by inquiring into my occupations more particularly than before. Winter, spring, and summer passed away during my labours; but I did not watch the blossom or the expanding leaves — sights which before always yielded me supreme delight — so deeply was I engrossed in my occupation. The leaves of that year had withered before my work drew near to a close[4]; and now every day showed me more plainly how well I had succeeded. But my enthusiasm was checked by my anxiety, and I appeared rather like one doomed by slavery to toil in the mines, or any other unwholesome trade, than an artist occupied by his favourite employment. Every night I was oppressed by a slow fever[5], and I became nervous to a most painful degree; the fall of a leaf startled me, and I shunned[6] my fellow-creatures as if I had been guilty of a crime. Sometimes I grew alarmed at the wreck[7] I perceived that I had become; the energy of my purpose alone sustained me: my labours would soon end, and I believed that exercise and amusement would then drive away incipient[8] disease; and I promised myself both of these when my creation should be complete.

---

1 empires of Mexico and Peru had not been destroyed: 과거에 융성하였다 결국 멸망하게 된 마야, 잉카, 아즈텍 문명을 지칭.
2 moralising: 설교하는. 도덕적 교훈을 말하는.
3 reproach: 꾸짖음. 비난.
4 drew near to a close: 거의 다 끝나다.
5 slow fever: 장티푸스(일반적으로 Typhoid fever라고 불림).
6 shunned: 피하다. 외면하다.
7 wreck: 수척해진 몸.
8 incipient: 초기의.

CHAPTER V

It was on a dreary night of November[1] that I beheld the accomplishment of my toils. With an anxiety that almost amounted to[2] agony, I collected the instruments of life around me, that I might infuse[3] a spark of being into the lifeless thing that lay at my feet. It was already one in the morning; the rain pattered dismally against the panes, and my candle was nearly burnt out, when, by the glimmer of the half-extinguished light, I saw the dull yellow eye of the creature open; it breathed hard, and a convulsive motion agitated its limbs.

How can I describe my emotions at this catastrophe, or how delineate[4] the wretch whom with such infinite pains and care I had endeavoured to form? His limbs were in proportion,[5] and I had selected his features as beautiful. Beautiful! — Great God! His yellow skin scarcely covered the work of muscles and arteries beneath; his hair was of a lustrous black, and flowing; his teeth of a pearly whiteness; but these luxuriances[6] only formed a more horrid contrast with his watery eyes, that seemed almost of the same colour as the dun[7] white sockets in which they were set, his shrivelled complexion and straight black lips.

The different accidents of life are not so changeable as the feelings of human nature. I had worked hard for nearly two years, for the sole purpose of infusing life into an inanimate body. For this I had deprived myself of rest and health. I had desired it with an ardour that far exceeded moderation[8]; but now that I had finished, the beauty of

---

1 It was on a dreary night of November: 메리는 원래 이 이야기를 이 문장으로 시작하였다고 한다.
2 amounted to: …(상태에) 이르다.
3 infuse: 불어넣다.
4 delineate: 묘사하다.
5 in proportion: 균형을 이룸.
6 luxuriances: 화려함.
7 dun: 암갈색(의).
8 moderation: 중용.

the dream vanished, and breathless horror and disgust filled my heart. Unable to endure the aspect of the being I had created, I rushed out of the room, and continued a long time traversing[1] my bedchamber, unable to compose my mind to sleep. At length lassitude[2] succeeded to the tumult[3] I had before endured; and I threw myself on the bed in my clothes, endeavouring to seek a few moments of forgetfulness. But it was in vain: I slept, indeed, but I was disturbed by the wildest dreams. I thought I saw Elizabeth, in the bloom of health,[4] walking in the streets of Ingolstadt. Delighted and surprised, I embraced her; but as I imprinted the first kiss on her lips, they became livid[5] with the hue of death; her features appeared to change, and I thought that I held the corpse of my dead mother in my arms; a shroud enveloped her form,[6] and I saw the grave-worms crawling in the folds of the flannel. I started[7] from my sleep with horror; a cold dew covered my forehead, my teeth chattered, and every limb became convulsed: when, by the dim and yellow light of the moon, as it forced its way through the window shutters, I beheld the wretch — the miserable monster whom I had created. He held up the curtain of the bed; and his eyes, if eyes they may be called, were fixed on me. His jaws opened, and he muttered some inarticulate[8] sounds, while a grin wrinkled his cheeks. He might have spoken, but I did not hear; one hand was stretched out, seemingly to detain[9] me, but I escaped and

---

1 traversing: 여기저기 걷다. 구석구석으로 거닐다.

2 lassitude: 피로(fatigue).

3 tumult: 흥분. 정신적 혼란.

4 in the bloom of health: 한창 건강한 상태에서.

5 livid: 창백한. 납빛의.

6 I thought that I held the corpse ⋯ a shroud enveloped her form: 엘리자베스의 죽음에 관한 꿈은 프랑켄스타인이 만든 괴물에 의해 그녀가 희생될 것이란 앞으로의 일을 예시하고 있다.

7 started: 깜짝 놀라 일어나다.

8 inarticulate: 발음이 분명치 않은.

9 detain: 붙들다.

rushed downstairs. I took refuge in the courtyard belonging to the house which I inhabited; where I remained during the rest of the night, walking up and down in the greatest agitation, listening attentively, catching and fearing each sound as if it were to announce the approach of the demoniacal corpse to which I had so miserably given life.

Oh! no mortal could support[1] the horror of that countenance. A mummy again endued with animation could not be so hideous as that wretch. I had gazed on him while unfinished; he was ugly then; but when those muscles and joints[2] were rendered capable of motion, it became a thing such as even Dante[3] could not have conceived.

I passed the night wretchedly. Sometimes my pulse beat so quickly and hardly[4] that I felt the palpitation[5] of every artery; at others, I nearly sank to the ground through languor[6] and extreme weakness. Mingled with this horror, I felt the bitterness of disappointment; dreams that had been my food and pleasant rest for so long a space were now become a hell to me; and the change was so rapid, the overthrow[7] so complete!

Morning, dismal and wet, at length dawned, and discovered to my sleepless and aching eyes the church of Ingolstadt, its white steeple and clock, which indicated the sixth hour. The porter opened the gates of the court, which had that night been my asylum,[8] and I issued[9] into the streets, pacing them with quick steps, as if I sought to avoid the wretch whom I feared every turning of the street would present

---

1 support: 감당하다.
2 joints: 관절.
3 Dante: 이태리의 시인 '단테'(Dante Alighieri, 1265-1321)를 지칭. 그가 쓴 『신곡』(Divine Comedy)의 첫 권인 『지옥편』(The Inferno)은 지옥의 모습을 그리고 있다.
4 hardly: 여기서는 '강하게'란 의미.
5 palpitation: 맥박.
6 languor: 피로. 무기력감.
7 overthrow: 전복.
8 asylum: 도피처. 피난처.
9 issued: 나아가다.

to my view. I did not dare return to the apartment which I inhabited, but felt impelled to hurry on, although drenched by the rain which poured from a black and comfortless sky.

I continued walking in this manner for some time, endeavouring by bodily exercise, to ease[1] the load that weighed upon my mind. I traversed the streets, without any clear conception of where I was, or what I was doing. My heart palpitated in the sickness of fear; and I hurried on with irregular steps, not daring to look about me: —

> "Like one who, on a lonely road,
> Doth walk in fear and dread,
> And, having once turned round, walks on,
> And turns no more his head;
> Because he knows a frightful fiend
> Doth close behind him tread."[2]

Continuing thus, I came at length opposite to the inn at which the various diligences[3] and carriages usually stopped. Here I paused, I knew not why; but I remained some minutes with my eyes fixed on a coach that was coming towards me from the other end of the street. As it drew nearer, I observed that it was the Swiss diligence: it stopped just where I was standing, and, on the door being opened, I perceived Henry Clerval, who, on seeing me, instantly sprung out. "My dear Frankenstein," exclaimed he, "how glad I am to see you! how fortunate that you should be here at the very moment of my alighting!"

Nothing could equal my delight on seeing Clerval; his presence brought back to my thoughts my father, Elizabeth, and all those scenes of home so dear to my recollection. I grasped his hand, and in a moment forgot my horror and misfortune; I felt suddenly, and for

---

1 ease: (짐을) 덜다.

2 Like one who … behind him tread: 코울리지가 쓴 「노수부의 노래」중 446-451행에 나오는 구절.

3 diligences: (불어) (프랑스 등지에서 사용된) 승합 마차.

the first time during many months, calm and serene joy. I welcomed my friend, therefore, in the most cordial[1] manner, and we walked towards my college. Clerval continued talking for some time about our mutual friends, and his own good fortune in being permitted to come to Ingolstadt. "You may easily believe," said he, "how great was the difficulty to persuade my father that all necessary knowledge was not comprised[2] in the noble art of bookkeeping; and, indeed, I believe I left him incredulous to the last, for his constant answer to my un-wearied entreaties was the same as that of the Dutch schoolmaster in the Vicar of Wakefield[3]: — 'I have ten thousand florins[4] a year without Greek, I eat heartily without Greek.' But his affection for me at length overcame his dislike of learning, and he has permitted me to under-take a voyage of discovery to the land of knowledge."

"It gives me the greatest delight to see you; but tell me how you left my father, brothers, and Elizabeth."

"Very well, and very happy, only a little uneasy that they hear from you so seldom. By the by, I mean to lecture you a little upon their account myself. — But, my dear Frankenstein," continued he, stopping short[5] and gazing full in my face, "I did not before remark how very ill you appear; so thin and pale; you look as if you had been watching[6] for several nights."

"You have guessed right; I have lately been so deeply engaged in one occupation that I have not allowed myself sufficient rest, as you see: but I hope, I sincerely hope, that all these employments are now at an end, and that I am at length free."

---

1 cordial: 진심어린.

2 comprised: 담겨있다.

3 Vicar of Wakefield: 18세기 영국의 소설가 골드스미스(Oliver Goldsmith)가 쓴 소설; 다음에 나오는 구절은 이 소설에서 인용한 것이다.

4 florins: 프로렌스(Florence)에서 발행한 금화.

5 stopping short: 갑자기 말을 멈추면서.

6 watching: 밤샘 한.

I trembled excessively; I could not endure to think of, and far less to allude to,[1] the occurrences of the preceding night. I walked with a quick pace, and we soon arrived at my college. I then reflected, and the thought made me shiver, that the creature whom I had left in my apartment might still be there, alive, and walking about. I dreaded to behold this monster; but I feared still more that Henry should see him. Entreating him, therefore, to remain a few minutes at the bottom of the stairs, I darted up towards my own room. My hand was already on the lock of the door before I recollected myself. I then paused; and a cold shivering came over me. I threw the door forcibly open, as children are accustomed to do when they expect a spectre to stand in waiting for them on the other side; but nothing appeared. I stepped fearfully in: the apartment was empty; and my bedroom was also freed from its hideous guest. I could hardly believe that so great a good fortune could have befallen[2] me; but when I became assured that my enemy had indeed fled, I clapped my hands for joy, and ran down to Clerval.

We ascended into my room, and the servant presently brought breakfast; but I was unable to contain[3] myself. It was not joy only that possessed me; I felt my flesh tingle[4] with excess of sensitiveness, and my pulse beat rapidly. I was unable to remain for a single instant in the same place; I jumped over the chairs, clapped my hands, and laughed aloud. Clerval at first attributed my unusual spirits to joy on his arrival; but when he observed me more attentively he saw a wildness in my eyes for which he could not account; and my loud, unrestrained, heartless laughter, frightened and astonished him.

"My dear Victor," cried he, "what, for God's sake, is the matter? Do not laugh in that manner. How ill you are! What is the cause of all

---

1   allude to: …에 대해 언급하다.
2   befallen: …에게 일어나다.
3   contain: 억제하다.
4   tingle: 근질근질하다.

this?"

"Do not ask me," cried I, putting my hands before my eyes, for I thought I saw the dreaded spectre glide into the room; "he can tell. — Oh, save me! save me!" I imagined that the monster seized me; I struggled furiously, and fell down in a fit.[1]

Poor Clerval! what must have been his feelings? A meeting, which he anticipated with such joy, so strangely turned to bitterness. But I was not the witness of his grief; for I was lifeless, and did not recover my senses for a long, long time.

This was the commencement[2] of a nervous fever which confined me for several months. During all that time Henry was my only nurse. I afterwards learned that, knowing my father's advanced age,[3] and unfitness for so long a journey, and how wretched my sickness would make Elizabeth, he spared them this grief by concealing the extent of my disorder.[4] He knew that I could not have a more kind and attentive nurse than himself; and, firm in the hope he felt of my recovery, he did not doubt that, instead of doing harm, he performed the kindest action that he could towards them.

But I was in reality very ill; and surely nothing but the unbounded and unremitting attentions of my friend could have restored me to life. The form of the monster on whom I had bestowed existence was forever before my eyes, and I raved[5] incessantly concerning him. Doubtless my words surprised Henry: he at first believed them to be the wanderings[6] of my disturbed imagination; but the pertinacity[7] with which I continually recurred to the same subject, persuaded him

---

1 fit: 흥분. 졸도.

2 commencement: 시작.

3 advanced age: 고령.

4 disorder: 병.

5 raved: 헛소리를 하다. (미친 사람같이) 고함치다.

6 wanderings: 혼란한 생각 또는 말.

7 pertinacity: 집요함.

that my disorder indeed owed its origin to some uncommon and terrible event.

By very slow degrees, and with frequent relapses[1] that alarmed and grieved my friend, I recovered. I remember the first time I became capable of observing outward objects with any kind of pleasure, I perceived that the fallen leaves had disappeared, and that the young buds were shooting forth[2] from the trees that shaded my window. It was a divine[3] spring; and the season contributed greatly to my convalescence[4]. I felt also sentiments of joy and affection revive in my bosom; my gloom disappeared, and in a short time I became as cheerful as before I was attacked by the fatal passion.

"Dearest Clerval," exclaimed I, "how kind, how very good you are to me. This whole winter, instead of being spent in study, as you promised yourself, has been consumed in my sick room. How shall I ever repay you? I feel the greatest remorse[5] for the disappointment of which I have been the occasion; but you will forgive me."

"You will repay me entirely, if you do not discompose[6] yourself, but get well as fast as you can; and since you appear in such good spirits, I may speak to you on one subject, may I not?"

I trembled. One subject! what could it be? Could he allude to an object on whom I dared not even think?

"Compose yourself," said Clerval, who observed my change of colour, "I will not mention it, if it agitates you; but your father and cousin would be very happy if they received a letter from you in your own handwriting. They hardly know how ill you have been, and are uneasy at your long silence."

1　relapses: (의학) 재발. 병의 도짐.
2　shooting forth: (싹이) 나다.
3　divine: 멋진.
4　convalescence: (병으로 부터의) 회복.
5　remorse: 양심의 가책.
6　discompose: 마음의 평정을 잃게 하다. 흥분시키다.

"Is that all, my dear Henry? How could you suppose that my first thought would not fly towards those dear, dear friends whom I love, and who are so deserving of my love."

"If this is your present temper, my friend, you will perhaps be glad to see a letter that has been lying here some days for you; it is from your cousin, I believe."

CHAPTER VI

Clerval then put the following letter into my hands. It was from my own Elizabeth:

"My Dearest Cousin,

You have been ill, very ill, and even the constant letters of dear kind Henry are not sufficient to reassure[1] me on your account. You are forbidden to write — to hold a pen; yet one word from you, dear Victor, is necessary to calm our apprehensions. For a long time I have thought that each post would bring this line, and my persuasions have restrained my uncle from undertaking a journey to Ingolstadt. I have prevented his encountering the inconveniences and perhaps dangers of so long a journey; yet how often have I regretted not being able to perform it myself! I figure to myself that the task of attending on your sick bed has devolved on[2] some mercenary old nurse, who could never guess your wishes, nor minister[3] to them with the care and affection of your poor cousin. Yet that is over now: Clerval writes that indeed you are getting better. I eagerly hope that you will confirm this intelligence soon in your own handwriting.

---

1 reassure: 안심시키다.

2 devolved on: ···에게 맡겨지다.

3 minister: 보살펴주다(to). ···(에게) 도움이 되다(to).

"Get well — and return to us. You will find a happy, cheerful home, and friends who love you dearly. Your father's health is vigorous, and he asks but to see you — but to be assured that you are well; and not a care will ever cloud[1] his benevolent countenance. How pleased you would be to remark the improvement of our Ernest! He is now sixteen, and full of activity and spirit. He is desirous to be a true Swiss, and to enter into foreign service[2]; but we cannot part with him, at least until his elder brother returns to us. My uncle is not pleased with the idea of a military career in a distant country; but Ernest never had your powers of application.[3] He looks upon study as an odious fetter[4]; — his time is spent in the open air, climbing the hills or rowing on the lake. I fear that he will become an idler, unless we yield the point[5], and permit him to enter on the profession which he has selected.

"Little alteration, except the growth of our dear children, has taken place since you left us. The blue lake, and snow-clad[6] mountains, they never change; — and I think our placid home and our contented hearts are regulated by the same immutable laws. My trifling occupations take up my time and amuse me, and I am rewarded for any exertions by seeing none but happy, kind faces around me. Since you left us, but one change has taken place in our little household. Do you remember on what occasion Justine Moritz entered our family? Probably you do not; I will relate[7] her history, therefore, in a few words. Madame Moritz, her mother, was a widow with four children, of whom Justine was the third. This girl had always been the favourite

---

1 cloud: 얼굴빛을 어둡게 하다.
2 enter into foreign service: 입대하여 외국에 복무하다.
3 application: 지속적인 노력.
4 fetter: 족쇄.
5 yield the point: 상대방의 뜻에 따르다.
6 snow-clad: 눈으로 덮인.
7 relate: 진술하다.

of her father; but through a strange perversity[1], her mother could not
endure her, and after the death of M. Moritz, treated her very ill. My
aunt observed this; and, when Justine was twelve years of age, prevailed on[2] her mother to allow her to live at our house. The republican
institutions of our country have produced simpler and happier manners than those which prevail[3] in the great monarchies that surround
it. Hence there is less distinction between the several classes of its inhabitants; and the lower orders[4], being neither so poor nor so despised,
their manners are more refined and moral. A servant in Geneva does
not mean the same thing as a servant in France and England.[5] Justine,
thus received in our family, learned the duties of a servant; a condition which, in our fortunate country, does not include the idea of ignorance, and a sacrifice of the dignity of a human being.

"Justine, you may remember, was a great favourite of yours; and
I recollect you once remarked, that if you were in an ill-humour, one
glance from Justine could dissipate[6] it, for the same reason that Ariosto gives concerning the beauty of Angelica[7] — she looked so frank-
hearted[8] and happy. My aunt conceived a great attachment for her,
by which she was induced[9] to give her an education superior to that

---

1 perversity: (정상적이지 못한) 잘못된 일.
2 prevailed on: 설득하다.
3 prevail: 널리 행하여지다.
4 lower orders: 하층민. 하류계급.
5 A servant in Geneva does not mean the same thing as a servant in France and
   England: 제네바는 민주주의가 실행되고 있는 곳으로 만인이 그 직업이 어떻든 평등
   한 곳이라고 셸리는 생각하였다.
6 dissipate: 사라지게 하다.
7 Ariosto gives concerning the beauty of Angelica: 루도비코 아리오스토(Ludovico
   Ariosto, 1474-1533)가 152년에 쓴「광란의 오를란도」(Orlando Furioso)라는 시에는
   미모로 많은 사람들을 매혹시키는 안젤리카(Angelica)라는 여성이 등장한다,
8 frank-hearted: 저스틴(Justine)이라는 이름이 '정의로움'(Justice)을 의미한다는 점을
   상기해 보면 셸리가 왜 저스틴이 솔직한 마음을 가진 사람이라고 했는지 짐작해 볼
   수 있을 것이다.
9 induced: 유도되다.

which she had at first intended. This benefit was fully repaid; Justine was the most grateful little creature in the world: I do not mean that she made any professions[1]; I never heard one pass her lips; but you could see by her eyes that she almost adored her protectress. Although her disposition was gay, and in many respects inconsiderate[2], yet she paid the greatest attention to every gesture of my aunt. She thought her the model of all excellence, and endeavoured to imitate her phraseology[3] and manners, so that even now she often reminds me of her.

"When my dearest aunt died, every one was too much occupied in their own grief to notice poor Justine, who had attended her during her illness with the most anxious affection. Poor Justine was very ill; but other trials were reserved for her.

"One by one, her brothers and sister died; and her mother, with the exception of her neglected daughter, was left childless. The conscience of the woman was troubled[4]; she began to think that the deaths of her favourites was a judgement from heaven to chastise[5] her partiality. She was a Roman Catholic; and I believe her confessor confirmed the idea which she had conceived. Accordingly, a few months after your departure for Ingolstadt, Justine was called home by her repentant mother. Poor girl! she wept when she quitted our house; she was much altered since the death of my aunt; grief had given softness and a winning mildness to her manners, which had before been remarkable for vivacity[6]. Nor was her residence at her mother's house of a nature to restore her gaiety. The poor woman was very vacillating[7] in her repentance. She sometimes begged Justine to forgive her un-

---

1　professions: 공언. 선언.
2　inconsiderate: 별 신경을 쓰지 않는.
3　phraseology: 말씨. 어법.
4　troubled: (양심의) 가책을 느끼는.
5　chastise: 응징하다.
6　vivacity: 쾌활함. 활달함.
7　vacillating: 변화가 심한. (생각이) 왔다 갔다 하는.

kindness, but much oftener accused her of having caused the deaths of her brothers and sister. Perpetual fretting[1] at length threw Madame Moritz into a decline, which at first increased her irritability, but she is now at peace for ever. She died on the first approach of cold weather, at the beginning of this last winter. Justine has just returned to us; and I assure you I love her tenderly. She is very clever and gentle, and extremely pretty; as I mentioned before, her mien[2] and her expression continually remind me of my dear aunt.

"I must say also a few words to you, my dear cousin, of little darling William. I wish you could see him; he is very tall of his age[3], with sweet laughing blue eyes, dark eyelashes, and curling hair. When he smiles, two little dimples appear on each cheek, which are rosy with health. He has already had one or two little wives, but Louisa Biron is his favourite, a pretty little girl of five years of age.

"Now, dear Victor, I dare say you wish to be indulged in[4] a little gossip concerning the good people of Geneva. The pretty Miss Mansfield has already received the congratulatory visits on her approaching marriage with a young Englishman, John Melbourne, Esq.[5] Her ugly sister, Manon, married M. Duvillard, the rich banker, last autumn. Your favourite schoolfellow, Louis Manoir, has suffered several misfortunes since the departure of Clerval from Geneva. But he has already recovered his spirits, and is reported to be on the point of marrying a very lively pretty Frenchwoman, Madame Tavernier. She is a widow, and much older than Manoir; but she is very much admired, and a favourite with everybody.

"I have written myself into better spirits[6], dear cousin; but my

---

1 fretting: 안달복달함.
2 mien: 태도.
3 of his age: 그의 나이에 비해서.
4 indulged in: …을 즐기다.
5 Esq: 'Esquire'의 약자로 '님', '귀하'의 의미.
6 I have written myself into better spirits: 편지를 쓰기 시작하니 기분이 나아졌다는

anxiety returns upon me as I conclude. Write, dearest Victor — one line — one word will be a blessing to us. Ten thousand thanks to Henry for his kindness, his affection, and his many letters: we are sincerely grateful. Adieu! my cousin; take care of yourself; and, I entreat you, write!

ELIZABETH LAVENZA.

"GENEVA, March 18th, 17 — ."

"Dear, dear Elizabeth!" I exclaimed, when I had read her letter, "I will write instantly and relieve them from the anxiety they must feel." I wrote, and this exertion greatly fatigued me; but my convalescence[1] had commenced, and proceeded regularly. In another fortnight I was able to leave my chamber.

One of my first duties on my recovery was to introduce Clerval to the several professors of the university. In doing this, I underwent a kind of rough usage[2], ill befitting the wounds that my mind had sustained. Ever since the fatal night, the end of my labours, and the beginning of my misfortunes, I had conceived a violent antipathy even to the name of natural philosophy. When I was otherwise quite restored to health, the sight of a chemical instrument would renew all the agony of my nervous symptoms. Henry saw this, and had removed all my apparatus[3] from my view. He had also changed my apartment; for he perceived that I had acquired a dislike for the room which had previously been my laboratory. But these cares of Clerval were made of no avail[4] when I visited the professors. M. Waldman inflicted torture when he praised, with kindness and warmth, the astonishing progress I had made in the sciences. He soon perceived that I disliked the subject; but

---

의미.

1 convalescence: (병으로부터의) 회복.

2 usage: 취급.

3 apparatus: 장비.

4 of no avail: 소용없는.

not guessing the real cause, he attributed my feelings to modesty, and changed the subject from my improvement, to the science itself, with a desire, as I evidently saw, of drawing me out. What could I do? He meant to please, and he tormented me. I felt as if he had placed carefully, one by one, in my view those instruments which were to be afterwards used in putting me to a slow and cruel death. I writhed[1] under his words, yet dared not exhibit the pain I felt. Clerval, whose eyes and feelings were always quick in discerning the sensations of others, declined[2] the subject, alleging[3], in excuse, his total ignorance; and the conversation took a more general turn[4]. I thanked my friend from my heart, but I did not speak. I saw plainly that he was surprised, but he never attempted to draw my secret from me; and although I loved him with a mixture of affection and reverence that knew no bounds, yet I could never persuade myself to confide in him that event which was so often present to my recollection[5], but which I feared the detail to another would only impress more deeply.[6]

M. Krempe was not equally docile; and in my condition at that time, of almost insupportable sensitiveness, his harsh blunt encomiums[7] gave me even more pain than the benevolent approbation[8] of M. Waldman. "D — n the fellow!" cried he; "why, M. Clerval, I assure you he has outstript[9] us all. Ay, stare if you please; but it is nevertheless true. A youngster who, but a few years ago, believed in Cornelius Agrippa as firmly as in the gospel, has now set himself at the head of

---

1 writhed: (몸부림치며) 괴로워하다.
2 declined: 논하길 거부하다.
3 alleging: (변명으로) 내세우다.
4 took a more general turn: 일반적인 화제(주제)로 바뀌다.
5 often present to my recollection: 종종 떠오르는.
6 detail to another would only impress more deeply: 다른 사람에게 자세히 그 이야기를 한다면 그 일이 더 강하게 그의 뇌리에 새겨지게 될 것이란 의미.
7 encomiums: 칭찬(의 말).
8 approbation: 찬성. 칭찬.
9 outstript: 능가하다.

the university; and if he is not soon pulled down,[1] we shall all be out
of countenance[2]. — Ay, ay," continued he, observing my face expressive
of suffering, "M. Frankenstein is modest; an excellent quality in a young
man. Young men should be diffident of themselves, you know, M. Clerval: I was myself when young; but that wears out[3] in a very short time."

M. Krempe had now commenced an eulogy[4] on himself, which
happily turned the conversation from a subject that was so annoying
to me.

Clerval had never sympathised in my tastes for natural science; and
his literary pursuits differed wholly from those which had occupied
me. He came to the university with the design[5] of making himself
complete master of the oriental languages, and thus he should open
a field for[6] the plan of life he had marked out[7] for himself. Resolved
to pursue no inglorious career, he turned his eyes toward the East, as
affording scope for his spirit of enterprise. The Persian, Arabic, and
Sanscrit languages engaged his attention, and I was easily induced to
enter on the same studies. Idleness had ever been irksome to me, and
now that I wished to fly from reflection, and hated my former studies,
I felt great relief in being the fellow-pupil with my friend, and found
not only instruction but consolation in the works of the orientalists. I
did not, like him, attempt a critical[8] knowledge of their dialects, for I
did not contemplate making any other use of them than temporary
amusement. I read merely to understand their meaning, and they well
repaid my labours. Their melancholy is soothing, and their joy elevat-

---

1 pulled down: (권좌에서) 물러나다.
2 out of countenance: 면목을 잃은.
3 wears out: 사라지다,
4 eulogy: 칭송.
5 design: 목적. 의도.
6 open a field: 분야를 개척하다.
7 marked out: 선정하다.
8 critical: 중요한. 중대한 영향을 미치는.

ing, to a degree I never experienced in studying the authors of any other country. When you read their writings, life appears to consist in a warm sun and a garden of roses — in the smiles and frowns of a fair enemy, and the fire that consumes your own heart. How different from the manly and heroical poetry of Greece and Rome!

Summer passed away in these occupations, and my return to Geneva was fixed for the latter end of autumn; but being delayed by several accidents, winter and snow arrived, the roads were deemed impassable[1], and my journey was retarded until the ensuing spring. I felt this delay very bitterly; for I longed to see my native town and my beloved friends. My return had only been delayed so long from an unwillingness to leave Clerval in a strange place, before he had become acquainted with any of its inhabitants. The winter, however, was spent cheerfully; and although the spring was uncommonly late, when it came its beauty compensated for its dilatoriness[2].

The month of May had already commenced, and I expected the letter daily which was to fix the date of my departure, when Henry proposed a pedestrian[3] tour in the environs of Ingolstadt, that I might bid a personal farewell to the country I had so long inhabited. I acceded[4] with pleasure to this proposition: I was fond of exercise, and Clerval had always been my favourite companion in the rambles of this nature that I had taken among the scenes of my native country.

We passed a fortnight in these perambulations[5]: my health and spirits had long been restored, and they gained additional strength from the salubrious[6] air I breathed, the natural incidents of our progress, and the conversation of my friend. Study had before secluded me from

---

1 impassable: 통행할 수 없는.
2 dilatoriness: 지연. 지체.
3 pedestrian: 도보의. 걸어서 하는.
4 acceded: 동의하다.
5 perambulations: 걸어서 하는 여행. 산책.
6 salubrious: 건강에 좋은.

the intercourse of my fellow-creatures, and rendered me unsocial; but Clerval called forth the better feelings of my heart; he again taught me to love the aspect of nature[1], and the cheerful faces of children. Excellent friend! how sincerely you did love me, and endeavour to elevate my mind until it was on a level with your own! A selfish pursuit had cramped[2] and narrowed me, until your gentleness and affection warmed and opened my senses; I became the same happy creature who, a few years ago, loved and beloved by all, had no sorrow or care. When happy, inanimate nature had the power of bestowing on me the most delightful sensations. A serene sky and verdant[3] fields filled me with ecstasy. The present season was indeed divine; the flowers of spring bloomed in the hedges, while those of summer were already in bud. I was undisturbed by thoughts which during the preceding year had pressed upon me, notwithstanding my endeavours to throw them off, with an invincible[4] burden.

Henry rejoiced in my gaiety, and sincerely sympathised in my feelings: he exerted himself to amuse me, while he expressed the sensations that filled his soul. The resources of his mind on this occasion were truly astonishing: his conversation was full of imagination; and very often, in imitation of the Persian and Arabic writers, he invented tales of wonderful fancy and passion. At other times he repeated my favourite poems, or drew me out into arguments, which he supported with great ingenuity.

We returned to our college on a Sunday afternoon: the peasants were dancing, and every one we met appeared gay and happy. My own spirits were high, and I bounded along with feelings of unbridled joy and hilarity.

---

1 he again taught me to love the aspect of nature: 자연의 아름다움을 일깨워주는 클러벨(Clerval)은 자연을 예찬하는 낭만주의 시인의 면모를 갖고 있다.
2 cramped: 속박하다.
3 verdant: 초록의, 녹색의.
4 invincible: 벗어날(극복할) 수 없는.

Chapter VII

On my return, I found the following letter from my father:—

"My Dear Victor,

You have probably waited impatiently for a letter to fix the date of your return to us; and I was at first tempted to write only a few lines, merely mentioning the day on which I should expect you. But that would be a cruel kindness, and I dare not do it. What would be your surprise, my son, when you expected a happy and glad welcome, to behold, on the contrary, tears and wretchedness? And how, Victor, can I relate our misfortune? Absence cannot have rendered you callous[1] to our joys and griefs; and how shall I inflict pain on my long absent son? I wish to prepare you for the woeful news, but I know it is impossible; even now your eye skims[2] over the page to seek the words which are to convey to you the horrible tidings.

"William is dead!—that sweet child, whose smiles delighted and warmed my heart, who was so gentle, yet so gay! Victor, he is murdered! "I will not attempt to console you; but will simply relate the circumstances of the transaction[3].

"Last Thursday (May 7th), I, my niece, and your two brothers, went to walk in Plainpalais.[4] The evening was warm and serene, and we prolonged our walk farther than usual. It was already dusk before we thought of returning; and then we discovered that William and Ernest, who had gone on before, were not to be found. We accordingly rested on a seat until they should return. Presently Ernest came, and inquired if we had seen his brother: he said, that he had been

---

1 callous: 무감각한(insensible). …에 냉담한(to).
2 skims: 대강 훑어보다.
3 circumstances of the transaction: 일이 벌어진 상황.
4 Plainpalais: '플랭팔레'; 제네바 근방의 지역.

playing with him, that William had run away to hide himself, and that he vainly sought for him, and afterwards waited for a long time, but that he did not return.

"This account rather alarmed us, and we continued to search for him until night fell, when Elizabeth conjectured that he might have returned to the house. He was not there. We returned again, with torches; for I could not rest, when I thought that my sweet boy had lost himself, and was exposed to all the damps and dews of night; Elizabeth also suffered extreme anguish. About five in the morning I discovered my lovely boy, whom the night before I had seen blooming and active in health, stretched on the grass livid and motionless: the print of the murder's finger was on his neck.

"He was conveyed home, and the anguish that was visible in my countenance betrayed the secret to Elizabeth. She was very earnest to see the corpse. At first I attempted to prevent her; but she persisted, and entering the room where it lay, hastily examined the neck of the victim, and clasping her hands exclaimed, 'O God! I have murdered my darling child!'

"She fainted, and was restored with extreme difficulty. When she again lived, it was only to weep and sigh. She told me that that same evening William had teased her to let him wear a very valuable miniature[1] that she possessed of your mother. This picture is gone, and was doubtless the temptation which urged the murderer to the deed. We have no trace of him at present, although our exertions to discover him are unremitted[2]; but they will not restore my beloved William!

"Come, dearest Victor; you alone can console Elizabeth. She weeps continually, and accuses herself unjustly as the cause of his death; her words pierce my heart. We are all unhappy; but will not that be an additional motive for you, my son, to return and be our comforter?

---

1 miniature: 작은 그림. 축소화.
2 unremitted: 중단되지 않는.

Your dear mother! Alas, Victor! I now say, Thank God she did not live to witness the cruel, miserable death of her youngest darling!

"Come, Victor; not brooding[1] thoughts of vengeance against the assassin, but with feelings of peace and gentleness, that will heal, instead of festering[2], the wounds of our minds. Enter the house of mourning, my friend, but with kindness and affection for those who love you, and not with hatred for your enemies. — Your affectionate and afflicted father,

ALPHONSE FRANKENSTEIN.
"GENEVA, May 12th, 17 — ."

Clerval, who had watched my countenance as I read this letter, was surprised to observe the despair that succeeded the joy I at first expressed on receiving new from my friends. I threw the letter on the table, and covered my face with my hands.

"My dear Frankenstein," exclaimed Henry, when he perceived me weep with bitterness, "are you always to be unhappy? My dear friend, what has happened?"

I motioned him to take up the letter, while I walked up and down the room in the extremest agitation. Tears also gushed from the eyes of Clerval, as he read the account of my misfortune.

"I can offer you no consolation, my friend," said he; "your disaster is irreparable. What do you intend to do?"

"To go instantly to Geneva: come with me, Henry, to order the horses."

During our walk, Clerval endeavoured to say a few words of consolation; he could only express his heartfelt sympathy. "Poor William!" said he, "dear lovely child, he now sleeps with his angel mother! Who that had seen him bright and joyous in his young beauty, but must

---

1 brooding: 곰곰이 생각하다.
2 festering: (상처를) 곪게 하다.

weep over his untimely loss! To die so miserably; to feel the murderer's grasp! How much more a murderer that could destroy such radiant innocence! Poor little fellow! one only consolation have we; his friends mourn and weep, but he is at rest. The pang is over, his sufferings are at an end for ever. A sod covers his gentle form, and he knows no pain. He can no longer be a subject for pity; we must reserve that for his miserable survivors."

Clerval spoke thus as we hurried through the streets; the words impressed themselves on my mind and I remembered them after-wards in solitude. But now, as soon as the horses arrived, I hurried into a cabriolet,[1] and bade farewell to my friend.

My journey was very melancholy. At first I wished to hurry on, for I longed to console and sympathise with my loved and sorrowing friends; but when I drew near my native town, I slackened[2] my prog-ress. I could hardly sustain the multitude of feelings that crowded into my mind. I passed through scenes familiar to my youth, but which I had not seen for nearly six years. How altered every thing might be during that time! One sudden and desolating change had taken place; but a thousand little circumstances might have by degrees worked[3] oth-er alterations, which, although they were done more tranquilly, might not be the less decisive. Fear overcame me; I dared not advance, dread-ing a thousand nameless evils that made me tremble, although I was unable to define them. I remained two days at Lausanne,[4] in this pain-ful state of mind. I contemplated[5] the lake: the waters were placid; all around was calm; and the snowy mountains, "the palaces of nature,[6]"

---

1 cabriolet: (불어) 말 한필이 끄는 2륜 포장마차.
2 slackened: (속도를) 늦추다.
3 worked: (변화를) 일으키다.
4 Lausanne: 로잔(스위스 서부 레만 호반의 도시).
5 contemplated: 찬찬히 바라보다.
6 palaces of nature: 시인 셸리(Percy B. Shelley)와도 친분이 있던 영국의 낭만주의 시인 바이런(Lord Byron)은 자신의 대표작 『차일드 해롤드의 편력』(Childe Harold's Pilgri-mage, 1816)에서 알프스 산(Alps)을 "자연의 궁전"(palaces of Nature)이라고 칭하였다.

were not changed. By degrees the calm and heavenly scene restored me, and I continued my journey towards Geneva.

The road ran by the side of the lake, which became narrower as I approached my native town. I discovered more distinctly the black sides of Jura, and the bright summit of Mont Blanc.[1] I wept like a child. "Dear mountains! my own beautiful lake! how do you welcome your wanderer? Your summits are clear; the sky and lake are blue and placid. Is this to prognosticate[2] peace, or to mock at my unhappiness?"

I fear, my friend, that I shall render myself tedious by dwelling on these preliminary[3] circumstances; but they were days of comparative happiness, and I think of them with pleasure. My country, my beloved country! who but a native can tell the delight I took in again beholding thy streams, thy mountains, and, more than all, thy lovely lake!

Yet, as I drew nearer home, grief and fear again overcame me. Night also closed around[4]; and when I could hardly see the dark mountains, I felt still more gloomily. The picture appeared a vast and dim scene of evil, and I foresaw obscurely that I was destined to become the most wretched of human beings. Alas! I prophesied truly, and failed only in one single circumstance, that in all the misery I imagined and dreaded, I did not conceive the hundredth part of the anguish I was destined to endure.

It was completely dark when I arrived in the environs[5] of Geneva; the gates of the town were already shut; and I was obliged to pass the night at Secheron, a village at the distance of half a league from the city. The sky was serene; and, as I was unable to rest, I resolved to visit the spot where my poor William had been murdered. As I could not

---

1 Mont Blanc: '몽블랑'; 프랑스에 위치한 알프스 산맥 중 하나로 유럽에서 가장 높은 산이다. 시인 셸리는 이 산을 주제로 한 「몽블랑」(Mont Blanc, 1816)이란 시를 썼다.

2 prognosticate: …의 징후를 나타내다.

3 preliminary: 서론적인.

4 closed around: …주변을 에워싸다.

5 environs: 주변(의 지역). 근교.

pass through the town, I was obliged to cross the lake in a boat to arrive at Plainpalais. During this short voyage I saw the lightning playing on the summit of Mont Blanc in the most beautiful figures. The storm appeared to approach rapidly; and, on landing, I ascended a low hill, that I might observe its progress. It advanced; the heavens were clouded, and I soon felt the rain coming slowly in large drops, but its violence quickly increased.

I quitted my seat, and walked on, although the darkness and storm increased every minute, and the thunder burst with a terrific[1] crash[2] over my head. It was echoed from Salêve[3], the Juras, and the Alps of Savoy; vivid flashes of lightning dazzled my eyes, illuminating the lake, making it appear like a vast sheet of fire; then for an instant everything seemed of a pitchy darkness, until the eye recovered itself from the preceding flash. The storm, as is often the case in Switzerland, appeared at once in various parts of the heavens. The most violent storm hung exactly north of the town, over that part of the lake which lies between the promontory[4] of Belrive and the village of Copêt[5]. Another storm enlightened Jura with faint flashes; and another darkened and sometimes disclosed the Môle, a peaked mountain to the east of the lake.

While I watched the tempest, so beautiful yet terrific, I wandered on with a hasty step. This noble war in the sky elevated my spirits; I clasped my hands, and exclaimed aloud, "William, dear angel! this is thy funeral, this thy dirge[6]!" As I said these words, I perceived in the gloom a figure which stole[7] from behind a clump of trees near me; I

---

1 terrific: 무시무시한.

2 crash: 요란한 소리.

3 Salêve: 해발 1,400 미터의 제네바 위로 솟은 산.

4 promontory: 곶. 갑(岬).

5 Copêt: 제네바 북쪽 근교에 위치한 지역.

6 dirge: (장례식에서 부르는) 애도가.

7 stole: 살그머니 나오다.

stood fixed, gazing intently: I could not be mistaken. A flash of lightning illuminated the object, and discovered its shape plainly to me; its
gigantic stature, and the deformity of its aspect, more hideous than
belongs to humanity, instantly informed me that it was the wretch,
the filthy[1] dæmon, to whom I had given life. What did he there?
Could he be (I shuddered at the conception[2]) the murderer of my
brother? No sooner did that idea cross my imagination, than I became
convinced of its truth; my teeth chattered, and I was forced to lean
against a tree for support. The figure passed me quickly, and I lost it
in the gloom. Nothing in human shape could have destroyed the fair
child. He was the murderer! I could not doubt it. The mere presence
of the idea was an irresistible proof of the fact[3]. I thought of pursuing
the devil; but it would have been in vain, for another flash discovered
him to me hanging among the rocks of the nearly perpendicular ascent of Mont Salêve, a hill that bounds[4] Plainpalais on the south. He
soon reached the summit, and disappeared.

I remained motionless. The thunder ceased; but the rain still continued, and the scene was enveloped in an impenetrable darkness. I
revolved[5] in my mind the events which I had until now sought to
forget: the whole train of my progress toward the creation; the appearance of the work of my own hands alive at my bedside; its departure.
Two years had now nearly elapsed since the night on which he first
received life; and was this his first crime? Alas! I had turned loose[6]
into the world a depraved wretch, whose delight was in carnage[7] and

---

1 filthy: 추악한.

2 conception: 생각.

3 The mere presence of the idea was an irresistible proof of the fact: 그런 생각(괴물
이 윌리엄을 죽였을 거란 생각)이 떠올랐다는 것 자체가 그가 죽였다는 사실을 입증
한다는 의미.

4 bounds: 접경하다.

5 revolved: 곰곰이 생각하다.

6 turned loose: 풀어놓다.

7 carnage: 살육.

misery; had he not murdered my brother?

No one can conceive the anguish I suffered during the remainder of the night, which I spent, cold and wet, in the open air. But I did not feel the inconvenience of the weather; my imagination was busy in scenes of evil and despair. I considered the being whom I had cast among mankind, and endowed with the will and power to effect[1] purposes of horror, such as the deed which he had now done, nearly in the light of my own vampire[2], my own spirit let loose from the grave, and forced to destroy all that was dear to me.

Day dawned; and I directed my steps towards the town. The gates were open, and I hastened to my father's house. My first thought was to discover what I knew of the murderer, and cause instant pursuit to be made. But I paused when I reflected on the story that I had to tell. A being whom I myself had formed, and endued with life, had met me at midnight among the precipices[3] of an inaccessible mountain. I remembered also the nervous fever with which I had been seized just at the time that I dated[4] my creation, and which would give an air of delirium to a tale[5] otherwise so utterly improbable. I well knew that if any other had communicated such a relation[6] to me, I should have looked upon it as the ravings[7] of insanity. Besides, the strange nature of the animal would elude all pursuit, even if I were so far credited as to persuade my relatives to commence it. And then of what use would be pursuit? Who could arrest a creature capable of scaling[8] the over-

---

1 effect: 성취하다. 완수하다.

2 in the light of my own vampire: 여기서 뱀파이어(vampire)는 '되살아난 시체'라는 의미로 사용되었다; 즉 프랑켄스타인은 자신이 만든 괴물을 자신이 되살린 시신으로 간주하고 있다.

3 precipices: 절벽.

4 dated: 시기를 산정하다.

5 give an air of delirium to a tale: delirium는 '정신 착란', '헛소리하는 상태'; 즉 자신이 하는 이야기는 정신착란을 겪고 있는 사람이 하는 소리로 간주될 수 있을 것이란 의미.

6 relation: 진술.

7 ravings: 헛소리.

8 scaling: (산을) 기어오르다.

hanging[1] sides of Mont Salêve? These reflections determined me, and I resolved to remain silent.

It was about five in the morning when I entered my father's house. I told the servants not to disturb the family, and went into the library to attend their usual hour of rising.

Six years had elapsed, passed in a dream but for one indelible[2] trace, and I stood in the same place where I had last embraced my father before my departure for Ingolstadt. Beloved and venerable parent! He still remained to me. I gazed on the picture of my mother, which stood over the mantel-piece. It was an historical subject, painted at my father's desire, and represented Caroline Beaufort in an agony of despair, kneeling by the coffin of her dead father. Her garb was rustic, and her cheek pale; but there was an air of dignity and beauty, that hardly permitted the sentiment of pity. Below this picture was a miniature of William; and my tears flowed when I looked upon it. While I was thus engaged, Ernest entered: he had heard me arrive, and hastened to welcome me. He expressed a sorrowful delight to see me: "Welcome, my dearest Victor," said he. "Ah! I wish you had come three months ago, and then you would have found us all joyous and delighted! You come to us now to share a misery which nothing can alleviate[3]; yet you presence will, I hope, revive our father, who seems sinking[4] under his misfortune; and your persuasions will induce poor Elizabeth to cease her vain and tormenting self-accusations. — Poor William! he was our darling and our pride!"

Tears, unrestrained, fell from my brother's eyes; a sense of mortal[5] agony crept over my frame. Before, I had only imagined the wretchedness of my desolated home; the reality came on me as a new, and

---

1 overhanging: (90도 이상으로) 경사진.
2 indelible: 지울 수 없는. 지워지지 않는.
3 alleviate: 경감시키다.
4 sinking: 건강이 나빠지는. (몸이) 쇠약해지는.
5 mortal: 엄청나게 큰.

a not less terrible, disaster. I tried to calm Ernest; I inquired more minutely concerning my father and her I named my cousin.

"She most of all," said Ernest, "requires consolation; she accused
herself of having caused the death of my brother, and that made her
very wretched. But since the murderer has been discovered — "

"The murderer discovered! Good God! how can that be? who
could attempt to pursue him? It is impossible; one might as well try to
overtake the winds, or confine[1] a mountain-stream with a straw. I saw
him too; he was free last night!"

"I do not know what you mean," replied my brother, in accents of
wonder, "but to us the discovery we have made completes our misery.
No one would believe it at first; and even now Elizabeth will not be
convinced, notwithstanding all the evidence. Indeed, who would credit
that Justine Moritz, who was so amiable, and fond of all the family,
could suddenly become capable of so frightful, so appalling[2] a crime?"

"Justine Moritz! Poor, poor girl, is she the accused? But it is
wrongfully; every one knows that; no one believes it, surely, Ernest?"

"No one did at first; but several circumstances came out, that have
almost forced conviction upon us; and her own behaviour has been so
confused, as to add to the evidence of facts a weight that, I fear, leaves
no hope for doubt. But she will be tried to-day, and you will then
hear all."

He then related that, the morning on which the murder of poor
William had been discovered, Justine had been taken ill[3], and confined
to her bed for several days. During this interval, one of the servants,
happening to examine the apparel she had worn on the night of the
murder, had discovered in her pocket the picture of my mother, which
had been judged to be the temptation of the murderer. The servant
instantly showed it to one of the others, who, without saying a word

---

1 confine: 가두어두다.
2 appalling: 소름끼치는.
3 taken ill: 병이 든.

to any of the family, went to a magistrate[1]; and, upon their deposition[2], Justine was apprehended. On being charged with the fact[3], the poor girl confirmed the suspicion in a great measure by her extreme confusion of manner.

This was a strange tale, but it did not shake my faith; and I replied earnestly, "You are all mistaken; I know the murderer. Justine, poor, good Justine, is innocent."

At that instant my father entered. I saw unhappiness deeply impressed on his countenance, but he endeavoured to welcome me cheerfully; and, after we had exchanged our mournful greeting, would have introduced some other topic than that of our disaster, had not Ernest exclaimed, "Good God, papa! Victor says that he knows who was the murderer of poor William."

"We do also, unfortunately," replied my father; "for indeed I had rather have been for ever ignorant than have discovered so much depravity[4] and ingratitude in one I valued so highly."

"My dear father, you are mistaken; Justine is innocent."

"If she is, God forbid[5] that she should suffer as guilty. She is to be tried to-day, and I hope, I sincerely hope, that she will be acquitted."

This speech calmed me. I was firmly convinced in my own mind that Justine, and indeed every human being, was guiltless of this murder. I had no fear, therefore, that any circumstantial evidence[6] could be brought forward strong enough to convict her. My tale was not one to announce publicly; its astounding horror would be looked upon as madness by the vulgar[7]. Did any one indeed exist, except I, the

---

1 magistrate: 치안판사.
2 deposition: 선서 증언. 증언 조서.
3 fact: (범죄 등의) 사실. 범행.
4 depravity: 악행.
5 God forbid: 절대 …한 일이 벌어지면 안 된다.
6 circumstantial evidence: (법률) 상황증거.
7 vulgar: 일반사람.

creator,[1] who would believe, unless his senses convinced him, in the existence of the living monument of presumption[2] and rash ignorance which I had let loose upon the world?

We were soon joined by Elizabeth. Time had altered her since I last beheld her; it had endowed her with loveliness surpassing the beauty of her childish years. There was the same candour, the same vivacity, but it was allied to an expression more full of sensibility and intel-lect. She welcomed me with the greatest affection. "Your arrival, my dear cousin," said she, "fills me with hope. You perhaps will find some means to justify[3] my poor guiltless Justine. Alas! who is safe, if she be convicted of crime? I rely on her innocence as certainly as I do upon my own. Our misfortune is doubly hard to us; we have not only lost that lovely darling boy, but this poor girl, whom I sincerely love, is to be torn away by even a worse fate. If she is condemned,[4] I never shall know joy more. But she will not, I am sure she will not; and then I shall be happy again, even after the sad death of my little William."

"She is innocent, my Elizabeth," said I, "and that shall be proved; fear nothing, but let your spirits be cheered by the assurance of her acquittal.[5]"

"How kind and generous you are! every one else believes in her guilt, and that made me wretched, for I knew that it was impossible: and to see every one else prejudiced in so deadly a manner rendered me hopeless and despairing." She wept.

"Dearest niece," said my father, "dry your tears. If she is, as you believe, innocent, rely on the justice of our laws, and the activity with

---

1 the creator: 프랑켄스타인은 그가 만든 괴물의 입장에서 볼 때 창조주와 같은 존재다. 괴물이 그를 아버지라고 부르고, 『실낙원』에 나오는 아담과 자신을 비교하는 이유는 바로 그 때문이다.

2 presumption: '오만함'. '주제넘음': 프랑켄스타인이 인간창조라는 신의 영역에 도전하였기 때문에 이런 표현을 쓴 것이다.

3 justify: 결백을 증명하다.

4 condemned: 유죄를 선고받다.

5 acquittal: 석방. 무죄방면.

which I shall prevent the slightest shadow of partiality.[1]"

CHAPTER VIII

We passed a few sad hours, until eleven o'clock, when the trial was to commence. My father and the rest of the family being obliged to attend as witnesses, I accompanied them to the court. During the whole of this wretched mockery of justice I suffered living torture. It was to be decided, whether the result of my curiosity and lawless devices would cause the death of two of my fellow-beings: one a smiling babe, full of innocence and joy; the other far more dreadfully murdered, with every aggravation of infamy that could make the murder memorable in horror. Justine also was a girl of merit, and possessed qualities which promised to render her life happy: now all was to be obliterated[2] in an ignominious[3] grave; and I the cause! A thousand times rather would I have confessed myself guilty of the crime ascribed to[4] Justine; but I was absent when it was committed, and such a declaration would have been considered as the ravings[5] of a madman, and would not have exculpated[6] her who suffered through me.

The appearance of Justine was calm. She was dressed in mourning[7]; and her countenance, always engaging, was rendered, by the solemnity of her feelings, exquisitely[8] beautiful. Yet she appeared confident

---

1 prevent the slightest shadow of partiality: shadow는 '극히 조금', partiality는 '불공정한 행위'; 즉 조금의 불공정한 행위도 막겠다는 의미.
2 obliterated: 망각되어지다.
3 ignominious: 수치스러운. 불명예스러운.
4 ascribed to: …탓으로 돌려진.
5 ravings: 헛소리.
6 exculpated: 무죄를 증명하다. 죄에서 벗어나게 하다,
7 dressed in mourning: 상복을 입고 있는.
8 exquisitely: 몹시. 매우.

in innocence, and did not tremble, although gazed on and execrated[1]
by thousands; for all the kindness which her beauty might otherwise
have excited, was obliterated in the minds of the spectators by the
imagination of the enormity[2] she was supposed to have committed.
She was tranquil, yet her tranquillity was evidently constrained[3]; and
as her confusion had before been adduced[4] as a proof of her guilt, she
worked up her mind to an appearance of courage.[5] When she entered
the court, she threw her eyes round it, and quickly discovered where
we were seated. A tear seemed to dim her eye[6] when she saw us;
but she quickly recovered herself, and a look of sorrowful affection
seemed to attest[7] her utter guiltlessness.

The trial began; and, after the advocate[8] against her had stated
the charge[9], several witnesses were called. Several strange facts combined against her, which might have staggered[10] any one who had not
such proof of her innocence as I had. She had been out the whole of
the night on which the murder had been committed, and towards
morning had been perceived by a market-woman not far from the
spot where the body of the murdered child had been afterwards
found. The woman asked her what she did there; but she looked very
strangely, and only returned a confused and unintelligible[11] answer.
She returned to the house about eight o'clock; and when one inquired
where she had passed the night, she replied that she had been look-

---

1 execrated: 비난받다. 저주받다.
2 enormity: 극악(極惡)무도한 죄. 큰 죄.
3 constrained: 부자연스런.
4 adduced: (증거 따위로) 제시되다.
5 worked up her mind to an appearance of courage: 정신을 추슬러 용기 있게 보이다.
6 dim her eye: (눈물로) 눈을 흐리게 하다.
7 attest: 증명하다. 입증하다.
8 advocate: 검사.
9 charge: 죄과.
10 staggered: (생각을) 흔들리게 하다.
11 unintelligible: 알 수 없는. 이해할 수 없는.

ing for the child and demanded earnestly if anything had been heard concerning him. When shown the body, she fell into violent hysterics, and kept her bed for several days. The picture was then produced, which the servant had found in her pocket; and when Elizabeth, in a faltering voice, proved that it was the same which, an hour before the child had been missed, she had placed round his neck, a murmur of horror and indignation filled the court.

Justine was called on[1] for her defence. As the trial had proceeded, her countenance had altered. Surprise, horror, and misery were strongly expressed. Sometimes she struggled with her tears[2]; but, when she was desired to plead[3], she collected her powers, and spoke, in an audible, although variable voice.

"God knows," she said, "how entirely I am innocent. But I do not pretend that my protestations should acquit me: I rest my innocence on a plain and simple explanation of the facts which have been adduced against me; and I hope the character I have always borne will incline my judges to a favourable interpretation, where any circumstance appears doubtful or suspicious."

She then related that, by the permission of Elizabeth, she had passed the evening of the night on which the murder had been committed at the house of an aunt at Chêne, a village situated at about a league from Geneva. On her return, at about nine o'clock, she met a man, who asked her if she had seen anything of the child who was lost. She was alarmed by this account, and passed several hours in looking for him, when the gates of Geneva were shut, and she was forced to remain several hours of the night in a barn belonging to a cottage, being unwilling to call up the inhabitants, to whom she was well known. Most of the night she spent here watching; towards morning she believed that she slept for a few minutes; some steps dis-

---

1 called on: 발언이 허락되다.

2 struggled with her tears: 울지 않으려고 안간힘을 썼다는 의미.

3 plead: 변론하다. 항변하다.

turbed her, and she awoke. It was dawn, and she quitted her asylum[1], that she might again endeavour to find my brother. If she had gone near the spot where his body lay, it was without her knowledge. That she had been bewildered[2] when questioned by the market-woman was not surprising, since she had passed a sleepless night, and the fate of poor William was yet uncertain. Concerning the picture she could give no account.

"I know," continued the unhappy victim, "how heavily and fatally this one circumstance weighs against[3] me, but I have no power of explaining it; and when I have expressed my utter ignorance, I am only left to conjecture[4] concerning the probabilities by which it might have been placed in my pocket. But here also I am checked[5]. I believe that I have no enemy on earth, and none surely would have been so wicked as to destroy me wantonly[6]. Did the murderer place it there? I know of no opportunity afforded him for so doing; or, if I had, why should he have stolen the jewel, to part with[7] it again so soon?

"I commit my cause to the justice of my judges[8], yet I see no room[9] for hope. I beg permission to have a few witnesses examined concerning my character; and if their testimony shall not overweigh[10] my supposed guilt, I must be condemned, although I would pledge[11]

---

1 asylum: 은신처.
2 bewildered: 당황한.
3 weighs against: …에게 불리하게 작용하다.
4 conjecture: 추측하다.
5 checked: (생각이) 막히다.
6 wantonly: 악의적으로.
7 part with: …을 내어놓다.
8 commit my cause to the justice of my judges: cause는 '주장', '소명'(疏明); justice 는 '재판', '심판'; 즉 판사들의 심판에 자신의 주장이 타당한지를 맡기겠다는 의미.
9 room: 여지.
10 if their testimony shall not overweigh my supposed guilt: overweigh는 '압도하다'; 즉 증인들의 말이 자신이 죄를 지었다는 의혹을 누를 정도로 자신에게 유리한 말을 하 지 않는다면의 의미.
11 pledge: 담보로 걸다.

my salvation on my innocence."

Several witnesses were called, who had known her for many years, and they spoke well of her; but fear and hatred of the crime of which they supposed her guilty rendered them timorous, and unwilling to come forward[1]. Elizabeth saw even this last resource[2], her excellent dispositions and irreproachable[3] conduct, about to fail the accused, when, although violently agitated, she desired permission to address the court.

"I am," said she, "the cousin of the unhappy child who was murdered, or rather his sister, for I was educated by, and have lived with his parents ever since and even long before, his birth. It may, therefore, be judged indecent in me to come forward on this occasion; but when I see a fellow-creature about to perish through the cowardice of her pretended friends, I wish to be allowed to speak, that I may say what I know of her character. I am well acquainted with the accused. I have lived in the same house with her, at one time for five and at another for nearly two years. During all that period she appeared to me the most amiable and benevolent of human creatures. She nursed Madame Frankenstein, my aunt, in her last illness, with the greatest affection and care; and afterwards attended her own mother during a tedious illness, in a manner that excited the admiration[4] of all who knew her; after which she again lived in my uncle's house, where she was beloved by all the family. She was warmly attached to the child who is now dead, and acted towards him like a most affectionate mother. For my own part, I do not hesitate to say, that, notwithstanding all the evidence produced against her, I believe and rely on her perfect innocence. She had no temptation for such an action: as to the bauble[5] on which the chief proof rests, if she had earnestly desired it, I should have willingly

---

1 come forward: 앞으로 나서다.
2 last resource: 최후의 방책(resource).
3 irreproachable: 결점 없는. 탓할 데 없는.
4 excited the admiration: 감탄을 불러일으키다.
5 bauble: 하찮은 물건.

given it to her; so much do I esteem[1] and value her."

A murmur of approbation followed Elizabeth's simple and power-ful appeal; but it was excited by her generous interference[2], and not in favour of poor Justine, on whom the public indignation was turned with renewed violence, charging her with the blackest ingratitude[3]. She herself wept as Elizabeth spoke, but she did not answer. My own agitation and anguish was extreme during the whole trial. I believed in her innocence; I knew it. Could the dæmon, who had (I did not for a minute doubt) murdered my brother, also in his hellish sport[4] have betrayed the innocent to[5] death and ignominy[6]? I could not sustain the horror of my situation; and when I perceived that the popular voice, and the countenances of the judges, had already condemned my unhappy victim, I rushed out of the court in agony. The tortures of the accused did not equal mine; she was sustained by innocence, but the fangs of remorse[7] tore my bosom, and would not forgo their hold.[8]

I passed a night of unmingled wretchedness. In the morning I went to the court; my lips and throat were parched. I dared not ask the fatal question; but I was known, and the officer guessed the cause of my visit. The ballots[9] had been thrown; they were all black, and Justine was condemned.

I cannot pretend to[10] describe what I then felt. I had before expe-rienced sensations of horror; and I have endeavoured to bestow upon them adequate expressions, but words cannot convey an idea of the

---

1 esteem: 존경하다. 높이 평가하다.
2 interference: 반대의견.
3 blackest ingratitude: 극악무도한 배은망덕.
4 sport: 장난.
5 betrayed the innocent to: 죄 없는 사람을 속여 …을 겪게 하다.
6 ignominy: 치욕.
7 fangs of remorse: 양심의 가책(remorse)이라는 이빨(fang).
8 forgo their hold: (붙들던 것을) 놓다.
9 ballots: 비밀투표에 사용되는 작은 공.
10 pretend to: 감히 …하다.

heart-sickening despair that I then endured. The person to whom I addressed myself added, that Justine had already confessed her guilt. "That evidence," he observed, "was hardly required in so glaring[1] a case, but I am glad of it; and, indeed, none of our judges like to condemn a criminal upon circumstantial evidence, be it ever so decisive[2]."

This was strange and unexpected intelligence[3]; what could it mean? Had my eyes deceived me? and was I really as mad as the whole world would believe me to be, if I disclosed the object of my suspicions? I hastened to return home, and Elizabeth eagerly demanded[4] the result.

"My cousin," replied I, "it is decided as you may have expected; all judges had rather[5] that ten innocent should suffer, than that one guilty should escape. But she has confessed."

This was a dire[6] blow to poor Elizabeth, who had relied with firmness upon Justine's innocence. "Alas!" said she, "how shall I ever again believe in human goodness? Justine, whom I loved and esteemed as my sister, how could she put on those smiles of innocence only to betray? her mild eyes seemed incapable of any severity[7] or guile[8], and yet she has committed a murder."

Soon after we heard that the poor victim had expressed a desire to see my cousin. My father wished her not to go; but said, that he left it to her own judgment and feelings to decide. "Yes," said Elizabeth, "I will go, although she is guilty; and you, Victor, shall accompany me: I cannot go alone." The idea of this visit was torture to me, yet I could

---

1 glaring: 명백한. 빤한.
2 decisive: 의심할 여지없는. (증거가) 결정적인.
3 intelligence: 정보.
4 demanded: 문의하다.
5 had rather: …하기를 바란다.
6 dire: 끔찍한.
7 severity: 잔인한 행위.
8 guile: 간계한 행동.

not refuse.

We entered the gloomy prison-chamber and beheld Justine sitting on some straw at the farther end; her hands were manacled[1], and her head rested on her knees. She rose on seeing us enter; and when we were left alone with her, she threw herself at the feet of Elizabeth, weeping bitterly. My cousin wept also.

"Oh, Justine!" said she. "why did you rob me of my last consolation? I relied on your innocence; and although I was then very wretched, I was not so miserable as I am now."

"And do you also believe that I am so very, very wicked? Do you also join with my enemies to crush me, to condemn me as a murderer?" Her voice was suffocated[2] with sobs.

"Rise, my poor girl," said Elizabeth, "why do you kneel, if you are innocent? I am not one of your enemies; I believed you guiltless, notwithstanding every evidence, until I heard that you had yourself declared your guilt. That report, you say, is false; and be assured, dear Justine, that nothing can shake my confidence in you for a moment, but your own confession."

"I did confess; but I confessed a lie. I confessed, that I might obtain absolution[3]; but now that falsehood lies heavier at my heart[4] than all my other sins. The God of heaven forgive me! Ever since I was condemned, my confessor has besieged[5] me; he threatened and menaced, until I almost began to think that I was the monster that he said I was. He threatened excommunication[6] and hell fire in my last moments, if I continued obdurate[7]. Dear lady, I had none to support me;

1　manacled: 수갑이 채워진. 묶여진.
2　suffocated: 숨이 막히다.
3　absolution: 방면. 석방.
4　lies heavier at my heart: 더 무겁게 내 마음을 짓누른다.
5　besieged: (끊임없이) 괴롭히다.
6　excommunication: 파문.
7　obdurate: 뜻을 굽히지 않는.

all looked on me as a wretch doomed to ignominy and perdition[1]. What could I do? In an evil hour[2] I subscribed to[3] a lie; and now only am I truly miserable."

She paused, weeping, and then continued — "I thought with horror, my sweet lady, that you should believe your Justine, whom your blessed aunt had so highly honoured, and whom you loved, was a creature capable of a crime which none but the devil himself could have perpetrated. Dear William! dearest blessed child! I soon shall see you again in heaven, where we shall all be happy; and that consoles me, going as I am to suffer ignominy and death."

"Oh, Justine! forgive me for having for one moment distrusted you. Why did you confess? But do not mourn, dear girl. Do not fear. I will proclaim, I will prove your innocence. I will melt the stony hearts of your enemies by my tears and prayers. You shall not die! — You, my playfellow, my companion, my sister, perish on the scaffold! No! no! I never could survive so horrible a misfortune."

Justine shook her head mournfully. "I do not fear to die," she said; "that pang is past. God raises my weakness, and gives me courage to endure the worst. I leave a sad and bitter world; and if you remember me, and think of me as of one unjustly condemned, I am resigned to the fate awaiting me. Learn from me, dear lady, to submit in patience to the will of Heaven!"

During this conversation I had retired to a corner of the prison-room, where I could conceal the horrid anguish that possessed me. Despair! Who dared talk of that? The poor victim, who on the morrow was to pass the awful boundary between life and death, felt not, as I did, such deep and bitter agony. I gnashed[4] my teeth, and ground them together, uttering a groan that came from my inmost soul. Jus-

---

1 perdition: 멸망. 파멸.
2 In an evil hour: 운수 나쁘게. 불행히도.
3 subscribed to: …에 찬동하다.
4 gnashed: 이를 갈다.

tine started. When she saw who it was, she approached me, and said, "Dear sir, you are very kind to visit me; you, I hope, do not believe that I am guilty?"

I could not answer. "No, Justine," said Elizabeth; "he is more convinced of your innocence than I was; for even when he heard that you had confessed, he did not credit[1] it."

"I truly thank him. In these last moments I feel the sincerest gratitude towards those who think of me with kindness. How sweet is the affection of others to such a wretch as I am! It removes more than half my misfortune; and I feel as if I could die in peace, now that my innocence is acknowledged by you, dear lady, and your cousin."

Thus the poor sufferer tried to comfort others and herself. She indeed gained the resignation she desired. But I, the true murderer, felt the never-dying worm alive in my bosom, which allowed of no hope or consolation. Elizabeth also wept, and was unhappy; but her's also was the misery of innocence, which, like a cloud that passes over the fair moon, for a while hides but cannot tarnish[2] its brightness. Anguish and despair had penetrated into the core of my heart; I bore a hell within me[3], which nothing could extinguish. We stayed several hours with Justine; and it was with great difficulty that Elizabeth could tear herself away[4]. "I wish," cried she, "that I were to die with you; I cannot live in this world of misery."

Justine assumed an air[5] of cheerfulness, while she with difficulty repressed her bitter tears. She embraced Elizabeth, and said in a voice of half-suppressed emotion, "Farewell, sweet lady, dearest Elizabeth, my beloved and only friend; may heaven, in its bounty,[6] bless and

---

1 credit: 믿다.

2 tarnish: 흐리게 하다.

3 I bore a hell within me: 밀튼의 『실낙원』에 나오는 사탄이 이와 유사한 진술을 한다.

4 tear herself away: 석별(惜別)하다. 뿌리치고 떠나다.

5 air: 모습. 태도.

6 in its bounty: 보상으로서.

preserve you; may this be the last misfortune that you will ever suffer! Live, and be happy, and make others so."

And on the morrow Justine died. Elizabeth's heart-rending eloquence failed to move the judges from their settled conviction[1] in the criminality of the saintly sufferer. My passionate and indignant appeals were lost[2] upon them. And when I received their cold answers, and heard the harsh, unfeeling reasoning of these men, my purposed avowal[3] died away on my lips. Thus I might proclaim myself a madman, but not revoke[4] the sentence passed upon my wretched victim. She perished on the scaffold as a murderess!

From the tortures of my own heart, I turned to contemplate the deep and voiceless grief of my Elizabeth. This also was my doing! And my father's woe, and the desolation of that late so smiling home — all was the work of my thrice-accursed[5] hands! Ye weep, unhappy ones; but these are not your last tears! Again shall you raise the funeral wail[6], and the sound of your lamentations shall again and again be heard! Frankenstein, your son, your kinsman, your early, much-loved friend; he who would spend each vital drop of blood for your sakes — who has no thought nor sense of joy, except as it is mirrored also in your dear countenances — who would fill the air with blessings, and spend his life in serving you — he bids you weep — to shed countless tears; happy beyond his hopes, if thus inexorable[7] fate be satisfied, and if the destruction pause before the peace of the grave have succeeded to[8] your sad torments!

---

1 settled conviction: 확신.
2 lost: …에게는 아무 소용없는.
3 avowal: 공언. 언명.
4 revoke: 철회하다. 무효로 하다.
5 thrice-accursed: thrice는 '대단히', '매우'; accursed는 '저주받은': 즉 대단히 저주받은.
6 funeral wail: 장례식 때의 통곡소리.
7 inexorable: 무정한. 냉혹한.
8 succeeded to: 뒤따라 일어나다.

Thus spoke my prophetic soul, as, torn by remorse, horror, and despair, I beheld those I loved spend vain sorrow upon the graves of William and Justine, the first hapless victims to my unhallowed arts[1].

CHAPTER IX

Nothing is more painful to the human mind, than, after the feelings have been worked up[2] by a quick succession of events, the dead[3] calmness of inaction and certainty which follows, and deprives the soul both of hope and fear. Justine died; she rested; and I was alive. The blood flowed freely in my veins, but a weight of despair and remorse pressed on my heart, which nothing could remove. Sleep fled from my eyes; I wandered like an evil spirit, for I had committed deeds of mischief beyond description[4] horrible, and more, much more (I persuaded myself), was yet behind[5]. Yet my heart overflowed with kindness, and the love of virtue. I had begun life with benevolent intentions, and thirsted for the moment when I should put them in practice, and make myself useful to my fellow-beings. Now all was blasted[6]: instead of that serenity[7] of conscience, which allowed me to look back upon the past with self-satisfaction, and from thence to gather promise of new hopes, I was seized by remorse and the sense of guilt, which hurried me away to a hell of intense tortures, such as no language can describe.

This state of mind preyed upon[8] my health, which had perhaps

---

1 unhallowed arts: 신성치 않은(unhallowed) 학문(art).
2 worked up: 흥분되다. 부추겨지다.
3 dead: 절대적인. 완전한.
4 beyond description: 묘사할 수 없는.
5 yet behind: '앞으로 다가 올' 것이란 의미.
6 blasted: (희망이) 무너진.
7 serenity: 평온. 차분함.
8 preyed upon: (건강을) 해치다.

never entirely recovered from the first shock it had sustained[1]. I shunned[2] the face of man; all sound of joy or complacency[3] was torture to me; solitude was my only consolation — deep, dark, deathlike solitude.

My father observed with pain the alteration perceptible in my disposition and habits, and endeavoured by arguments deduced from[4] the feelings of his serene conscience and guiltless life, to inspire me with fortitude[5], and awaken in me the courage to dispel the dark cloud which brooded over[6] me. "Do you think, Victor," said he, "that I do not suffer also? No one could love a child more than I loved your brother" (tears came into his eyes as he spoke) "but is it not a duty to the survivors, that we should refrain from augmenting[7] their unhappiness by an appearance of immoderate[8] grief? It is also a duty owed to yourself; for excessive sorrow prevents improvement or enjoyment, or even the discharge[9] of daily usefulness, without which no man is fit for society."

This advice, although good, was totally inapplicable to my case; I should have been the first to hide my grief, and console my friends, if remorse had not mingled its bitterness, and terror its alarm with my other sensations. Now I could only answer my father with a look of despair, and endeavour to hide myself from his view.

About this time we retired to our house at Belrive. This change was particularly agreeable to me. The shutting of the gates regularly at ten o'clock, and the impossibility of remaining on the lake after that hour, had rendered our residence within the walls of Geneva very irk-

---

1 sustained: (충격을) 받다.
2 shunned: 피하다.
3 complacency: 만족(감).
4 deduced from: …으로부터 연유된.
5 fortitude: 용기. 강인한 정신.
6 brooded over: 뒤덮다.
7 augmenting: 확대시키다. 증가시키다.
8 immoderate: 과도한. 엄청난.
9 discharge: (의무의) 수행. 임무이행.

some[1] to me. I was now free. Often, after the rest of the family had retired for the night, I took the boat, and passed many hours upon the water. Sometimes, with my sails set, I was carried by the wind: and sometimes, after rowing into the middle of the lake, I left the boat to pursue its own course, and gave way to[2] my own miserable reflections. I was often tempted, when all was at peace around me, and I the only unquiet thing that wandered restless in a scene so beautiful and heavenly — if I except some bat, or the frogs, whose harsh and interrupted croaking[3] was heard only when I approached the shore — often, I say, I was tempted to plunge into the silent lake, that the waters might close over me and my calamities[4] for ever. But I was restrained, when I thought of the heroic and suffering Elizabeth, whom I tenderly loved, and whose existence was bound up in mine. I thought also of my father and surviving brother: should I by my base[5] desertion leave them exposed and unprotected to the malice of the fiend whom I had let loose among them?

At these moments I wept bitterly, and wished that peace would revisit my mind only that I might afford them consolation and happiness. But that could not be. Remorse extinguished every hope. I had been the author of unalterable evils; and I lived in daily fear, lest the monster whom I had created should perpetrate[6] some new wickedness. I had an obscure feeling that all was not over, and that he would still commit some signal[7] crime, which by its enormity should almost efface the recollection of the past. There was always scope[8] for fear,

---

1 irksome: 지루한.
2 gave way to: …에 빠지다(몰두하다).
3 croaking: (개구리 등의) 쉰 소리.
4 calamities: 불행. 비운.
5 base: 비열한.
6 perpetrate: 행하다. (죄를) 저지르다.
7 signal: 커다란.
8 scope: 여지.

so long as anything I loved remained behind. My abhorrence of this fiend cannot be conceived. When I thought of him, I gnashed my teeth, my eyes became inflamed, and I ardently wished to extinguish that life which I had so thoughtlessly bestowed. When I reflected on his crimes and malice, my hatred and revenge burst all bounds of moderation[1]. I would have made a pilgrimage to the highest peak of the Andes[2], could I, when there, have precipitated[3] him to their base. I wished to see him again, that I might wreak the utmost extent of abhorrence[4] on his head, and avenge the deaths of William and Justine.

Our house was the house of mourning. My father's health was deeply shaken by the horror of the recent events. Elizabeth was sad and desponding[5]; she no longer took delight in her ordinary occupations; all pleasure seemed to her sacrilege toward the dead; eternal woe and tears she then thought was the just tribute[6] she should pay to innocence so blasted and destroyed. She was no longer that happy creature, who in earlier youth wandered with me on the banks of the lake, and talked with ecstasy of our future prospects. The first of those sorrows which are sent to wean[7] us from the earth, had visited her, and its dimming influence quenched her dearest smiles.

"When I reflect, my dear cousin," said she, "on the miserable death of Justine Moritz, I no longer see the world and its works as they before appeared to me. Before, I looked upon the accounts of vice and injustice, that I read in books or heard from others, as tales of ancient days, or imaginary[8] evils; at least they were remote, and more familiar

---

1 moderation: 절제. 중용.
2 Andes: (남미에 있는) 안데스 산맥.
3 precipitated: 거꾸로 떨어뜨리다.
4 wreak: (분노를) 터뜨리다.
5 desponding: 낙담한. 의기소침한.
6 tribute: 조의.
7 wean: 버리게 하다. 단념시키다.
8 imaginary: 상상 속에서만 존재하는.

to reason than to the imagination; but now misery has come home[1], and men appear to me as monsters thirsting for each other's blood. Yet I am certainly unjust. Everybody believed that poor girl to be guilty; and if she could have committed the crime for which she suffered, as-suredly[2] she would have been the most depraved[3] of human creatures. For the sake of a few jewels, to have murdered the son of her bene-factor and friend, a child whom she had nursed from its birth, and appeared to love as if it had been her own! I could not consent to the death of any human being; but certainly I should have thought such a creature unfit to remain in the society of men. But she was innocent. I know, I feel she was innocent; you are of the same opinion, and that confirms me. Alas! Victor, when falsehood can look so like the truth, who can assure themselves of[4] certain happiness? I feel as if I were walking on the edge of a precipice, towards which thousands are crowding, and endeavouring to plunge me into the abyss. William and Justine were assassinated, and the murderer escapes; he walks about the world free, and perhaps respected. But even if I were condemned to suffer on the scaffold for the same crimes, I would not change places with such a wretch."

I listened to this discourse with the extremest agony. I, not in deed, but in effect[5], was the true murderer. Elizabeth read my anguish in my countenance, and kindly taking my hand, said, "My dearest friend, you must calm yourself. These events have affected me, God knows how deeply; but I am not so wretched as you are. There is an expression of despair, and sometimes of revenge[6], in your countenance, that makes me tremble. Dear Victor, banish these dark passions. Remember the friends

---

1 come home: 가슴에 와 닿다. 확실하게 이해되다.

2 assuredly: 확실히. 의심할 바 없이.

3 depraved: 타락한. 사악한.

4 assure themselves of: …을 확신하다.

5 not in deed, but in effect: 행위를 저지른 건 아니지만 실제적인 면에서는.

6 revenge: 원한.

around you, who centre all their hopes in you. Have we lost the power of rendering you happy? Ah! while we love — while we are true to each other, here in this land of peace and beauty, your native country, we may reap every tranquil blessing — what can disturb our peace?"

And could not such words from her whom I fondly prized[1] before every other gift of fortune, suffice to chase away the fiend that lurked[2] in my heart? Even as she spoke I drew near to her, as if in terror; lest at that very moment the destroyer had been near to rob me of her.

Thus not the tenderness of friendship, nor the beauty of earth, nor of heaven, could redeem[3] my soul from woe: the very accents of love were ineffectual. I was encompassed by a cloud which no beneficial influence could penetrate. The wounded deer dragging its fainting[4] limbs to some untrodden brake[5], there to gaze upon the arrow which had pierced it, and to die — was but a type[6] of me.

Sometimes I could cope with[7] the sullen despair that overwhelmed me: but sometimes the whirlwind passions of my soul drove me to seek, by bodily exercise and by change of place, some relief from my intolerable sensations. It was during an access[8] of this kind that I suddenly left my home, and bending my steps towards[9] the near Alpine valleys, sought in the magnificence, the eternity of such scenes, to forget myself and my ephemeral[10], because human, sorrows. My wanderings were directed towards the valley of Chamounix[11]. I had visited it

---

1 prized: 소중히 여기다.
2 lurked: 숨어있다.
3 redeem: 구제(회복)하다.
4 fainting: 약해져가는. 기운을 잃어 가는.
5 brake: 숲. 덤불.
6 type: 대변하는 것.
7 cope with: …을 극복하다(이겨내다).
8 access: (병·노여움 등의) 발작. 격발.
9 bending my steps towards: 발길을 …로 돌리다.
10 ephemeral: 일시적인.
11 Chamounix: 몽블랑 북쪽에 위치한 계곡이다.

frequently during my boyhood. Six years had passed since then: I was a wreck — but nought[1] had changed in those savage and enduring scenes.

I performed the first part of my journey on horseback. I afterwards hired a mule, as the more sure-footed[2], and least liable to[3] receive injury on these rugged roads. The weather was fine: it was about the middle of the month of August, nearly two months after the death of Justine; that miserable epoch from which I dated all my woe. The weight upon my spirit was sensibly lightened as I plunged[4] yet deeper in the ravine[5] of Arve[6]. The immense mountains and precipices that overhung me on every side — the sound of the river raging[7] among the rocks, and the dashing of the waterfalls around, spoke of a power mighty as Omnipotence — and I ceased to fear, or to bend[8] before any being less almighty than that which had created and ruled the elements, here displayed in their most terrific guise[9]. Still, as I ascended higher, the valley assumed a more magnificent and astonishing character. Ruined castles hanging on the precipices of piny[10] mountains; the impetuous[11] Arve, and cottages every here and therefrom peeping forth[12] among the trees, formed a scene of singular[13] beauty. But it was augmented and rendered sublime by the mighty Alps, whose white

---

1   nought: 'nothing'의 의미.
2   sure-footed: 자빠지지 않는. 믿음직한
3   liable to: (까딱하면) …하기 쉬운.
4   plunged: 뛰어들다.
5   ravine: 협곡. 계곡.
6   Arve: '아르브강'; 프랑스 론알프주 오트사부아(Haute-Savoie) 데파르트망과 스위스를 흐르는 강으로 론강(Rhône River)의 왼쪽 지류.
7   raging: 사납게 흐르는.
8   bend: 굴복하다.
9   guise: 외관. 모습.
10   piny: 소나무가 무성한.
11   impetuous: 격렬한. 맹렬한.
12   peeping forth: 슬쩍슬쩍 그 모습을 드러내다.
13   singular: 기묘한. 독특한.

and shining pyramids and domes[1] towered[2] above all, as belonging to another earth, the habitations of another race of beings.

I passed the bridge of Pélissier, where the ravine, which the river forms, opened before me, and I began to ascend the mountain that overhangs it. Soon after I entered the valley of Chamounix. This valley is more wonderful and sublime, but not so beautiful and picturesque, as that of Servox, through which I had just passed. The high and snowy mountains were its immediate boundaries; but I saw no more ruined castles and fertile fields. Immense glaciers approached the road; I heard the rumbling thunder of the falling avalanche[3], and marked the smoke of its passage. Mont Blanc, the supreme and magnificent Mont Blanc, raised itself from the surrounding aiguilles[4], and its tremendous dôme overlooked the valley.

A tingling[5] long-lost sense of pleasure often came across me during this journey. Some turn in the road, some new object suddenly perceived and recognised, reminded me of days gone by, and were associated with the light-hearted gaiety of boyhood. The very winds whispered in soothing accents, and maternal nature bade me weep no more. Then again the kindly influence ceased to act — I found myself fettered[6] again to grief, and indulging in all the misery of reflection. Then I spurred on[7] my animal, striving so to forget the world, my fears, and, more than all, myself — or, in a more desperate fashion, I alighted, and threw myself on the grass, weighed down[8] by horror and despair.

---

1 domes: 둥근 마루터기.
2 towered: 우뚝 솟다.
3 avalanche: 눈사태.
4 aiguilles: 뾰족한 산봉우리.
5 tingling: 흥분하게 만드는. 설레게 하는.
6 fettered: 족쇄에 차인.
7 spurred on: …에 박차를 가하다. 질주하게 하다.
8 weighed down: 침울케 되다.

At length I arrived at the village of Chamounix. Exhaustion succeeded to the extreme fatigue both of body and of mind which I had
endured. For a short space of time I remained at the window, watching the pallid[1] lightnings that played above Mont Blanc, and listening
to the rushing of the Arve, which pursued its noisy way beneath. The
same lulling[2] sounds acted as a lullaby to my too keen[3] sensations:
when I placed my head upon my pillow, sleep crept over me; I felt it
as it came, and blessed the giver of oblivion.

Chapter X

I spent the following day roaming[4] through the valley. I stood beside
the sources of the Arveiron[5], which take their rise[6] in a glacier, that
with slow pace is advancing down from the summit of the hills, to
barricade the valley. The abrupt[7] sides of vast mountains were before me; the icy wall of the glacier overhung me; a few shattered
pines were scattered around; and the solemn silence of this glorious
presence-chamber[8] of imperial Nature was broken only by the brawling[9] waves, or the fall of some vast fragment, the thunder sound of
the avalanche, or the cracking reverberated along the mountains of
the accumulated ice, which, through the silent working of immutable
laws, was ever and anon[10] rent and torn, as if it had been but a play-

---

1 pallid: 희미한.
2 lulling: 달래는. 어르는.
3 keen: 예민한. 민감한.
4 roaming: 배회하다.
5 Arveiron: 몽블랑 산 근처에 위치한 강으로 빙하에 의해 만들어졌다.
6 take their rise in: …에서 기원하다.
7 abrupt: 가파른.
8 presence-chamber: (왕을 만나는) 알현실.
9 brawling: 떠들썩한.
10 ever and anon: 때때로. 가끔.

thing in their hands. These sublime and magnificent scenes afforded me the greatest consolation that I was capable of receiving. They elevated me from all littleness of feeling[1]; and although they did not remove my grief, they subdued and tranquillised[2] it. In some degree, also, they diverted my mind from the thoughts over which it had brooded for the last month. I retired to rest at night; my slumbers, as it were, waited on and ministered to[3] by the assemblance[4] of grand shapes which I had contemplated during the day. They congregated[5] round me; the unstained snowy mountain-top, the glittering pinnacle[6], the pine woods, and ragged[7] bare ravine; the eagle, soaring amidst the clouds — they all gathered round me and bade me be at peace.

Where had they fled when the next morning I awoke? All of soul-inspiriting[8] fled with sleep, and dark melancholy clouded every thought. The rain was pouring in torrents, and thick mists hid the summits of the mountains, so that I even saw not the faces of those mighty friends. Still I would penetrate their misty veil, and seek them in their cloudy retreats[9]. What were rain and storm to me? My mule was brought to the door, and I resolved to ascend to the summit of Montanvert[10]. I remembered the effect that the view of the tremendous and ever-moving glacier had produced upon my mind when I first saw it. It had then filled me with a sublime ecstasy that gave wings to[11] the soul, and allowed it to soar from the obscure world to light and

---

1 littleness of feeling: '사소한 (인간의) 감정'.
2 tranquillised: 진정시키다. 누그러뜨리다.
3 ministered to: 돌보아지다.
4 assemblance: 집합물.
5 congregated: 모이다. 집합하다.
6 pinnacle: 산봉우리.
7 ragged: 울퉁불퉁한.
8 soul-inspiriting: 원기(용기)를 북돋우는.
9 retreats: 은신처.
10 Montanvert: '몽탕베르'; 몽블랑에 있는 3개의 큰 빙하 중 하나.
11 gave wings to: …을 비상하게 하다.

joy. The sight of the awful and majestic in nature had indeed always the effect of solemnising[1] my mind, and causing me to forget the passing cares of life. I determined to go without a guide, for I was well acquainted with the path, and the presence of another would destroy the solitary grandeur of the scene.

The ascent is precipitous[2], but the path is cut into continual and short windings, which enable you to surmount the perpendicularity of the mountain[3]. It is a scene terrifically desolate. In a thousand spots the traces of the winter avalanche may be perceived, where trees lie broken and strewed[4] on the ground; some entirely destroyed, others bent, leaning upon the jutting[5] rocks of the mountain, or transversely[6] upon other trees. The path, as you ascend higher, is intersected by ravines of snow, down which stones continually roll from above; one of them is particularly dangerous, as the slightest sound, such as even speaking in a loud voice, produces a concussion[7] of air sufficient to draw destruction upon[8] the head of the speaker. The pines are not tall or luxuriant[9], but they are sombre[10], and add an air of severity to the scene. I looked on the valley beneath; vast mists were rising from the rivers which ran through it, and curling in thick wreaths[11] around the opposite mountains, whose summits were hid in the uniform clouds, while rain poured from the dark sky, and added to the melancholy

---

1 solemnising: 장엄(숭고)하게 하다.

2 precipitous: 가파른.

3 surmount the perpendicularity of the mountain: surmount는 '완전히 오르다'; per-pendicularity는 '수직'; 즉 '수직으로 산을 완전히 오르다'란 의미.

4 strewed: 여기 저기 널려진.

5 jutting: 튀어나온.

6 transversely: 가로질러.

7 concussion: 큰 진동. 강한 흔들림.

8 draw destruction upon: …에게 파멸(죽음)을 가져오다.

9 luxuriant: (나뭇잎이) 울창하게 자라난.

10 sombre: 거무스름한. 어두운.

11 in thick wreaths: 짙은 소용돌이의 형태로.

impression I received from the objects around me. Alas! why does man boast of sensibilities superior to those apparent in the brute; it only renders them more necessary beings. If our impulses were confined to hunger, thirst, and desire, we might be nearly free; but now we are moved by every wind that blows, and a chance word or scene that that word may convey to us.

> "We rest; a dream has power to poison sleep.
>   We rise; one wandering thought pollutes the day.
> We feel, conceive, or reason; laugh or weep,
>   Embrace fond woe, or cast our cares away;
>
> It is the same: for, be it joy or sorrow,
>   The path of its departure still is free.
> Man's yesterday may ne'er be like his morrow;
>   Nought may endure but mutability!"[1]

It was nearly noon when I arrived at the top of the ascent[2]. For some time I sat upon the rock that overlooks the sea of ice[3]. A mist covered both that and the surrounding mountains. Presently a breeze dissipated[4] the cloud, and I descended upon the glacier. The surface is very uneven, rising like the waves of a troubled sea[5], descending low, and interspersed by rifts[6] that sink deep. The field[7] of ice is almost a league in width, but I spent nearly two hours in crossing it. The opposite mountain is a bare perpendicular rock. From the side where I now stood Montanvert was

---

1   P. B. 셸리의 시 「무상에 관해서」(On Mutability)의 마지막 8행.

2   ascent: 오르막.

3   sea of ice: 불어로 'Mer de Glace'라고 불리는 이 빙산은 몽블랑에서 하강한 빙산 중 하나로 매리 셸리는 자신의 일기장에 이 빙산이 "이 세상에서 가장 황량한 곳"이라고 기술하고 있다. (1816년 7월 25일자 일기)

4   dissipated: 흩뜨리다.

5   troubled sea: 거친 바다.

6   interspersed by rifts: 갈라진 틈(rift)이 군데군데 있는(interspersed).

7   field: 지면.

exactly opposite, at the distance of a league; and above it rose Mont Blanc, in awful majesty. I remained in a recess[1] of the rock, gazing on this wonderful and stupendous[2] scene. The sea, or rather[3] the vast river of ice, wound among its dependent mountains, whose aerial[4] summits hung over its recesses. Their icy and glittering peaks shone in the sunlight over the clouds. My heart, which was before sorrowful, now swelled with something like joy; I exclaimed—"Wandering spirits, if indeed ye wander, and do not rest in your narrow beds, allow me this faint[5] happiness, or take me, as your companion, away from the joys of life."

As I said this, I suddenly beheld the figure of a man, at some distance, advancing towards me with superhuman speed. He bounded over[6] the crevices in the ice, among which I had walked with caution; his stature, also, as he approached, seemed to exceed that of man. I was troubled: a mist came over my eyes, and I felt a faintness seize me[7]; but I was quickly restored by the cold gale of the mountains. I perceived, as the shape came nearer (sight tremendous and abhorred!) that it was the wretch whom I had created. I trembled with rage and horror, resolving to wait his approach, and then close with[8] him in mortal combat[9]. He approached; his countenance bespoke[10] bitter anguish, combined with disdain and malignity, while its unearthly[11] ugliness rendered it almost too horrible for human eyes. But I scarcely

---

1 recess: 구석. 움푹 들어간 곳.
2 stupendous: 엄청난. 굉장한.
3 or rather: 보다 정확히 말하자면.
4 aerial: 높이 치솟아있는.
5 faint: 약간의.
6 bounded over: …위를 뛰어넘어가다.
7 faintness seize me: 정신이 흐릿해지기 시작하였다는 의미.
8 close with: …와 맞붙어 싸우다.
9 mortal combat: 목숨을 건 싸움.
10 bespoke: …을 나타내다.
11 unearthly: 이 세상 것이 아닌.

observed this; rage and hatred had at first deprived me of utterance[1], and I recovered only to overwhelm him with words expressive of furious detestation and contempt.

"Devil," I exclaimed, "do you dare approach me? and do not you fear the fierce vengeance of my arm wreaked on your miserable head? Begone, vile insect[2]! or rather, stay, that I may trample you to dust! and, oh! that I could, with the extinction of your miserable existence, restore those victims whom you have so diabolically murdered!"

"I expected this reception," said the dæmon. "All men hate the wretched; how, then, must I be hated, who am miserable beyond all living things! Yet you, my creator, detest and spurn[3] me, thy creature, to whom thou art[4] bound by ties only dissoluble[5] by the annihilation of one of us. You purpose to kill me. How dare you sport thus with[6] life? Do your duty towards me, and I will do mine towards you and the rest of mankind. If you will comply with my conditions, I will leave them and you at peace; but if you refuse, I will glut[7] the maw[8] of death, until it be satiated[9] with the blood of your remaining friends."

"Abhorred monster! fiend that thou art! the tortures of hell are too mild a vengeance for thy crimes. Wretched devil! you reproach me with your creation; come on, then, that I may extinguish the spark which I so negligently[10] bestowed."

My rage was without bounds; I sprang on[11] him, impelled by all the

---

1 utterance: 말. 진술.
2 insect: 벌레 같은 인간.
3 spurn: 경멸하다.
4 art: 'are'의 의미.
5 dissoluble: 단절될 수 있는.
6 sport thus with: …을 가지고 장난치다.
7 glut: 가득 채우다. 배불리 먹이다,
8 maw: 위(胃). 입.
9 satiated: 물릴 정도로 채워지다.
10 negligently: 별 생각 없이. 부주의하게.
11 sprang on: …에게 달려들다.

feelings which can arm one being against the existence of another.

He easily eluded me and said,

"Be calm! I entreat you to hear me, before you give vent to[1] your hatred on my devoted[2] head. Have I not suffered enough that you seek to increase my misery? Life, although it may only be an accumulation of anguish, is dear to me, and I will defend it. Remember, thou[3] hast[4] made me more powerful than thyself; my height is superior to thine; my joints more supple[5]. But I will not be tempted to set myself in opposition to thee. I am thy creature, and I will be even mild and docile to my natural lord and king, if thou wilt[6] also perform thy part, the which thou owest me. Oh, Frankenstein, be not equitable[7] to every other, and trample upon me alone, to whom thy justice, and even thy clemency[8] and affection, is most due. Remember, that I am thy creature; I ought to be thy Adam[9]; but I am rather the fallen angel[10], whom thou drivest from joy for no misdeed. Everywhere I see bliss, from which I alone am irrevocably[11] excluded. I was benevolent and good; misery made me a fiend. Make me happy, and I shall again be virtuous."

"Begone! I will not hear you. There can be no community[12] be-

---

1 give vent to: ···을 터뜨리다(나타내다).
2 devoted: 저주 받은.
3 thou: 'you'의 의미.
4 hast: 'have'의 2인칭·단수·직설법·현재형.
5 supple: 유연한.
6 wilt: 'will'의 2인칭 단수형.
7 equitable: 공정한. 정당한.
8 clemency: 관대함, 자비(로운 행동).
9 I ought to be thy Adam: 프랑켄스타인이 만든 괴물은 프랑켄스타인을 기독교의 신으로 자신을 신이 최초로 창조한 피조물인 아담에 비유하고 있는데, 그가 이런 생각을 한 데에는 그가 실제의 일을 다룬 이야기라고 믿는 「실낙원」을 읽었기 때문이다.
10 fallen angel: 여기서 말하는 '타락한 천사'(fallen angel)는 밀튼의 「실낙원」에서 하늘나라에서 쫓겨난 천사장인 루시퍼(Lucifer)를 연상시킨다. 신에게 반란을 일으키다 지옥으로 떨어진 루시퍼는 후에 사탄(Satan)이라는 이름을 얻게 된다.
11 irrevocably: 돌이킬 수 없게.
12 community: 공통점. 공감할 수 있는 영역.

tween you and me; we are enemies. Begone, or let us try our strength in a fight, in which one must fall."

"How can I move thee? Will no entreaties cause thee to turn a favourable eye upon thy creature, who implores thy goodness and compassion? Believe me, Frankenstein: I was benevolent; my soul glowed with love and humanity: but am I not alone, miserably alone? You, my creator, abhor me; what hope can I gather from your fellow-creatures, who owe me nothing? they spurn and hate me. The desert[1] mountains and dreary glaciers are my refuge. I have wandered here many days; the caves of ice, which I only do not fear, are a dwelling to me, and the only one which man does not grudge[2]. These bleak skies I hail[3], for they are kinder to me than your fellow-beings. If the multitude of mankind knew of my existence, they would do as you do, and arm themselves for my destruction. Shall I not then hate them who abhor me? I will keep no terms with[4] my enemies. I am miserable, and they shall share my wretchedness. Yet it is in your power to recompense[5] me, and deliver them from an evil which it only remains for you to make so great that not only you and your family, but thousands of others, shall be swallowed up in the whirlwinds of its rage. Let your compassion be moved, and do not disdain me. Listen to my tale: when you have heard that, abandon or commiserate[6] me, as you shall judge that I deserve. But hear me. The guilty are allowed, by human laws, bloody as they are, to speak in their own defence before they are condemned. Listen to me, Frankenstein. You accuse me of murder; and yet you would, with a satisfied conscience[7], destroy your

---

1 desert: 사람이 살지 않는.
2 grudge: (주기를) 싫어하다(아까워하다).
3 hail: 환호하여 맞이하다.
4 keep no terms with: …와 관련(관계)을 맺지 않다.
5 recompense: 보상해주다.
6 commiserate: 동정하다.
7 conscience: 속마음(감정).

own creature. Oh, praise the eternal justice of man! Yet I ask you not to spare me: listen to me; and then, if you can, and if you will, destroy the work of your hands."

"Why do you call to my remembrance[1]," I rejoined, "circumstances, of which I shudder to reflect, that I have been the miserable origin and author? Cursed be the day, abhorred devil, in which you first saw light! Cursed (although I curse myself) be the hands that formed you! You have made me wretched beyond expression. You have left me no power to consider whether I am just to you or not. Begone! relieve me from the sight of your detested form."

"Thus I relieve thee, my creator," he said, and placed his hated hands before my eyes, which I flung from me with violence; "thus I take from thee a sight which you abhor. Still thou canst listen to me, and grant me thy compassion. By the virtues that I once possessed, I demand this from you. Hear my tale; it is long and strange, and the temperature of this place is not fitting to your fine[2] sensations; come to the hut upon the mountain. The sun is yet high in the heavens; before it descends to hide itself behind your snowy precipices and illuminate another world, you will have heard my story, and can decide. On you it rests whether I quit forever the neighbourhood of man, and lead a harmless life, or become the scourge[3] of your fellow-creatures, and the author[4] of your own speedy ruin."

As he said this, he led the way across the ice: I followed. My heart was full, and I did not answer him; but as I proceeded, I weighed[5] the various arguments that he had used, and determined at least to listen to his tale. I was partly urged by curiosity, and compassion confirmed[6]

---

1 call to my remembrance: ⋯을 생각나게 하다.
2 fine: 민감한. 예민한.
3 scourge: 응징. 불행을 가져오는 존재.
4 author: 장본인.
5 weighed: 곰곰이 생각해보다.
6 confirmed: (결심을) 굳히다.

my resolution. I had hitherto supposed him to be the murderer of my brother, and I eagerly sought a confirmation or denial of this opinion. For the first time, also, I felt what the duties of a creator towards his creature were, and that I ought to render him happy before I complained of his wickedness. These motives urged me to comply with his demand. We crossed the ice, therefore, and ascended the opposite rock. The air was cold, and the rain again began to descend: we entered the hut, the fiend with an air of exultation[1], I with a heavy heart and depressed spirits. But I consented to listen; and, seating myself by the fire which my odious[2] companion had lighted, he thus began his tale.

CHAPTER XI

"It is with considerable difficulty that I remember the original era of my being; all the events of that period appear confused and indistinct. A strange multiplicity of sensations seized me, and I saw, felt, heard, and smelt, at the same time; and it was, indeed, a long time before I learned to distinguish between the operations of my various senses. By degrees, I remember, a stronger light pressed upon my nerves, so that I was obliged to shut my eyes. Darkness then came over me, and troubled me; but hardly had I felt this, when, by opening my eyes, as I now suppose, the light poured in upon me again. I walked, and, I believe, descended; but I presently found a great alteration in my sensations. Before, dark and opaque[3] bodies had surrounded me, impervious to my touch or sight[4]; but I now found that I could wander

---

1 exultation: 광희(狂喜). 환희.
2 odious: 혐오스런.
3 opaque: 불투명한.
4 impervious to my touch or sight: 촉감으로나 시각으로 느낄 수 없는.

on at liberty[1], with no obstacles which I could not either surmount or avoid. The light became more and more oppressive to me; and, the heat wearying[2] me as I walked, I sought a place where I could receive shade. This was the forest near Ingolstadt; and here I lay by the side of a brook[3] resting from my fatigue, until I felt tormented by hunger and thirst. This roused me from my nearly dormant[4] state, and I ate some berries which I found hanging on the trees, or lying on the ground. I slaked[5] my thirst at the brook; and then lying down, was overcome by sleep.

"It was dark when I awoke; I felt cold also, and half frightened, as it were instinctively, finding myself so desolate. Before I had quitted your apartment, on a sensation of cold, I had covered myself with some clothes; but these were insufficient to secure me from the dews of night. I was a poor, helpless, miserable wretch; I knew, and could distinguish, nothing; but feeling pain invade me on all sides, I sat down and wept.

"Soon a gentle light stole over[6] the heavens, and gave me a sensation of pleasure. I started up, and beheld a radiant form rise from among the trees. I gazed with a kind of wonder. It moved slowly, but it enlightened my path; and I again went out in search of berries. I was still cold, when under one of the trees I found a huge cloak, with which I covered myself, and sat down upon the ground. No distinct ideas occupied my mind; all was confused. I felt light, and hunger, and thirst, and darkness; innumerable sounds rang in my ears, and on all sides various scents saluted me[7]: the only object that I could distinguish was the bright moon, and I fixed my eyes on that with pleasure.

---

1 at liberty: 자유로이.
2 wearying: 지치게 하다.
3 brook: 시내.
4 dormant: 졸린. 잠에 취한 듯한.
5 slaked: 갈증을 풀다.
6 stole over: 어느새 엄습하다(뒤덮다).
7 various scents saluted me: 여러 냄새가 났다는 의미.

"Several changes of day and night passed, and the orb of night[1] had greatly lessened, when I began to distinguish my sensations from each other. I gradually saw plainly the clear stream that supplied me with drink, and the trees that shaded me with their foliage[2]. I was delighted when I first discovered that a pleasant sound, which often saluted my ears[3], proceeded from the throats of the little winged animals who had often intercepted the light from my eyes. I began also to observe, with greater accuracy, the forms that surrounded me and to perceive the boundaries of the radiant roof of light which canopied[4] me. Sometimes I tried to imitate the pleasant songs of the birds, but was unable. Sometimes I wished to express my sensations in my own mode, but the uncouth[5] and inarticulate sounds which broke[6] from me frightened me into silence again.

"The moon had disappeared from the night, and again, with a lessened form, showed itself, while I still remained in the forest. My sensations had, by this time become distinct, and my mind received every day additional ideas. My eyes became accustomed to the light, and to perceive objects in their right forms; I distinguished the insect from the herb, and, by degrees, one herb from another. I found that the sparrow uttered none but harsh notes, whilst those of the blackbird and thrush were sweet and enticing.[7]

"One day, when I was oppressed[8] by cold, I found a fire which had been left by some wandering beggars, and was overcome with delight at the warmth I experienced from it. In my joy I thrust my hand into

---

1 orb of night: '달'을 지칭.
2 foliage: 잎.
3 saluted my ears: 내 귀에 들리다.
4 canopied: 덮다.
5 uncouth: 거친. 조야한.
6 broke: (소리가) 터져 나오다.
7 enticing: 마음을 끄는. 매혹적인.
8 oppressed: 고통당하는.

the live embers[1], but quickly drew it out again with a cry of pain. How strange, I thought, that the same cause should produce such opposite effects! I examined the materials of the fire, and to my joy found it to be composed of wood. I quickly collected some branches; but they were wet, and would not burn. I was pained at this, and sat still watching the operation of the fire. The wet wood which I had placed near the heat dried, and itself became inflamed. I reflected on this; and by touching the various branches, I discovered the cause, and busied myself in collecting a great quantity of wood, that I might dry it, and have a plentiful supply of fire. When night came on, and brought sleep with it, I was in the greatest fear lest my fire should be extinguished. I covered it carefully with dry wood and leaves, and placed wet branches upon it; and then, spreading my cloak, I lay on the ground, and sunk into sleep[2].

"It was morning when I awoke, and my first care was to visit the fire. I uncovered it, and a gentle breeze quickly fanned it into a flame. I observed this also, and contrived[3] a fan of branches, which roused the embers when they were nearly extinguished. When night came again, I found, with pleasure, that the fire gave light as well as heat; and that the discovery of this element was useful to me in my food; for I found some of the offals[4] that the travellers had left had been roasted, and tasted much more savoury[5] than the berries I gathered from the trees. I tried, therefore, to dress[6] my food in the same man- ner, placing it on the live embers. I found that the berries were spoiled by this operation, and the nuts and roots much improved.

"Food, however, became scarce; and I often spent the whole day

---

1 embers: 타다 남은 불. 깜부기불.
2 sunk into sleep: 잠에 빠져들었다.
3 contrived: 이럭저럭 만들어내다.
4 offals: 남은 부스러기 음식.
5 savoury: 맛 좋은.
6 dress: (음식을) 조리하다.

searching in vain for a few acorns to assuage[1] the pangs of hunger. When I found this, I resolved to quit the place that I had hitherto inhabited, to seek for one where the few wants I experienced would be more easily satisfied. In this emigration[2], I exceedingly lamented the loss of the fire which I had obtained through accident, and knew not how to reproduce it. I gave several hours to the serious consideration of this difficulty; but I was obliged to relinquish[3] all attempt to supply it; and, wrapping myself up in my cloak, I struck[4] across the wood towards the setting sun. I passed three days in these rambles, and at length discovered the open country. A great fall of snow had taken place the night before, and the fields were of one uniform white; the appearance was disconsolate[5], and I found my feet chilled by the cold damp substance that covered the ground.

"It was about seven in the morning, and I longed to obtain food and shelter; at length I perceived a small hut, on a rising ground, which had doubtless been built for the convenience of some shepherd. This was a new sight to me; and I examined the structure[6] with great curiosity. Finding the door open, I entered. An old man sat in it, near a fire, over which he was preparing his breakfast. He turned on hearing a noise; and, perceiving me, shrieked loudly, and, quitting the hut, ran across the fields with a speed of which his debilitated[7] form hardly appeared capable. His appearance, different from any I had ever before seen, and his flight, somewhat surprised me. But I was enchanted by the appearance of the hut: here the snow and rain could not penetrate; the ground was dry; and it presented to me then as exquisite and di-

---

1 assuage: 감소시키다.
2 emigration: 이동.
3 relinquish: 포기하다.
4 struck: 가다. 지나다.
5 disconsolate: 쓸쓸한. 황량한.
6 structure: 구조물. 건축물.
7 debilitated: 허약한.

vine a retreat as Pandæmonium[1] appeared to the dæmons of hell after their sufferings in the lake of fire. I greedily devoured the remnants of the shepherd's breakfast, which consisted of bread, cheese, milk, and wine; the latter, however, I did not like. Then, overcome by fatigue, I lay down among some straw, and fell asleep.

"It was noon when I awoke; and allured[2], by the warmth of the sun, which shone brightly on the white ground, I determined to re-commence[3] my travels; and, depositing the remains of the peasant's breakfast in a wallet[4] I found, I proceeded across the fields for several hours, until at sunset I arrived at a village. How miraculous did this appear! the huts, the neater cottages, and stately houses, engaged my admiration[5] by turns. The vegetables in the gardens, the milk and cheese that I saw placed at the windows of some of the cottages, al-lured my appetite. One of the best of these I entered; but I had hardly placed my foot within the door, before the children shrieked, and one of the women fainted. The whole village was roused; some fled, some attacked me, until, grievously[6] bruised by stones and many other kinds of missile[7] weapons, I escaped to the open country, and fearfully took refuge in a low hovel[8], quite bare, and making a wretched appear-ance[9] after the palaces I had beheld in the village. This hovel, however, joined a cottage of a neat and pleasant appearance; but after my late dearly bought[10] experience, I dared not enter it. My place of refuge was

---

1 Pandæmonium: '복마전'. '지옥': '모든 악마가 모여 사는 곳'이란 의미로 밀튼의 『실낙원』에서 루시퍼와 그의 일행이 하늘나라에서 떨어져 당도한 곳이다.
2 allured: 이끌리어.
3 recommence: 다시 시작하다.
4 wallet: (나그네, 여행객 등의) 전대(纏帶).
5 engaged my admiration: 나의 감탄을 자아냈다.
6 grievously: 심하게. 가혹하게.
7 missile: 던질 수 있는.
8 hovel: 헛간.
9 making a wretched appearance: 볼품없어 보이다.
10 bought: (대가를 치루고) 얻은.

constructed of wood, but so low that I could with difficulty sit upright in it. No wood, however, was placed on the earth, which formed the floor, but it was dry; and although the wind entered it by innumerable chinks[1], I found it an agreeable asylum from the snow and rain.

"Here then I retreated, and lay down happy to have found a shelter, however miserable, from the inclemency[2] of the season, and still more from the barbarity of man.

"As soon as morning dawned, I crept from my kennel[3], that I might view the adjacent[4] cottage, and discover if I could remain in the habitation I had found. It was situated against the back of the cottage, and surrounded on the sides which were exposed by a pig-sty[5] and a clear pool of water. One part was open, and by that I had crept in; but now I covered every crevice[6] by which I might be perceived with stones and wood, yet in such a manner that I might move them on occasion to pass out: all the light I enjoyed came through the sty, and that was sufficient for me.

"Having thus arranged my dwelling, and carpeted it with clean straw, I retired; for I saw the figure of a man at a distance, and I remembered too well my treatment the night before to trust myself in his power. I had first, however, provided for my sustenance[7] for that day, by a loaf of coarse bread, which I purloined[8], and a cup with which I could drink, more conveniently than from my hand, of the pure water which flowed by my retreat. The floor was a little raised, so that it was kept perfectly dry, and by its vicinity[9] to the chimney of

---

1 chinks: 틈.
2 inclemency: 험악한(매서운) 날씨.
3 kennel: 허름한 헛간.
4 adjacent: 인접한.
5 pig-sty: 돼지우리.
6 crevice: 갈라진 틈.
7 sustenance: 생명유지.
8 purloined: 훔치다.
9 vicinity: 인접.

the cottage it was tolerably warm.

"Being thus provided, I resolved to reside in this hovel until something should occur which might alter my determination. It was indeed a paradise compared to the bleak forest, my former residence, the rain-dropping branches, and dank[1] earth. I ate my breakfast with pleasure, and was about to remove a plank to procure myself a little water, when I heard a step, and looking through a small chink, I beheld a young creature, with a pail on her head, passing before my hovel. The girl was young, and of gentle demeanour, unlike what I have since found cottagers and farm-house servants to be. Yet she was meanly[2] dressed, a coarse blue petticoat and a linen jacket being her only garb[3]; her fair hair was plaited, but not adorned: she looked patient, yet sad. I lost sight of her; and in about a quarter of an hour she returned, bearing the pail, which was now partly filled with milk. As she walked along, seemingly incommoded[4] by the burden, a young man met her, whose countenance expressed a deeper despondence[5]. Uttering a few sounds with an air of melancholy, he took the pail from her head, and bore it to the cottage himself. She followed, and they disappeared. Presently I saw the young man again, with some tools in his hand, cross the field behind the cottage; and the girl was also busied, sometimes in the house, and sometimes in the yard.

"On examining my dwelling, I found that one of the windows of the cottage had formerly occupied a part of it, but the panes had been filled up with wood. In one of these was a small and almost imperceptible chink, through which the eye could just penetrate. Through this crevice a small room was visible, whitewashed[6] and clean, but

---

1 dank: 축축한.
2 meanly: 초라하게.
3 garb: 의상.
4 incommoded: 불편을 느끼면서.
5 despondence: 낙담. 의기소침.
6 whitewashed: 흰 도료가 칠해진.

very bare of[1] furniture. In one corner, near a small fire, sat an old man, leaning his head on his hands in a disconsolate attitude. The young girl was occupied in arranging the cottage; but presently she took something out of a drawer, which employed her hands, and she sat down beside the old man, who, taking up an instrument, began to play, and to produce sounds sweeter than the voice of the thrush or the nightingale. It was a lovely sight, even to me, poor wretch! who had never beheld aught[2] beautiful before. The silver hair and benevolent countenance of the aged cottager won my reverence, while the gentle manners of the girl enticed[3] my love. He played a sweet mournful air[4], which I perceived drew tears from the eyes of his amiable companion, of which the old man took no notice, until she sobbed audibly; he then pronounced a few sounds, and the fair creature, leaving her work, knelt at his feet. He raised her, and smiled with such kindness and affection that I felt sensations of a peculiar and overpowering nature: they were a mixture of pain and pleasure, such as I had never before experienced, either from hunger or cold, warmth or food; and I withdrew from the window, unable to bear these emotions.

"Soon after this the young man returned, bearing on his shoulders a load of wood. The girl met him at the door, helped to relieve him of his burden, and, taking some of the fuel into the cottage, placed it on the fire; then she and the youth went apart into a nook[5] of the cottage, and he showed her a large loaf and a piece of cheese. She seemed pleased, and went into the garden for some roots and plants, which she placed in water, and then upon the fire. She afterwards continued her work, whilst the young man went into the garden, and appeared

---

1 bare of: …이 없는.
2 aught: 'anything'의 의미.
3 enticed: 부추기다.
4 air: 노래. 음악.
5 nook: 구석. 모퉁이.

busily employed in digging and pulling up roots. After he had been employed thus about an hour, the young woman joined him, and they entered the cottage together.

"The old man had, in the meantime, been pensive[1]; but, on the appearance of his companions, he assumed a more cheerful air, and they sat down to eat. The meal was quickly despatched[2]. The young woman was again occupied in arranging the cottage; the old man walked before the cottage in the sun for a few minutes, leaning on the arm of the youth. Nothing could exceed in beauty the contrast between these two excellent creatures. One was old, with silver hairs and a countenance beaming[3] with benevolence and love: the younger was slight and graceful in his figure, and his features[4] were moulded with the finest symmetry: yet his eyes and attitude expressed the utmost sadness and despondency. The old man returned to the cottage; and the youth, with tools different from those he had used in the morning, directed his steps across the fields.

"Night quickly shut in[5]; but to my extreme wonder, I found that the cottagers had a means of prolonging light by the use of tapers[6], and was delighted to find that the setting of the sun did not put an end to the pleasure I experienced in watching my human neighbours. In the evening, the young girl and her companion were employed in various occupations which I did not understand; and the old man again took up the instrument which produced the divine sounds that had enchanted[7] me in the morning. So soon as he had finished, the youth began, not to play, but to utter sounds that were monotonous,

---

1 pensive: 생각(수심)에 잠긴.
2 despatched: (식사를) 끝마치다.
3 beaming: 환한 미소를 짓는.
4 features: 얼굴 생김새. 용모.
5 shut in: (어둠이) 내리다.
6 tapers: 초.
7 enchanted: 매료시키다.

and neither resembling the harmony of the old man's instrument nor the songs of the birds: I since found that he read aloud, but at that time I knew nothing of the science of words or letters.

"The family, after having been thus occupied for a short time, extinguished their lights, and retired, as I conjectured, to rest.

CHAPTER XII

"I lay on my straw, but I could not sleep. I thought of the occurrences of the day. What chiefly struck[1] me was the gentle manners of these people; and I longed to join them, but dared not. I remembered too well the treatment I had suffered the night before from the barbarous villagers, and resolved, whatever course of conduct I might hereafter think it right to pursue, that for the present I would remain quietly in my hovel, watching, and endeavouring to discover the motives which influenced their actions.

"The cottagers arose the next morning before the sun. The young woman arranged the cottage, and prepared the food; and the youth departed after the first meal.

"This day was passed in the same routine as that which preceded it. The young man was constantly employed out of doors, and the girl in various laborious occupations within. The old man, whom I soon perceived to be blind, employed his leisure hours on his instrument or in contemplation. Nothing could exceed the love and respect which the younger cottagers exhibited towards their venerable[2] companion. They performed towards him every little office[3] of affection and duty with gentleness; and he rewarded them by his benevolent smiles.

---

1 struck: 감명을 주다.
2 venerable: 존경할 만한. 훌륭한.
3 office: 임무. 직무.

"They were not entirely happy. The young man and his companion often went apart, and appeared to weep. I saw no cause for their unhappiness; but I was deeply affected by it. If such lovely creatures were miserable, it was less strange that I, an imperfect and solitary being, should be wretched. Yet why were these gentle beings unhappy? They possessed a delightful house (for such it was in my eyes) and every luxury; they had a fire to warm them when chill, and delicious viands[1] when hungry; they were dressed in excellent clothes; and, still more, they enjoyed one another's company and speech, interchanging each day looks of affection and kindness. What did their tears imply? Did they really express pain? I was at first unable to solve these questions; but perpetual attention and time explained to me many appearances which were at first enigmatic.

"A considerable period elapsed before I discovered one of the causes of the uneasiness of this amiable family: it was poverty; and they suffered that evil in a very distressing degree. Their nourishment[2] consisted entirely of the vegetables of their garden, and the milk of one cow, which gave very little during the winter, when its masters could scarcely procure food to support it. They often, I believe, suffered the pangs of hunger very poignantly[3], especially the two younger cottagers; for several times they placed food before the old man when they reserved none for themselves.

"This trait of kindness moved me sensibly[4]. I had been accustomed, during the night, to steal a part of their store[5] for my own consumption; but when I found that in doing this I inflicted pain on the cottagers, I abstained[6], and satisfied myself with berries, nuts, and roots,

---

1 viands: 음식. 양식.
2 nourishment: 음식물. 식량.
3 poignantly: 통렬하게.
4 moved me sensibly: 나를 상당히(sensibly) 감동시켰다(moved).
5 store: '비축한 음식'을 지칭.
6 abstained: 그만두다.

which I gathered from a neighbouring wood.

"I discovered also another means through which I was enabled to assist their labours. I found that the youth spent a great part of each day in collecting wood for the family fire; and during the night, I often took his tools, the use of which I quickly discovered, and brought home firing[1] sufficient for the consumption of several days.

"I remember the first time that I did this the young woman, when she opened the door in the morning, appeared greatly astonished on seeing a great pile of wood on the outside. She uttered some words in a loud voice, and the youth joined her, who also expressed surprise. I observed, with pleasure, that he did not go to the forest that day, but spent it in repairing the cottage and cultivating[2] the garden.

"By degrees I made a discovery of still greater moment. I found that these people possessed a method of communicating their experience and feelings to one another by articulate[3] sounds. I perceived that the words they spoke sometimes produced pleasure or pain, smiles or sadness, in the minds and countenances of the hearers. This was indeed a godlike science, and I ardently desired to become acquainted with it. But I was baffled[4] in every attempt I made for this purpose. Their pronunciation was quick; and the words they uttered, not having any apparent connection with visible objects, I was unable to discover any clue by which I could unravel[5] the mystery of their reference. By great application[6], however, and after having remained during the space of several revolutions of the moon in my hovel, I discovered the names that were given to some of the most familiar objects of discourse; I learned and applied the words, fire, milk, bread, and wood.

---

1 firing: 연료. 땔감.

2 cultivating: 재배하다.

3 articulate: 분명하게 발음된.

4 baffled: 좌절된.

5 unravel: 해결하다. 풀다.

6 application: 근면.

I learned also the names of the cottagers themselves. The youth and his companion had each of them several names, but the old man had only one, which was father. The girl was called sister, or Agatha[1]; and the youth Felix[2], brother, or son. I cannot describe the delight I felt when I learned the ideas appropriated[3] to each of these sounds, and was able to pronounce them. I distinguished several other words without being able as yet to understand or apply them; such as good, dearest, unhappy.

"I spent the winter in this manner. The gentle manners and beauty of the cottagers greatly endeared[4] them to me: when they were unhappy, I felt depressed; when they rejoiced, I sympathised in their joys. I saw few human beings besides them; and if any other happened to enter the cottage, their harsh manners and rude gait[5] only enhanced to me the superior accomplishments[6] of my friends. The old man, I could perceive, often endeavoured to encourage his children, as sometimes I found that he called them, to cast off their melancholy. He would talk in a cheerful accent, with an expression of goodness that bestowed pleasure even upon me. Agatha listened with respect, her eyes sometimes filled with tears, which she endeavoured to wipe away unperceived; but I generally found that her countenance and tone were more cheerful after having listened to the exhortations[7] of her father. It was not thus with Felix. He was always the saddest of the group; and even to my unpractised senses, he appeared to have suffered more deeply than his friends. But if his countenance was more sorrowful, his voice was more cheerful than that of his sister, especially when he

---

1 Agatha: 그리스어로 '아름답다'는 의미가 있다.
2 Felix: '행운이 있는'이라는 의미가 있다.
3 appropriated: …에 전적으로 할당된.
4 endeared: 사랑받게 하다.
5 gait: 걸음걸이.
6 accomplishments: 교양.
7 exhortations: 훈계. 충고.

addressed the old man.

I could mention innumerable instances, which, although slight, marked[1] the dispositions of these amiable cottagers. In the midst of poverty and want[2], Felix carried with pleasure to his sister the first little white flower that peeped out[3] from beneath the snowy ground. Early in the morning, before she had risen, he cleared away the snow that obstructed her path to the milk-house, drew water from the well, and brought the wood from the out-house[4], where, to his perpetual astonishment, he found his store always replenished[5] by an invisible hand. In the day, I believe, he worked sometimes for a neighbouring farmer, because he often went forth, and did not return until dinner, yet brought no wood with him. At other times he worked in the garden; but as there was little to do in the frosty season, he read to the old man and Agatha.

"This reading had puzzled me extremely at first; but, by degrees, I discovered that he uttered many of the same sounds when he read as when he talked. I conjectured, therefore, that he found on the paper signs for speech which he understood, and I ardently longed to comprehend these also; but how was that possible, when I did not even understand the sounds for which they stood as signs? I improved, however, sensibly[6] in this science, but not sufficiently to follow up any kind of conversation, although I applied my whole mind to the endeavour; for I easily perceived that, although I eagerly longed to discover myself to the cottagers, I ought not to make the attempt until I had first become master of their language; which knowledge might enable me to make them overlook the deformity of my figure; for

---

1 marked: 분명하게 나타내다.
2 want: 가난. 곤궁.
3 peeped out: (바깥으로) '모습을 드러나다'; 즉 '꽃이 피기 시작했다'는 의미.
4 out-house: 딴채. 헛간.
5 replenished: 다시 채우다.
6 sensibly: 두드러지게. 꽤.

with this also the contrast perpetually presented to my eyes had made me acquainted.

"I had admired the perfect forms of my cottagers — their grace, beauty, and delicate complexions: but how was I terrified when I viewed myself in a transparent pool! At first I started back[1], unable to believe that it was indeed I who was reflected in the mirror; and when I became fully convinced that I was in reality the monster that I am, I was filled with the bitterest sensations of despondence and mortification[2]. Alas! I did not yet entirely know the fatal effects of this miserable deformity.

"As the sun became warmer, and the light of day longer, the snow vanished, and I beheld the bare trees and the black earth. From this time Felix was more employed; and the heart-moving indications of impending[3] famine disappeared. Their food, as I afterwards found, was coarse, but it was wholesome; and they procured a sufficiency of it. Several new kinds of plants sprung up in the garden, which they dressed; and these signs of comfort increased daily as the season advanced.

"The old man, leaning on his son, walked each day at noon, when it did not rain, as I found it was called when the heavens poured forth its waters. This frequently took place; but a high wind quickly dried the earth, and the season became far more pleasant than it had been.

"My mode of life in my hovel was uniform. During the morning, I attended the motions of the cottagers; and when they were dispersed[4] in various occupations I slept: the remainder of the day was

---

1 started back: '놀라서 뒤로 물러서다'; 물에 비친 자신의 흉측한 모습에 놀라는 괴물
   은 『실낙원』에서 물에 비친 자신의 아름다운 모습에 감탄하는 이브(Eve)와 대조를 이
   룬다.
2 mortification: 치욕. 굴욕.
3 impending: 절박한. 박두한.
4 dispersed: 뿔뿔이 흩어지다.

spent in observing my friends. When they had retired to rest, if there was any moon, or the night was star-light[1], I went into the woods, and collected my own food and fuel for the cottage. When I returned, as often as it was necessary, I cleared their path from the snow, and performed those offices that I had seen done by Felix. I afterwards found that these labours, performed by an invisible hand, greatly astonished them; and once or twice I heard them, on these occasions, utter the words good spirit, wonderful; but I did not then understand the signification[2] of these terms.

"My thoughts now became more active, and I longed to discover the motives and feelings of these lovely creatures; I was inquisitive to know why Felix appeared so miserable and Agatha so sad. I thought (foolish wretch!) that it might be in my power to restore happiness to these deserving people. When I slept, or was absent, the forms of the venerable blind father, the gentle Agatha, and the excellent Felix flitted[3] before me. I looked upon them as superior beings, who would be the arbiters[4] of my future destiny. I formed in my imagination a thousand pictures of presenting myself to them, and their reception of me. I imagined that they would be disgusted, until, by my gentle demeanour and conciliating[5] words, I should first win their favour, and afterwards their love.

"These thoughts exhilarated[6] me, and led me to apply with fresh ardour to the acquiring the art of language. My organs were indeed harsh, but supple; and although my voice was very unlike the soft music of their tones, yet I pronounced such words as I understood

---

1 star-light: 별빛이 밝은.
2 signification: 의미.
3 flitted: 문뜩 스쳐지나가다.
4 arbiters: 심판자. 결정권자.
5 conciliating: 환심을 사는. 제 편으로 끌어들이는.
6 exhilarated: 기분을 돋우다. 유쾌하게 하다.

with tolerable[1] ease. It was as the ass and the lap-dog[2]; yet surely the gentle ass whose intentions were affectionate, although his manners were rude, deserved better treatment than blows and execration[3].

"The pleasant showers and genial[4] warmth of spring greatly altered the aspect of the earth. Men, who before this change seemed to have been hid in caves, dispersed themselves, and were employed in various arts of cultivation. The birds sang in more cheerful notes, and the leaves began to bud forth[5] on the trees. Happy, happy earth! fit habitation for gods, which, so short a time before, was bleak, damp, and unwholesome. My spirits were elevated by the enchanting appearance of nature; the past was blotted[6] from my memory, the present was tranquil, and the future gilded[7] by bright rays of hope and anticipations of joy."

CHAPTER XIII

"I now hasten to the more moving[8] part of my story. I shall relate events that impressed me with feelings which, from what I had been, have made me what I am.

"Spring advanced rapidly; the weather became fine, and the skies cloudless. It surprised me that what before was desert and gloomy should now bloom with the most beautiful flowers and verdure[9]. My senses were gratified[10] and refreshed by a thousand scents of delight,

---

1 tolerable: 웬만한.
2 the ass and the lap-dog: 이솝(Aesop)우화에서 자신보다 팔자가 좋다고 생각한 애완견 흉내를 내다 몽둥이로 얻어맞고 죽은 당나귀 이야기를 연상시킨다.
3 execration: 욕설.
4 genial: 기분 좋은.
5 bud forth: 봉오리를 맺다.
6 blotted: 지워지다.
7 gilded: '금빛 나는'; 즉 미래의 전망이 아주 좋은 것처럼 느껴졌다는 의미.
8 moving: 애처로운. 가슴 뭉클한.
9 verdure: 신록.
10 gratified: 만족시키다. (욕망을) 채우다.

and a thousand sights of beauty.

"It was on one of these days, when my cottagers periodically rested from labour — the old man played on his guitar, and the children listened to him — that I observed the countenance of Felix was melancholy beyond expression; he sighed frequently; and once his father paused in his music, and I conjectured by his manner that he inquired the cause of his son's sorrow. Felix replied in a cheerful accent, and the old man was recommencing his music when some one tapped[1] at the door.

"It was a lady on horseback, accompanied by a country-man as a guide. The lady was dressed in a dark suit, and covered with a thick black veil. Agatha asked a question; to which the stranger only replied by pronouncing, in a sweet accent, the name of Felix. Her voice was musical, but unlike that of either of my friends. On hearing this word, Felix came up hastily to the lady; who, when she saw him, threw up her veil, and I beheld a countenance of angelic beauty and expression. Her hair of a shining raven[2] black, and curiously braided[3]; her eyes were dark, but gentle, although animated; her features of a regular proportion, and her complexion wondrously fair, each cheek tinged[4] with a lovely pink.

"Felix seemed ravished[5] with delight when he saw her, every trait[6] of sorrow vanished from his face, and it instantly expressed a degree of ecstatic joy, of which I could hardly have believed it capable; his eyes sparkled as his cheek flushed with pleasure; and at that moment I thought him as beautiful as the stranger. She appeared affected by different feelings; wiping a few tears from her lovely eyes, she held

---

1 tapped: (문) 두드리다.
2 raven: 칠흑의.
3 curiously braided: 기묘하게 (머리를) 딴.
4 tinged: 엷게 물들여진.
5 ravished: 몹시 기쁜.
6 trait: 기미. 흔적.

out her hand to Felix, who kissed it rapturously[1], and called her, as well as I could distinguish, his sweet Arabian. She did not appear to understand him, but smiled. He assisted her to dismount, and dismissing[2] her guide, conducted her into the cottage. Some conversation took place between him and his father; and the young stranger knelt at the old man's feet, and would have kissed his hand, but he raised her, and embraced her affectionately.

"I soon perceived that, although the stranger uttered articulate sounds, and appeared to have a language of her own, she was neither understood by, nor herself understood, the cottagers. They made many signs which I did not comprehend; but I saw that her presence diffused[3] gladness through the cottage, dispelling their sorrow as the sun dissipates the morning mists. Felix seemed peculiarly happy, and with smiles of delight welcomed his Arabian. Agatha, the ever-gentle Agatha, kissed the hands of the lovely stranger; and, pointing to her brother, made signs which appeared to me to mean that he had been sorrowful until she came. Some hours passed thus, while they, by their countenances, expressed joy, the cause of which I did not comprehend. Presently I found, by the frequent recurrence[4] of some sound which the stranger repeated after them, that she was endeavouring to learn their language; and the idea instantly occurred to me that I should make use of the same instructions to the same end. The stranger learned about twenty words at the first lesson, most of them, indeed, were those which I had before understood, but I profited by the others.

"As night came on, Agatha and the Arabian retired early. When they separated, Felix kissed the hand of the stranger, and said, 'Good night, sweet Safie.' He sat up much longer, conversing with his father;

---

1 rapturously: 환희에 넘쳐서.
2 dismissing: 돌려보내다.
3 diffused: 퍼트리다.
4 recurrence: 반복.

and, by the frequent repetition of her name, I conjectured that their lovely guest was the subject of their conversation. I ardently desired to understand them, and bent every faculty[1] towards that purpose, but found it utterly impossible.

"The next morning Felix went out to his work; and, after the usual occupations of Agatha were finished, the Arabian sat at the feet of the old man, and, taking his guitar, played some airs so entrancingly[2] beautiful that they at once drew tears of sorrow and delight from my eyes. She sang, and her voice flowed in a rich cadence[3], swelling or dying away[4], like a nightingale of the woods.

"When she had finished, she gave the guitar to Agatha, who at first declined it. She played a simple air, and her voice accompanied it in sweet accents, but unlike the wondrous strain[5] of the stranger. The old man appeared enraptured, and said some words, which Agatha endeavoured to explain to Safie, and by which he appeared to wish to express that she bestowed on him the greatest delight by her music.

"The days now passed as peaceably as before, with the sole alteration that joy had taken place of sadness in the countenances of my friends. Safie was always gay and happy; she and I improved rapidly in the knowledge of language, so that in two months I began to comprehend most of the words uttered by my protectors.

"In the meanwhile also the black ground was covered with herbage[6], and the green banks interspersed with innumerable flowers, sweet to the scent and the eyes, stars of pale radiance[7] among the moonlight

---

1 bent every faculty: bent는 '(노력을) 기울이다'; faculty는 '신체 기능'; 즉 '나의 모든 신체 기능을 집중시켰다'는 의미.

2 entrancingly: 정신을 빼앗을 정도로.

3 cadence: 리듬. 억양.

4 swelling or dying away: 노래 소리가 커지거나(swell) 작아져서 점차 사라지는 것(dying away)을 지칭.

5 strain: 가락. 선율.

6 herbage: 풀. 목초.

7 stars of pale radiance: 희미하게 빛나는 별들.

woods; the sun became warmer, the nights clear and balmy[1]; and my nocturnal[2] rambles were an extreme pleasure to me, although they were considerably shortened by the late setting and early rising of the sun; for I never ventured abroad during daylight, fearful of meeting with the same treatment I had formerly endured in the first village which I entered.

"My days were spent in close attention, that I might more speedily master the language; and I may boast that I improved more rapidly than the Arabian, who understood very little, and conversed in broken accents, whilst I comprehended and could imitate almost every word that was spoken.

"While I improved in speech, I also learned the science of letters, as it was taught to the stranger; and this opened before me a wide field for wonder and delight.

"The book from which Felix instructed Safie was Volney's *Ruins of Empires*[3]. I should not have understood the purport[4] of this book, had not Felix, in reading it, given very minute explanations. He had chosen this work, he said, because the declamatory[5] style was framed in imitation of the Eastern authors. Through this work I obtained a cursory[6] knowledge of history, and a view of the several empires at present existing in the world; it gave me an insight into the manners, governments, and religions of the different nations of the earth. I heard of the slothful[7] Asiatics; of the stupendous[8] genius and men-

---

1 balmy: 향긋한. 기분 좋은.
2 nocturnal: 밤에 하는.
3 Volney's Ruins of Empires: 프랑스의 철학자이자 역사학자인 Volney 백작(Constantin François Chasseboeuf, 1757-1820)이 쓴 저서로 원 제목은 Les Ruines, ou Meditations sur les Revolutions des Empires (1791)이다.
4 purport: 의미. 요지.
5 declamatory: 연설조의.
6 cursory: 대강의.
7 slothful: 게으른.
8 stupendous: 엄청난. 거대한.

tal activity of the Grecians[1]; of the wars and wonderful virtue of the early Romans — of their subsequent degenerating[2] — of the decline of that mighty empire; of chivalry, Christianity, and kings. I heard of the discovery of the American hemisphere, and wept with Safie over the hapless fate of its original inhabitants.

"These wonderful narrations inspired me with strange feelings. Was man, indeed, at once so powerful, so virtuous and magnificent, yet so vicious and base? He appeared at one time a mere scion[3] of the evil principle, and at another as all that can be conceived of noble and godlike. To be a great and virtuous man appeared the highest honour that can befall a sensitive being; to be base and vicious, as many on record[4] have been, appeared the lowest degradation[5], a condition more abject[6] than that of the blind mole or harmless worm. For a long time I could not conceive how one man could go forth to murder his fellow, or even why there were laws and governments; but when I heard details of vice and bloodshed[7], my wonder ceased, and I turned away with disgust and loathing.

"Every conversation of the cottagers now opened new wonders to me. While I listened to the instructions which Felix bestowed upon the Arabian, the strange system of human society was explained to me. I heard of the division of property; of immense wealth and squalid[8] poverty, of rank, descent[9], and noble blood.

"The words induced me to turn towards myself. I learned that the possessions most esteemed by your fellow-creatures were high and

---

1 Grecians: 그리스인.
2 degenerating: 퇴보.
3 scion: 자손.
4 on record: 기록상의.
5 degradation: 불명예.
6 abject: 굴욕적인. 비참한.
7 bloodshed: 살상. 학살.
8 squalid: 비참한.
9 descent: 혈통. 출신.

unsullied[1] descent united with riches. A man might be respected with only one of these advantages; but without either, he was considered, except in very rare instances, as a vagabond and a slave, doomed to waste his powers for the profits of the chosen few! And what was I? Of my creation and creator I was absolutely ignorant; but I knew that I possessed no money, no friends, no kind of property. I was, besides, endued[2] with a figure hideously deformed and loathsome; I was not even of the same nature as man. I was more agile[3] than they, and could subsist upon[4] coarser diet; I bore the extremes of heat and cold with less injury to my frame; my stature far exceeded theirs. When I looked around, I saw and heard of none like me. Was I then a monster, a blot[5] upon the earth, from which all men fled, and whom all men disowned[6]?

"I cannot describe to you the agony that these reflections inflicted upon me: I tried to dispel them, but sorrow only increased with knowledge. Oh, that[7] I had forever remained in my native wood, nor known nor felt beyond the sensations of hunger, thirst, and heat!

"Of what a strange nature is knowledge! It clings to the mind, when it has once seized on it, like a lichen[8] on the rock. I wished sometimes to shake off all thought and feeling; but I learned that there was but one means to overcome the sensation of pain, and that was death — a state which I feared yet did not understand. I admired virtue and good feelings, and loved the gentle manners and amiable qualities of my cottagers; but I was shut out from intercourse with

---

1 unsullied: 순수한.
2 endued: 부여받은.
3 agile: (몸이) 재빠른.
4 subsist upon: ⋯을 먹고 살아가다(생명을 보존하다).
5 blot: 오점.
6 disowned: 합법성을 인정치 않다.
7 Oh, that: ⋯하였으면 좋았으련만!
8 lichen: 이끼.

them, except through means which I obtained by stealth[1], when I was unseen and unknown, and which rather increased than satisfied the desire I had of becoming one among my fellows. The gentle words of Agatha, and the animated smiles of the charming Arabian were not for me. The mild exhortations of the old man, and the lively conversation of the loved Felix, were not for me. Miserable, unhappy wretch!

"Other lessons were impressed upon me even more deeply. I heard of the difference of sexes; and the birth and growth of children; how the father doated on [2]the smiles of the infant, and the lively sallies[3] of the older child; how all the life and cares of the mother were wrapped up in the precious charge; how the mind of youth expanded and gained knowledge; of brother, sister, and all the various relationships which bind one human being to another in mutual bonds[4].

"But where were my friends and relations? No father had watched my infant days, no mother had blessed me with smiles and caresses; or if they had, all my past life was now a blot, a blind vacancy in which I distinguished nothing. From my earliest remembrance I had been as I then was in height and proportion. I had never yet seen a being resembling me, or who claimed any intercourse with me. What was I? The question again recurred, to be answered only with groans.

"I will soon explain to what these feelings tended[5]; but allow me now to return to the cottagers, whose story excited in me such various feelings of indignation[6], delight, and wonder, but which all terminated in additional love and reverence for my protectors (for so I loved, in an innocent, half-painful self-deceit, to call them).

---

1 by stealth: 은밀히. 몰래.

2 doated on: …을 무척 좋아하다.

3 sallies: 돌발적 행동이나 말.

4 mutual bonds: '서로간의 유대감'; 여기서 괴물은 자신이 혼자라는 사실을 더욱 더 뼈저리게 느끼게 된다.

5 tended: 향하다.

6 indignation: 분개.

CHAPTER XIV

"Some time elapsed before I learned the history of my friends. It was one which could not fail to impress itself deeply on my mind, unfolding as it did a number of circumstances, each interesting and wonderful to one so utterly inexperienced as I was.

"The name of the old man was De Lacey. He was descended from[1] a good family in France, where he had lived for many years in affluence[2], respected by his superiors and beloved by his equals. His son was bred in the service of his country; and Agatha had ranked with[3] ladies of the highest distinction[4]. A few months before my arrival they had lived in a large and luxurious city called Paris, surrounded by friends, and possessed of every enjoyment which virtue, refinement of intellect, or taste, accompanied by a moderate fortune, could afford.

"The father of Safie had been the cause of their ruin. He was a Turkish merchant, and had inhabited Paris for many years, when, for some reason which I could not learn, he became obnoxious[5] to the government. He was seized and cast into prison the very day that Safie arrived from Constantinople[6] to join him. He was tried and condemned to death. The injustice of his sentence was very flagrant[7]; all Paris was indignant; and it was judged that his religion and wealth, rather than the crime alleged[8] against him, had been the cause of his condemnation.

"Felix had accidentally been present at the trial; his horror and

---

1 descended from: ⋯출신인.
2 in affluence: 부유하게.
3 ranked with: ⋯와 대등하다.
4 distinction: 고귀함. 저명함.
5 obnoxious: 미움 받고 있는.
6 Constantinople: '콘스탄티노플'; 터키의 옛 수도.
7 flagrant: 극악(무도)한.
8 alleged: (근거 없이) 주장된.

indignation were uncontrollable when he heard the decision of the court. He made, at that moment, a solemn vow to deliver him, and then looked around for the means. After many fruitless attempts to gain admittance to the prison, he found a strongly grated[1] window in an unguarded part of the building which lighted the dungeon of the unfortunate Mahometan[2]; who, loaded with chains, waited in despair the execution of the barbarous sentence. Felix visited the grate at night, and made known to the prisoner his intentions in his favour. The Turk, amazed and delighted, endeavoured to kindle the zeal of his deliverer by promises of reward and wealth. Felix rejected his offers with contempt; yet when he saw the lovely Safie, who was allowed to visit her father, and who, by her gestures, expressed her lively gratitude, the youth could not help owning[3] to his own mind that the captive possessed a treasure which would fully reward his toil and hazard.

"The Turk quickly perceived the impression that his daughter had made on the heart of Felix, and endeavoured to secure him more entirely in his interests by the promise of her hand in marriage[4], so soon as he should be conveyed to a place of safety. Felix was too delicate to accept this offer; yet he looked forward to the probability of the event as to the consummation[5] of his happiness.

"During the ensuing days, while the preparations were going forward[6] for the escape of the merchant, the zeal of Felix was warmed by several letters that he received from this lovely girl, who found means to express her thoughts in the language of her lover by the aid of an old man, a servant of her father, who understood French. She thanked

---

1 grated: 쇠창살을 댄.
2 Mahometan: 이슬람교도.
3 owning: 고백하다. 인정하다.
4 promise of her hand in marriage: 자신의 딸을 그에게 시집보내겠다는 약속을 의미.
5 consummation: 완성. 달성.
6 going forward: 진행되다.

him in the most ardent terms for his intended services towards her parent; and at the same time she gently deplored her own fate.

"I have copies of these letters; for I found means, during my residence in the hovel, to procure the implements of writing; and the letters were often in the hands of Felix or Agatha. Before I depart, I will give them to you, they will prove the truth of my tale; but at present, as the sun is already far declined, I shall only have time to repeat the substance[1] of them to you.

"Safie related that her mother was a Christian Arab, seized and made a slave by the Turks; recommended[2] by her beauty, she had won the heart of the father of Safie, who married her. The young girl spoke in high and enthusiastic terms of her mother, who, born in freedom, spurned[3] the bondage to which she was now reduced. She instructed her daughter in the tenets[4] of her religion, and taught her to aspire to higher powers of intellect, and an independence of spirit, forbidden to the female followers of Mahomet. This lady died; but her lessons were indelibly[5] impressed on the mind of Safie, who sickened[6] at the prospect of again returning to Asia and being immured[7] within the walls of a harem, allowed only to occupy herself with infantile amusements, ill suited to the temper of her soul, now accustomed to grand ideas and a noble emulation[8] for virtue. The prospect of marrying a Christian, and remaining in a country where women were allowed to take a rank[9] in society, was enchanting to her.

---

1 substance: 요지. 골자.

2 recommended: 호감을 사게 되다. 마음에 들게 되다.

3 spurned: '경멸하다'; 억압으로부터의 해방과 자유에 대한 추구는 셸리의 이상주의적 목표 중 하나다.

4 tenets: 주의(主義). 교의(敎義).

5 indelibly: 지워지지 않게.

6 sickened: 혐오감을 느끼다.

7 immured: 가두어진.

8 emulation: 모방. 야망.

9 take a rank: 나름대로의 독자적인 지위를 차지한다는 의미.

"The day for the execution[1] of the Turk was fixed; but, on the night previous to it, he quitted his prison, and before morning was distant many leagues from Paris. Felix had procured passports in the name of his father, sister, and himself. He had previously communicated his plan to the former, who aided the deceit[2] by quitting his house, under the pretence of a journey, and concealed himself, with his daughter, in an obscure[3] part of Paris.

"Felix conducted the fugitives[4] through France to Lyons[5], and across Mont Cenis[6] to Leghorn, where the merchant had decided to wait a favourable opportunity of passing into some part of the Turkish dominions.

"Safie resolved to remain with her father until the moment of his departure, before which time the Turk renewed his promise that she should be united to his deliverer; and Felix remained with them in expectation of that event; and in the meantime he enjoyed the society of the Arabian, who exhibited towards him the simplest and tenderest affection. They conversed with one another through the means of an interpreter, and sometimes with the interpretation of looks; and Safie sang to him the divine airs of her native country.

"The Turk allowed this intimacy to take place, and encouraged the hopes of the youthful lovers, while in his heart he had formed far other plans. He loathed the idea that his daughter should be united to a Christian; but he feared the resentment of Felix, if he should appear lukewarm[7]; for he knew that he was still in the power of his deliverer, if he should choose to betray[8] him to the Italian state which they

---

1 execution: 사형집행. 처형.
2 deceit: 책략.
3 obscure: 잘 알려지지 않은.
4 fugitives: 도망자.
5 Lyons: 리용(프랑스 남동부의 도시).
6 Mont Cenis: 몽스니 고개(알프스 서부에 위치).
7 lukewarm: (마음이) 내키지 않는.
8 betray: 밀고하다.

inhabited. He revolved[1] a thousand plans by which he should be enabled to prolong the deceit until it might be no longer necessary, and secretly to take his daughter with him when he departed. His plans were facilitated[2] by the news which arrived from Paris.

"The government of France were greatly enraged at the escape of their victim, and spared no pains[3] to detect and punish his deliverer. The plot of Felix was quickly discovered, and De Lacey and Agatha were thrown into prison. The news reached Felix, and roused him from his dream of pleasure. His blind and aged father, and his gentle sister, lay in a noisome[4] dungeon, while he enjoyed the free air and the society of her whom he loved. This idea was torture to him. He quickly arranged with the Turks that if the latter should find a favourable opportunity for escape before Felix could return to Italy, Safie should remain as a boarder[5] at a convent at Leghorn; and then, quitting the lovely Arabian, he hastened to Paris, and delivered himself up[6] to the vengeance of the law, hoping to free De Lacey and Agatha by this proceeding.

"He did not succeed. They remained confined for five months before the trial took place; the result of which deprived them of their fortune, and condemned them to a perpetual exile[7] from their native country.

"They found a miserable asylum in the cottage in Germany where I discovered them. Felix soon learned that the treacherous[8] Turk, for whom he and his family endured such unheard-of oppression, on

---

1 revolved: 궁리하다. 곰곰이 생각하다.
2 facilitated: (도움을 얻어) 손쉽게 이루어지다.
3 spared no pains: 노력을 아끼지 않았다.
4 noisome: 혐오스러운.
5 boarder: 기숙인.
6 delivered himself up: 자수하다.
7 exile: 추방,
8 treacherous: 믿을 수 없는,

discovering that his deliverer was thus reduced to poverty and ruin, became a traitor to good feeling and honour, and had quitted Italy with his daughter, insultingly sending Felix a pittance[1] of money, to aid him, as he said, in some plan of future maintenance[2].

"Such were the events that preyed on the heart of Felix, and rendered him, when I first saw him, the most miserable of his family. He could have endured poverty; and while this distress had been the meed[3] of his virtue, he gloried in[4] it; but the ingratitude[5] of the Turk, and the loss of his beloved Safie, were misfortunes more bitter and irreparable. The arrival of the Arabian now infused[6] new life into his soul.

"When the news reached Leghorn that Felix was deprived of his wealth and rank, the merchant commanded his daughter to think no more of her lover, but to prepare to return to her native country. The generous nature of Safie was outraged[7] by this command; she attempted to expostulate with[8] her father, but he left her angrily, reiterating[9] his tyrannical mandate[10].

"A few days after, the Turk entered his daughter's apartment, and told her hastily that he had reason to believe that his residence at Leghorn had been divulged[11], and that he should speedily be delivered up to the French government; he had, consequently, hired a vessel to convey him to Constantinople, for which city he should sail in a few

---

1 pittance: 소량. 약간의 돈.
2 maintenance: 생계.
3 meed: 당연히 받을 것.
4 gloried in: …을 자랑으로 여기다.
5 ingratitude: 배은망덕.
6 infused: 불어넣다.
7 outraged: 격노한.
8 expostulate with: 설득하다.
9 reiterating: 반복해서 말하다.
10 mandate: 명령.
11 divulged: 누설되다. 밝혀지다.

hours. He intended to leave his daughter under the care of a confidential servant, to follow at her leisure[1] with the greater part of his property, which had not yet arrived at Leghorn.

"When alone, Safie resolved in her own mind the plan of conduct that it would become her to pursue in this emergency. A residence in Turkey was abhorrent to her; her religion and her feelings were alike averse[2] to it. By some papers of her father, which fell into her hands, she heard of the exile of her lover, and learnt the name of the spot where he then resided. She hesitated some time, but at length she formed her determination. Taking with her some jewels that belonged to her, and a sum of money, she quitted Italy with an attendant[3], a native of Leghorn, but who understood the common language of Turkey, and departed for Germany.

"She arrived in safety at a town about twenty leagues from the cottage of De Lacey, when her attendant fell dangerously ill. Safie nursed her with the most devoted affection; but the poor girl died, and the Arabian was left alone, unacquainted with the language of the country, and utterly ignorant of the customs of the world. She fell, however, into good hands[4]. The Italian had mentioned the name of the spot for which they were bound; and, after her death, the woman of the house in which they had lived took care that[5] Safie should arrive in safety at the cottage of her lover.

---

1 at her leisure: (그녀가) 편리한 때에.
2 averse: 싫어하는. 반대하는.
3 attendant: 수행원. 안내원.
4 She fell, however, into good hands: 좋은 사람들을 만나게 되었다는 의미.
5 took care that: …하도록 신경 쓰다.

CHAPTER XV

"Such was the history of my beloved cottagers. It impressed me deeply. I learned, from the views of social life which it developed, to admire their virtues, and to deprecate[1] the vices of mankind.

"As yet I looked upon crime as a distant evil; benevolence and generosity were ever present before me, inciting[2] within me a desire to become an actor in the busy scene where so many admirable qualities were called forth and displayed. But, in giving an account of the progress of my intellect, I must not omit a circumstance which occurred in the beginning of the month of August of the same year.

"One night, during my accustomed visit to the neighbouring wood, where I collected my own food, and brought home firing for my protectors, I found on the ground a leathern portmanteau[3], containing several articles[4] of dress and some books. I eagerly seized the prize[5], and returned with it to my hovel. Fortunately the books were written in the language the elements of which I had acquired at the cottage; they consisted of *Paradise Lost*, a volume of *Plutarch's Lives*, and the *Sorrows of Werter*[6]. The possession of these treasures gave me extreme delight; I now continually studied and exercised my mind upon these histories, whilst my friends were employed in their ordinary occupations.

"I can hardly describe to you the effect of these books. They pro-

---

1 deprecate: 비난하다. 못마땅하게 여기다.
2 inciting: 불러일으키다.
3 portmanteau: 대형 여행용 가방.
4 several articles: (의류) 몇 점.
5 prize: 노획물.
6 *Paradise Lost*, a volume of *Plutarch's Lives*, and the *Sorrows of Werter*: 17세기 영국의 시인 밀튼(Milton1608-74)이 쓴 『실낙원』; 플루타크(Plutarch 46-120)가 그리스와 로마의 영웅들에 관해 쓴 『플루타크 영웅전』(Plutarch's Lives); 독일의 문호 괴테(Johann Wolfgang von Goethe 1749-1832)가 1774년 출판한 『베르테르의 슬픔』 등을 각각 지칭한다.

duced in me an infinity of new images and feelings that sometimes raised me to ecstasy, but more frequently sunk me into the lowest dejection[1]. In the *Sorrows of Werter*, besides the interest of its simple and affecting story, so many opinions are canvassed[2], and so many lights thrown upon what had hitherto been to me obscure subjects, that I found in it a never-ending source of speculation and astonishment. The gentle and domestic manners it described, combined with lofty sentiments and feelings, which had for their object something out of self, accorded[3] well with my experience among my protectors, and with the wants which were for ever alive in my own bosom. But I thought Werter himself a more divine being than I had ever beheld or imagined; his character contained no pretension[4], but it sunk deep. The disquisitions[5] upon death and suicide were calculated to fill me with wonder. I did not pretend to enter into[6] the merits of the case, yet I inclined towards[7] the opinions of the hero, whose extinction I wept, without precisely understanding it.

"As I read, however, I applied much personally to my own feelings and condition. I found myself similar, yet at the same time strangely unlike to the beings concerning whom I read, and to whose conversation I was a listener. I sympathised with, and partly understood them, but I was unformed in mind; I was dependent on none and related to none. 'The path of my departure was free;' and there was none to lament my annihilation[8]. My person[9] was hideous and my stature gigantic. What did this mean? Who was I? What was I? Whence did

---

1 dejection: 낙담. 실의.
2 canvassed: 점검되다. 논의되다.
3 accorded: 일치하다. 조화하다.
4 pretension: 가장. 허식.
5 disquisitions: 논리적인 이론.
6 enter into: …을 깊이 파고들다,
7 inclined towards: …로 마음이 기울다.
8 annihilation: 흔적도 없이 사라짐.
9 person: 외모.

I come? What was my destination? These questions continually recurred, but I was unable to solve them.

"The volume of *Plutarch's Lives*, which I possessed, contained the histories of the first founders of the ancient republics[1]. This book had a far different effect upon me from the *Sorrows of Werter*. I learned from Werter's imaginations despondency and gloom[2]: but Plutarch taught me high thoughts; he elevated me above the wretched sphere of my own reflections to admire and love the heroes of past ages. Many things I read surpassed[3] my understanding and experience. I had a very confused knowledge of kingdoms, wide extents of country, mighty rivers, and boundless seas. But I was perfectly unacquainted with towns, and large assemblages of men. The cottage of my protectors had been the only school in which I had studied human nature[4]; but this book developed new and mightier scenes of action. I read of men concerned in public affairs, governing or massacring[5] their species. I felt the greatest ardour for virtue rise within me, and abhorrence for vice, as far as I understood the signification of those terms, relative as they were, as I applied them, to pleasure and pain alone. Induced by these feelings, I was of course led to admire peaceable lawgivers, Numa[6], Solon[7], and Lycurgus[8], in preference to Romulus and Theseus[9]. The patriarchal[10] lives of my protectors caused these im-

---

1 ancient republics: 그리스와 로마를 지칭.

2 gloom: 침울. 슬픔.

3 surpassed: 넘어서다.

4 human nature: 인간의 본성.

5 massacring: 대량학살하다.

6 Numa: 뉘마 폼필리우스(Numa Pompilius, 753-673 B.C); 로마의 두 번째 왕으로 절제된 삶을 살며 사치를 혐오하였다고 한다.

7 Solon: 솔론(640?-560 B.C.); 아테네의 정치가이자 시인으로 '솔론의 개혁'이라 불리는 여러 개혁을 단행.

8 Lycurgus: 리쿠르구스는 기원전 7세기경에 활동했던 스파르타(Sparta)의 지도자.

9 Romulus and Theseus: 로물루스(Romulus)는 로마의 건국자이자 통치자; 테세우스(Theseus)는 아테네의 왕.

10 patriarchal: 존경할 만한.

pressions to take a firm hold on my mind; perhaps, if my first introduction to humanity had been made by a young soldier, burning for
glory and slaughter, I should have been imbued with different sensations.

"But *Paradise Lost* excited different and far deeper emotions. I read
it, as I had read the other volumes which had fallen into my hands[1],
as a true history. It moved every feeling of wonder and awe that the
picture of an omnipotent God warring with his creatures was capable
of exciting. I often referred the several situations, as their similarity
struck me, to my own. Like Adam, I was apparently united by no link
to any other being in existence[2]; but his state was far different from
mine in every other respect. He had come forth from the hands of
God a perfect creature, happy and prosperous, guarded by the especial care of his Creator; he was allowed to converse with, and acquire
knowledge from, beings of a superior nature: but I was wretched,
helpless, and alone. Many times I considered Satan as the fitter emblem[3] of my condition; for often, like him, when I viewed the bliss of
my protectors, the bitter gall[4] of envy rose within me.

"Another circumstance strengthened and confirmed these feelings.
Soon after my arrival in the hovel, I discovered some papers in the
pocket of the dress which I had taken from your laboratory. At first I
had neglected them; but now that I was able to decipher[5] the characters in which they were written, I began to study them with diligence.
It was your journal of the four months that preceded my creation. You
minutely described in these papers every step you took in the progress of your work; this history was mingled with accounts of domestic
occurrences. You, doubtless, recollect these papers. Here they are. Ev-

---

1 had fallen into my hands: 내 수중에 떨어지다.
2 in existence: 존재하고 있는.
3 emblem: 상징.
4 gall: 쓴 맛.
5 decipher: 해독하다.

erything is related in them which bears reference to[1] my accursed origin; the whole detail of that series of disgusting circumstances which produced it is set in view; the minutest description of my odious and loathsome person is given, in language which painted[2] your own horrors and rendered mine indelible. I sickened as I read. 'Hateful day when I received life!' I exclaimed in agony. 'Accursed creator! Why did you form a monster so hideous that even you turned from me in disgust? God, in pity, made man beautiful and alluring[3], after his own image; but my form is a filthy type of yours, more horrid even from the very resemblance. Satan had his companions, fellow-devils, to admire and encourage him; but I am solitary and abhorred.'

"These were the reflections of my hours of despondency and solitude; but when I contemplated the virtues of the cottagers, their amiable and benevolent dispositions, I persuaded myself[4] that when they should become acquainted with my admiration of their virtues, they would compassionate me, and overlook my personal deformity. Could they turn from their door one, however monstrous, who solicited[5] their compassion and friendship? I resolved, at least, not to despair, but in every way to fit myself for an interview with them which would decide my fate. I postponed this attempt for some months longer; for the importance attached to its success inspired me with a dread lest I should fail. Besides, I found that my understanding improved so much with every day's experience that I was unwilling to commence this undertaking until a few more months should have added to my sagacity[6].

"Several changes, in the meantime, took place in the cottage. The

---

1 bears reference to: …와 관련이 있는.
2 painted: 묘사하다.
3 alluring: 유혹적인,
4 persuaded myself: 확신하다.
5 solicited: 간청하다. 갈구하다.
6 sagacity: 정보. 현명함.

presence of Safie diffused happiness among its inhabitants; and I also found that a greater degree of plenty reigned[1] there. Felix and Agatha spent more time in amusement and conversation, and were assisted in their labours by servants. They did not appear rich, but they were contented and happy; their feelings were serene and peaceful, while mine became every day more tumultuous[2]. Increase of knowledge only discovered to me more clearly what a wretched outcast I was. I cherished hope, it is true; but it vanished when I beheld my person reflected in water, or my shadow in the moonshine, even as that frail image and that inconstant shade.

"I endeavoured to crush these fears, and to fortify myself[3] for the trial which in a few months I resolved to undergo; and sometimes I allowed my thoughts, unchecked by reason, to ramble in the fields of Paradise, and dared to fancy amiable and lovely creatures sympathising with my feelings, and cheering[4] my gloom; their angelic countenances breathed[5] smiles of consolation. But it was all a dream; no Eve soothed my sorrows, nor shared my thoughts; I was alone. I remembered Adam's supplication[6] to his Creator. But where was mine? He had abandoned me: and, in the bitterness of my heart, I cursed him.

"Autumn passed thus. I saw, with surprise and grief, the leaves decay and fall, and nature again assume the barren and bleak appearance it had worn when I first beheld the woods and the lovely moon. Yet I did not heed the bleakness of the weather; I was better fitted by my conformation[7] for the endurance of cold than heat. But my chief delights were the sight of the flowers, the birds, and all the gay ap-

---

1 reigned: 퍼지다. 우세해지다.

2 tumultuous: 동요된. 격앙된.

3 fortify myself: 나의 마음을 굳건히 하다.

4 cheering my gloom: 위로하여 '우울함'(gloom)을 덜어준다는 의미.

5 breathed: (미소를) 발산하다.

6 supplication: '탄원'. '애원'; 성경에서 아담이 신에게 자신의 짝을 만들어 달라고 탄원한 사실을 괴물은 염두에 두고 말하고 있다.

7 conformation: 몸 구조. 형태.

parel[1] of summer; when those deserted me, I turned with more attention towards the cottagers. Their happiness was not decreased by the absence of summer. They loved, and sympathised with one another; and their joys, depending on each other, were not interrupted by the casualties[2] that took place around them. The more I saw of them, the greater became my desire to claim their protection and kindness; my heart yearned to be known and loved by these amiable creatures: to see their sweet looks directed towards me with affection was the utmost limit[3] of my ambition. I dared not think that they would turn them from me with disdain and horror. The poor that stopped at their door were never driven away. I asked, it is true, for greater treasures than a little food or rest: I required kindness and sympathy; but I did not believe myself utterly unworthy of it.

"The winter advanced, and an entire revolution[4] of the seasons had taken place since I awoke into life. My attention, at this time, was solely directed towards my plan of introducing myself into the cottage of my protectors. I revolved many projects; but that on which I finally fixed was, to enter the dwelling when the blind old man should be alone. I had sagacity enough to discover that the unnatural hideousness of my person was the chief object of horror with those who had formerly beheld me. My voice, although harsh, had nothing terrible in it; I thought, therefore, that if, in the absence of his children, I could gain the good-will and mediation[5] of the old De Lacey, I might, by his means be tolerated by my younger protectors.

"One day, when the sun shone on the red leaves that strewed the ground, and diffused cheerfulness, although it denied warmth, Safie, Agatha, and Felix departed on a long country walk, and the old man,

---

1 apparel: 의상.
2 casualties: 사상자.
3 utmost limit: 극한계선.
4 revolution: 순환.
5 mediation: 중재. 조정.

at his own desire[1], was left alone in the cottage. When his children had departed, he took up his guitar, and played several mournful but sweet airs, more sweet and mournful than I had ever heard him play before. At first his countenance was illuminated with pleasure, but as he continued, thoughtfulness and sadness succeeded; at length, laying aside the instrument, he sat absorbed in reflection.

"My heart beat quick; this was the hour and moment of trial which would decide my hopes or realise my fears. The servants were gone to a neighbouring fair. All was silent in and around the cottage; it was an excellent opportunity; yet, when I proceeded to execute my plan, my limbs failed me[2], and I sank to the ground. Again I rose; and, exerting all the firmness of which I was master, removed the planks which I had placed before my hovel to conceal my retreat. The fresh air revived me, and, with renewed determination, I approached the door of their cottage.

"I knocked. 'Who is there?' said the old man—'Come in.'

"I entered; 'Pardon this intrusion,' said I: 'I am a traveller in want of a little rest; you would greatly oblige me if you would allow me to remain a few minutes before the fire.'

"'Enter,' said De Lacey; 'and I will try in what manner I can to relieve your wants; but, unfortunately, my children are from home, and, as I am blind, I am afraid I shall find it difficult to procure food for you.'

"'Do not trouble yourself, my kind host, I have food; it is warmth and rest only that I need.'

"I sat down, and a silence ensued. I knew that every minute was precious to me, yet I remained irresolute[3] in what manner to commence the interview; when the old man addressed me—

"'By your language, stranger, I suppose you are my country-

---

1 at his own desire: 그 자신의 요청에 따라. 그가 바라는 대로.
2 my limbs failed me: '나의 다리가 나를 지탱해 주지 못하였다'; 즉 '쓰러졌다'는 의미.
3 irresolute: 망설이는. 결심이 서지 못한.

man; — are you French?'

" 'No; but I was educated by a French family, and understand that language only. I am now going to claim the protection of some friends, whom I sincerely love, and of whose favour I have some hopes.'

" 'Are they Germans?'

" 'No, they are French. But let us change the subject. I am an unfortunate and deserted creature; I look around, and I have no relation or friend upon earth. These amiable people to whom I go have never seen me, and know little of me. I am full of fears; for if I fail there, I am an outcast in the world for ever.'

" 'Do not despair. To be friendless is indeed to be unfortunate; but the hearts of men, when unprejudiced by any obvious self-interest, are full of brotherly love and charity. Rely, therefore, on your hopes; and if these friends are good and amiable, do not despair.'

" 'They are kind — they are the most excellent creatures in the world; but, unfortunately, they are prejudiced against me. I have good dispositions; my life has been hitherto harmless, and in some degree beneficial; but a fatal prejudice clouds their eyes, and where they ought to see a feeling and kind friend, they behold only a detestable monster.'

" 'That is indeed unfortunate; but if you are really blameless, cannot you undeceive[1] them?'

" 'I am about to undertake that task; and it is on that account that I feel so many overwhelming terrors. I tenderly love these friends; I have, unknown to them, been for many months in the habits of daily kindness towards them; but they believe that I wish to injure them, and it is that prejudice which I wish to overcome.'

" 'Where do these friends reside?'

" 'Near this spot.'

---

1 undeceive: (잘못을) 깨닫게 하다.

"The old man paused, and then continued, 'If you will unreserv-edly[1] confide to me the particulars[2] of your tale, I perhaps may be of use in undeceiving them. I am blind, and cannot judge of your coun-tenance, but there is something in your words which persuades me that you are sincere. I am poor, and an exile; but it will afford me true pleasure to be in any way serviceable to a human creature.'

" 'Excellent man! I thank you, and accept your generous offer. You raise me from the dust by this kindness; and I trust that, by your aid, I shall not be driven from the society and sympathy of your fellow-creatures.'

" 'Heaven forbid! even if you were really criminal; for that can only drive you to desperation, and not instigate you to virtue. I also am unfortunate; I and my family have been condemned, although in-nocent: judge, therefore, if I do not feel for your misfortunes.'

" 'How can I thank you, my best and only benefactor? From your lips first have I heard the voice of kindness directed towards me; I shall be for ever grateful; and your present humanity assures me of success with those friends whom I am on the point of meeting.'

" 'May I know the names and residence of those friends?'

"I paused. This, I thought, was the moment of decision, which was to rob me of, or bestow happiness on me for ever. I struggled vainly for firmness sufficient to answer him, but the effort destroyed all my remaining strength; I sank on the chair, and sobbed aloud. At that moment I heard the steps of my younger protectors. I had not a mo-ment to lose; but seizing the hand of the old man, I cried, 'Now is the time! — save and protect me! You and your family are the friends whom I seek. Do not you desert me in the hour of trial!'

" 'Great God!' exclaimed the old man, 'who are you?'

"At that instant the cottage door was opened, and Felix, Safie,

---

1 unreservedly: 툭 터놓고.
2 particulars: 세세한(구체적인) 내용.

and Agatha entered. Who can describe their horror and consterna-tion[1] on beholding me? Agatha fainted; and Safie, unable to attend to her friend, rushed out of the cottage. Felix darted[2] forward, and with supernatural force tore me from his father, to whose knees I clung: in a transport of fury[3], he dashed me to the ground[4] and struck me violently with a stick. I could have torn him limb from limb, as the lion rends[5] the antelope. But my heart sank within me as with bitter sickness, and I refrained. I saw him on the point of repeating his blow, when, overcome by pain and anguish, I quitted the cottage and in the general tumult[6] escaped unperceived to my hovel.

CHAPTER XVI

"Cursed, cursed creator! Why did I live? Why, in that instant, did I not extinguish the spark of existence which you had so wantonly[7] be-stowed? I know not; despair had not yet taken possession of me; my feelings were those of rage and revenge. I could with pleasure have destroyed the cottage and its inhabitants, and have glutted myself with[8] their shrieks and misery.

"When night came, I quitted my retreat, and wandered in the wood; and now, no longer restrained by the fear of discovery, I gave vent to my anguish in fearful howlings[9]. I was like a wild beast that

---

1 consternation: 대경실색. 소스라치게 놀람.
2 darted: 달려들다.
3 in a transport of fury: 몹시 분노해서.
4 dashed me to the ground: 나를 바닥에 내동댕이치다.
5 rends: (사지를) 찢다.
6 in the general tumult: 모든 사람들이 소란 피는 가운데.
7 wantonly: 제멋대로.
8 glutted myself with: …을 실컷 누리다(맛보다).
9 howlings: 울부짖음.

had broken the toils[1]; destroying the objects that obstructed me, and ranging[2] through the wood with a stag-like swiftness. O! what a miserable night I passed! the cold stars shone in mockery, and the bare trees waved their branches above me: now and then the sweet voice of a bird burst forth amidst the universal stillness[3]. All, save[4] I, were at rest or in enjoyment: I, like the arch-fiend[5], bore a hell within me; and finding myself unsympathised with, wished to tear up the trees, spread havoc[6] and destruction around me, and then to have sat down and enjoyed the ruin.

"But this was a luxury of sensation that could not endure; I became fatigued with excess of bodily exertion, and sank on the damp grass in the sick impotence[7] of despair. There was none among the myriads[8] of men that existed who would pity or assist me; and should I feel kindness towards my enemies? No: from that moment I declared everlasting war against the species[9], and, more than all, against him who had formed me. and sent me forth to this insupportable misery.

"The sun rose; I heard the voices of men, and knew that it was impossible to return to my retreat during that day. Accordingly I hid myself in some thick underwood, determining to devote the ensuing hours to reflection on my situation.

"The pleasant sunshine, and the pure air of day, restored me to some degree of tranquillity; and when I considered what had passed at the cottage, I could not help believing that I had been too hasty in my conclusions. I had certainly acted imprudently. It was apparent

---

1   toils: 덫. 함정.

2   ranging: (떼)돌아다니다.

3   amidst the universal stillness: 모든 것이 조용한 가운데.

4   save: 'except'의 의미.

5   arch-fiend: 마왕. 사탄.

6   havoc: 대 파괴.

7   impotence: 무기력.

8   myriads: 무수히 많은 사람들.

9   species: '인간'을 지칭.

that my conversation had interested the father in my behalf, and I was a fool in having exposed my person to the horror of his children. I ought to have familiarised the old De Lacey to me, and by degrees to have discovered myself to the rest of his family, when they should have been prepared for my approach. But I did not believe my errors to be irretrievable[1]; and, after much consideration, I resolved to return to the cottage, seek the old man, and by my representations win him to my party[2].

"These thoughts calmed me, and in the afternoon I sank into a profound sleep; but the fever of my blood did not allow me to be visited by peaceful dreams. The horrible scene of the preceding day was for ever acting before my eyes; the females were flying, and the enraged Felix tearing me from his father's feet. I awoke exhausted; and, finding that it was already night, I crept forth from my hiding-place, and went in search of food.

"When my hunger was appeased[3], I directed my steps towards the well-known path that conducted to[4] the cottage. All there was at peace. I crept into my hovel, and remained in silent expectation of the accustomed[5] hour when the family arose. That hour passed, the sun mounted high in the heavens, but the cottagers did not appear. I trembled violently, apprehending some dreadful misfortune. The inside of the cottage was dark, and I heard no motion; I cannot describe the agony of this suspense.

"Presently two countrymen passed by; but pausing near the cottage, they entered into conversation, using violent gesticulations[6]; but I did not understand what they said, as they spoke the language of the

---

1 irretrievable: 돌이킬 수없는.
2 win him to my party: 그를 내편으로 만들다.
3 appeased: 진정시키다. 누그러뜨리다.
4 conducted to: …로 이어지다.
5 accustomed: 익숙해진.
6 gesticulations: 몸짓. 손짓.

country, which differed from that of my protectors. Soon after, however, Felix approached with another man: I was surprised, as I knew that he had not quitted the cottage that morning, and waited anxiously to discover, from his discourse, the meaning of these unusual appearances.

" 'Do you consider,' said his companion to him, 'that you will be obliged to pay three months' rent, and to lose the produce[1] of your garden? I do not wish to take any unfair advantage, and I beg therefore that you will take some days to consider of your determination.'

" 'It is utterly useless,' replied Felix; 'we can never again inhabit your cottage. The life of my father is in the greatest danger, owing to the dreadful circumstance that I have related. My wife and my sister will never recover from their horror. I entreat you not to reason with[2] me any more. Take possession of your tenement[3], and let me fly from this place.'

"Felix trembled violently as he said this. He and his companion entered the cottage, in which they remained for a few minutes, and then departed. I never saw any of the family of De Lacey more.

"I continued for the remainder of the day in my hovel in a state of utter and stupid despair. My protectors had departed, and had broken the only link that held me to the world. For the first time the feelings of revenge and hatred filled my bosom, and I did not strive to control them; but, allowing myself to be borne away by the stream[4], I bent my mind towards[5] injury and death. When I thought of my friends, of the mild voice of De Lacey, the gentle eyes of Agatha, and the exquisite beauty of the Arabian, these thoughts vanished, and a gush of tears[6] somewhat soothed me. But again, when I reflected that they had

---

1　produce: 생산물.

2　reason with: 설득하다.

3　tenement: 집.

4　stream: 복수심(revenge)과 분노(fury)라는 감정의 소용돌이를 지칭.

5　bent my mind towards: …에 전념하다(신경을 집중하다).

6　gush of tears: 솟구치는 눈물.

spurned and deserted me, anger returned, a rage of anger; and, unable to injure anything human, I turned my fury towards inanimate objects. As night advanced, I placed a variety of combustibles[1] around the cottage; and after having destroyed every vestige[2] of cultivation in the garden, I waited with forced impatience[3] until the moon had sunk to commence my operations.

"As the night advanced, a fierce wind arose from the woods, and quickly dispersed the clouds that had loitered[4] in the heavens: the blast tore[5] along like a mighty avalanche, and produced a kind of insanity in my spirits that burst all bounds of reason and reflection. I lighted the dry branch of a tree, and danced with fury around the devoted[6] cottage, my eyes still fixed on the western horizon, the edge of which the moon nearly touched. A part of its orb was at length hid, and I waved my brand[7]; it sank, and, with a loud scream, I fired the straw, and heath, and bushes, which I had collected. The wind fanned the fire, and the cottage was quickly enveloped by the flames, which clung to it, and licked[8] it with their forked and destroying tongues.

"As soon as I was convinced that no assistance could save any part of the habitation, I quitted the scene[9] and sought for refuge in the woods.

"And now, with the world before me, whither should I bend my steps[10]? I resolved to fly far from the scene of my misfortunes; but to

---

1 combustibles: 연소물. 가연물.
2 vestige: 흔적.
3 with forced impatience: 억지로 참아내면서.
4 loitered: 느릿느릿 움직이다.
5 tore: 빠르게 움직이다.
6 devoted: 파멸을 맞이할(doomed).
7 brand: 불이 붙은 나무.
8 licked: (불길이) 널름거리다.
9 quit the scene: '떠나다'. '퇴장하다'; 『실낙원』의 말미에 나오는 에덴동산의 파괴를 연상시킨다.
10 with the world before me, whither should I bend my steps: 에덴동산이 파괴된 후

me, hated and despised, every country must be equally horrible. At length the thought of you crossed my mind. I learned from your papers that you were my father, my creator; and to whom could I apply with more fitness than to him who had given me life? Among the lessons that Felix had bestowed upon Safie, geography had not been omitted. I had learned from these the relative situations of the different countries of the earth. You had mentioned Geneva as the name of your native town; and towards this place I resolved to proceed.

"But how was I to direct myself? I knew that I must travel in a south-westerly direction to reach my destination; but the sun was my only guide. I did not know the names of the towns that I was to pass through, nor could I ask information from a single human being; but I did not despair. From you only could I hope for succour[1], although towards you I felt no sentiment but that of hatred. Unfeeling, heartless creator! you had endowed me with perceptions and passions, and then cast me abroad an object for the scorn and horror of mankind. But on you only had I any claim for pity and redress[2], and from you I determined to seek that justice which I vainly attempted to gain from any other being that wore the human form.

"My travels were long, and the sufferings I endured intense. It was late in autumn when I quitted the district where I had so long resided. I travelled only at night, fearful of encountering the visage[3] of a human being. Nature decayed around me, and the sun became heatless; rain and snow poured around me; mighty rivers were frozen; the surface of the earth was hard, and chill, and bare, and I found no shelter. Oh, earth! how often did I imprecate[4] curses on the cause of my be-

---

어디로 가야할지 고민하는 아담의 모습을 연상시키는 구절로 여기서 괴물은 자신을 거주할 곳을 잃은 아담에 비유하고 있다.

1 succour: 도움.
2 redress: 배상. 구제(책).
3 visage: 얼굴.
4 imprecate: (저주를 내려달라고) 빌다.

ing! The mildness of my nature had fled, and all within me was turned to gall[1] and bitterness. The nearer I approached to your habitation, the more deeply did I feel the spirit of revenge enkindled[2] in my heart. Snow fell, and the waters were hardened; but I rested not. A few incidents now and then directed me, and I possessed a map of the country; but I often wandered wide from my path. The agony of my feelings allowed me no respite[3]: no incident occurred from which my rage and misery could not extract its food; but a circumstance that happened when I arrived on the confines[4] of Switzerland, when the sun had recovered its warmth, and the earth again began to look green, confirmed in an especial manner the bitterness and horror of my feelings.

"I generally rested during the day, and travelled only when I was secured by night from the view of man. One morning, however, finding that my path lay through a deep wood, I ventured to continue my journey after the sun had risen; the day, which was one of the first of spring, cheered even me by the loveliness of its sunshine and the balminess[5] of the air. I felt emotions of gentleness and pleasure, that had long appeared dead, revive within me. Half surprised by the novelty of these sensations, I allowed myself to be borne away by them; and, forgetting my solitude and deformity, dared to be happy. Soft tears again bedewed[6] my cheeks, and I even raised my humid eyes with thankfulness towards the blessed sun which bestowed such joy upon me.

"I continued to wind among the paths of the wood, until I came to its boundary, which was skirted[7] by a deep and rapid river, into which many of the trees bent their branches, now budding with the

---

1 gall: 증오(심).
2 enkindled: 불이 붙은.
3 respite: 휴식,
4 confines: 경계. 국경.
5 balminess: 향기가 그윽함.
6 bedewed: 눈물로 적시다.
7 skirted: 둘러싸인.

fresh spring. Here I paused, not exactly knowing what path to pursue, when I heard the sound of voices that induced me to conceal myself under the shade of a cypress[1]. I was scarcely hid, when a young girl came running towards the spot where I was concealed, laughing, as if she ran from some one in sport[2]. She continued her course along the precipitous sides of the river, when suddenly her foot slipt, and she fell into the rapid stream. I rushed from my hiding-place; and, with extreme labour from the force of the current, saved her, and dragged her to shore. She was senseless; and I endeavoured by every means in my power to restore animation, when I was suddenly interrupted by the approach of a rustic[3], who was probably the person from whom she had playfully fled. On seeing me, he darted towards me, and tearing the girl from my arms, hastened towards the deeper parts of the wood. I followed speedily, I hardly knew why; but when the man saw me draw near, he aimed a gun, which he carried, at my body, and fired. I sunk to the ground, and my injurer, with increased swiftness, escaped into the wood.

"This was then the reward of my benevolence! I had saved a human being from destruction, and, as a recompense[4], I now writhed[5] under the miserable pain of a wound, which shattered the flesh and bone. The feelings of kindness and gentleness which I had entertained but a few moments before gave place to[6] hellish rage and gnashing of teeth[7]. Inflamed[8] by pain, I vowed eternal hatred and vengeance to all mankind. But the agony of my wound overcame me; my pulses

---

1 cypress: 삼(杉)나무의 일종.
2 in sport: 장난으로.
3 rustic: 시골사람. 농부.
4 recompense: 보상. 배상.
5 writhed: 몸부림치며 괴로워하다.
6 gave place to: …으로 바뀌다.
7 gnashing of teeth: 이를 감.
8 Inflamed: 감정이 격해져.

paused, and I fainted.

"For some weeks I led a miserable life in the woods, endeavouring to cure the wound which I had received. The ball[1] had entered my shoulder, and I knew not whether it had remained there or passed through; at any rate I had no means of extracting it. My sufferings were augmented also by the oppressive[2] sense of the injustice and ingratitude of their infliction. My daily vows rose for revenge— a deep and deadly revenge, such as would alone compensate for the outrages[3] and anguish I had endured.

"After some weeks my wound healed, and I continued my journey. The labours I endured were no longer to be alleviated[4] by the bright sun or gentle breezes of spring; all joy was but a mockery[5], which insulted my desolate state, and made me feel more painfully that I was not made for the enjoyment of pleasure.

"But my toils[6] now drew near a close; and in two months from this time I reached the environs of Geneva.

"It was evening when I arrived, and I retired to a hiding-place among the fields that surround it, to meditate in what manner I should apply to you. I was oppressed by fatigue and hunger and far too unhappy to enjoy the gentle breezes of evening, or the prospect[7] of the sun setting behind the stupendous mountains of Jura.

"At this time a slight sleep relieved me from the pain of reflection, which was disturbed by the approach of a beautiful child, who came running into the recess[8] I had chosen, with all the sportiveness of in-

---

1 ball: 총알.
2 oppressive: 견디기 힘든.
3 outrages: 능욕. 유린.
4 alleviated: 완화된. (고통이) 누그러진,
5 mockery: 조소의 대상.
6 toils: 노고. 고생,
7 prospect: 전망. 경치.
8 recess: 구석. 후미진 곳.

fancy. Suddenly, as I gazed on him, an idea seized me, that this little creature was unprejudiced, and had lived too short a time to have imbibed[1] a horror of deformity. If, therefore, I could seize him, and educate him as my companion and friend, I should not be so desolate in this peopled earth.

"Urged by this impulse, I seized on the boy as he passed and drew him towards me. As soon as he beheld my form, he placed his hands before his eyes and uttered a shrill scream: I drew his hand forcibly from his face, and said, 'Child, what is the meaning of this? I do not intend to hurt you; listen to me.'

"He struggled violently. 'Let me go,' he cried; 'monster! ugly wretch! you wish to eat me, and tear me to pieces — You are an ogre[2] — Let me go, or I will tell my papa.'

"'Boy, you will never see your father again; you must come with me.'

"'Hideous monster! let me go. My papa is a Syndic[3] — he is M. Frankenstein — he will punish you. You dare not keep me.'

"'Frankenstein! you belong then to my enemy — to him towards whom I have sworn eternal revenge; you shall be my first victim.'

"The child still struggled, and loaded me with epithets[4] which carried despair to my heart; I grasped his throat to silence him, and in a moment he lay dead at my feet.

"I gazed on my victim, and my heart swelled with exultation and hellish triumph: clapping my hands, I exclaimed, 'I too can create desolation; my enemy is not invulnerable[5]; this death will carry despair to him, and a thousand other miseries shall torment and destroy him.'

"As I fixed my eyes on the child, I saw something glittering on his breast. I took it; it was a portrait of a most lovely woman. In spite

---

1 imbibed: 받아들이다,
2 ogre: (동화에 나오는) 사람 잡아먹는 괴물.
3 Syndic: 지방 행정관.
4 epithets: 모멸적인 말.
5 invulnerable: 상처 입지 않는. 죽지 않는.

of my malignity, it softened and attracted me. For a few moments I gazed with delight on her dark eyes, fringed by deep lashes, and her lovely lips; but presently my rage returned: I remembered that I was for ever deprived of the delights that such beautiful creatures could bestow; and that she whose resemblance I contemplated would, in regarding me, have changed that air of divine benignity to one expressive of disgust and affright[1].

"Can you wonder that such thoughts transported[2] me with rage? I only wonder that at that moment, instead of venting my sensations in exclamations[3] and agony, I did not rush among mankind and perish in the attempt to destroy them.

"While I was overcome by these feelings, I left the spot where I had committed the murder, and seeking a more secluded hiding-place, I entered a barn which had appeared to me to be empty. A woman was sleeping on some straw; she was young: not indeed so beautiful as her whose portrait I held; but of an agreeable aspect, and blooming in the loveliness of youth and health. Here, I thought, is one of those whose joy-imparting[4] smiles are bestowed on all but me. And then I bent over her and whispered, 'Awake, fairest, thy lover is near — he who would give his life but to obtain one look of affection from thine eyes: my beloved, awake!'

"The sleeper stirred; a thrill of terror ran through me. Should she indeed awake, and see me, and curse me, and denounce[5] the murderer? Thus would she assuredly act, if her darkened eyes opened and she beheld me. The thought was madness; it stirred the fiend[6] within me — not I, but she shall suffer: the murder I have committed because

---

1 affright: 공포,
2 transported: 제정신이 아니게 만들다.
3 exclamations: 외침. 절규.
4 joy-imparting: 기쁨을 주는.
5 denounce: 비난(공격)하다.
6 the fiend: '악마성': 즉 내 마음에 존재하는 악마성을 일깨웠다는 의미.

I am for ever robbed of all that she could give me, she shall atone[1]. The crime had its source in her: be hers the punishment! Thanks to the lessons of Felix and the sanguinary[2] laws of man, I had learned now to work mischief[3]. I bent over her, and placed the portrait securely in one of the folds of her dress. She moved again, and I fled.

"For some days I haunted[4] the spot where these scenes had taken place; sometimes wishing to see you, sometimes resolved to quit the world and its miseries forever. At length I wandered towards these mountains, and have ranged through their immense recesses, consumed[5] by a burning passion which you alone can gratify[6]. We may not part until you have promised to comply with my requisition[7]. I am alone, and miserable; man will not associate with[8] me; but one as deformed and horrible as myself would not deny herself[9] to me. My companion must be of the same species, and have the same defects. This being you must create."

CHAPTER XVII

The being finished speaking, and fixed his looks upon me in the expectation of a reply. But I was bewildered, perplexed, and unable to arrange my ideas sufficiently to understand the full extent of his proposition[10]. He continued —

1　atone: 죄를 씻다.
2　sanguinary: 피비린내 나는. 피 보기를 즐기는.
3　work mischief: 재난을 가져오다. 해를 입히다.
4　haunted: 자주 들르다.
5　consumed: …에 사로잡혀서.
6　gratify: 충족시키다.
7　requisition: 요구.
8　associate with: 사귀다.
9　deny herself: 그녀 자신에게 접근하는 것을 허용하지 않다.
10　unable to arrange … full extent of his proposition: 그가 어느 정도까지의 요구를 하

"You must create a female for me, with whom I can live in the interchange of those sympathies necessary for my being. This you alone can do; and I demand it of you as a right which you must not refuse to concede[1]."

The latter part of his tale had kindled anew in me the anger that had died away while he narrated his peaceful life among the cottagers, and as he said this, I could no longer suppress[2] the rage that burned within me.

"I do refuse it," I replied; "and no torture shall ever extort[3] a consent from me. You may render me the most miserable of men, but you shall never make me base in my own eyes. Shall I create another like yourself, whose joint wickedness might desolate[4] the world! Begone! I have answered you; you may torture me, but I will never consent."

"You are in the wrong," replied the fiend; "and, instead of threatening, I am content to reason with you. I am malicious because I am miserable. Am I not shunned and hated by all mankind? You, my creator, would tear me to pieces, and triumph; remember that, and tell me why I should pity man more than he pities me? You would not call it murder if you could precipitate[5] me into one of those ice-rifts[6], and destroy my frame, the work of your own hands. Shall I respect man when he contemns[7] me? Let him live with me in the interchange of kindness; and instead of injury, I would bestow every benefit upon

---

는지 이해할 수가 없었다는 의미.

1 I demand it of you as a right which you must not refuse to concede: concede는 '인정하다'. '부여하다'; 여자 괴물을 만들어 주는 것이 프랑켄스타인의 의무라고 하는 괴물의 말은 성경에서 아담이 신에게 자신의 짝을 만들어 달라고 요청한 것과 그 맥을 같이 한다.

2 suppress: 억누르다.

3 extort: 강압적으로 얻어내다.

4 desolate: 황폐하게 만들다. 사람이 살지 못하게 하다.

5 precipitate: 거꾸로 집어 던지다.

6 ice-rifts: 얼음 사이의 갈라진 틈.

7 contemns: 경멸하다. 업신여기다.

him with tears of gratitude at his acceptance. But that cannot be; the human senses are insurmountable[1] barriers to our union. Yet mine shall not be the submission of abject[2] slavery. I will revenge my injuries: if I cannot inspire love, I will cause fear; and chiefly towards you my arch-enemy, because my creator, do I swear inextinguishable hatred. Have a care[3]: I will work at[4] your destruction, nor finish until I desolate your heart, so that you shall curse the hour of your birth."

A fiendish rage animated him as he said this; his face was wrinkled into contortions[5] too horrible for human eyes to behold; but presently he calmed himself and proceeded —

"I intended to reason[6]. This passion is detrimental[7] to me; for you do not reflect that you are the cause of its excess. If any being felt emotions of benevolence towards me, I should return them an hundred and an hundred fold; for that one creature's sake, I would make peace with the whole kind! But I now indulge in dreams of bliss[8] that cannot be realised. What I ask of you is reasonable and moderate; I demand a creature of another sex, but as hideous as myself; the gratification is small, but it is all that I can receive, and it shall content me. It is true we shall be monsters, cut off from all the world; but on that account we shall be more attached to one another. Our lives will not be happy, but they will be harmless, and free from the misery I now feel. Oh! my creator, make me happy; let me feel gratitude towards you for one benefit! Let me see that I excite the sympathy of some existing thing; do not deny me my request!"

---

1 insurmountable: 극복할 수 없는.
2 abject: 비굴한.
3 Have a care: 주의(조심)하라.
4 work at: …하는데 힘쓰다.
5 contortions: (얼굴의) 일그러짐. 찡그림.
6 reason: 논리적으로 생각하다.
7 detrimental: …에게 유해한(손해되는).
8 bliss: 커다란 행복.

I was moved. I shuddered when I thought of the possible consequences of my consent; but I felt that there was some justice in his argument. His tale, and the feelings he now expressed, proved him to be
a creature of fine[1] sensations; and did I not as his maker owe him all
the portion of happiness that it was in my power to bestow? He saw
my change of feeling and continued —

"If you consent, neither you nor any other human being shall ever
see us again: I will go to the vast wilds of South America. My food is not
that of man; I do not destroy the lamb and the kid to glut my appetite[2];
acorns and berries afford me sufficient nourishment. My companion
will be of the same nature as myself, and will be content with the same
fare[3]. We shall make our bed of dried leaves; the sun will shine on us as
on man, and will ripen our food. The picture I present to you is peaceful and human, and you must feel that you could deny it only in the
wantonness of power and cruelty. Pitiless as you have been towards me,
I now see compassion in your eyes; let me seize the favourable moment,
and persuade you to promise what I so ardently desire."

"You propose," replied I, "to fly from the habitations of man, to dwell
in those wilds where the beasts of the field will be your only companions. How can you, who long for the love and sympathy of man, persevere[4] in this exile? You will return, and again seek their kindness, and
you will meet with[5] their detestation; your evil passions will be renewed,
and you will then have a companion to aid you in the task of destruction. This may not be: cease to argue the point[6], for I cannot consent."

"How inconstant are your feelings! but a moment ago you were

---

1 fine: 섬세한.

2 I do not destroy the lamb and the kid to glut my appetite: glut는 (욕망, 식욕을)
'채우다'; 괴물은 시인 셸리처럼 채식주의자이다.

3 fare: 음식. 요리.

4 persevere: 참고 버티다. 지속적으로 이어가다.

5 meet with: …을 받다(겪다).

6 argue the point: 이 문제에 대한 논쟁을 벌이다.

moved by my representations[1], and why do you again harden yourself to[2] my complaints? I swear to you, by the earth which I inhabit, and by you that made me, that, with the companion you bestow, I will quit the neighbourhood of man, and dwell as it may chance in the most savage of places. My evil passions will have fled, for I shall meet with sympathy! my life will flow quietly away, and, in my dying moments, I shall not curse my maker."

His words had a strange effect upon me. I compassionated, him and sometimes felt a wish to console him; but when I looked upon him, when I saw the filthy mass that moved and talked, my heart sickened, and my feelings were altered to those of horror and hatred. I tried to stifle[3] these sensations; I thought that, as I could not sympathise with him, I had no right to withhold from him the small portion of happiness which was yet in my power to bestow.

"You swear," I said, "to be harmless; but have you not already shown a degree of malice that should reasonably make me distrust you? May not even this be a feint[4] that will increase your triumph by affording a wider scope for your revenge?"

"How is this? I must not be trifled with[5]: and I demand an answer. If I have no ties and no affections, hatred and vice must be my portion[6]; the love of another will destroy the cause of my crimes, and I shall become a thing of whose existence every one will be ignorant. My vices are the children of a forced solitude that I abhor; and my virtues will necessarily arise when I live in communion with[7] an equal. I shall feel the affections of a sensitive being, and become linked to

---

1 representations: 설명. 진술.
2 harden yourself to: …에 대해 듣지 않으려 하다.
3 stifle: 억누르다.
4 feint: 속임수. 거짓꾸밈.
5 trifled with: 농락하다.
6 portion: 운명. (감당해야 할) 몫.
7 in communion with : …와 소통하며.

the chain of existence and events, from which I am now excluded."

I paused some time to reflect on all he had related, and the various arguments which he had employed. I thought of the promise of virtues which he had displayed on the opening of his existence[1], and the subsequent blight[2] of all kindly feeling by the loathing and scorn which his protectors had manifested towards him. His power and threats were not omitted in my calculations: a creature who could exist in the ice-caves of the glaciers, and hide himself from pursuit among the ridges[3] of inaccessible precipices, was a being possessing faculties it would be vain to cope with[4]. After a long pause of reflection, I concluded that the justice due both to him and my fellow-creatures demanded of me that I should comply with his request. Turning to him, therefore, I said —

"I consent to your demand, on your solemn oath to quit Europe for ever, and every other place in the neighbourhood of man, as soon as I shall deliver into your hands a female who will accompany you in your exile."

"I swear," he cried, "by the sun, and by the blue sky of Heaven, and by the fire of love that burns my heart, that if you grant my prayer, while they exist you shall never behold me again. Depart to your home, and commence your labours: I shall watch their progress with unutterable anxiety; and fear not but that when you are ready I shall appear."

Saying this, he suddenly quitted me, fearful, perhaps, of any change in my sentiments. I saw him descend the mountain with greater speed than the flight of an eagle, and quickly lost among the undulations[5] of the sea of ice.

---

1 on the opening of his existence: 그의 존재가 시작될 때; 즉 그가 생명을 갖기 시작한 순간.
2 blight: 파괴.
3 ridges: 튀어나온 부분.
4 cope with: 대항하다. 맞서다.
5 undulations: 파도.

His tale had occupied the whole day; and the sun was upon the verge of the horizon when he departed. I knew that I ought to hasten my descent towards the valley, as I should soon be encompassed[1] in darkness; but my heart was heavy, and my steps slow. The labour of winding among the little paths of the mountains, and fixing my feet firmly as I advanced, perplexed me, occupied as I was by the emotions which the occurrences of the day had produced. Night was far advanced when I came to the half-way[2] resting-place, and seated myself beside the fountain. The stars shone at intervals, as the clouds passed from over them; the dark pines rose before me, and every here and there a broken tree lay on the ground: it was a scene of wonderful solemnity[3], and stirred strange thoughts within me. I wept bitterly; and clasping my hands in agony, I exclaimed, "Oh! stars, and clouds, and winds, ye[4] are all about to mock me: if ye really pity me, crush sensation and memory; let me become as nought; but if not, depart, depart, and leave me in darkness."

These were wild and miserable thoughts; but I cannot describe to you how the eternal twinkling of the stars weighed upon[5] me, and how I listened to every blast[6] of wind as if it were a dull ugly siroc[7] on its way to consume[8] me.

Morning dawned before I arrived at the village of Chamounix; I took no rest, but returned immediately to Geneva. Even in my own heart I could give no expression to my sensations — they weighed on me with a mountain's weight, and their excess destroyed my agony

---

1 encompassed: 둘러싸인.
2 half-way: 도중에 있는.
3 solemnity: 장엄함.
4 ye: 'thou'의 복수형.
5 weighed upon: 압박하다.
6 blast: 돌풍.
7 siroc: 열풍(북 아프리카에서 지중해를 거쳐 남유럽으로 몰아쳐 오는 바람).
8 consume: 다 태워버리다. 없애버리다.

beneath them. Thus I returned home, and entering the house, presented myself to the family. My haggard[1] and wild appearance awoke intense alarm; but I answered no question, scarcely did I speak. I felt as if I were placed under a ban[2] — as if I had no right to claim their sympathies — as if never more might I enjoy companionship with them. Yet even thus I loved them to adoration[3]; and to save them, I resolved to dedicate myself to my most abhorred task. The prospect of such an occupation made every other circumstance of existence pass before me like a dream; and that thought only had to me the reality of life.

CHAPTER XVIII

Day after day, week after week, passed away on my return to Geneva; and I could not collect the courage to recommence my work. I feared the vengeance of the disappointed fiend, yet I was unable to overcome my repugnance[4] to the task which was enjoined[5] me. I found that I could not compose a female without again devoting several months to profound study and laborious disquisition[6]. I had heard of some discoveries having been made by an English philosopher, the knowledge of which was material[7] to my success, and I sometimes thought of obtaining my father's consent to visit England for this purpose; but I clung to every pretence[8] of delay, and shrunk from[9] taking the

---

1 haggard: 수척한. 초췌한.
2 ban: 추방.
3 to adoration: 숭배할 정도로.
4 repugnance: 혐오감.
5 enjoined: 강요된. 요구된.
6 disquisition: 연구. 조사.
7 material: 중요한.
8 pretence: 구실. 핑계.
9 shrunk from: 피하다.

first step in an undertaking whose immediate necessity began to appear less absolute to me. A change indeed had taken place in me: my health, which had hitherto declined, was now much restored; and my spirits, when unchecked[1] by the memory of my unhappy promise, rose proportionably[2]. My father saw this change with pleasure, and he turned his thoughts towards[3] the best method of eradicating[4] the remains of my melancholy, which every now and then would return by fits[5], and with a devouring blackness overcast[6] the approaching sunshine. At these moments I took refuge in the most perfect solitude. I passed whole days on the lake alone in a little boat, watching the clouds, and listening to the rippling[7] of the waves, silent and listless[8]. But the fresh air and bright sun seldom failed to restore me to some degree of composure[9]; and, on my return, I met the salutations[10] of my friends with a readier smile and a more cheerful heart.

It was after my return from one of these rambles, that my father, calling me aside, thus addressed me:—

"I am happy to remark, my dear son, that you have resumed[11] your former pleasures, and seem to be returning to yourself. And yet you are still unhappy, and still avoid our society[12]. For some time I was lost in conjecture[13] as to the cause of this; but yesterday an idea struck me,

---

1 unchecked: 억눌림에서 풀려난.
2 proportionably: 비례하여.
3 turned his thoughts towards: …로 그의 생각을 집중하다.
4 eradicating: 근절하다.
5 by fits: 발작적으로.
6 overcast: 어둡게 하다.
7 rippling: 잔물결.
8 listless: 멍하게. 힘없이.
9 composure: 마음의 평정. 침착.
10 salutations: 인사말.
11 resumed: 다시 시작하다.
12 society: 만남. 교류.
13 lost in conjecture: 짐작하지 못하겠다는 의미.

and if it is well founded, I conjure[1] you to avow[2] it. Reserve[3] on such a point would be not only useless, but draw[4] down treble[5] misery on us all."

I trembled violently at his exordium[6], and my father continued —

"I confess, my son, that I have always looked forward to your marriage with our dear Elizabeth as the tie[7] of our domestic comfort, and the stay of my declining years[8]. You were attached to each other from your earliest infancy; you studied together, and appeared, in dispositions and tastes, entirely suited to one another. But so blind is the experience of man that what I conceived to be the best assistants to my plan may have entirely destroyed it. You, perhaps, regard her as your sister, without any wish that she might become your wife. Nay[9], you may have met with another whom you may love; and, considering yourself as bound in honour[10] to Elizabeth, this struggle may occasion the poignant[11] misery which you appear to feel."

"My dear father, reassure[12] yourself. I love my cousin tenderly and sincerely. I never saw any woman who excited, as Elizabeth does, my warmest admiration and affection. My future hopes and prospects are entirely bound up in[13] the expectation of our union."

"The expression of your sentiments of this subject, my dear Vic-

---

1 conjure: 탄원하다. 부탁하다.
2 avow: 인정하다.
3 Reserve: '(마음에) 숨김'; 즉 마음에만 담고 입 밖에 내지 않았다는 의미.
4 draw: 가져오다.
5 treble: 세배의.
6 exordium: 서두. 서설.
7 tie: 기반.
8 stay of my declining years: 내 노년(declining years)의 버팀목(stay).
9 Nay: 아니. 오히려 뿐만 아니라.
10 in honour: 도의상.
11 poignant: 통렬한.
12 reassure: 안심시키다.
13 bound up in: …와 깊이 관계하다.

tor, gives me more pleasure than I have for some time experienced. If you feel thus, we shall assuredly¹ be happy, however present events may cast a gloom over² us. But it is this gloom, which appears to have taken so strong a hold of³ your mind, that I wish to dissipate⁴. Tell me, therefore, whether you object to an immediate solemnisation⁵ of the marriage. We have been unfortunate, and recent events have drawn us from that every-day tranquillity befitting my years and infirmities⁶. You are younger; yet I do not suppose, possessed as you are of a competent⁷ fortune, that an early marriage would at all interfere with any future plans of honour and utility that you may have formed. Do not suppose, however, that I wish to dictate⁸ happiness to you, or that a delay on your part would cause me any serious uneasiness. Interpret my words with candour, and answer me, I conjure you, with confidence and sincerity."

I listened to my father in silence, and remained for some time incapable of offering any reply. I revolved rapidly in my mind a multitude of thoughts, and endeavoured to arrive at some conclusion. Alas! to me the idea of an immediate union with my Elizabeth was one of horror and dismay⁹. I was bound by a solemn promise, which I had not yet fulfilled, and dared not break; or, if I did, what manifold miseries might not impend¹⁰ over me and my devoted¹¹ family! Could I en-

---

1 assuredly: 확실히. 의심의 여지없이.

2 cast a gloom over: 어두운 그림자를(암영을) 드리우다.

3 taken so strong a hold of: …을 강하게 사로잡다(지배하다).

4 dissipate: 몰아내다.

5 solemnisation: (결혼식 등의) 엄숙한 거행.

6 infirmities: 병.

7 competent: 충분한. 상당한.

8 dictate: '지시하다'; 즉 어떻게 하면 행복해 질 수 있는지 지시를 내리지 않겠다는 의미.

9 dismay: 당황. 경악.

10 impend: 곧 일어나려 하다. 임박하다.

11 devoted: '사랑하는'. '저주받은'; 문맥상 이 단어는 이 두 가지 의미를 동시에 갖고 있다.

ter into a festival with this deadly weight yet hanging round my neck[1], and bowing me to the ground[2]. I must perform my engagement, and let the monster depart with his mate, before I allowed myself to[3] enjoy the delight of a union from which I expected peace.

I remembered also the necessity imposed upon[4] me of either journeying to England, or entering into a long correspondence with those philosophers of that country, whose knowledge and discoveries were of indispensable use to me in my present undertaking[5]. The latter method of obtaining the desired intelligence was dilatory[6] and unsatisfactory: besides, I had an insurmountable aversion[7] to the idea of engaging myself in my loathsome task in my father's house, while in habits of familiar intercourse with those I loved. I knew that a thousand fearful accidents might occur, the slightest of which would disclose a tale to thrill all connected with me with horror. I was aware also that I should often lose all self-command[8], all capacity of hiding the harrowing[9] sensations that would possess me during the progress of my unearthly[10] occupation. I must absent myself from all I loved while thus employed. Once commenced, it would quickly be achieved, and I might be restored to my family in peace and happiness. My promise fulfilled, the monster would depart forever. Or (so my fond[11] fancy imaged) some accident might meanwhile occur to destroy him,

---

1 with this deadly weight yet hanging round my neck: 코울리지의 『노수부의 노래』에서 노수부가 활로 쏴서 죽인 알바트로스는 그의 목 주위에 달라붙어 그의 저주가 풀리기 전까지는 떨어지지 않는다.
2 bowing me to the ground: 날 바닥까지 몸을 굽히게 만들면서.
3 allowed myself to: 감히 …하다. 큰마음 먹고 …하다.
4 imposed upon: …에게 부과된.
5 undertaking: 임무. 부여된 과업.
6 dilatory: 지연하는. 시간을 끄는.
7 aversion: 혐오.
8 self-command: 자제(력).
9 harrowing: 괴로운. 가슴 아픈.
10 unearthly: 섬뜩한.
11 fond: 어리석은. 바보 같은.

and put an end to my slavery for ever.

These feelings dictated my answer to my father. I expressed a wish to visit England; but concealing the true reasons of this request, I clothed my desires under a guise[1] which excited[2] no suspicion, while I urged[3] my desire with an earnestness that easily induced my father to comply. After so long a period of an absorbing[4] melancholy, that resembled madness in its intensity and effects, he was glad to find that I was capable of taking pleasure in the idea of such a journey, and he hoped that change of scene and varied amusement would, before my return, have restored me entirely to myself.

The duration of my absence was left to my own choice; a few months, or at most a year, was the period contemplated[5]. One paternal kind precaution[6] he had taken to ensure my having a companion. Without previously communicating with me, he had, in concert with[7] Elizabeth, arranged[8] that Clerval should join me at Strasburgh. This interfered with the solitude I coveted[9] for the prosecution[10] of my task; yet at the commencement of my journey the presence of my friend could in no way be an impediment[11], and truly I rejoiced that thus I should be saved many hours of lonely, maddening reflection. Nay, Henry might stand between me and the intrusion of my foe. If I were alone, would he not at times force his abhorred presence[12] on me, to

---

1 guise: 외관. 외양.
2 excited: 불러일으키다.
3 urge: 주장하다. 강조하다.
4 absorbing: 온 정신을 빼앗는.
5 contemplated: 계획된. 의도된.
6 precaution: 사전 대응책.
7 in concert with: …와 협력하여(힘을 모아).
8 arranged: …하도록 조정하다.
9 coveted: 열망하다.
10 prosecution: 실행. 수행.
11 impediment: 방해물.
12 presence: 출현.

remind me of my task, or to contemplate[1] its progress?

To England, therefore, I was bound[2], and it was understood that my union with Elizabeth should take place immediately on my return. My father's age rendered him extremely averse to delay. For myself, there was one reward I promised myself from my detested toils — one consolation for my unparalleled[3] sufferings; it was the prospect of that day when, enfranchised[4] from my miserable slavery, I might claim Elizabeth, and forget the past in my union with her.

I now made arrangements for my journey; but one feeling haunted[5] me, which filled me with fear and agitation. During my absence I should leave my friends unconscious of the existence of their enemy, and unprotected from his attacks, exasperated[6] as he might be by my departure. But he had promised to follow me wherever I might go; and would he not accompany me to England? This imagination was dreadful in itself, but soothing, inasmuch as[7] it supposed[8] the safety of my friends. I was agonised with the idea of the possibility that the reverse of this might happen. But through the whole period during which I was the slave of my creature, I allowed myself to be governed by the impulses of the moment; and my present sensations strongly intimated[9] that the fiend would follow me, and exempt[10] my family from the danger of his machinations[11].

It was in the latter end of September that I again quitted my na-

---

1 contemplate: 관찰하다.
2 bound: …로 향하여 나아가는.
3 unparalleled: 전대미문의. 미증유의.
4 enfranchised: 해방된. 자유롭게 된.
5 haunted: 떠나지 않다.
6 exasperated: 화가 난.
7 inasmuch as: 'because'의 의미.
8 supposed: 전제로 하다. 필요조건으로 하다.
9 intimated: 암시하다. 제시하다.
10 exempt: 면제하다.
11 machinations: 간계. 음모.

tive country. My journey had been my own suggestion, and Elizabeth, therefore, acquiesced[1]: but she was filled with disquiet at the idea of my suffering, away from her, the inroads[2] of misery and grief. It had been her care which provided me a companion in Clerval — and yet a man is blind to a thousand minute circumstances, which call forth a woman's sedulous[3] attention. She longed to bid me hasten my return, — a thousand conflicting emotions rendered her mute as she bade me a tearful silent farewell.

I threw myself into the carriage that was to convey me away, hardly knowing whither I was going, and careless of what was passing[4] around. I remembered only, and it was with a bitter anguish that I reflected on it, to order that my chemical instruments should be packed to go with me. Filled with dreary[5] imaginations, I passed through many beautiful and majestic scenes; but my eyes were fixed and unobserving. I could only think of the bourne[6] of my travels, and the work which was to occupy me whilst they endured.

After some days spent in listless indolence[7], during which I traversed many leagues, I arrived at Strasburgh[8], where I waited two days for Clerval. He came. Alas, how great was the contrast between us! He was alive[9] to every new scene; joyful when he saw the beauties of the setting sun, and more happy when he beheld it rise, and recommence a new day. He pointed out to me the shifting colours of the landscape, and the appearances of the sky. "This is what it is to live," he cried,

---

1 acquiesced: 받아들이다. (마지못해) 따르다.
2 inroads: 침입. 습격.
3 sedulous: 세심한. 꼼꼼한.
4 passing: (일이) 벌어지다.
5 dreary: 울적한. 비참한.
6 bourne: 목적지.
7 indolence: 아무 일도 하지 않음.
8 Strasburgh: 주요 하항(河港) 중 하나로 이들이 가는 여정은 1814년 매리와 셸리가 라인 강을 따라 내려간 경로와 일치한다.
9 alive: 민감하게 반응하는.

"now I enjoy existence! But you, my dear Frankenstein, wherefore are you desponding[1] and sorrowful!" In truth, I was occupied by gloomy thoughts, and neither saw the descent of the evening star, nor the golden sunrise reflected in the Rhine[2]. — And you, my friend, would be far more amused with the journal of Clerval, who observed the scenery with an eye of feeling and delight, than in listening to my reflections. I, a miserable wretch, haunted by a curse that shut up every avenue[3] to enjoyment.

We had agreed to descend the Rhine in a boat from Strasburgh to Rotterdam[4], whence we might take shipping[5] for London. During this voyage, we passed many willowy islands, and saw several beautiful towns. We stayed a day at Manheim[6], and, on the fifth from our departure from Strasburgh, arrived at Mayence. The course of the Rhine below Mayence[7] becomes much more picturesque[8]. The river descends rapidly, and winds between hills, not high, but steep, and of beautiful forms. We saw many ruined castles standing on the edges of precipices, surrounded by black woods, high and inaccessible. This part of the Rhine, indeed, presents a singularly variegated[9] landscape. In one spot you view rugged[10] hills, ruined castles overlooking tremendous precipices, with the dark Rhine rushing beneath; and, on the sudden turn of a promontory, flourishing vineyards[11], with green sloping banks, and

---

1 desponding: 낙담한. 기운 없는.
2 Rhine: 라인 강(독일에 있는 주요 강의 하나).
3 avenue: 접근로. 접근방법.
4 Rotterdam: 로테르담(네덜란드 남서부의 항구 도시).
5 shipping: 선박.
6 Manheim: 만하임(독일의 도시).
7 Mayence: 마인쯔(Mainz)의 프랑스 명으로 라인 강과 메인(Main) 강의 합류점에 있는 도시.
8 picturesque: 그림과 같은. 그림처럼 아름다운.
9 variegated: 다양한.
10 rugged: 바위투성이의.
11 flourishing vineyards: 포도가 주렁주렁 열린 포도밭.

a meandering[1] river, and populous towns occupy the scene.

We travelled at the time of the vintage[2], and heard the song of the labourers, as we glided[3] down the stream. Even I, depressed in mind, and my spirits continually agitated by gloomy feelings, even I was pleased. I lay at the bottom of the boat, and, as I gazed on the cloudless blue sky, I seemed to drink in a tranquillity to which I had long been a stranger. And if these were my sensations, who can describe those of Henry? He felt as if he had been transported[4] to Fairyland, and enjoyed a happiness seldom tasted by man. "I have seen," he said, "the most beautiful scenes of my own country; I have visited the lakes of Lucerne and Uri[5], where the snowy mountains descend almost perpendicularly to the water, casting black and impenetrable shades, which would cause a gloomy and mournful appearance, were it not for the most verdant islands that relieve the eye by their gay appearance; I have seen this lake agitated by a tempest, when the wind tore up whirlwinds[6] of water, and gave you an idea of what the waterspout[7] must be on the great ocean; and the waves dash[8] with fury the base of the mountain, where the priest and his mistress[9] were overwhelmed by an avalanche, and where their dying voices are still said to be heard amid the pauses of the nightly wind;[10] I have seen

---

1 meandering: 굽이쳐 흐르는.
2 vintage: 포도수확기.
3 glided: (배를 타고) 미끄러지듯 나아가다.
4 transported: '황홀경에 취하게 되다'. '운반되다'; 이 문장에서 이 단어는 이 두 가지 의미를 동시에 지니고 있다.
5 Uri: 스위스에 있는 호수.
6 whirlwinds: 회오리바람.
7 waterspout: 바다 회오리. 물기둥.
8 dash: 부딪치다.
9 mistress: 여왕. 여지배자.
10 the priest and his mistress were overwhelmed by an avalanche … said to be heard amid the pauses of the nightly wind: 매리 셸리는 유럽 여행을 다녀온 뒤 쓴 『6주간의 여행 이야기』(History of a Six Weeks' Tour, 1817)에서 어느 사제와 그의 애인에 관한 이야기를 소개하고 있는데, 그 요지는 주위의 핍박을 피해 달아난 사제와 그의 애인이

the mountains of La Valais, and the Pays de Vaud: but this country, Victor, pleases me more than all those wonders. The mountains of Switzerland are more majestic and strange; but there is a charm in the banks of this divine river, that I never before saw equalled. Look at that castle which overhangs[1] yon[2] precipice; and that also on the island, almost concealed amongst the foliage of those lovely trees; and now that group of labourers coming from among their vines; and that village half hid in the recess of the mountain. Oh, surely, the spirit that inhabits and guards this place has a soul more in harmony with man than those who pile the glacier, or retire to the inaccessible peaks of the mountains of our own country."

Clerval! beloved friend! even now it delights me to record your words, and to dwell on[3] the praise of which you are so eminently deserving. He was a being formed in the "very poetry of nature."[4] His wild and enthusiastic imagination was chastened[5] by the sensibility of his heart. His soul overflowed with ardent affections, and his friendship was of that devoted and wondrous nature that the worldly-minded teach us to look for only in the imagination. But even human sympathies were not sufficient to satisfy his eager mind. The scenery of external nature, which others regard only with admiration, he loved with ardour[6]: —

어느 오두막에서 거쳐하게 되었는데, 어느 겨울날 눈사태가 이들을 덮쳐 오두막에 있던 이들은 결국 목숨을 잃게 되었지만, 폭풍이 부는 밤이면 도와달라는 이들의 목소리가 들려온다는 것이었다.

1 overhangs: …위에 있다.
2 yon: 'yonder'의 의미; 즉 '저기'.
3 dwell on: …을 길게 논하다(강조하다).
4 He was a being formed in the "very poetry of nature.": 이 구절은 19세기 영국의 평론가이자 시인인 레이 헌트(Leigh Hunt)의 「리미니」(Limini)라는 장시에 나오는 것이다.
5 chastened: 누그러지게 되다. 순화되다.
6 ardour: 열정. 열의.

> The sounding cataract
> Haunted him like a passion: the tall rock,
> The mountain, and the deep and gloomy wood,
> Their colours and their forms, were then to him
> An appetite; a feeling, and a love,
> That had no need of a remoter charm,
> By thought supplied, or any interest
> Unborrow'd from the eye."[1]

And where does he now exist? Is this gentle and lovely being lost forever? Has this mind, so replete[2] with ideas, imaginations fanciful and magnificent, which formed a world, whose existence depended on the life of its creator;—has this mind perished? Does it now only exist in my memory? No, it is not thus; your form so divinely wrought, and beaming[3] with beauty, has decayed, but your spirit still visits and consoles your unhappy friend.

Pardon this gush of sorrow[4]; these ineffectual words are but a slight tribute[5] to the unexampled[6] worth of Henry, but they soothe my heart, overflowing with the anguish which his remembrance creates. I will proceed with my tale.

Beyond Cologne[7] we descended to the plains of Holland; and we resolved to post[8] the remainder of our way; for the wind was contrary[9], and the stream of the river was too gentle to aid us.

---

1 19세기 영국의 낭만주의 시인 윌리엄 워즈워드(William Wordsworth)가 쓴 「틴턴 수 도원」(Tintern Abbey)의 77-84행; sounding cataract은 '큰 소리를 내며 떨어지는 폭 포'라는 의미.
2 replete: 가득 찬. 충만한.
3 beaming: 빛을 발하는.
4 gush of sorrow: 솟구치는 슬픔.
5 tribute: 찬사. 칭찬.
6 unexampled: 유례(전례)없는.
7 Cologne: 쾰른(독일의 라인 강변에 있는 도시).
8 post: 파발마(馬)로 여행하다.
9 contrary: (진행방향과) 반대로 부는.

Our journey here lost the interest arising from beautiful scenery; but we arrived in a few days at Rotterdam,[1] whence we proceeded by sea to England. It was on a clear morning, in the latter days of December, that I first saw the white cliffs of Britain[2]. The banks of the Thames presented a new scene; they were flat, but fertile, and almost every town was marked by the remembrance of some story. We saw Tilbury Fort[3], and remembered the Spanish armada[4]; Gravesend,[5] Woolwich,[6] and Greenwich, places which I had heard of even in my country.

At length we saw the numerous steeples of London, St. Paul's towering above all, and the Tower[7] famed in English history.

CHAPTER XIX

London was our present point of rest; we determined to remain several months in this wonderful and celebrated city. Clerval desired the intercourse of the men of genius and talent who flourished at this time[8]; but this was with me a secondary object; I was principally occupied with the means of obtaining the information necessary for the completion of my promise, and quickly availed myself of[9] the letters

---

1 Rotterdam: 로테르담(네덜란드 남서부의 항구 도시).

2 I first saw the white cliffs of Britain: 처음으로 볼 수 있는 영국 해협은 도버(Dover) 해협이다.

3 Tilbury Fort: '틸버리 요새'; 스페인과의 전쟁 시 바다로부터의 공격에서 런던을 보호하기 위해 만든 요새.

4 Spanish armada: 1588년 영국 침략을 꾀했다가 격멸된 스페인 함대로 일명 무적함대라고 불리곤 하였다.

5 Gravesend: 그레이브젠드(템스강 하구의 우안에 위치한 하항(河港))

6 Woolwich: 울위치(대런던(Greater London) 남동부의 한 지구의 옛 수도구).

7 Tower: '런던 타워'(London Tower)를 지칭.

8 men of genius and talent who flourished at this time: 매리 셸리는 이 당시 유명하였던 영국의 사상가 예술가들을 의미하고 있는데 그 중에서도 영국 낭만주의의 사상적 기반을 제공하며 당대 사상가로서도 이름을 널리 알렸던 그녀의 아버지 고드윈을 염두에 두고 있는 듯하다.

9 availed myself of: …을 이용하다.

of introduction that I had brought with me, addressed to the most distinguished natural philosophers.

If this journey had taken place during my days of study and happiness, it would have afforded me inexpressible pleasure. But a blight[1] had come over my existence, and I only visited these people for the sake of the information they might give me on the subject in which my interest[2] was so terribly profound[3]. Company[4] was irksome to me; when alone, I could fill my mind with the sights of heaven and earth; the voice of Henry soothed me, and I could thus cheat myself into a transitory[5] peace. But busy uninteresting joyous faces brought back despair to my heart. I saw an insurmountable barrier placed between me and my fellow-men; this barrier was sealed[6] with the blood of William and Justine; and to reflect on the events connected with those names filled my soul with anguish.

But in Clerval I saw the image of my former self[7]; he was inquisitive, and anxious to gain experience and instruction. The difference of manners which he observed was to him an inexhaustible source of instruction and amusement. He was also pursuing an object he had long had in view[8]. His design[9] was to visit India, in the belief that he had in his knowledge of its various languages, and in the views he

---

1 blight: (앞날의) 어두운 그림자.

2 interest: 이해관계. 사리(私利).

3 profound: …에 뿌리 깊이 근거를 둔(in).

4 Company: 사람들과의 만남(회합).

5 transitory: 일시적인.

6 sealed: 확고히 되다.

7 in Clerval I saw the image of my former self: 클러밸의 낭만주의 시인같은 모습은 프랑켄스타인이 괴물을 창조하던 시기 이전의 모습과 비슷하다. 허나 이 구절은 워즈워드의「틴턴 수도원」의 117-121행의 구절과 유사하다. "My dear, dear Freind … in thy voice I catch / The language of my former heart, and read / My former pleasures … what I was once."

8 had in view: 목표로 삼다.

9 design: 구상. 의도. 목적.

had taken of its society, the means of materially[1] assisting the progress
of European colonisation and trade[2]. In Britain only could he further
the execution of his plan. He was for ever busy; and the only check[3]
to his enjoyments was my sorrowful and dejected[4] mind. I tried to
conceal this as much as possible, that I might not debar[5] him from the
pleasures natural to one who was entering on a new scene of life[6], undisturbed by any care or bitter recollection. I often refused to accompany him, alleging[7] another engagement, that I might remain alone. I
now also began to collect the materials necessary for my new creation,
and this was to me like the torture of single drops of water continually falling on the head. Every thought that was devoted to it was an
extreme anguish, and every word that I spoke in allusion to[8] it caused
my lips to quiver, and my heart to palpitate[9].

After passing some months in London, we received a letter from a
person in Scotland, who had formerly been our visitor at Geneva. He
mentioned the beauties of his native country, and asked us if those
were not sufficient allurements[10] to induce us to prolong our journey
as far north as Perth[11], where he resided. Clerval eagerly desired to accept this invitation; and I, although I abhorred society, wished to view
again mountains and streams, and all the wondrous works with which
Nature adorns her chosen dwelling-places.

---

1 materially: 실질적으로. 구체적으로.
2 assisting the progress of European colonisation and trade: 클러밸은 유럽문명의 우
   월성을 당연시하고 동양을 서양의 문명을 통해 개화시켜야 할 대상으로 보고 있다. 이
   점에서 그는 제국주의적인 신념을 갖고 있다고도 볼 수 있다.
3 check: 방해. 저지.
4 dejected: 기운 없는. 의기소침한.
5 debar: 방해하다. 금하다.
6 entering on a new scene of life: 새로운 삶(의 환경)으로 진입하다.
7 alleging: (변명으로) 내세우다. 거짓 구실을 내세우다.
8 in allusion to: 암암리에 …을 가리켜.
9 palpitate: (가슴이) 뛰다.
10 allurements: 유혹(물).
11 Perth: 퍼스(스코틀랜드의 중심부에 있는 도시).

We had arrived in England at the beginning of October[1], and it was now February. We accordingly determined to commence our journey towards the north at the expiration of another month. In this expedition[2] we did not intend to follow the great road to Edinburgh[3], but to visit Windsor, Oxford, Matlock, and the Cumberland[4] lakes, resolving[5] to arrive at the completion of this tour about the end of July. I packed up my chemical instruments, and the materials I had collected, resolving to finish my labours in some obscure nook[6] in the northern highlands[7] of Scotland.

We quitted London on the 27th of March, and remained a few days at Windsor, rambling in its beautiful forest. This was a new scene to us mountaineers; the majestic oaks, the quantity of game[8], and the herds of stately deer, were all novelties[9] to us.

From thence we proceeded to Oxford. As we entered this city, our minds were filled with the remembrance of the events that had been transacted[10] there more than a century and a half before. It was here that Charles I[11] had collected his forces. This city had remained faith-

---

1   had arrived in England at the beginning of October: 프랑켄스타인은 전 장(chap-ter)에서 영국에 12월 하반기에 도착하였다고 말하였으므로 이 말은 시간상 모순이 된다.

2   expedition: 긴 여행.

3   Edinburgh: 에든버러(스코틀랜드의 수도).

4   Windsor, Oxford, Matlock … and Cumberland: 윈저(런던 서부의 도시); 매틀록 (Matlock)은 영국 잉글랜드에 있는 더비셔카운티(Derbyshire county)의 카운티타운 (county town); 컴벌랜드(이전의 잉글랜드 북서부의 주(州)).

5   resolving: 결심하다.

6   nook: 외진 곳. 벽지(僻地).

7   highlands: 스코틀랜드 북부의 고지.

8   game: 사냥감.

9   novelties: 색다른 것(일). 새로운 경험.

10   transacted: (사건이) 벌어지다.

11   It was here that Charles I: 찰스 1세(1625-1649)는 권리청원이 제출되자, 의회를 해산하고 11년간 의회를 소집하지 않았다. 그러다 스코틀랜드의 반란처리 비용을 충당하기 위해 의회를 소집하였다가 의회와 대립하여 결국 이로 인해 확대된 크롬웰(Cromwell)이 이끄는 청교도 혁명으로 인해 처형당하였다. 청교도들과의 싸움 당시 찰스 1세는 옥

ful to him, after the whole nation had forsaken his cause[1] to join the standard[2] of parliament and liberty. The memory of that unfortunate king, and his companions, the amiable Falkland[3], the insolent Goring[4], his queen, and son, gave a peculiar interest to every part of the city, which they might be supposed to have inhabited. The spirit of elder days[5] found a dwelling here, and we delighted to trace its footsteps. If these feelings had not found an imaginary gratification, the appearance of the city had yet in itself sufficient beauty to obtain our admiration. The colleges are ancient and picturesque; the streets are almost magnificent; and the lovely Isis[6], which flows beside it through meadows of exquisite verdure, is spread forth into a placid expanse of waters[7], which reflects its majestic assemblage of towers, and spires[8], and domes, embosomed[9] among aged trees.

I enjoyed this scene; and yet my enjoyment was embittered both by the memory of the past, and the anticipation of the future. I was formed for peaceful happiness. During my youthful days discontent never visited my mind; and if I was ever overcome by ennui[10], the sight of what is beautiful in nature, or the study of what is excellent

---

스퍼드에 기지를 치며 전쟁을 치렀다.

1 forsaken his cause: '그의 뜻을 저버리다'; 즉, 찰스 1세에 대한 지지를 철회하였다는 의미.

2 standard: 기치. 주의.

3 Falkland: 1st Viscount Falkland (c. 1575- 1633)를 지칭; 찰스 1세의 고문 중 한 사람 이었던 그는 1643년 전쟁에서 죽음을 맞이한다. 메리 셸리의 부친 윌리엄 고드윈은 자 신의 정치적 견해를 담은 『캐럽 윌리엄즈』(Caleb Williams)라는 소설에서 주요 등장인 물에게 포클랜드라는 이름을 부여하였다.

4 Goring: 찰스 1세의 휘하에 있던 장군 중 하나로 크롬웰이 이끄는 세력에게 찰스 1세 의 계획을 알려주었다. 여기서 매리는 절대 왕정을 표방하였던 찰스 1세에 대한 동정심 을 표방하고 그를 파멸로 이끈 세력에 대해 비우호적으로 생각하고 있는 것 같다.

5 elder days: 과거.

6 Isis: 옥스퍼드에서 부르는 템즈 강의 이름.

7 expanse of waters: 광활한 강.

8 spires: 뾰족탑.

9 embosomed: (감싸듯) 둘러싸인.

10 ennui: 권태.

and sublime in the productions of man, could always interest[1] my heart, and communicate elasticity[2] to my spirits. But I am a blasted[3] tree; the bolt has entered my soul; and I felt then that I should survive to exhibit, what I shall soon cease to be — a miserable spectacle of wrecked humanity[4], pitiable to others, and intolerable to myself.

We passed a considerable period at Oxford, rambling among its environs, and endeavouring to identify every spot which might relate to the most animating epoch of English history. Our little voyages of discovery were often prolonged by the successive objects that presented themselves. We visited the tomb of the illustrious Hampden[5], and the field on which that patriot fell. For a moment my soul was elevated from its debasing and miserable fears, to contemplate the divine ideas of liberty and self-sacrifice, of which these sights[6] were the monuments and the remembrancers[7]. For an instant I dared to shake off my chains, and look around me with a free and lofty spirit; but the iron had eaten into my flesh[8], and I sank again, trembling and hopeless, into my miserable self.

We left Oxford with regret, and proceeded to Matlock, which was our next place of rest. The country in the neighbourhood of this village resembled, to a greater degree, the scenery of Switzerland; but everything is on a lower scale[9], and the green hills want the crown of distant white Alps, which always attend[10] on the piny mountains of

---

1   interest: 관심을 끌다.

2   elasticity: 명랑. 쾌활.

3   blasted: 시든. 해를 입은.

4   miserable spectacle of wrecked humanity: 파멸한 인간의 비참한 모습.

5   Hampden: 햄던(1594-1643); 의회주의자이며 크롬웰의 지지지로 옥스퍼드 근처에서 벌어진 전투에서 사망했다.

6   sights: 명소. 명승지.

7   remembrancers: 생각나게 하는 것. 기념물.

8   iron had eaten into my flesh: 족쇄(iron)가 내 살 속까지 파고들었다.

9   on a lower scale: 소규모로.

10   attend: 동반하다. 같이 있다.

my native country. We visited the wondrous cave, and the little cabinets[1] of natural history, where the curiosities[2] are disposed in the same manner as in the collections at Servox and Chamounix. The latter name made me tremble when pronounced by Henry; and I hastened to quit Matlock, with which that terrible scene was thus associated.

From Derby, still journeying northward, we passed two months in Cumberland and Westmorland[3]. I could now almost fancy myself among the Swiss mountains. The little patches of snow which yet lingered[4] on the northern sides of the mountains, the lakes, and the dashing of the rocky streams, were all familiar and dear sights to me. Here also we made some acquaintances, who almost contrived[5] to cheat me into happiness. The delight of Clerval was proportionably greater than mine; his mind expanded in the company of men of talent[6], and he found in his own nature greater capacities and resources than he could have imagined himself to have possessed while he associated with his inferiors. "I could pass my life here," said he to me; "and among these mountains I should scarcely regret[7] Switzerland and the Rhine."

But he found that a traveller's life is one that includes much pain amidst its enjoyments. His feelings are forever on the stretch[8]; and when he begins to sink into repose[9], he finds himself obliged to quit

---

1 cabinets: 작은 방. (박물관의) 소 진열실.
2 curiosities: 진기한 물건,
3 Westmorland: 웨스트몰랜드(잉글랜드 북서부의 옛 주).
4 lingered: 남아 있다.
5 contrived: 노력하다.
6 men of talent: 구(舊)컴벌랜드 남부와 구(舊)웨스트몰랜드 서부에 걸쳐 있는 레이크 디스트릭트(Lake District)에는 여러 개의 빙하호가 경관을 이루고 있어 '호반의 시인' 으로 널리 알려진 19세기 낭만주의 시인인 윌리엄 워즈워스(William Wordsworth), 코 울리지가 몹시 좋아하였던 곳이다. 따라서 여기서 말하는 '재능 있는 사람들'(men of talent)은 이들 낭만주의 시인들을 간접적으로 지칭하고 있는 듯하다.
7 regret: 아쉬워하다. 그리워하다.
8 on the stretch: 긴밀히 활동하는.
9 repose: 휴식.

that on which he rests in pleasure for something new, which again engages[1] his attention, and which also he forsakes for other novelties.

We had scarcely visited the various lakes of Cumberland and Westmorland, and conceived an affection for some of the inhabitants, when the period of our appointment with our Scotch friend approached, and we left them to travel on. For my own part I was not sorry. I had now neglected my promise for some time, and I feared the effects of the dæmon's disappointment. He might remain in Switzerland, and wreak his vengeance on[2] my relatives. This idea pursued me, and tormented me at every moment from which I might otherwise have snatched repose[3] and peace. I waited for my letters with feverish impatience: if they were delayed, I was miserable, and overcome by a thousand fears; and when they arrived and I saw the superscription[4] of Elizabeth or my father, I hardly dared to read and ascertain[5] my fate. Sometimes I thought that the fiend followed me, and might expedite my remissness[6] by murdering my companion. When these thoughts possessed me, I would not quit Henry for a moment, but followed him as his shadow, to protect him from the fancied rage of his destroyer. I felt as if I had committed some great crime, the consciousness of which haunted me. I was guiltless, but I had indeed drawn down a horrible curse upon my head, as mortal as that of crime.

I visited Edinburgh with languid[7] eyes and mind; and yet that city might have interested the most unfortunate being. Clerval did not like it so well as Oxford: for the antiquity of the latter city was more pleasing to him. But the beauty and regularity of the new town of

---

1   engages: (주의를) 끌다.
2   wreak his vengeance on: …에게 복수를 하다.
3   snatched repose: 가까스로(틈틈이) 쉬다.
4   superscription: 수신인의 이름과 주소를 쓰는 것.
5   ascertain: 확인하다.
6   expedite my remissness: '태만함'(remissness)에서 벗어나 일을 빨리 하도록 '재촉하다'(expedite)는 의미.
7   languid: 기력이 없는.

Edinburgh, its romantic castle, and its environs, the most delightful in the world, Arthur's Seat[1], St. Bernard's Well[2], and the Pentland Hills[3], compensated him for the change, and filled him with cheerfulness and admiration. But I was impatient to arrive at the termination[4] of my journey.

We left Edinburgh in a week, passing through Coupar, St. Andrew's, and along the banks of the Tay, to Perth, where our friend expected us. But I was in no mood to laugh and talk with strangers, or enter into their feelings[5] or plans with the good humour expected from a guest; and accordingly I told Clerval that I wished to make the tour of Scotland alone. "Do you," said I, "enjoy yourself, and let this be our rendezvous[6]. I may be absent a month or two; but do not interfere with my motions, I entreat you: leave me to peace and solitude for a short time; and when I return, I hope it will be with a lighter heart, more congenial[7] to your own temper."

Henry wished to dissuade me; but seeing me bent on[8] this plan, ceased to remonstrate[9]. He entreated me to write often. "I had rather be with you," he said, "in your solitary rambles, than with these Scotch people, whom I do not know: hasten, then, my dear friend, to return, that I may again feel myself somewhat at home, which I cannot do in your absence."

---

1 Arthur's Seat: 아서(Arthur)는 5세기 말에서 6세기 초에 살며(혹은 전설상의) 색슨족에 저항하였던 영국의 왕; seat는 '중심지', '근거지'의 의미.
2 St. Bernard's Well: 에든버러(Edinburgh) 스톡브리지(Stockbridge) 근방에 있는 우물로 이곳 광천수는 의학적인 효능이 있는 것으로 알려졌다.
3 Pentland Hills: 에든버러의 남서쪽으로 이어진 구릉 지대로 그 길이는 20마일 정도에 다다른다.
4 termination: 끝.
5 enter into their feelings: 그들과 공감하다.
6 rendezvous: (약속으로 정한) 회합 장소.
7 congenial: 적합한. 어울리는.
8 bent on: …을 하겠다고 결심히 확고한.
9 remonstrate: 이의를 제기하다. 항의하다.

Having parted from my friend, I determined to visit some remote spot of Scotland, and finish my work in solitude. I did not doubt but that the monster followed me, and would discover himself[1] to me when I should have finished, that he might receive his companion.

With this resolution I traversed the northern highlands, and fixed on one of the remotest of the Orkneys[2] as the scene of my labours. It was a place fitted for such a work, being hardly more than a rock, whose high sides were continually beaten upon by the waves. The soil was barren, scarcely affording pasture[3] for a few miserable cows, and oatmeal for its inhabitants, which consisted of five persons, whose gaunt[4] and scraggy[5] limbs gave tokens of[6] their miserable fare. Vegetables and bread, when they indulged in such luxuries, and even fresh water, was to be procured from the mainland, which was about five miles distant.

On the whole island there were but three miserable huts, and one of these was vacant when I arrived. This I hired[7]. It contained but two rooms, and these exhibited all the squalidness[8] of the most miserable penury[9]. The thatch[10] had fallen in[11], the walls were unplastered[12], and the door was off its hinges[13]. I ordered it to be repaired, bought some furniture, and took possession; an incident which would, doubtless

---

1 discover himself: 자신의 모습을 드러내다.
2 Orkneys: 스코틀랜드 북쪽 해안 근처에 위치한 섬.
3 pasture: 목초지.
4 gaunt: 야윈.
5 scraggy: 말라빠진. 빈약한.
6 gave tokens of: …을 알려주다(나타내다).
7 hired: 임대하다.
8 squalidness: 비참함.
9 penury: 빈곤.
10 thatch: 초가지붕.
11 fallen in: 내려(주저)앉다.
12 unplastered: 모르타르를 바르지 않은.
13 off its hinges: 돌쩌귀가 빠진.

have occasioned some surprise, had not all the senses of the cottagers been benumbed[1] by want and squalid poverty. As it was, I lived un-gazed at and unmolested[2], hardly thanked for the pittance of food and clothes which I gave; so much does suffering blunt[3] even the coarsest sensations of men.

In this retreat I devoted the morning to labour; but in the evening, when the weather permitted, I walked on the stony beach of the sea, to listen to the waves as they roared and dashed at my feet. It was a monotonous yet ever-changing scene. I thought of Switzerland; it was far different from this desolate and appalling landscape. Its hills are covered with vines, and its cottages are scattered thickly in the plains. Its fair lakes reflect a blue and gentle sky; and when troubled[4] by the winds, their tumult is but as the play of a lively infant, when com-pared to the roarings of the giant ocean.

In this manner I distributed[5] my occupations when I first arrived; but, as I proceeded in my labour, it became every day more horrible and irksome to me. Sometimes I could not prevail on myself to[6] enter my laboratory for several days; and at other times I toiled day and night in order to complete my work. It was, indeed, a filthy[7] process in which I was engaged. During my first experiment, a kind of enthu-siastic frenzy[8] had blinded me to the horror of my employment; my mind was intently fixed on the consummation of my labour, and my eyes were shut to the horror of my proceedings. But now I went to it in cold blood[9], and my heart often sickened at the work of my hands.

---

1 benumbed: 무감각하게 된.
2 unmolested: 간섭받지 않은 채.
3 blunt: 무디게 하다. 둔감하게 하다.
4 troubled: 물결이 일다.
5 distributed: 나누다. 분배하다.
6 prevail on myself to: 나 자신을 타일러 …하도록 하다.
7 filthy: 몹시 싫은.
8 frenzy: 흥분.
9 in cold blood: 아무 열의 없이.

Thus situated, employed in the most detestable occupation, immersed[1] in a solitude where nothing could for an instant call my attention from the actual scene in which I was engaged, my spirits became unequal[2]; I grew restless[3] and nervous. Every moment I feared to meet my persecutor[4]. Sometimes I sat with my eyes fixed on the ground, fearing to raise them, lest they should encounter the object which I so much dreaded to behold. I feared to wander from the sight of my fellow-creatures, lest when alone he should come to claim his companion.

In the meantime I worked on, and my labour was already considerably advanced. I looked towards its completion with a tremulous and eager hope, which I dared not trust myself to question, but which was intermixed with obscure forebodings[5] of evil, that made my heart sicken in my bosom.

CHAPTER XX

I sat one evening in my laboratory; the sun had set, and the moon was just rising from the sea; I had not sufficient light for my employment[6], and I remained idle[7], in a pause of consideration of whether I should leave my labour for the night, or hasten its conclusion by an unremitting[8] attention to it. As I sat, a train of reflection occurred to me, which led me to consider the effects of what I was now doing.

---

1 immersed in: …에 몰두하여(깊이 빠져).
2 unequal: 한결같지 않은.
3 restless: 침착하지 못한.
4 persecutor: 박해자. 학대자.
5 obscure forebodings: 분명치 않은 예감. 전조(forebodings).
6 employment: 일.
7 idle: 아무 일도 하지 않는.
8 unremitting: 멈추지 않는.

Three years before I was engaged in the same manner, and had created a fiend whose unparalleled barbarity had desolated[1] my heart, and filled it for ever with the bitterest remorse[2]. I was now about to form another being, of whose dispositions I was alike[3] ignorant; she might become ten thousand times more malignant than her mate, and delight, for its own sake, in murder and wretchedness[4]. He had sworn to quit the neighbourhood of man, and hide himself in deserts; but she had not; and she, who in all probability[5] was to become a thinking and reasoning animal, might refuse to comply with a compact[6] made before her creation. They might even hate each other; the creature who already lived loathed his own deformity, and might he not conceive a greater abhorrence for it when it came before his eyes in the female form? She also might turn with disgust from him to the superior beauty of man; she might quit him, and he be again alone, exasperated[7] by the fresh provocation[8] of being deserted by one of his own species.

Even if they were to leave Europe, and inhabit the deserts of the new world, yet one of the first results of those sympathies for which the dæmon thirsted would be children, and a race of devils would be propagated[9] upon the earth who might make the very existence of the species of man a condition precarious[10] and full of terror. Had I right, for my own benefit, to inflict[11] this curse upon everlasting generations?

---

1 desolated: 망연자실하게 만들다(devastate).
2 remorse: 후회. 양심의 가책.
3 alike: (이번에도) 마찬가지로.
4 wretchedness: 비열함. 비열한 행동.
5 in all probability: 십중팔구는.
6 compact: 계약. 맹약.
7 exasperated: 격양되어서.
8 provocation: 도발. 자극적인(화나게 하는) 일.
9 propagated: 번식되다.
10 precarious: 불안정한. 불안(不安)한.
11 inflict: (저주를) 내리다.

I had before been moved by the sophisms[1] of the being I had created; I had been struck senseless[2] by his fiendish threats: but now, for the first time, the wickedness of my promise burst upon[3] me; I shuddered to think that future ages might curse me as their pest, whose selfishness had not hesitated to buy its own peace at the price, perhaps, of the existence of the whole human race.

I trembled, and my heart failed within me; when, on looking up, I saw, by the light of the moon, the dæmon at the casement[4]. A ghastly[5] grin wrinkled his lips as he gazed on me, where I sat fulfilling the task which he had allotted to me. Yes, he had followed me in my travels; he had loitered in forests, hid himself in caves, or taken refuge in wide and desert heaths[6]; and he now came to mark my progress, and claim the fulfillment of my promise.

As I looked on him, his countenance expressed the utmost extent of malice and treachery. I thought with a sensation of madness on my promise of creating another like to him, and trembling with passion, tore to pieces the thing on which I was engaged. The wretch saw me destroy the creature on whose future existence he depended for happiness, and, with a howl of devilish despair and revenge, withdrew.

I left the room, and, locking the door, made a solemn vow in my own heart never to resume my labours; and then, with trembling steps, I sought my own apartment. I was alone; none were near me to dissipate the gloom, and relieve me from the sickening oppression of the most terrible reveries[7].

Several hours passed, and I remained near my window gazing on

---

1 sophisms: 궤변.
2 had been struck senseless: 놀라서 분별을 잃었다.
3 burst upon: 엄습하다.
4 casement: 두 짝 여닫이 창.
5 ghastly: 소름끼치는. 무시무시한.
6 heaths: 히스가 무성한 황야.
7 reveries: 공상. 몽상.

the sea; it was almost motionless, for the winds were hushed, and all nature reposed under the eye of the quiet moon. A few fishing vessels alone specked[1] the water, and now and then the gentle breeze wafted[2] the sound of voices, as the fishermen called to one another. I felt the silence, although I was hardly conscious of its extreme profundity, until my ear was suddenly arrested[3] by the paddling[4] of oars near the shore, and a person landed close to my house.

In a few minutes after, I heard the creaking[5] of my door, as if some one endeavoured to open it softly. I trembled from head to foot; I felt a presentiment[6] of who it was, and wished to rouse one of the peasants who dwelt in a cottage not far from mine; but I was overcome by the sensation of helplessness, so often felt in frightful dreams, when you in vain endeavour to fly from an impending danger, and was rooted to the spot[7].

Presently I heard the sound of footsteps along the passage; the door opened, and the wretch whom I dreaded appeared. Shutting the door, he approached me and said, in a smothered voice[8] —

"You have destroyed the work which you began; what is it that you intend? Do you dare to break your promise? I have endured toil and misery: I left Switzerland with you; I crept along the shores of the Rhine, among its willow islands, and over the summits of its hills. I have dwelt many months in the heaths of England, and among the deserts of Scotland. I have endured incalculable[9] fatigue, and cold, and hunger; do you dare destroy my hopes?"

---

1 specked: …에 점점이 위치해 있다.
2 wafted: 가볍게 실어 나르다.
3 arrested: …에 사로잡히다.
4 paddling: 노 젓는 소리.
5 creaking: (문이) 삐걱거리는 소리.
6 presentiment: (불길한) 예감.
7 rooted to the spot: 꼼짝 못하고 그 자리에 머문다.
8 in a smothered voice: 감정을 억누른 목소리로.
9 incalculable: 헤아릴 수 없는. 엄청난.

"Begone! I do break my promise; never will I create another like yourself, equal in deformity and wickedness."

"Slave, I before reasoned with you, but you have proved yourself unworthy of my condescension[1]. Remember that I have power; you believe yourself miserable, but I can make you so wretched that the light of day will be hateful to you. You are my creator, but I am your master; — obey!"

"The hour of my irresolution[2] is past, and the period of your power is arrived. Your threats cannot move me to do an act of wickedness; but they confirm me in a determination of not creating you a companion in vice[3]. Shall I, in cool blood, set loose upon the earth a dæmon whose delight is in death and wretchedness? Begone! I am firm, and your words will only exasperate my rage."

The monster saw my determination in my face, and gnashed his teeth in the impotence of anger. "Shall each man," cried he, "find a wife for his bosom, and each beast have his mate, and I be alone? I had feelings of affection, and they were requited[4] by detestation and scorn. Man! you may hate; but beware! your hours will pass in dread and misery, and soon the bolt will fall which must ravish[5] from you your happiness forever. Are you to be happy while I grovel[6] in the intensity of my wretchedness? You can blast my other passions; but revenge remains — revenge, henceforth dearer than light or food! I may die; but first you, my tyrant and tormentor, shall curse the sun that gazes on your misery. Beware; for I am fearless, and therefore power-

---

1 condescension: '지체를 낮추기'; 즉 아랫사람에게 자신을 낮추어 동등하게 상대해 주었다는 의미. 괴물은 자신이 프랑켄스타인의 피조물이지만 힘에 있어서는 프랑켄스타인 보다 우월하다며 이렇게 말하고 있는 것이다.

2 irresolution: 우유부단. 망설임.

3 companion in vice: 악행을 같이 하는 동반자.

4 requited: 처벌받다.

5 ravish: 앗아가다.

6 grovel: 넙죽 엎드리며 지내다. 비굴하게 살다.

ful. I will watch with the wiliness[1] of a snake, that I may sting with its venom. Man, you shall repent of the injuries you inflict."

"Devil, cease; and do not poison the air with these sounds of malice. I have declared my resolution to you, and I am no coward to bend[2] beneath words. Leave me; I am inexorable[3]."

"It is well. I go; but remember, I shall be with you on your wedding-night."

I started forward, and exclaimed, "Villain! before you sign my death-warrant[4], be sure that you are yourself safe."

I would have seized him; but he eluded me, and quitted the house with precipitation[5]. In a few moments I saw him in his boat, which shot across the waters with an arrowy swiftness[6], and was soon lost amidst the waves.

All was again silent; but his words rung in my ears. I burned with rage to pursue the murderer of my peace and precipitate him into the ocean. I walked up and down my room hastily and perturbed[7], while my imagination conjured up a thousand images to torment and sting me. Why had I not followed him, and closed with him in mortal strife? But I had suffered him to depart, and he had directed his course towards the main land. I shuddered to think who might be the next victim sacrificed to his insatiate[8] revenge. And then I thought again of his words — "I will be with you on your wedding-night." That then was the period fixed for the fulfillment of my destiny. In that hour I should die, and at once satisfy and extinguish his malice[9].

---

1 wiliness: 간교함. 교활함.

2 bend: 굴복하다.

3 inexorable: (간청을) 들어주지 않는.

4 death-warrant: 사형집행 영장.

5 with precipitation: 부랴부랴. 재빨리.

6 with an arrowy swiftness: 화살처럼 빠르게.

7 perturbed: 마음이 어지러운(혼란스러운).

8 insatiate: 만족을 모르는.

9 malice: 적의(敵意). 원한.

The prospect did not move me to fear; yet when I thought of my be-loved Elizabeth, — of her tears and endless sorrow, when she should find her lover so barbarously snatched from her, — tears, the first I had shed for many months, streamed from my eyes, and I resolved not to fall before my enemy without a bitter struggle.

The night passed away, and the sun rose from the ocean; my feel-ings became calmer, if it may be called calmness, when the violence of rage sinks into the depths of despair. I left the house, the horrid scene of the last night's contention[1], and walked on the beach of the sea, which I almost regarded as an insuperable[2] barrier between me and my fellow-creatures; nay, a wish that such should prove the fact stole across me. I desired that I might pass my life on that barren rock, wearily, it is true, but uninterrupted by any sudden shock of misery. If I returned, it was to be sacrificed, or to see those whom I most loved die under the grasp of a dæmon whom I had myself created.

I walked about the isle like a restless spectre, separated from all it loved, and miserable in the separation. When it became noon, and the sun rose higher, I lay down on the grass, and was overpowered by a deep sleep. I had been awake the whole of the preceding night, my nerves were agitated, and my eyes inflamed by watching and misery. The sleep into which I now sank refreshed me; and when I awoke, I again felt as if I belonged to a race of human beings like myself, and I began to reflect upon what had passed with greater composure; yet still the words of the fiend rung in my ears like a death-knell[3]; they appeared like a dream, yet distinct and oppressive as a reality.

The sun had far descended, and I still sat on the shore, satisfying my appetite, which had become ravenous[4], with an oaten cake, when I saw a fishing-boat land close to me, and one of the men brought

---

1 contention: 싸움. 말다툼.

2 insuperable: 극복할 수 없는.

3 death-knell: 장례식 때 울리는 종소리.

4 ravenous: (식욕이) 몹시 왕성한.

me a packet[1]; it contained letters from Geneva, and one from Clerval, entreating me to join him. He said that he was wearing away[2] his time fruitlessly where he was; that letters from the friends he had formed in London desired his return to complete the negotiation they had entered into for his Indian enterprise. He could not any longer delay his departure; but as his journey to London might be followed, even sooner than he now conjectured, by his longer voyage, he entreated me to bestow as much of my society on him as I could spare. He besought me, therefore, to leave my solitary isle, and to meet him at Perth, that we might proceed southwards together. This letter in a degree recalled me to life[3], and I determined to quit my island at the expiration of two days.

Yet, before I departed, there was a task to perform, on which I shuddered to reflect: I must pack up my chemical instruments; and for that purpose I must enter the room which had been the scene of my odious work, and I must handle those utensils[4], the sight of which was sickening to me. The next morning, at daybreak, I summoned sufficient courage, and unlocked the door of my laboratory. The remains of the half-finished creature, whom I had destroyed, lay scattered on the floor, and I almost felt as if I had mangled[5] the living flesh of a human being. I paused to collect myself[6], and then entered the chamber. With trembling hand I conveyed the instruments out of the room; but I reflected that I ought not to leave the relics[7] of my work to excite the horror and suspicion of the peasants; and I accordingly put them into a basket, with a great quantity of stones, and, lay-

---

1 packet: 한 묶음. 한 다발.
2 wearing away: (시간을) 빈둥빈둥 보내다.
3 recalled me to life: 나를 소생시켰다.
4 utensils: 기구. 도구.
5 mangled: 토막토막 베다. 난도질하다.
6 collect myself: 마음을 가라앉히다.
7 relics: 잔여물.

ing them up, determined to throw them into the sea that very night; and in the meantime I sat upon the beach, employed in cleaning and arranging my chemical apparatus[1].

Nothing could be more complete than the alteration that had taken place in my feelings since the night of the appearance of the dæmon. I had before regarded my promise with a gloomy despair, as a thing that, with whatever consequences, must be fulfilled; but I now felt as if a film had been taken from before my eyes, and that I, for the first time, saw clearly. The idea of renewing my labours did not for one instant occur to me; the threat I had heard weighed on my thoughts, but I did not reflect that a voluntary act of mine could avert it. I had resolved in my own mind, that to create another like the fiend I had first made would be an act of the basest and most atrocious[2] selfishness; and I banished from my mind every thought that could lead to a different conclusion.

Between two and three in the morning the moon rose; and I then, putting my basket aboard a little skiff[3], sailed out about four miles from the shore. The scene was perfectly solitary: a few boats were returning towards land, but I sailed away from them. I felt as if I was about the commission[4] of a dreadful crime, and avoided with shuddering anxiety any encounter with my fellow-creatures. At one time the moon, which had before been clear, was suddenly overspread[5] by a thick cloud, and I took advantage of the moment of darkness, and cast my basket into the sea: I listened to the gurgling sound[6] as it sunk, and then sailed away from the spot. The sky became clouded; but the air was pure, although chilled by the north-east breeze that

---

1 chemical apparatus: 화학 기계.
2 atrocious: 극악무도한.
3 skiff: 작은 배. 작은 범선.
4 commission: 죄를 저지름.
5 overspread: …으로 뒤덮인.
6 gurgling sound: (물이 차서) 꼴깍꼴깍하는 소리.

was then rising. But it refreshed me, and filled me with such agreeable sensations, that I resolved to prolong my stay on the water; and fixing the rudder[1] in a direct position, stretched myself at the bottom of the boat. Clouds hid the moon, everything was obscure, and I heard only the sound of the boat, as its keel[2] cut through the waves; the murmur[3] lulled me, and in a short time I slept soundly.

I do not know how long I remained in this situation, but when I awoke I found that the sun had already mounted considerably. The wind was high, and the waves continually threatened the safety of my little skiff. I found that the wind was north-east, and must have driven me far from the coast from which I had embarked[4]. I endeavoured to change my course, but quickly found that, if I again made the attempt, the boat would be instantly filled with water. Thus situated, my only resource was to drive before the wind[5]. I confess that I felt a few sensations of terror. I had no compass with me, and was so slenderly[6] acquainted with the geography of this part of the world, that the sun was of little benefit to me. I might be driven into the wide Atlantic, and feel all the tortures of starvation, or be swallowed up in the immeasurable waters that roared and buffeted[7] around me. I had already been out many hours, and felt the torment of a burning thirst, a prelude to[8] my other sufferings. I looked on the heavens, which were covered by clouds that flew before the wind, only to be replaced by others: I looked upon the sea, it was to be my grave. "Fiend," I exclaimed, "your task is already fulfilled!" I thought of Elizabeth, of my father,

---

1 rudder: (배의) 키.

2 keel: (배의) 용골(龍骨).

3 murmur: 낮고 불분명하게 계속되는 소리의 의미로 여기서는 배의 용골에 파도가 부딪힐 때 나는 소리를 지칭한다.

4 embarked: 배를 타다.

5 before the wind: 바람을 따라서.

6 slenderly: 조금. 약간.

7 buffeted: (파도가) 몰아치다(밀려들다).

8 prelude to: …에 대한 서곡.

and of Clerval; all left behind, on whom the monster might satisfy his sanguinary and merciless passions. This idea plunged me into a reverie, so despairing and frightful, that even now, when the scene is on the point of closing before me for ever, I shudder to reflect on it.

Some hours passed thus; but by degrees, as the sun declined towards the horizon, the wind died away into a gentle breeze, and the sea became free from breakers[1]. But these gave place to a heavy swell[2]: I felt sick, and hardly able to hold the rudder, when suddenly I saw a line of high land towards the south.

Almost spent[3], as I was, by fatigue, and the dreadful suspense I endured for several hours, this sudden certainty of life rushed like a flood of warm joy to my heart, and tears gushed[4] from my eyes.

How mutable[5] are our feelings, and how strange is that clinging love we have of life even in the excess of misery! I constructed another sail with a part of my dress, and eagerly steered[6] my course towards the land. It had a wild and rocky appearance: but as I approached nearer, I easily perceived the traces of cultivation. I saw vessels near the shore, and found myself suddenly transported back to the neighbourhood of civilised man. I carefully traced the windings[7] of the land, and hailed a steeple which I at length saw issuing from behind a small promontory. As I was in a state of extreme debility[8], I resolved to sail directly towards the town, as a place where I could most easily procure nourishment. Fortunately I had money with me. As I turned the promontory, I perceived a small neat[9] town and a good harbour,

---

1 breakers: (해안·암초 따위의) 부서지는 파도.
2 swell: 큰 파도. 놀.
3 spent: 기진맥진한.
4 gushed: 솟구쳐 나오다.
5 mutable: 변화무쌍한.
6 steered: 조종하다.
7 windings: 굴곡. 꾸불꾸불 한 지역.
8 debility: 약함. 쇠약.
9 neat: 아담하고 깨끗한.

which I entered, my heart bounding[1] with joy at my unexpected escape.

As I was occupied in fixing the boat and arranging the sails, several people crowded towards the spot. They seemed much surprised at my appearance; but instead of offering me any assistance, whispered together with gestures that at any other time might have produced in me a slight sensation of alarm. As it was, I merely remarked that they spoke English; and I therefore addressed them in that language: "My good friends," said I, "will you be so kind as to tell me the name of this town, and inform me where I am?"

"You will know that soon enough," replied a man with a hoarse voice. "May be you are come to a place that will not prove much to your taste[2]; but you will not be consulted as to your quarters[3], I promise you."

I was exceedingly surprised on receiving so rude an answer from a stranger; and I was also disconcerted[4] on perceiving the frowning and angry countenances of his companions. "Why do you answer me so roughly?" I replied; "surely it is not the custom of Englishmen to receive strangers so inhospitably[5]."

"I do not know," said the man, "what the custom of the English may be; but it is the custom of the Irish to hate villains."

While this strange dialogue continued, I perceived the crowd rapidly increase. Their faces expressed a mixture of curiosity and anger, which annoyed, and in some degree alarmed me. I inquired the way to the inn; but no one replied. I then moved forward, and a murmuring sound arose from the crowd as they followed and surrounded me;

---

1 bounding: (가슴이) 뛰다.

2 will not prove much to your taste: '당신 취향에 맞지 않을 것이다'; 즉 싫어하게 될 것이다란 의미.

3 quarters: 숙소. 거처.

4 disconcerted: 당황한.

5 inhospitably: 불친절하게.

when an ill-looking man approaching, tapped me on the shoulder, and said, "Come, sir, you must follow me to Mr. Kirwin's, to give an account of yourself."

"Who is Mr. Kirwin? Why am I to give an account of myself? Is not this a free country?"

"Ay, sir, free enough for honest folks. Mr. Kirwin is a magistrate; and you are to give an account of the death of a gentleman who was found murdered here last night."

This answer startled[1] me; but I presently recovered myself. I was innocent; that could easily be proved: accordingly I followed my conductor in silence, and was led to one of the best houses in the town. I was ready to sink from fatigue and hunger; but, being surrounded by a crowd, I thought it politic[2] to rouse all my strength, that no physical debility might be construed[3] into apprehension[4] or conscious guilt. Little did I then expect the calamity[5] that was in a few moments to overwhelm me, and extinguish in horror and despair all fear of ignominy or death.

I must pause here; for it requires all my fortitude[6] to recall the memory of the frightful events which I am about to relate, in proper detail, to my recollection.

CHAPTER XXI

I was soon introduced into the presence of the magistrate, an old benevolent man, with calm and mild manners. He looked upon me,

---

1 startled: 놀라게 하다.
2 politic: 현명한.
3 construed: …으로 해석되다(into).
4 apprehension: 염려. 불안.
5 calamity: 재앙. 불행. 비운(悲運).
6 fortitude: 강인한 정신.

however, with some degree of severity[1]: and then, turning towards my conductors, he asked who appeared as witnesses on this occasion.

About half a dozen men came forward; and one being selected by the magistrate, he deposed[2] that he had been out fishing the night before with his son and brother-in-law, Daniel Nugent, when, about ten o' clock, they observed a strong northerly blast rising, and they accordingly put in for[3] port. It was a very dark night, as the moon had not yet risen; they did not land at the harbour, but, as they had been accustomed, at a creek[4] about two miles below. He walked on first, carrying a part of the fishing tackle[5], and his companions followed him at some distance. As he was proceeding along the sands, he struck his foot against something, and fell at his length[6] on the ground. His companions came up to assist him; and, by the light of their lantern, they found that he had fallen on the body of a man who was to all appearance[7] dead. Their first supposition was that it was the corpse of some person who had been drowned, and was thrown on shore by the waves; but on examination, they found that the clothes were not wet, and even that the body was not then cold. They instantly carried it to the cottage of an old woman near the spot, and endeavoured, but in vain, to restore it to life. It appeared to be a handsome young man, about five and twenty years of age. He had apparently been strangled; for there was no sign of any violence, except the black mark of fingers on his neck.

The first part of this deposition[8] did not in the least interest me;

---

1 severity: 엄격. 엄중.
2 deposed: 선서 증언하다.
3 put in for: 기항하다.
4 creek: (해안 · 강기슭 등의) 후미. 작은 항구.
5 fishing tackle: 낚시 도구.
6 at his length: 길게 누워.
7 to all appearance: 아무리 보아도. 어느 모로 보나.
8 deposition: 선서 증언.

but when the mark of the fingers was mentioned, I remembered the murder of my brother, and felt myself extremely agitated; my limbs trembled, and a mist came over my eyes[1], which obliged me to lean on a chair for support. The magistrate observed me with a keen eye, and of course drew an unfavourable augury[2] from my manner.

The son confirmed his father's account: but when Daniel Nugent was called, he swore positively that, just before the fall of his companion, he saw a boat, with a single man in it, at a short distance from the shore; and, as far as he could judge by the light of a few stars, it was the same boat in which I had just landed.

A woman deposed that she lived near the beach, and was standing at the door of her cottage, waiting for the return of the fishermen, about an hour before she heard of the discovery of the body, when she saw a boat, with only one man in it, push off from that part of the shore where the corpse was afterwards found.

Another woman confirmed the account of the fishermen having brought the body into her house; it was not cold. They put it into a bed, and rubbed it; and Daniel went to the town for an apothecary[3], but life was quite gone.

Several other men were examined concerning my landing; and they agreed that, with the strong north wind that had arisen during the night, it was very probable that I had beaten about[4] for many hours, and had been obliged to return nearly to the same spot from which I had departed. Besides, they observed that it appeared that I had brought the body from another place, and it was likely that, as I did not appear to know the shore, I might have put into[5] the harbour ignorant of the distance of the town of — from the place where I had

---

1 mist came over my eyes: 내 시야가 흐려졌다는 의미.
2 augury: 징조.
3 apothecary: 약제사.
4 beaten about: 바람을 거슬러 나아가다.
5 put into: …에 입항하다.

deposited[1] the corpse.

Mr. Kirwin, on hearing this evidence, desired that I should be taken into the room where the body lay for interment[2], that it might be observed what effect the sight of it would produce upon me. This idea was probably suggested by the extreme agitation I had exhibited when the mode of the murder had been described. I was accordingly conducted, by the magistrate and several other persons, to the inn. I could not help being struck by the strange coincidences that had taken place during this eventful night; but, knowing that I had been conversing with several persons in the island I had inhabited about the time that the body had been found, I was perfectly tranquil as to the consequences of the affair.

I entered the room where the corpse lay, and was led up to the coffin. How can I describe my sensations on beholding it? I feel yet parched[3] with horror, nor can I reflect on that terrible moment without shuddering and agony. The examination, the presence of the magistrate and witnesses, passed like a dream from my memory, when I saw the lifeless form of Henry Clerval stretched before me. I gasped for breath[4]; and, throwing myself on the body, I exclaimed, "Have my murderous machinations deprived you also, my dearest Henry, of life? Two I have already destroyed; other victims await their destiny: but you, Clerval, my friend, my benefactor — "

The human frame could no longer support the agonies that I endured, and I was carried out of the room in strong convulsions[5].

A fever succeeded to this. I lay for two months on the point of death[6]: my ravings, as I afterwards heard, were frightful; I called my-

---

1 deposited: 내려놓다.
2 interment: 매장(burial).
3 parched: 목(입술)이 마른.
4 gasped for breath: 숨이 차다.
5 in strong convulsions: 강한 경련을 일으키며.
6 on the point of death: 죽음의 경계에 있는. 사경을 헤매는.

self the murderer of William, of Justine, and of Clerval. Sometimes I entreated my attendants to assist me in the destruction of the fiend by whom I was tormented; and at others I felt the fingers of the monster already grasping my neck, and screamed aloud with agony and terror. Fortunately, as I spoke my native language, Mr. Kirwin alone understood me; but my gestures and bitter cries were sufficient to affright[1] the other witnesses.

Why did I not die? More miserable than man ever was before, why did I not sink into forgetfulness and rest? Death snatches away many blooming children, the only hopes of their doating parents: how many brides and youthful lovers have been one day in the bloom of health and hope, and the next a prey for worms and the decay of the tomb! Of what materials was I made, that I could thus resist so many shocks, which, like the turning of the wheel, continually renewed the torture?

But I was doomed to live; and, in two months, found myself as awaking from a dream, in a prison, stretched on a wretched bed, surrounded by gaolers[2], turnkeys[3], bolts, and all the miserable apparatus of a dungeon. It was morning, I remember, when I thus awoke to understanding: I had forgotten the particulars of what had happened, and only felt as if some great misfortune had suddenly overwhelmed me; but when I looked around, and saw the barred windows, and the squalidness[4] of the room in which I was, all flashed[5] across my memory, and I groaned bitterly.

This sound disturbed an old woman who was sleeping in a chair beside me. She was a hired nurse, the wife of one of the turnkeys, and her countenance expressed all those bad qualities which often characterise

---

1 affright: 놀라게 하다.
2 gaolers: 교도관.
3 turnkeys: 감옥을 지키는 사람.
4 squalidness: 지저분함.
5 flashed: 섬광처럼 스쳐가다.

that class. The lines of her face were hard and rude, like that of persons accustomed to see without sympathising in sights of misery. Her tone expressed her entire indifference; she addressed me in English, and the voice struck me as one that I had heard during my sufferings: —

"Are you better now, sir?" said she.

I replied in the same language, with a feeble[1] voice, "I believe I am; but if it be all true, if indeed I did not dream, I am sorry that I am still alive to feel this misery and horror."

"For that matter," replied the old woman, "if you mean about the gentleman you murdered, I believe that it were better for you if you were dead, for I fancy it will go hard with you! However, that's none of my business; I am sent to nurse you, and get you well; I do my duty with a safe conscience[2]; it were well if everybody did the same."

I turned with loathing[3] from the woman who could utter so un-feeling a speech to a person just saved, on the very edge of death[4]; but I felt languid, and unable to reflect on all that had passed. The whole series of my life appeared to me as a dream; I sometimes doubted if indeed it were all true, for it never presented itself to my mind with the force of reality.

As the images that floated before me became more distinct, I grew feverish; a darkness pressed[5] around me: no one was near me who soothed me with the gentle voice of love; no dear hand supported me. The physician came and prescribed[6] medicines, and the old woman prepared them for me; but utter carelessness was visible in the first, and the expression of brutality was strongly marked in the visage[7] of

---

1 feeble: 힘없는. 약한.
2 with a safe conscience: 안전하게.
3 loathing: 혐오감.
4 on the very edge of death: 죽음의 문턱에 있던.
5 pressed: 밀어닥치다.
6 prescribed: 처방하다.
7 visage: 얼굴.

the second. Who could be interested in the fate of a murderer, but the hangman who would gain his fee?

These were my first reflections; but I soon learned that Mr. Kirwin had shown me extreme kindness. He had caused the best room in the prison to be prepared for me (wretched indeed was the best); and it was he who had provided a physician and a nurse. It is true, he seldom came to see me; for although he ardently desired to relieve the sufferings of every human creature, he did not wish to be present at the agonies and miserable ravings of a murderer. He came, therefore, sometimes to see that I was not neglected; but his visits were short, and with long intervals.

One day, while I was gradually recovering, I was seated in a chair, my eyes half open, and my cheeks livid like those in death. I was overcome by gloom and misery, and often reflected I had better seek death than desire to remain in a world which to me was replete with wretchedness. At one time I considered whether I should not declare myself guilty, and suffer the penalty of the law, less innocent than poor Justine had been. Such were my thoughts when the door of my apartment was opened and Mr. Kirwin entered. His countenance expressed sympathy and compassion; he drew a chair close to mine and addressed me in French —

"I fear that this place is very shocking to you; can I do anything to make you more comfortable?"

"I thank you; but all that you mention is nothing to me: on the whole earth there is no comfort which I am capable of receiving."

"I know that the sympathy of a stranger can be but of little relief[1] to one borne down[2] as you are by so strange a misfortune. But you will, I hope, soon quit this melancholy abode[3]; for, doubtless, evidence can easily be brought to free you from the criminal charge."

---

1   of little relief: 별 위로가 되지 않는.
2   borne down: 압도당한.
3   abode: 거처.

"That is my least concern: I am, by a course of strange events, become the most miserable of mortals. Persecuted and tortured as I am and have been, can death be any evil to me?"

"Nothing indeed could be more unfortunate and agonising than the strange chances that have lately occurred. You were thrown, by some surprising accident, on this shore renowned for its hospitality, seized immediately, and charged with murder. The first sight that was presented to your eyes was the body of your friend, murdered in so unaccountable[1] a manner, and placed, as it were, by some fiend across your path."

As Mr. Kirwin said this, notwithstanding the agitation I endured on this retrospect[2] of my sufferings, I also felt considerable surprise at the knowledge he seemed to possess concerning me. I suppose some astonishment was exhibited in my countenance; for Mr. Kirwin hastened to say —

"Immediately upon your being taken ill[3], all the papers that were on your person were brought me, and I examined them that I might discover some trace by which I could send to your relations[4] an account of your misfortune and illness. I found several letters, and, among others, one which I discovered from its commencement to be from your father. I instantly wrote to Geneva: nearly two months have elapsed since the departure of my letter. — But you are ill; even now you tremble: you are unfit for agitation of any kind."

"This suspense is a thousand times worse than the most horrible event: tell me what new scene of death has been acted, and whose murder I am now to lament?"

"Your family is perfectly well," said Mr. Kirwin with gentleness; "and some one, a friend, is come to visit you."

---

1 unaccountable: 설명할 수 없는. 이상한.
2 retrospect: 회고. 회상.
3 taken ill: 병에 걸린.
4 relations: 친척.

I know not by what chain of thought the idea presented itself, but it instantly darted into my mind that the murderer had come to mock at my misery, and taunt[1] me with the death of Clerval, as a new incitement[2] for me to comply with his hellish desires. I put my hand before my eyes, and cried out in agony — "Oh! take him away! I cannot see him; for God's sake, do not let him enter!"

Mr. Kirwin regarded me with a troubled countenance. He could not help regarding my exclamation as a presumption[3] of my guilt, and said, in rather a severe tone —

"I should have thought, young man, that the presence of your father would have been welcome instead of inspiring such violent repugnance[4]."

"My father!" cried I, while every feature and every muscle was relaxed from anguish to pleasure: "is my father indeed come? How kind, how very kind! But where is he, why does he not hasten to me?"

My change of manner surprised and pleased the magistrate; perhaps he thought that my former exclamation was a momentary return of delirium[5], and now he instantly resumed his former benevolence. He rose and quitted the room with my nurse, and in a moment my father entered it.

Nothing, at this moment, could have given me greater pleasure than the arrival of my father. I stretched out my hand to him and cried — "Are you then safe — and Elizabeth — and Ernest?"

My father calmed me with assurances of their welfare, and endeavoured, by dwelling on these subjects so interesting to my heart, to raise my desponding spirits; but he soon felt that a prison cannot be

---

1 taunt: 조롱하다.
2 incitement: 동기.
3 presumption: 추정의 근거.
4 repugnance: 강한 반감.
5 delirium: 정신착란.

the abode of cheerfulness. "What a place is this that you inhabit, my son!" said he, looking mournfully at the barred windows and wretched appearance of the room. "You travelled to seek happiness, but a fatality[1] seems to pursue you. And poor Clerval—"

The name of my unfortunate and murdered friend was an agitation too great to be endured in my weak state; I shed tears.

"Alas! yes, my father," replied I; "some destiny of the most horrible kind hangs over me, and I must live to fulfil it, or surely I should have died on the coffin of Henry."

We were not allowed to converse for any length of time, for the precarious state of my health rendered every precaution necessary that could ensure[2] tranquillity. Mr. Kirwin came in and insisted that my strength should not be exhausted by too much exertion. But the appearance of my father was to me like that of my good angel, and I gradually recovered my health.

As my sickness quitted me, I was absorbed by a gloomy and black melancholy that nothing could dissipate. The image of Clerval was for ever before me, ghastly and murdered. More than once the agitation into which these reflections threw me made my friends dread a dangerous relapse[3]. Alas! why did they preserve so miserable and detested a life? It was surely that I might fulfil my destiny, which is now drawing to a close. Soon, oh! very soon, will death extinguish these throbbings[4], and relieve me from the mighty weight of anguish that bears me to the dust; and, in executing the award[5] of justice, I shall also sink to rest. Then the appearance of death was distant although the wish was ever present to my thoughts; and I often sat for hours motionless and speechless, wishing for some mighty revolution that might bury

---

1 fatality: 참사. 죽음. 불행.
2 ensure: 확보하다.
3 relapse: (병의) 재발.
4 throbbings: 심장박동.
5 award: 심사. 판정.

me and my destroyer in its ruins.

The season of the assizes[1] approached. I had already been three months in prison; and although I was still weak, and in continual danger of a relapse, I was obliged to travel nearly a hundred miles to the country-town where the court was held. Mr. Kirwin charged himself with[2] every care of collecting witnesses and arranging my defence. I was spared the disgrace of appearing publicly as a criminal, as the case was not brought before the court that decides on life and death. The grand jury[3] rejected the bill[4] on its being proved that I was on the Orkney Islands at the hour the body of my friend was found; and a fortnight after my removal I was liberated from prison.

My father was enraptured on finding me freed from the vexations[5] of a criminal charge, that I was again allowed to breathe the fresh atmosphere, and permitted to return to my native country. I did not participate in these feelings; for to me the walls of a dungeon or a palace were alike hateful. The cup of life was poisoned for ever[6]; and although the sun shone upon me as upon the happy and gay of heart, I saw around me nothing but a dense and frightful darkness, penetrated by no light but the glimmer of two eyes that glared[7] upon me. Sometimes they were the expressive eyes of Henry languishing[8] in death, the dark orbs nearly covered by the lids, and the long black lashes that fringed them; sometimes it was the watery, clouded eyes of the monster as I first saw them in my chamber at Ingolstadt.

My father tried to awaken in me the feelings of affection. He talk-

---

1　assizes: 순회재판.
2　charged himself with: 스스로 …을 떠맡다. …의 책임을 맡다.
3　grand jury: 대배심.
4　bill: 기소장.
5　vexations: 고통의 원인. 짜증스런 일.
6　The cup of life was poisoned for ever: 인생에서 즐거움을 찾지 못하고 고통만 느끼게 되었다는 의미.
7　glared: 노려보다.
8　languishing: 괴로워하다. 번민하다.

ed of Geneva, which I should soon visit — of Elizabeth and Ernest; but these words only drew deep groans from me. Sometimes, indeed, I felt a wish for happiness; and thought, with melancholy delight, of my beloved cousin; or longed, with a devouring[1] maladie du pays[2], to see once more the blue lake and rapid Rhone that had been so dear to me in early childhood: but my general state of feeling was a torpor[3] in which a prison was as welcome a residence as the divinest scene in nature; and these fits were seldom interrupted but by paroxysms[4] of anguish and despair. At these moments I often endeavoured to put an end to the existence I loathed; and it required unceasing attendance and vigilance[5] to restrain me from committing some dreadful act of violence.

Yet one duty remained to me, the recollection of which finally triumphed over my selfish despair. It was necessary that I should return without delay to Geneva, there to watch over the lives of those I so fondly loved; and to lie in wait for[6] the murderer, that if any chance led me to the place of his concealment, or if he dared again to blast me by his presence, I might, with unfailing aim[7], put an end to the existence of the monstrous Image which I had endued with the mockery of a soul[8] still more monstrous. My father still desired to delay our departure, fearful that I could not sustain the fatigues of a journey: for I was a shattered wreck[9] — the shadow of a human being[10]. My strength

---

1 devouring: 괴롭히는.
2 maladie du pays: (불어) 향수(鄕愁).
3 torpor: 무감각. 무감동.
4 paroxysms: 발작. (감정 등의) 격발.
5 vigilance: 경계. 감시.
6 lie in wait for: …을 숨어서 기다리다.
7 with unfailing aim: 겨냥이 빗나가지 않고.
8 mockery of a soul: '흉내 낸 영혼'; 즉 프랑켄스타인은 자신이 괴물에게 부여한 것은 진정한 영혼이 아니라 흉내 낸 가짜 영혼에 불과하다고 말하고 있는 것이다.
9 shattered wreck: 몸이 엉망이 된 상태의 사람을 의미.
10 shadow of a human being: shadow는 '이름뿐인 것'; 즉 이름뿐인 인간.

was gone. I was a mere skeleton; and fever night and day preyed upon my wasted frame[1].

Still, as I urged our leaving Ireland with such inquietude[2] and impatience, my father thought it best to yield. We took our passage on board a vessel bound for Havre-de-Grace, and sailed with a fair wind[3] from the Irish shores. It was midnight. I lay on the deck looking at the stars and listening to the dashing of the waves. I hailed[4] the darkness that shut Ireland from my sight; and my pulse beat with a feverish joy when I reflected that I should soon see Geneva. The past appeared to me in the light of a frightful dream; yet the vessel in which I was, the wind that blew me from the detested shore of Ireland, and the sea which surrounded me, told me too forcibly that I was deceived by no vision, and that Clerval, my friend and dearest companion, had fallen a victim to me and the monster of my creation. I repassed[5], in my memory, my whole life; my quiet happiness while residing with my family in Geneva, the death of my mother, and my departure for Ingolstadt. I remembered, shuddering, the mad enthusiasm that hurried me on to the creation of my hideous enemy, and I called to mind[6] the night in which he first lived. I was unable to pursue the train of thought; a thousand feelings pressed upon me, and I wept bitterly.

Ever since my recovery from the fever I had been in the custom of taking every night a small quantity of laudanum[7], for it was by means of this drug only that I was enabled to gain the rest necessary for the preservation of life. Oppressed by the recollection of my various misfortunes, I now swallowed double my usual quantity and soon

---

1 wasted frame: 쇠약해진 몸.
2 inquietude: 불안. 동요.
3 fair wind: 순풍.
4 hailed: 반가이 맞이하다.
5 repassed: 다시 경험하다.
6 called to mind: 떠올리다. 상기하다.
7 laudanum: 안정제로 사용되던 것으로 알코올에 녹인 아편이다.

slept profoundly. But sleep did not afford me respite from thought and misery; my dreams presented a thousand objects that scared me. Towards morning I was possessed by a kind of nightmare[1]; I felt the fiend's grasp in my neck, and could not free myself from it; groans and cries rung in my ears. My father, who was watching over me, perceiving my restlessness, awoke me; the dashing waves were around: the cloudy sky above; the fiend was not here: a sense of security, a feeling that a truce[2] was established between the present hour and the irresistible, disastrous future, imparted to me a kind of calm forgetfulness, of which the human mind is by its structure peculiarly susceptible[3].

CHAPTER XXII

The voyage came to an end. We landed and proceeded to Paris. I soon found that I had overtaxed[4] my strength, and that I must repose before I could continue my journey. My father's care and attentions were indefatigable[5]; but he did not know the origin of my sufferings, and sought erroneous methods to remedy the incurable ill. He wished me to seek amusement in society[6]. I abhorred the face of man. Oh, not abhorred! they were my brethren, my fellow beings, and I felt attracted even to the most repulsive[7] among them as to creatures of an angelic nature and celestial mechanism. But I felt that I had no right

---

1 nightmare: '악몽'이라는 뜻의 이 단어는 어원적으로 볼 때 '잠자는 동안 공격하는 사악한 영혼'이란 의미다. 프랑켄스타인이 악몽을 꾼 다음날 악마가 자신의 목을 조였다고 생각하는 것은 이런 맥락에서 이해될 수 있다.

2 truce: 정전(휴전) 협정.

3 susceptible: 빠져들기 쉬운.

4 overtaxed: 지나치게 사용하다.

5 indefatigable: 지칠 줄 모르는.

6 in society: 사람들과의 만남을 통해서.

7 repulsive: 혐오스런.

to share their intercourse. I had unchained an enemy among them, whose joy it was to shed their blood and to revel in[1] their groans. How they would, each and all[2], abhor me, and hunt me from the world, did they know my unhallowed acts and the crimes which had their source[3] in me!

My father yielded at length to my desire to avoid society, and strove by various arguments to banish my despair. Sometimes he thought that I felt deeply the degradation[4] of being obliged to answer a charge of murder, and he endeavoured to prove to me the futility of pride.

"Alas! my father," said I, "how little do you know me. Human beings, their feelings and passions, would indeed be degraded if such a wretch as I felt pride.

Justine, poor unhappy Justine, was as innocent as I, and she suffered the same charge; she died for it; and I am the cause of this—I murdered her. William, Justine, and Henry—they all died by my hands."

My father had often, during my imprisonment, heard me make the same assertion; when I thus accused myself he sometimes seemed to desire an explanation, and at others he appeared to consider it as the offspring[5] of delirium, and that, during my illness, some idea of this kind had presented itself to my imagination, the remembrance of which I preserved in my convalescence[6]. I avoided explanation, and maintained a continual silence concerning the wretch I had created. I had a persuasion[7] that I should be supposed mad; and this in itself would for ever have chained my tongue. But, besides, I could

1 revel in: …을 한껏 즐기다.
2 each and all: 각자 모두.
3 source: 근원(지).
4 degradation: 체면손상.
5 offspring: 소산(fruit). 결과물.
6 convalescence: (병의) 회복.
7 persuasion: 확신.

not bring myself to[1] disclose a secret which would fill my hearer with consternation[2], and make fear and unnatural horror the inmates[3] of his breast. I checked, therefore, my impatient thirst for sympathy, and was silent when I would have given the world to have confided[4] the fatal secret. Yet, still, words like those I have recorded would burst uncontrollably from me. I could offer no explanation of them; but their truth in part relieved the burden of my mysterious woe.

Upon this occasion my father said, with an expression of unbounded wonder, "My dearest Victor, what infatuation[5] is this? My dear son, I entreat you never to make such an assertion again."

"I am not mad," I cried energetically; "the sun and the heavens, who have viewed my operations, can bear witness of[6] my truth. I am the assassin of those most innocent victims; they died by my machinations[7]. A thousand times would I have shed my own blood, drop by drop, to have saved their lives; but I could not, my father, indeed I could not sacrifice the whole human race."

The conclusion of this speech convinced my father that my ideas were deranged[8], and he instantly changed the subject of our conversation and endeavoured to alter the course of my thoughts. He wished as much as possible to obliterate the memory of the scenes that had taken place in Ireland, and never alluded to[9] them, or suffered[10] me to speak of my misfortunes.

As time passed away I became more calm: misery had her dwell-

---

1 could not bring myself to: 도저히 …할 수가 없었다.
2 consternation: 당혹(감).
3 inmates: 내재해 있는 존재.
4 confided: 비밀을 털어놓다.
5 infatuation: 제정신이 아님. 비정상적인 정신상태.
6 bear witness of: …을 입증하다(…의 증인이 되다).
7 machinations: 간계. 음모.
8 deranged: 혼란된. 제정신이 아닌.
9 alluded to: …에 대해 언급하다(암시하다).
10 suffered: 허용하다(allow).

ing in my heart, but I no longer talked in the same incoherent manner of my own crimes; sufficient for me was the consciousness of them. By the utmost self-violence[1], I curbed[2] the imperious[3] voice of wretchedness, which sometimes desired to declare itself to the whole world; and my manners were calmer and more composed than they had ever been since my journey to the sea of ice.[4]

A few days before we left Paris on our way to Switzerland, I received the following letter from Elizabeth: —

"MY DEAR FRIEND,

It gave me the greatest pleasure to receive a letter from my uncle dated at Paris; you are no longer at a formidable[5] distance, and I may hope to see you in less than a fortnight. My poor cousin, how much you must have suffered! I expect to see you looking even more ill than when you quitted Geneva. This winter has been passed most miserably, tortured as I have been by anxious suspense[6]; yet I hope to see peace in your countenance, and to find that your heart is not totally void of comfort and tranquillity.

"Yet I fear that the same feelings now exist that made you so miserable a year ago, even perhaps augmented by time. I would not disturb you at this period when so many misfortunes weigh upon you; but a conversation that I had with my uncle previous to his departure renders some explanation necessary before we meet.

"Explanation! you may possibly say; what can Elizabeth have to explain? If you really say this, my questions are answered, and all my

---

1 self-violence: 스스로에 대한 억압.
2 curbed: 억제하다. 구속하다.
3 imperious: 요구하는.
4 sea of ice: 프랑켄스타인이 괴물과 만나는 몽블랑에서 내려온 빙하를 지칭한다.
5 formidable: 엄청난.
6 suspense: 걱정. 불안.

doubts satisfied[1]. But you are distant from me, and it is possible that you may dread, and yet be pleased with this explanation; and, in a probability of this being the case, I dare not any longer postpone writing what, during your absence, I have often wished to express to you, but have never had the courage to begin.

"You well know, Victor, that our union had been the favourite plan of your parents ever since our infancy. We were told this when young, and taught to look forward to it as an event that would certainly take place. We were affectionate playfellows during childhood, and, I believe, dear and valued friends to one another as we grew older. But as brother and sister often entertain[2] a lively affection towards each other without desiring a more intimate union, may not such also be our case? Tell me, dearest Victor. Answer me, I conjure[3] you, by our mutual happiness, with simple truth — Do you not love another?

"You have travelled; you have spent several years of your life at Ingolstadt; and I confess to you, my friend, that when I saw you last autumn so unhappy, flying to solitude, from the society of every creature, I could not help supposing that you might regret our connection, and believe yourself bound in honour to fulfil the wishes of your parents although they opposed themselves to your inclinations. But this is false reasoning. I confess to you, my friend, that I love you, and that in my airy[4] dreams of futurity you have been my constant friend and companion. But it is your happiness I desire as well as my own when I declare to you that our marriage would render me eternally miserable unless it were the dictate of your own free choice[5]. Even now I weep to

---

1 satisfied: 의심을 풀다.

2 entertain: (감정을) 품다(가지다).

3 conjure: 간청(기원)하다.

4 airy: 허황된. 공상적인.

5 dictate of your own free choice: dictate는 (양심· 이성의) '명령', '지시'; 즉 자신의 자유로운 선택에 의한 것이란 의미.

think that, borne down[1] as you are by the cruellest misfortunes, you may stifle[2], by the word honour, all hope of that love and happiness which would alone restore you to yourself. I, who have so disinterested an affection for you, may increase your miseries tenfold by being an obstacle to your wishes. Ah! Victor, be assured that[3] your cousin and playmate has too sincere a love for you not to be made miserable by this supposition. Be happy, my friend; and if you obey me in this one request, remain satisfied that nothing on earth will have the power to interrupt my tranquillity.

"Do not let this letter disturb you; do not answer tomorrow, or the next day, or even until you come, if it will give you pain. My uncle will send me news of your health; and if I see but one smile on your lips when we meet, occasioned by this or any other exertion of mine, I shall need no other happiness.

"ELIZABETH LAVENZA
GENEVA, May 18th, 17 — ."

This letter revived in my memory what I had before forgotten, the threat of the fiend — "I will be with you on your wedding-night!" Such was my sentence[4], and on that night would the dæmon employ every art[5] to destroy me, and tear me from the glimpse of happiness which promised partly to console my sufferings. On that night he had determined to consummate[6] his crimes by my death. Well, be it so; a deadly struggle would then assuredly take place, in which if he were victorious I should be at peace, and his power over me be at an end.

---

1 borne down: 압도당한(꺾인).
2 stifle: 억누르다.
3 be assured that: ···라는 것에 대해선 확신하라.
4 sentence: 선고.
5 art: 간계. 계략.
6 consummate: 성취(완성)하다.

If he were vanquished[1], I should be a free man. Alas! what freedom? such as the peasant enjoys when his family have been massacred before his eyes, his cottage burnt, his lands laid waste[2], and he is turned adrift[3], homeless, penniless, and alone, but free. Such would be my liberty except that in my Elizabeth I possessed a treasure; alas! balanced by those horrors of remorse and guilt which would pursue me until death.

Sweet and beloved Elizabeth! I read and re-read her letter and some softened feelings stole into[4] my heart and dared to whisper paradisiacal dreams of love and joy; but the apple was already eaten, and the angel's arm bared to drive me from all hope[5]. Yet I would die to make her happy. If the monster executed his threat, death was inevitable; yet, again, I considered whether my marriage would hasten my fate. My destruction might indeed arrive a few months sooner; but if my torturer should suspect that I postponed it influenced by his menaces he would surely find other, and perhaps more dreadful, means of revenge. He had vowed to be with me on my wedding-night, yet he did not consider that threat as binding him to peace in the meantime[6]; for as if to show me that he was not yet satiated with blood, he had murdered Clerval immediately after the enunciation[7] of his threats. I resolved, therefore, that if my immediate union with my cousin would conduce[8] either to hers or my father's happiness, my adversary's designs against my life[9]

---

1 vanquished: 패배시키다.

2 laid waste: 황폐화시키다.

3 turned adrift: 떠돌아다니게 되다. 방황하다.

4 stole into: 어느새 엄습하다(스며들다).

5 apple was already eaten, and the angel's arm bared to drive me from all hope: 사과를 먹었다는 말은 금지된 열매를 먹은 아담과 이브를 떠올리게 하며, 천사가 모든 희망으로부터 나를 쫓아내기 위해 팔을 걷어 부쳤다는 구절은 밀튼의 『실낙원』의 한 장면과 유사하다; 여기서 금지된 열매(사과)를 이미 먹었단 의미는 프랑켄스타인이 생명창조라는 인간에게는 금지된 일을 한 사실을 암시한다.

6 in the meantime: 그 동안에.

7 enunciation: 선언.

8 conduce: 도움이 되다. 이바지하다(to).

9 designs against my life: 나의 목숨을 노리려는 기도(의도).

should not retard[1] it a single hour.

In this state of mind I wrote to Elizabeth. My letter was calm and affectionate. "I fear, my beloved girl," I said, "little happiness remains for us on earth; yet all that I may one day enjoy is centred in you. Chase away[2] your idle[3] fears; to you alone do I consecrate[4] my life and my endeavours for contentment. I have one secret, Elizabeth, a dreadful one; when revealed to you it will chill[5] your frame with horror, and then, far from being surprised at my misery, you will only wonder that I survive what I have endured. I will confide this tale of misery and terror to you the day after our marriage shall take place; for, my sweet cousin, there must be perfect confidence between us. But until then, I conjure you, do not mention or allude to it. This I most earnestly entreat, and I know you will comply."

In about a week after the arrival of Elizabeth's letter we returned to Geneva. The sweet girl welcomed me with warm affection; yet tears were in her eyes as she beheld my emaciated frame and feverish cheeks. I saw a change in her also. She was thinner and had lost much of that heavenly vivacity[6] that had before charmed me; but her gentleness and soft looks of compassion made her a more fit companion for one blasted and miserable as I was.

The tranquillity which I now enjoyed did not endure[7]. Memory brought madness with it; and when I thought of what had passed a real insanity possessed me; sometimes I was furious and burnt with rage; sometimes low[8] and despondent[9]. I neither spoke nor looked at

1 retard: 늦추다.
2 Chase away: 몰아내다.
3 idle: 쓸데없는. 근거 없는.
4 consecrate: 바치다. 희생하다.
5 chill: 오싹하게 하다.
6 vivacity: 활달. 명랑.
7 endure: 지속되다.
8 low: 침울한(depressed).
9 despondent: 낙담한. 의기소침한.

any one, but sat motionless, bewildered by the multitude of miseries that overcame me.

Elizabeth alone had the power to draw me from these fits; her gentle voice would soothe me when transported[1] by passion, and inspire me with human feelings when sunk in torpor[2]. She wept with me and for me. When reason returned she would remonstrate[3] and endeavour to inspire me with resignation[4]. Ah! it is well for the unfortunate to be resigned, but for the guilty there is no peace. The agonies of remorse poison the luxury there is otherwise sometimes found in indulging the excess of grief.

Soon after my arrival, my father spoke of my immediate marriage with Elizabeth. I remained silent.

"Have you, then, some other attachment[5]?"

"None on earth. I love Elizabeth, and look forward to our union with delight. Let the day therefore be fixed; and on it I will consecrate myself, in life or death, to the happiness of my cousin."

"My dear Victor, do not speak thus. Heavy[6] misfortunes have befallen us; but let us only cling closer to what remains, and transfer our love for those whom we have lost to those who yet live. Our circle[7] will be small, but bound close by the ties of affection and mutual misfortune. And when time shall have softened your despair, new and dear objects of care will be born to replace those of whom we have been so cruelly deprived."

Such were the lessons of my father. But to me the remembrance of the threat returned: nor can you wonder that, omnipotent as the

1 transported: 이성을 잃은.
2 sunk in torpor: 무력감에 빠지다.
3 remonstrate: 충고하다. 간언하다.
4 resignation: 포기. 단념. 체념.
5 attachment: 사랑(하는 사람).
6 heavy: 견디기 어려운. 괴로운.
7 circle: 여기서는 '가족'을 지칭.

fiend had yet been in his deeds of blood[1], I should almost regard him as invincible, and that when he had pronounced the words, "I shall be with you on your wedding-night," I should regard the threatened fate as unavoidable. But death was no evil[2] to me if the loss of Elizabeth were balanced[3] with it; and I therefore, with a contented and even cheerful countenance, agreed with my father that, if my cousin would consent, the ceremony should take place in ten days, and thus put, as I imagined, the seal to my fate[4].

Great God! if for one instant I had thought what might be the hellish[5] intention of my fiendish adversary, I would rather have banished myself for ever from my native country, and wandered a friendless outcast over the earth, than have consented to this miserable marriage. But, as if possessed of magic powers, the monster had blinded me to[6] his real intentions; and when I thought that I had prepared only my own death, I hastened that of a far dearer victim.

As the period fixed for our marriage drew nearer, whether from cowardice or a prophetic feeling, I felt my heart sink[7] within me. But I concealed my feelings by an appearance of hilarity[8], that brought smiles and joy to the countenance of my father, but hardly deceived the everwatchful and nicer[9] eye of Elizabeth. She looked forward to our union with placid contentment, not unmingled with a little fear, which past misfortunes had impressed[10], that what now appeared cer-

---

1 deeds of blood: 잔인무도한 행위.
2 evil: 재앙.
3 balanced: 이해득실을 따지다.
4 put … the seal to my fate: 나의 운명을 결정지었다.
5 hellish: 흉악한.
6 blinded me to: 나로 하여금 …을 못 보게 하다.
7 heart sink: 가슴이 철렁 내려앉다.
8 hilarity: 환희. 기분이 좋아 떠들어 댐.
9 nicer: 보다 민감한(섬세한).
10 impressed: 통감하게 하다.

tain and tangible[1] happiness might soon dissipate into[2] an airy dream, and leave no trace but deep and everlasting regret.

Preparations were made for the event; congratulatory visits were received; and all wore a smiling appearance. I shut up, as well as I could, in my own heart the anxiety that preyed[3] there, and entered with seeming earnestness into the plans[4] of my father, although they might only serve as the decorations of my tragedy. Through my father's exertions, a part of the inheritance of Elizabeth had been restored to her by the Austrian government. A small possession on the shores of Como belonged to her. It was agreed that, immediately after our union, we should proceed to Villa Lavenza, and spend our first days of happiness beside the beautiful lake near which it stood.

In the meantime I took every precaution to defend my person in case the fiend should openly attack me. I carried pistols and a dagger constantly about me, and was ever on the watch[5] to prevent artifice[6]; and by these means gained a greater degree of tranquillity. Indeed, as the period approached, the threat appeared more as a delusion, not to be regarded as worthy to disturb my peace, while the happiness I hoped for in my marriage wore a greater appearance of certainty as the day fixed for its solemnisation drew nearer and I heard it continually spoken of as an occurrence which no accident could possibly prevent.

Elizabeth seemed happy; my tranquil demeanour contributed greatly to calm her mind. But on the day that was to fulfil my wishes and my destiny, she was melancholy, and a presentiment of evil pervaded her; and perhaps also she thought of the dreadful secret which

---

1 tangible: 확실한. 현실의.

2 dissipate into: 사라져 …으로 변하다.

3 preyed: 괴롭히다.

4 entered with seeming earnestness into: '보기에는 진지하게'(with seeming earnestness) '계획에 참여하였다'(enter into the plans)는 의미.

5 on the watch: 경계하고 있는.

6 artifice: 책략. 술책.

I had promised to reveal to her on the following day. My father was in the meantime overjoyed, and, in the bustle[1] of preparation, only recognised in the melancholy of his niece the diffidence[2] of a bride.

After the ceremony was performed a large party assembled at my father's; but it was agreed that Elizabeth and I should commence our journey by water[3], sleeping that night at Evian, and continuing our voyage on the following day. The day was fair[4], the wind favourable, all smiled on our nuptial embarkation[5].

Those were the last moments of my life during which I enjoyed the feeling of happiness. We passed rapidly along: the sun was hot, but we were sheltered from its rays by a kind of canopy[6], while we enjoyed the beauty of the scene, sometimes on one side of the lake, where we saw Mont Salêve, the pleasant banks of Montalègre, and at a distance, surmounting all, the beautiful Mont Blanc, and the assemblage of snowy mountains that in vain endeavour to emulate[7] her; sometimes coasting[8] the opposite banks, we saw the mighty Jura[9] opposing its dark side to the ambition that would quit its native country, and an almost insurmountable barrier to the invader who should wish to enslave it[10].

I took the hand of Elizabeth: "You are sorrowful, my love. Ah! if you knew what I have suffered, and what I may yet endure, you

---

1 bustle: 부산함.

2 diffidence: 자신 없음. 망설임.

3 by water: 수로로. 배로.

4 fair: (날씨가) 맑게 갠.

5 nuptial embarkation: 결혼생활의 시작.

6 canopy: 차양.

7 emulate: 경쟁하다.

8 coasting: (연안을) 항행하다.

9 Jura: 쥐라 산맥 (프랑스와 스위스 사이에 위치).

10 insurmountable barrier to the invader who should wish to enslave it: 1798년 스위스를 정복하기 위해 침공했던 나폴레옹에 대한 간접적인 언급; 영국의 많은 작가들은 전제 군주제를 타파한 프랑스 혁명을 지지하였지만 이를 계기로 정권을 잡고 스스로를 황제라고 칭한 나폴레옹에게 큰 실망을 하고 있었다.

would endeavour to let me taste the quiet and freedom from despair that this one day at least permits me to enjoy."

"Be happy, my dear Victor," replied Elizabeth; "there is, I hope, nothing to distress you; and be assured that if a lively joy is not painted in my face, my heart is contented. Something whispers to me not to depend too much on the prospect that is opened before us; but I will not listen to such a sinister[1] voice. Observe how fast we move along, and how the clouds, which sometimes obscure and sometimes rise above the dome of Mont Blanc, render this scene of beauty still more interesting. Look also at the innumerable fish that are swimming in the clear waters, where we can distinguish every pebble that lies at the bottom. What a divine[2] day! how happy and serene all nature appears!"

Thus Elizabeth endeavoured to divert her thoughts and mine from all reflection upon melancholy subjects. But her temper was fluctuating[3]; joy for a few instants shone in her eyes, but it continually gave place to distraction[4] and reverie.

The sun sank lower in the heavens: we passed the river Drance, and observed its path through the chasms of the higher, and the glens[5] of the lower hills. The Alps here come closer to the lake, and we approached the amphitheatre[6] of mountains which forms its eastern boundary. The spire of Evian shone under the woods that surrounded it, and the range of mountain above mountain by which it was overhung.

The wind, which had hitherto carried us along with amazing rapidity, sunk at sunset to a light breeze[7]; the soft air just ruffled[8]

---

1 sinister: 불길한.
2 divine: 멋진.
3 temper was fluctuating: 기분(temper)이 들쭉날쭉 하였다(fluctuate).
4 distraction: (마음이) 산란함.
5 glens: 골짜기. 협곡.
6 amphitheatre: 분지.
7 sunk at sunset to a light breeze: (바람이) '해질 무렵에는'(at sunset)에는 약해져서 (sunk) '약한 산들바람'(light breeze)으로 변하였다는 의미.
8 ruffled: 물결을 일으키다.

the water, and caused a pleasant motion among the trees as we approached the shore, from which it wafted the most delightful scent of flowers and hay. The sun sunk beneath the horizon as we landed; and as I touched[1] the shore, I felt those cares and fears revive which soon were to clasp[2] me and cling to me for ever.

Chapter XXIII

It was eight o'clock when we landed; we walked for a short time on the shore enjoying the transitory light, and then retired to the inn and contemplated the lovely scene of waters, woods, and mountains, obscured[3] in darkness, yet still displaying their black outlines.

The wind, which had fallen in the south, now rose with great violence in the west. The moon had reached her summit in the heavens and was beginning to descend; the clouds swept[4] across it swifter than the flight of the vulture[5] and dimmed her rays, while the lake reflected the scene of the busy heavens, rendered still busier by the restless waves that were beginning to rise. Suddenly a heavy storm of rain[6] descended.

I had been calm during the day; but so soon as night obscured the shapes of objects, a thousand fears arose in my mind. I was anxious and watchful, while my right hand grasped a pistol which was hidden in my bosom; every sound terrified me; but I resolved that I would sell my life dearly, and not shrink from[7] the conflict until my own life,

---

1 touched: (배가) 기항하다. (육지에) 닿다.
2 clasp: (옥)죄다(사로잡다).
3 obscured: 가려진. 잘 보이지 않게 된.
4 swept: 휙 지나가다.
5 vulture: 독수리.
6 storm of rain: 폭우.
7 shrink from: 피하다.

or that of my adversary, was extinguished.

Elizabeth observed my agitation for some time in timid and fearful silence; but there was something in my glance which communicated terror to her, and trembling she asked, "What is it that agitates you, my dear Victor? What is it you fear?"

"Oh! peace, peace, my love," replied I; "this night and all will be safe: but this night is dreadful, very dreadful."

I passed an hour in this state of mind, when suddenly I reflected how fearful the combat which I momentarily[1] expected would be to my wife, and I earnestly entreated her to retire, resolving not to join her until I had obtained some knowledge as to the situation of my enemy.

She left me, and I continued some time walking up and down the passages of the house, and inspecting every corner that might afford a retreat to my adversary. But I discovered no trace of him, and was beginning to conjecture that some fortunate chance had intervened to prevent the execution of his menaces, when suddenly I heard a shrill and dreadful scream. It came from the room into which Elizabeth had retired. As I heard it, the whole truth rushed into my mind[2], my arms dropped, the motion of every muscle and fibre[3] was suspended; I could feel the blood trickling in my veins and tingling[4] in the extremities of my limbs. This state lasted but for an instant; the scream was repeated, and I rushed into the room.

Great God! why did I not then expire[5]! Why am I here to relate the destruction of the best hope and the purest creature on earth? She was there, lifeless and inanimate[6], thrown across the bed, her head

---

1 momentarily: 시시각각의. 언제라도 일어날 것 같은.

2 whole truth rushed into my mind: '진상을 갑자기 깨닫게 되었다'는 의미.

3 fibre: 신경(근육) 섬유.

4 tingling: 얼얼함. 욱신욱신한 느낌.

5 expire: 숨을 거두다. 죽다.

6 inanimate: 생명 없는.

hanging down, and her pale and distorted features half covered by her hair.[1] Everywhere I turn I see the same figure — her bloodless arms and relaxed[2] form flung by the murderer on its bridal bier[3]. Could I behold this and live? Alas! life is obstinate[4] and clings closest where it is most hated. For a moment only did I lose recollection; I fell sense-less on the ground.

When I recovered, I found myself surrounded by the people of the inn; their countenances expressed a breathless[5] terror: but the horror of others appeared only as a mockery, a shadow of the feelings that oppressed me. I escaped from them to the room where lay the body of Elizabeth, my love, my wife, so lately living, so dear, so worthy. She had been moved from the posture in which I had first beheld her; and now, as she lay, her head upon her arm, and a handkerchief thrown across her face and neck, I might have supposed her asleep. I rushed towards her, and embraced her with ardour; but the deadly languor and coldness of the limbs told me that what I now held in my arms had ceased to be the Elizabeth whom I had loved and cherished. The murderous mark of the fiend's grasp was on her neck, and the breath had ceased to issue from her lips.

While I still hung over her in the agony of despair, I happened to look up. The windows of the room had before been darkened, and I felt a kind of panic on seeing the pale yellow light of the moon il-luminate the chamber. The shutters had been thrown back; and with a sensation of horror not to be described, I saw at the open window a figure the most hideous and abhorred. A grin was on the face of the

---

1 She was there, lifeless and inanimate ⋯ distorted features half covered by her hair: 침대 바깥으로 머리가 나온 채 축 쳐져 누워있는 엘리자베스의 모습은 헨리 퓨젤리(Henry Fuseli 1741-1825)의 그림 「악몽」(Nightmare)을 연상시킨다.

2 relaxed: 축 늘어진.

3 bier: 관.

4 obstinate: 끈질긴.

5 breathless: 마음 조이는.

monster; he seemed to jeer[1] as with his fiendish finger he pointed towards the corpse of my wife. I rushed towards the window and, drawing a pistol from my bosom, fired; but he eluded me, leaped from his station, and, running with the swiftness of lightning, plunged into the lake.

The report[2] of the pistol brought a crowd into the room. I pointed to the spot where he had disappeared, and we followed the track with boats; nets were cast, but in vain. After passing several hours, we returned hopeless, most of my companions believing it to have been a form conjured up by my fancy. After having landed, they proceeded to search the country, parties going in different directions among the woods and vines.

I attempted to accompany them, and proceeded a short distance from the house; but my head whirled[3] round, my steps were like those of a drunken man, I fell at last in a state of utter exhaustion[4]; a film covered my eyes[5], and my skin was parched with the heat of fever. In this state I was carried back and placed on a bed, hardly conscious of what had happened; my eyes wandered round the room as if to seek something that I had lost.

After an interval I arose, and as if by instinct, crawled into the room where the corpse of my beloved lay. There were women weeping around — I hung over it, and joined my sad tears to theirs — all this time no distinct idea presented itself to my mind; but my thoughts rambled to various subjects, reflecting confusedly on my misfortunes and their cause. I was bewildered in a cloud of wonder and horror[6].

---

1 jeer: 조소(야유)하다.

2 report: 총소리.

3 whirled: (머리가) 핑 돌다.

4 exhaustion: (기력의) 소진.

5 film covered my eyes: film은 '(눈의) 흐려짐'; 즉 눈의 흐려져 앞이 보이지 않게 되었다는 의미.

6 in a cloud of wonder and horror: 놀람과 공포로 망연자실하여(멍한 상태에 놓여).

The death of William, the execution of Justine, the murder of Clerval, and lastly of my wife; even at that moment I knew not that my only remaining friends were safe from the malignity of the fiend; my father even now might be writhing under his grasp, and Ernest might be dead at his feet. This idea made me shudder and recalled me to action[1]. I started up and resolved to return to Geneva with all possible speed.

There were no horses to be procured, and I must return by the lake; but the wind was unfavourable, and the rain fell in torrents. However, it was hardly morning, and I might reasonably hope to arrive by night. I hired men to row, and took an oar myself; for I had always experienced relief from mental torment in bodily exercise. But the overflowing[2] misery I now felt, and the excess of agitation that I endured, rendered me incapable of any exertion. I threw down the oar, and leaning my head upon my hands, gave way to[3] every gloomy idea that arose. If I looked up, I saw scenes which were familiar to me in my happier time, and which I had contemplated but the day before in the company of her who was now but a shadow and a recollection. Tears streamed from my eyes. The rain had ceased for a moment, and I saw the fish play in the waters as they had done a few hours before; they had then been observed by Elizabeth. Nothing is so painful to the human mind as a great and sudden change. The sun might shine or the clouds might lower: but nothing could appear to me as it had done the day before. A fiend had snatched from me every hope of future happiness: no creature had ever been so miserable as I was; so frightful an event is single in the history of man.

But why should I dwell upon the incidents that followed this last overwhelming event? Mine has been a tale of horrors; I have reached their acme[4], and what I must now relate can but be tedious to you.

---

1 recalled me to action: 나로 하여금 정신 차리게 해 행동하게 만들었다는 의미.
2 overflowing: 과다한. 지나친.
3 gave way to: …에 빠지게 되다.
4 acme: 정점.

Know that, one by one, my friends were snatched away[1]; I was left desolate. My own strength is exhausted; and I must tell, in a few words, what remains of my hideous narration.

I arrived at Geneva. My father and Ernest yet lived; but the former sunk[2] under the tidings[3] that I bore. I see him now, excellent and venerable old man! his eyes wandered in vacancy[4], for they had lost their charm and their delight— his Elizabeth, his more than daughter, whom he doted on with all that affection which a man feels, who in the decline of life, having few affections, clings more earnestly to those that remain. Cursed, cursed be the fiend that brought misery on his grey hairs, and doomed him to waste[5] in wretchedness! He could not live under the horrors that were accumulated around him; the springs of existence suddenly gave way[6]: he was unable to rise from his bed, and in a few days he died in my arms.

What then became of[7] me? I know not; I lost sensation, and chains and darkness were the only objects that pressed upon me. Sometimes, indeed, I dreamt that I wandered in flowery meadows and pleasant vales[8] with the friends of my youth; but I awoke, and found myself in a dungeon. Melancholy followed, but by degrees I gained a clear conception of my miseries and situation, and was then released from my prison. For they had called me mad; and during many months, as I understood, a solitary cell had been my habitation.

Liberty, however, had been an useless gift to me had I not, as I awakened to reason, at the same time awakened to revenge. As the

---

1 snatched away: 죽임을 당한.

2 sunk: 맥없이 쓰러지다. (의기(意氣)가) 꺾이다.

3 tidings: 소식.

4 in vacancy: 공허하게. 허탈하게.

5 waste: 쇠약해지다. 기력을 잃다.

6 springs of existence suddenly gave way: 삶의 원동력(spring)이 꺾이다(gave way).

7 became of: …에게 일이 벌어지다(happen to).

8 vales: 골짜기. 계곡.

memory of past misfortunes pressed upon me, I began to reflect on their cause — the monster whom I had created, the miserable dæmon whom I had sent abroad into the world for my destruction. I was possessed by a maddening rage when I thought of him, and desired and ardently prayed that I might have him within my grasp[1] to wreak a great and signal[2] revenge on his cursed head.

Nor did my hate long confine itself to useless wishes; I began to reflect on the best means of securing[3] him; and for this purpose, about a month after my release, I repaired[4] to a criminal judge in the town, and told him that I had an accusation[5] to make; that I knew the destroyer of my family; and that I required him to exert his whole authority[6] for the apprehension[7] of the murderer.

The magistrate listened to me with attention and kindness: — "Be assured, sir," said he, "no pains or exertions on my part shall be spared to discover the villain."

"I thank you," replied I; "listen, therefore, to the deposition that I have to make. It is indeed a tale so strange that I should fear you would not credit it were there not something in truth which, however wonderful, forces conviction. The story is too connected to be mistaken for a dream, and I have no motive for falsehood." My manner, as I thus addressed him, was impressive but calm; I had formed in my own heart a resolution to pursue my destroyer to death; and this purpose quieted my agony, and for an interval reconciled me to life[8]. I now related my history, briefly, but with firmness and precision,

---

1　have him within my grasp: '그를 수중에 넣다'; 즉 그를 붙잡다.
2　signal: 확실한.
3　securing: 붙잡다.
4　repaired: …로 가다.
5　accusation: 고발(告發). 고소.
6　exert his whole authority: 그의 모든 권한을 발휘하다.
7　apprehension: 체포.
8　reconciled me to life: 마지못해 목숨을 이어가기로 결정하였다는 의미.

marking the dates with accuracy, and never deviating into[1] invective[2] or exclamation.

The magistrate appeared at first perfectly incredulous, but as I continued he became more attentive and interested; I saw him sometimes shudder with horror, at others a lively surprise, unmingled with disbelief, was painted on his countenance.

When I had concluded my narration, I said, "This is the being whom I accuse, and for whose seizure[3] and punishment I call upon you to exert your whole power. It is your duty as a magistrate, and I believe and hope that your feelings as a man will not revolt from[4] the execution of those functions[5] on this occasion."

This address caused a considerable change in the physiognomy[6] of my own auditor[7]. He had heard my story with that half kind of belief that is given to a tale of spirits and supernatural events; but when he was called upon to act officially in consequence, the whole tide of his incredulity returned[8]. He, however, answered mildly, "I would willingly afford you every aid in your pursuit; but the creature of whom you speak appears to have powers which would put all my exertions to defiance[9]. Who can follow an animal which can traverse the sea of ice, and inhabit caves and dens where no man would venture to intrude? Besides, some months have elapsed since the commission[10] of his crimes, and no one can conjecture to what place he has wandered

---

1 deviating into: 하던 일에서 '일탈하여 …하게 되다'.

2 invective: 욕설. 독설.

3 seizure: 체포.

4 revolt from: 몹시 싫어 외면하다.

5 execution of those functions: 그 '임무'(functions)의 '수행'(execution).

6 physiognomy: 얼굴.

7 auditor: '듣는 사람'; 여기서는 프랑켄스타인의 설명을 듣고 있던 치안판사를 지칭.

8 whole tide of his incredulity returned: 믿지 못하겠다는(incredulity) 태도로 다시 변하였다는 의미.

9 put all my exertions to defiance: 나의 모든 노력을 헛되게 만든다.

10 commission: (범행을) 저지름.

or what region he may now inhabit."

"I do not doubt that he hovers[1] near the spot which I inhabit; and if he has indeed taken refuge in the Alps, he may be hunted like the chamois[2], and destroyed as a beast of prey[3]. But I perceive your thoughts: you do not credit my narrative, and do not intend to pursue my enemy with the punishment which is his desert[4]."

As I spoke, rage sparkled in my eyes; the magistrate was intimidated[5]: — "You are mistaken," said he. "I will exert myself[6]; and if it is in my power to seize the monster, be assured that he shall suffer punishment proportionate to[7] his crimes. But I fear, from what you have yourself described to be his properties[8], that this will prove impracticable[9]; and thus, while every proper measure is pursued, you should make up your mind to disappointment[10]."

"That cannot be; but all that I can say will be of little avail. My revenge is of no moment[11] to you; yet, while I allow it to be a vice, I confess that it is the devouring and only passion of my soul. My rage is unspeakable when I reflect that the murderer, whom I have turned loose upon society, still exists. You refuse my just demand: I have but one resource; and I devote myself, either in my life or death, to his destruction."

I trembled with excess of agitation as I said this; there was a frenzy[12] in my manner and something, I doubt not, of that haughty fierce-

---

1 hovers: 주변을 맴돌다.
2 chamois: 몸집이 작은 산 영양류.
3 beast of prey: 맹수. 육식동물.
4 desert: '당연히 받아야 할 것'; 즉 '당연한(응분의) 벌'.
5 intimidated: 위협을 느낀.
6 exert myself: 노력하다.
7 proportionate to: …에 비례한(합당한).
8 properties: 속성. 본질.
9 impracticable: 실행 불가능한.
10 make up your mind to disappointment: 실패를 (체념하고) 받아들이다.
11 of no moment: 중요하지 않은.
12 frenzy: 격앙. 광란.

ness which the martyrs of old are said to have possessed. But to a Genevan magistrate, whose mind was occupied by far other ideas than those of devotion[1] and heroism, this elevation of mind[2] had much the appearance of madness. He endeavoured to soothe me as a nurse does a child, and reverted to my tale as the effects of delirium.[3]

"Man," I cried, "how ignorant art thou in thy pride of wisdom! Cease; you know not what it is you say."

I broke from[4] the house angry and disturbed, and retired to meditate on some other mode of action.

CHAPTER XXIV

My present situation was one in which all voluntary thought was swallowed up and lost. I was hurried away by fury; revenge alone endowed me with strength and composure; it moulded my feelings, and allowed me to be calculating[5] and calm, at periods when otherwise delirium or death would have been my portion[6].

My first resolution was to quit Geneva for ever; my country, which, when I was happy and beloved, was dear to me, now, in my adversity[7], became hateful. I provided myself with a sum of money, together with a few jewels which had belonged to my mother, and departed.

And now my wanderings began, which are to cease but with life.

---

1 devotion: 헌신.

2 elevation of mind: 정신적 고양.

3 reverted to my tale as the effects of delirium: reverted to는 '처음 생각으로 돌아가다'. 즉 내 이야기가 나의 정신착란(delirium)의 결과(effect)라는 처음 생각으로 돌아갔다는 의미.

4 broke from: …로부터 갑자기 뛰어나가다.

5 calculating: 빈틈없는. 앞뒤를 살피는.

6 portion: 운명.

7 adversity: 역경.

I have traversed a vast portion of the earth, and have endured all the hardships which travellers, in deserts and barbarous countries, are wont to[1] meet. How I have lived I hardly know; many times have I stretched my failing[2] limbs upon the sandy plain and prayed for death. But revenge kept me alive; I dared not die and leave my adversary in being[3].

When I quitted Geneva my first labour was to gain some clue by which I might trace the steps of my fiendish enemy. But my plan was unsettled; and I wandered many hours round the confines of the town, uncertain what path I should pursue. As night approached, I found myself at the entrance of the cemetery where William, Elizabeth, and my father reposed. I entered it and approached the tomb which marked their graves. Everything was silent, except the leaves of the trees, which were gently agitated by the wind; the night was nearly dark; and the scene would have been solemn and affecting[4] even to an uninterested observer. The spirits of the departed seemed to flit around[5] and to cast a shadow, which was felt but not seen, around the head of the mourner.

The deep grief which this scene had at first excited quickly gave way to[6] rage and despair. They were dead, and I lived; their murderer also lived, and to destroy him I must drag out my weary existence.[7] I knelt on the grass and kissed the earth, and with quivering lips exclaimed, "By the sacred earth on which I kneel, by the shades[8] that wander near me, by the deep and eternal grief that I feel, I swear; and

---

1 wont to: 늘 …하는.
2 failing: 힘이 약해져가는.
3 in being: 생존해 있는.
4 affecting: 애처로운. 마음에 찡한.
5 flit around: …주위를 (날아) 돌아다니다.
6 gave way to: …으로 바뀌다.
7 drag out my weary existence: drag out는 '(싫으면서도) 억지로 이어가다'; 즉 억지로 삶을 이어간다는 의미.
8 shades: 망령. 영혼.

by thee, O Night, and the spirits that preside over[1] thee, to pursue the dæmon who caused this misery until he or I shall perish in mortal conflict. For this purpose I will preserve my life: to execute this dear revenge will I again behold the sun and tread the green herbage[2] of earth, which otherwise should vanish from my eyes for ever. And I call on[3] you, spirits of the dead; and on you, wandering ministers of vengeance[4], to aid and conduct me in my work. Let the cursed and hellish monster drink deep of[5] agony; let him feel the despair that now torments me."

I had begun my adjuration[6] with solemnity and an awe which almost assured me that the shades of my murdered friends heard and approved my devotion[7]; but the furies possessed me as I concluded, and rage choked my utterance[8].

I was answered through the stillness of night by a loud and fiendish laugh. It rung on my ears long and heavily; the mountains re-echoed it, and I felt as if all hell surrounded me with mockery and laughter. Surely in that moment I should have been possessed by frenzy, and have destroyed my miserable existence, but that my vow was heard and that I was reserved for vengeance. The laughter died away; when a well-known and abhorred voice, apparently close to my ear, addressed me in an audible whisper — "I am satisfied: miserable wretch! you have determined to live, and I am satisfied."

I darted towards the spot from which the sound proceeded; but the devil eluded my grasp. Suddenly the broad disk of the moon arose

---

1 preside over: 통할하다. 관장하다.
2 herbage: 초본. 풀.
3 call on: 요구(요청)하다.
4 ministers of vengeance: 복수를 대행해 주는 존재.
5 drink deep of: …을 흠뻑 마시다.
6 adjuration: 간원.
7 devotion: 기도.
8 rage choked my utterance: 너무 화가나 말을 할 수 없었다는 의미.

and shone full upon his ghastly and distorted shape as he fled with
more than mortal speed[1].

I pursued him; and for many months this has been my task. Guided by a slight clue I followed the windings of the Rhone[2], but vainly.
The blue Mediterranean appeared; and by a strange chance, I saw the
fiend enter by night and hide himself in a vessel bound for[3] the Black
Sea. I took my passage in[4] the same ship; but he escaped, I know not
how.

Amidst the wilds of Tartary[5] and Russia, although he still evaded
me, I have ever followed in his track. Sometimes the peasants, scared
by this horrid apparition[6], informed me of his path; sometimes he
himself, who feared that if I lost all trace of him I should despair and
die, left some mark to guide me. The snows descended on my head,
and I saw the print of his huge step on the white plain. To you first
entering on life[7], to whom care is new and agony unknown, how can
you understand what I have felt and still feel? Cold, want, and fatigue
were the least pains which I was destined to endure; I was cursed
by some devil, and carried about with me my eternal hell[8]; yet still a
spirit of good followed and directed my steps; and when I most murmured[9], would suddenly extricate[10] me from seemingly insurmount-

---

1 mortal speed: 인간이 달릴 수 있는 최대한의 속도.
2 Rhone: 론 강(알프스의 론(Rhone) 빙하에서 시작하여 프랑스를 지나 지중해로 흘러
   드는 강).
3 bound for: …로 향하는.
4 took my passage in: …을 타고 도항하다.
5 Tartary: 타타르 (지방).
6 apparition: 불가사의한 형상. 허깨비같은 존재.
7 first entering on life: 생을 이제 처음 시작하는.
8 carried about with me my eternal hell: 『실낙원』에 나오는 사탄의 말과 유사하다;
   괴물도 이런 표현을 앞서 사용하였고 프랑켄스타인도 이 표현을 사용한다는 사실
   은 이 둘이 서로 적대적 관계이면서도 동시에 서로가 또 다른 자아 즉 알터이고(Alter
   Ego)의 관계임을 시사한다.
9 murmured: 불평하다. 투덜대다.
10 extricate: 구출(救出)하다. 벗어나게 해주다.

able difficulties. Sometimes, when nature,[1] overcome by hunger, sunk under the exhaustion, a repast[2] was prepared for me in the desert that restored and inspirited[3] me. The fare was, indeed, coarse, such as the peasants of the country ate; but I will not doubt that it was set there by the spirits that I had invoked to aid me. Often, when all was dry, the heavens cloudless, and I was parched by thirst, a slight cloud would bedim the sky, shed the few drops that revived me, and vanish.

I followed, when I could, the courses of the rivers; but the dæmon generally avoided these, as it was here that the population of the country chiefly collected[4]. In other places human beings were seldom seen; and I generally subsisted on[5] the wild animals that crossed my path. I had money with me, and gained the friendship of the villagers by distributing it; or I brought with me some food that I had killed, which, after taking a small part, I always presented to those who had provided me with fire and utensils for cooking.

My life, as it passed thus, was indeed hateful to me, and it was during sleep alone that I could taste joy. O blessed sleep! often, when most miserable, I sank to repose, and my dreams lulled[6] me even to rapture. The spirits that guarded me had provided these moments, or rather hours, of happiness, that I might retain strength to fulfil my pilgrimage. Deprived of this respite, I should have sunk under my hardships. During the day I was sustained and inspirited by the hope of night: for in sleep I saw my friends, my wife, and my beloved country; again I saw the benevolent countenance of my father, heard the silver[7] tones of my Elizabeth's voice, and beheld Clerval enjoying

---

1 nature: 체력. 생명력.
2 repast: 식사.
3 inspirited: 분발시키다. 힘나게 하다.
4 collected: 모이다.
5 subsisted on: …을 먹고 생명을 이어가다.
6 lulled: 달래다.
7 silver: (소리가) 맑은.

health and youth. Often, when wearied by a toilsome march, I persuaded myself that I was dreaming until night should come, and that I should then enjoy reality in the arms of my dearest friends. What agonising fondness did I feel for them! how did I cling to their dear forms, as sometimes they haunted even my waking hours, and persuade myself that they still lived! At such moments vengeance, that burned within me, died in my heart, and I pursued my path towards the destruction of the dæmon more as a task enjoined[1] by heaven, as the mechanical impulse of some power of which I was unconscious, than as the ardent desire of my soul.

What his feelings were whom I pursued I cannot know. Sometimes, indeed, he left marks in writing on the barks of the trees, or cut[2] in stone, that guided me and instigated[3] my fury. "My reign is not yet over" (these words were legible[4] in one of these inscriptions[5]); "you live, and my power is complete. Follow me; I seek the everlasting ices of the north, where you will feel the misery of cold and frost to which I am impassive[6]. You will find near this place, if you follow not too tardily, a dead hare; eat and be refreshed[7]. Come on, my enemy; we have yet to wrestle for our lives but many hard and miserable hours must you endure until that period shall arrive."

Scoffing[8] devil! Again do I vow vengeance; again do I devote thee, miserable fiend, to torture and death[9]. Never will I give up my search until he or I perish; and then with what ecstasy shall I join my Eliza-

---

1 enjoined: 명을 받은.
2 cut: 새겨 넣은.
3 instigated: 부추기다.
4 legible: 읽을 수 있는.
5 inscriptions: 새겨진 글.
6 impassive: 고통을 느끼지 않는. 무감각한.
7 be refreshed: 기운을 되찾아라.
8 Scoffing: 조롱하는. 비웃는.
9 devote thee, miserable fiend, to torture and death: devote는 '…로 몰아넣다'; 즉 너 비천한 악마(miserable fiend)를 고통과 죽음으로 몰아넣겠다는 의미.

beth and my departed[1] friends, who even now prepare for me the reward of my tedious toil and horrible pilgrimage[2]!

As I still pursued my journey to the northward, the snows thickened and the cold increased in a degree almost too severe to support. The peasants were shut up[3] in their hovels, and only a few of the most hardy[4] ventured forth[5] to seize the animals whom starvation had forced from their hiding-places to seek for prey. The rivers were covered with ice and no fish could be procured; and thus I was cut off from my chief article of maintenance[6].

The triumph of my enemy increased with the difficulty of my labours. One inscription that he left was in these words: — "Prepare! your toils only begin: wrap yourself in furs and provide food; for we shall soon enter upon[7] a journey where your sufferings will satisfy my everlasting hatred."

My courage and perseverance were invigorated[8] by these scoffing words; I resolved not to fail in my purpose; and, calling on Heaven to support me, I continued with unabated fervour[9] to traverse immense deserts until the ocean appeared at a distance and formed the utmost[10] boundary of the horizon. Oh! how unlike it was to the blue seas of the south! Covered with ice, it was only to be distinguished from land by its superior wildness and ruggedness. The Greeks wept for joy when they beheld the Mediterranean from the hills of Asia, and hailed with rapture[11]

---

1 departed: (최근에) 죽은.

2 pilgrimage: 긴 여행.

3 shut up: 틀어 박혀있는.

4 hardy: 대담한 사람. 배짱 좋은 사람.

5 ventured forth: 과감히 나오다.

6 article of maintenance: 생계에 필요한 품목(음식).

7 enter upon: 착수하다. 시작하다.

8 invigorated: 힘을 얻다.

9 with unabated fervour: 줄지 않는(unabated) 열의(fervour)로.

10 utmost: 맨 끝(의).

11 with rapture: 황홀경에 빠져.

the boundary of their toils[1]. I did not weep; but I knelt down and, with a full heart[2], thanked my guiding spirit for conducting me in safety to the place where I hoped, notwithstanding my adversary's gibe[3], to meet and grapple with[4] him.

Some weeks before this period I had procured a sledge[5] and dogs, and thus traversed the snows with inconceivable[6] speed. I know not whether the fiend possessed the same advantages; but I found that, as before I had daily lost ground[7] in the pursuit, I now gained on[8] him: so much so that[9], when I first saw the ocean, he was but one day's journey in advance, and I hoped to intercept[10] him before he should reach the beach. With new courage, therefore, I pressed on[11], and in two days arrived at a wretched hamlet[12] on the sea-shore. I inquired of the inhabitants concerning the fiend, and gained accurate information. A gigantic monster, they said, had arrived the night before, armed with a gun and many pistols, putting to flight[13] the inhabitants of a solitary cottage through fear of his terrific[14] appearance. He had car-

---

1 The Greeks wept for joy ⋯ the boundary of their toils: 그리스의 역사가이자 장군인 크세노폰(Xenophon, 434?-355? B.C)은 기원전 400년에 고국에서 1,500km 떨어진 곳에 있던 자기 부대를 이끌고 이민족과 싸움을 벌이면서 바다와 아르메니아 지역을 지나, 마침내 흑해 연안에 있는 그리스 도시 트라페주스에 도착했는데 이 일은 그의 책『소아시아 원정기』(Anabasis)에 자세히 기록되어 있다; 괴물을 쫓아 험난한 여정에 들어선 프랑켄스타인은 자신의 고난을 크세노폰의 고난에 비유하고 있는 것이다.

2 with a full heart: 벅찬 가슴으로.

3 gibe: 비웃음. 조롱.

4 grapple with: ⋯와 맞붙어 싸우다.

5 sledge: (말·개·순록이 끄는) 썰매.

6 inconceivable: 믿을 수 없을 정도의.

7 lost ground: 뒤지다.

8 gained on: 능가하다.

9 so much so that: 아주 그러하므로 ⋯하다.

10 intercept: 도중에 붙잡다.

11 pressed on: 서두르다. 급히 가다.

12 wretched hamlet: 초라한(wretched) 작은 마을(hamlet).

13 putting to flight: 도망가게 만들다.

14 terrific: 무시무시한(terrible). 소름끼치는.

ried off their store[1] of winter food, and placing it in a sledge, to draw
which he had seized on a numerous drove[2] of trained dogs, he had
harnessed[3] them, and the same night, to the joy of the horror-struck
villagers, had pursued his journey across the sea in a direction that led
to no land; and they conjectured that he must speedily be destroyed
by the breaking of the ice or frozen by the eternal frosts.

On hearing this information, I suffered a temporary access[4]
of despair. He had escaped me; and I must commence a destructive and almost endless journey across the mountainous ices of the
ocean — amidst cold that few of the inhabitants could long endure,
and which I, the native of a genial[5] and sunny climate, could not
hope to survive. Yet at the idea that the fiend should live and be tri-
umphant, my rage and vengeance returned, and like a mighty tide,
overwhelmed every other feeling. After a slight repose, during which
the spirits of the dead hovered round and instigated me to toil and
revenge, I prepared for my journey.

I exchanged my land-sledge for one fashioned[6] for the inequalities
of the Frozen Ocean; and purchasing a plentiful stock of provisions[7], I
departed from land.

I cannot guess how many days have passed since then; but I have
endured misery which nothing but the eternal sentiment of a just retribution[8] burning within my heart could have enabled me to support.
Immense and rugged mountains of ice often barred up[9] my passage,

---

1 store: 비축물.

2 drove: 가축의 떼.

3 harnessed: (썰매를 끄는) 도구를 달다.

4 access: (노여움·절망 등의) 발작. 격발.

5 genial: (기후) 온화한.

6 fashioned: 만들어진(made).

7 provisions: 식량.

8 retribution: 징벌. 보복.

9 barred up: 가로 막다.

and I often heard the thunder[1] of the ground sea[2] which threatened my destruction. But again the frost came and made the paths of the sea secure.

By the quantity of provision which I had consumed, I should guess that I had passed three weeks in this journey; and the continual protraction[3] of hope, returning back upon the heart, often wrung[4] bitter drops of despondency[5] and grief from my eyes. Despair had indeed almost secured her prey, and I should soon have sunk beneath this misery. Once, after the poor animals that conveyed me had with incredible toil gained[6] the summit of a sloping ice-mountain, and one, sinking under his fatigue, died, I viewed the expanse[7] before me with anguish, when suddenly my eye caught a dark speck upon the dusky plain. I strained my sight[8] to discover what it could be, and uttered a wild cry of ecstasy when I distinguished a sledge and the distorted proportions of a well-known form within. Oh! with what a burning gush[9] did hope revisit my heart! warm tears filled my eyes, which I hastily wiped away that they might not intercept the view I had of the dæmon; but still my sight was dimmed by the burning drops[10] until, giving way to the emotions that oppressed me, I wept aloud.

But this was not the time for delay: I disencumbered[11] the dogs of their dead companion, gave them a plentiful portion of food; and after an hour's rest, which was absolutely necessary, and yet which

---

1   thunder: 우레 같은 소리. 큰 소리.
2   ground sea: 큰 놀. 큰 파도.
3   protraction: 연장.
4   wrung: (눈물을) 짜내다.
5   despondency: 낙담.
6   gained: 도달하다. 이르다.
7   expanse: 광활한 공간(구역).
8   strained my sight: (잘 보려고) 눈을 부릅뜨다.
9   gush: 복받치는 감정.
10   burning drops: '뜨거운 눈물'을 지칭.
11   disencumbered: 풀어주다. 빼내다.

was bitterly irksome to me, I continued my route. The sledge was still visible; nor did I again lose sight of it except at the moments when for a short time some ice-rock concealed it with its intervening crags[1]. I indeed perceptibly[2] gained on[3] it; and when, after nearly two days' journey, I beheld my enemy at no more than a mile distant, my heart bounded within me.

But now, when I appeared almost within grasp of[4] my foe, my hopes were suddenly extinguished, and I lost all trace of him more utterly than I had ever done before. A ground sea was heard; the thunder of its progress, as the waters rolled[5] and swelled beneath me, became every moment more ominous[6] and terrific. I pressed on, but in vain. The wind arose; the sea roared; and, as with the mighty shock of an earthquake, it split and cracked with a tremendous and overwhelming sound. The work was soon finished: in a few minutes a tumultuous sea rolled between me and my enemy, and I was left drifting[7] on a scattered piece of ice, that was continually lessening, and thus preparing for me a hideous death.

In this manner many appalling[8] hours passed; several of my dogs died; and I myself was about to sink under the accumulation of distress when I saw your vessel riding at anchor[9], and holding forth[10] to me hopes of succour[11] and life. I had no conception that vessels ever came so far north, and was astounded at the sight. I quickly destroyed

---

1 crags: 돌출한 바위.
2 perceptibly: 상당한(눈에 띌) 정도로.
3 gained on: 접근하다. 따라붙다.
4 within grasp of: …을 잡을 수 있을 거리에 있는.
5 rolled: (파도 따위가) 굽이치다.
6 ominous: 불길한.
7 drifting: 표류하다. 떠돌아다니다.
8 appalling: 끔직스런.
9 riding at anchor: 정박해 있다.
10 holding forth: 제시하다.
11 succour: 구조. 구원.

part of my sledge to construct oars; and by these means was enabled, with infinite fatigue, to move my ice-raft[1] in the direction of your ship. I had determined, if you were going southward, still to trust myself to the mercy of the seas[2] rather than abandon my purpose. I hoped to induce you to grant me a boat with which I could pursue my enemy. But your direction was northward. You took me on board when my vigour[3] was exhausted, and I should soon have sunk under my multiplied hardships into a death which I still dread — for my task is unfulfilled.

Oh! when will my guiding spirit, in conducting me to the dæmon, allow me the rest I so much desire; or must I die and he yet live? If I do, swear to me, Walton, that he shall not escape; that you will seek him and satisfy my vengeance[4] in his death. And do I dare to ask of you to undertake my pilgrimage, to endure the hardships that I have undergone? No; I am not so selfish. Yet, when I am dead, if he should appear, if the ministers of vengeance should conduct him to you, swear that he shall not live — swear that he shall not triumph over[5] my accumulated woes, and survive to add to the list of his dark crimes. He is eloquent and persuasive; and once his words had even power over my heart: but trust him not. His soul is as hellish as his form, full of treachery and fiend-like malice. Hear him not; call on the manes[6] of William, Justine, Clerval, Elizabeth, my father, and of the wretched Victor, and thrust your sword into his heart. I will hover near and direct the steel[7] aright[8].

---

1 ice-raft: 얼음으로 만든 뗏목.

2 trust myself to the mercy of the seas: '나를 바다의 처분에 맡기었다'; 즉 내 운명을 바다에 맡긴다는 의미.

3 vigour: 체력.

4 satisfy my vengeance: 나의 복수를 해주다.

5 triumph over: ···에 대해 의기양양한 태도를 보이다.

6 manes: 죽은 사람의 영혼.

7 steel: 칼.

8 aright: 정확히.

WALTON, in continuation.

August 26th, 17 —.

You have read this strange and terrific story, Margaret; and do you not feel your blood congeal[1] with horror like that which even now curdles[2] mine? Sometimes, seized with[3] sudden agony, he could not continue his tale; at others, his voice broken[4], yet piercing, uttered with difficulty the words so replete with anguish. His fine and lovely eyes were now lighted up with indignation, now subdued to downcast[5] sorrow, and quenched in infinite wretchedness. Sometimes he commanded[6] his countenance and tones, and related the most horrible incidents with a tranquil voice, suppressing every mark of agitation; then, like a volcano bursting forth, his face would suddenly change to an expression of the wildest rage, as he shrieked out imprecations on his persecutor[7].

His tale is connected[8], and told with an appearance of the simplest truth; yet I own[9] to you that the letters of Felix and Safie, which he showed me, and the apparition of the monster seen from our ship, brought to me a greater conviction of the truth of his narrative than his asseverations[10], however earnest and connected. Such a monster has then really existence! I cannot doubt it; yet I am lost in[11] surprise and admira-

---

1 congeal: (피가) 얼어붙다.
2 curdles: 응결시키다.
3 seized with: …에 사로잡혀.
4 broken: 띄엄띄엄 이어지는.
5 downcast: 풀이 죽은.
6 commanded: 제어(통제)하다.
7 shrieked out imprecations on his persecutor: shrieked out는 '날카로운 소리로 소리치다'; imprecations은 '저주'; persecutor는 '박해자'. '학대자'.
8 connected: 조리 있는.
9 own: 인정(자백)하다.
10 asseverations: 단호한 주장.
11 lost in: …에 몰두하고 있는(빠져있는).

tion. Sometimes I endeavoured to gain from Frankenstein the particulars of his creature's formation: but on this point he was impenetrable[1].

"Are you mad, my friend?" said he; "or whither does your senseless[2] curiosity lead you? Would you also create for yourself and the world a demoniacal enemy? Peace, peace! learn my miseries, and do not seek to increase your own."

Frankenstein discovered that I made notes concerning his history: he asked to see them, and then himself corrected and augmented[3] them in many places; but principally in giving the life and spirit to[4] the conversations he held with his enemy. "Since you have preserved my narration," said he, "I would not that[5] a mutilated[6] one should go down to posterity[7]."

Thus has a week passed away, while I have listened to the strangest tale that ever imagination formed. My thoughts, and every feeling of my soul, have been drunk up by the interest for my guest, which this tale, and his own elevated[8] and gentle manners, have created. I wish to soothe him; yet can I counsel one so infinitely miserable, so destitute of[9] every hope of consolation, to live? Oh, no! the only joy that he can now know will be when he composes his shattered spirit to peace and death. Yet he enjoys one comfort, the offspring of solitude and delirium: he believes that, when in dreams he holds converse with his friends and derives from that communion[10] consolation

---

1 impenetrable: (요구 등을) 받아들이지 않는.
2 senseless: 어리석은.
3 augmented: 보완하다. 늘이다.
4 giving the life and spirit to: …에 생기를 불어넣다.
5 would not that: …하는 것을 바라지 않는다(do not wish that).
6 mutilated: (일부 문장이 삭제되어) 불완전한.
7 go down to posterity: 후세(posterity)에 전해지다(go down).
8 elevated: 고결한.
9 destitute of: …이 없는.
10 communion: (영적) 교섭.

for his miseries or excitements to his vengeance[1], that they are not the creations of his fancy, but the beings themselves who visit him from the regions of a remote world[2]. This faith gives a solemnity to his reveries that render them to me almost as imposing[3] and interesting as truth.

Our conversations are not always confined to his own history and misfortunes. On every point of general literature he displays unbounded knowledge and a quick and piercing[4] apprehension. His eloquence is forcible and touching[5]; nor can I hear him, when he relates a pathetic incident, or endeavours to move[6] the passions of pity or love, without tears. What a glorious creature must he have been in the days of his prosperity when he is thus noble and godlike in ruin![7] He seems to feel his own worth and the greatness of his fall.

"When younger," said he, "I believed myself destined for some great enterprise[8]. My feelings are profound; but I possessed a coolness of judgment that fitted me for illustrious achievements[9]. This sentiment of the worth of my nature supported me when others would have been oppressed; for I deemed it criminal to throw away in useless grief those talents that might be useful to my fellow-creatures. When I reflected on the work I had completed, no less a one than the creation of a sensitive[10] and rational animal, I could not rank myself with[11] the

---

1 excitements to his vengeance: 복수를 하라는 자극(제).
2 regions of a remote world: '저승'을 암시.
3 imposing: 인상적인.
4 piercing: 통찰력 있는.
5 forcible and touching: 설득력 있는(forcible) 그리고 감동적인(touching).
6 move: (감정을) 일으키다.
7 What a glorious creature … thus noble and godlike in ruin!: 이 구절은 『실낙원』에 나오는 사탄에 대한 묘사와 유사하다.
8 enterprise: 대담한(야심찬) 계획.
9 illustrious achievements: 빛나는(illustrious) 위업(achievement).
10 sensitive: 감각이 있는.
11 rank myself with: …와 나 자신을 같은 부류에 두다.

herd of common projectors[1]. But this thought, which supported me in the commencement of my career, now serves only to plunge[2] me lower in the dust. All my speculations[3] and hopes are as nothing; and, like the archangel who aspired to omnipotence[4], I am chained in an eternal hell. My imagination was vivid, yet my powers of analysis and application were intense; by the union of these qualities I conceived[5] the idea and executed the creation of a man. Even now I cannot recollect without passion my reveries while the work was incomplete. I trod heaven in my thoughts, now exulting in[6] my powers, now burning with the idea of their effects. From my infancy I was imbued with high hopes and a lofty ambition; but how am I sunk! Oh! my friend, if you had known me as I once was you would not recognise me in this state of degradation. Despondency rarely visited my heart; a high destiny seemed to bear me on until I fell, never, never again to rise."

Must I then lose this admirable being? I have longed for a friend; I have sought one who would sympathise with and love me. Behold, on these desert[7] seas I have found such a one; but I fear I have gained him only to know his value and lose him. I would reconcile him to life, but he repulses the idea[8].

"I thank you, Walton," he said, "for your kind intentions towards so miserable a wretch; but when you speak of new ties and fresh affections, think you that any can replace those who are gone? Can any man be to me as Clerval was; or any woman another Elizabeth? Even where the affections are not strongly moved by any superior

---

1 projectors: 계획자. 실험가.

2 plunge: 내몰다. 내동댕이치다. 빠져들게 하다.

3 speculations: (숙고 끝에 얻은) 결론(이론).

4 archangel who aspired to omnipotence: 전능의 신(omnipotence)의 위치까지 올라가기 바랐던 대천사(archangel)는 『실낙원』에 나오는 사탄을 연상시킨다.

5 conceived: 구상하다.

6 exulting in: …에 대해 무척 기뻐하다.

7 desert: 황량한. 사람이 살지 않는.

8 repulses the idea: 생각 자체를 거부한다.

excellence, the companions of our childhood always possess a certain power over our minds which hardly any later friend can obtain. They know our infantine dispositions, which, however they may be afterwards modified, are never eradicated[1]; and they can judge of our actions with more certain conclusions as to the integrity[2] of our motives. A sister or a brother can never, unless indeed such symptoms have been shown early, suspect the other of fraud[3] or false dealing, when another friend, however strongly he may be attached, may, in spite of himself[4], be contemplated with suspicion. But I enjoyed friends, dear not only through habit and association[5], but from their own merits; and wherever I am the soothing voice of my Elizabeth and the conversation of Clerval will be ever whispered in my ear. They are dead, and but one feeling in such a solitude can persuade me to preserve my life. If I were engaged in any high undertaking[6] or design[7], fraught with[8] extensive utility to my fellow-creatures, then could I live to fulfil it. But such is not my destiny; I must pursue and destroy the being to whom I gave existence; then my lot on earth will be fulfilled, and I may die."

September 2nd.

MY BELOVED SISTER,

I write to you encompassed by peril and ignorant whether I am ever doomed to see again dear England, and the dearer friends that inhabit

---

1 eradicated: 근절되다.
2 integrity: 본래의 모습. 고결함.
3 fraud: 사기행위.
4 in spite of himself: 그 자신도 모르게. 무심코.
5 association: 교제. 친밀(한 관계).
6 undertaking: 떠맡은 일.
7 design: 계획.
8 fraught with: …으로 가득 찬.

it. I am surrounded by mountains of ice[1] which admit of no escape
and threaten every moment to crush my vessel. The brave fellows
whom I have persuaded to be my companions look towards me for
aid; but I have none to bestow. There is something terribly appalling in our situation, yet my courage and hopes do not desert me[2]. Yet
it is terrible to reflect that the lives of all these men are endangered
through me. If we are lost, my mad schemes are the cause.

And what, Margaret, will be the state of your mind? You will not
hear of my destruction, and you will anxiously await my return. Years
will pass, and you will have visitings of despair[3], and yet be tortured
by hope. Oh! my beloved sister, the sickening failing of your heart-felt
expectations[4] is, in prospect[5], more terrible to me than my own death.
But you have a husband and lovely children; you may be happy:
Heaven bless you and make you so!

My unfortunate guest regards me with the tenderest compassion.
He endeavours to fill me with hope; and talks as if life were a possession which he valued. He reminds me how often the same accidents
have happened to other navigators who have attempted this sea, and,
in spite of myself, he fills me with cheerful auguries[6]. Even the sailors feel the power of his eloquence: when he speaks they no longer
despair; he rouses their energies and, while they hear his voice, they
believe these vast mountains of ice are mole-hills which will vanish
before the resolutions[7] of man. These feelings are transitory; each day
of expectation delayed fills them with fear, and I almost dread a mu-

---

1 I am surrounded by mountains of ice: 「노수부의 노래」에서 노수부가 탄 배가 남극
   에 도달하였을 때 커다란 얼음덩이에 둘러 쌓이는 상황에 직면하게 된다.

2 my courage and hopes do not desert me: 난 용기와 희망을 잃지 않았다는 의미.

3 visitings of despair: 절망감의 엄습.

4 failing of your heart-felt expectations: failing은 '좌절'(이루어지지 않음); heart-felt
   는 '진심어린'; 즉 당신의 진심어린 기대의 좌절.

5 in prospect: '예상에 따르면'; 즉 예상컨대.

6 auguries: 전조. 조짐.

7 resolutions: 확고한 결의.

tiny[1] caused by this despair.

                                        September 5 th
A scene has just passed[2] of such uncommon interest that although it
is highly probable that these papers may never reach you, yet I cannot
forbear recording it.

We are still surrounded by mountains of ice, still in imminent[3]
danger of being crushed in their conflict[4]. The cold is excessive, and
many of my unfortunate comrades have already found a grave[5] amidst
this scene of desolation. Frankenstein has daily declined in health: a
feverish fire still glimmers in his eyes; but he is exhausted and when
suddenly roused to any exertion, he speedily sinks again into apparent
lifelessness.

I mentioned in my last letter the fears I entertained[6] of a mutiny. This morning, as I sat watching the wan[7] countenance of my
friend — his eyes half closed, and his limbs hanging listlessly[8] — I
was roused by half a dozen of the sailors who demanded admission
into the cabin. They entered, and their leader addressed me. He told
me that he and his companions had been chosen by the other sailors to come in deputation[9] to me, to make me a requisition[10] which,
in justice[11], I could not refuse. We were immured[12] in ice and should

---

1 mutiny: 선상반란.
2 passed: (일이) 벌어지다(일어나다).
3 imminent: 언제 닥칠지 모르는.
4 conflict: (물체의) 충돌.
5 found a grave: 죽을 자리를 얻다(죽다).
6 entertained: (생각을) 품다.
7 wan: 창백한.
8 listlessly: 힘없이.
9 in deputation: 대표(자격으)로.
10 requisition: 요구.
11 in justice: 도의적인 측면에서.
12 immured: 갇힌.

probably never escape; but they feared that if, as was possible, the ice should dissipate[1], and a free passage be opened, I should be rash enough to continue my voyage and lead them into fresh dangers after they might happily have surmounted this. They insisted, therefore, that I should engage[2] with a solemn promise that if the vessel should be freed I would instantly direct my course southward.

This speech troubled me. I had not despaired; nor had I yet conceived the idea of returning if set free. Yet could I, in justice, or even in possibility, refuse this demand? I hesitated before I answered; when Frankenstein, who had at first been silent, and, indeed, appeared hardly to have force enough to attend, now roused himself; his eyes sparkled, and his cheeks flushed with momentary vigour. Turning towards the men he said—

"What do you mean? What do you demand of your captain? Are you then so easily turned from your design? Did you not call this a glorious expedition[3]? And wherefore was it glorious? Not because the way was smooth and placid as a southern sea, but because it was full of dangers and terror; because at every new incident your fortitude was to be called forth[4] and your courage exhibited; because danger and death surrounded it, and these you were to brave[5] and overcome. For this was it a glorious, for this was it an honourable undertaking. You were hereafter to be hailed[6] as the benefactors of your species; your names adored as belonging to brave men who encountered death for honour and the benefit of mankind. And now, behold, with the first imagination of danger[7], or, if you will, the first mighty and terrific

---

1 dissipate: 흩어져 없어지다.
2 engage: 보증하다.
3 expedition: 원정.
4 called forth: 요구되다.
5 brave: 용감히 맞서다.
6 hailed: …라고 불리다(환호되다).
7 with the first imagination of danger: 위험할 것이라는 생각이 들자마자.

trial[1] of your courage, you shrink away, and are content to be handed down as[2] men who had not strength enough to endure cold and peril; and so, poor souls, they were chilly and returned to their warm firesides. Why, that requires not this preparation; ye need not have come thus far, and dragged your captain to the shame of a defeat, merely to prove yourselves cowards. Oh! be men, or be more than men. Be steady to your purposes and firm as a rock. This ice is not made of such stuff as your hearts may be; it is mutable[3] and cannot withstand you if you say that it shall not. Do not return to your families with the stigma of disgrace marked on your brows[4]. Return as heroes who have fought and conquered, and who know not what it is to turn their backs on the foe[5]."

He spoke this with a voice so modulated to[6] the different feelings expressed in his speech, with an eye so full of lofty design and heroism, that can you wonder that these men were moved? They looked at one another and were unable to reply. I spoke; I told them to retire and consider of what had been said: that I would not lead them farther north if they strenuously[7] desired the contrary; but that I hoped that, with reflection[8], their courage would return.

---

1 trial: 시험.

2 handed down as: …라고 판결(언도)되다.

3 mutable: 변하기 쉬운.

4 with the stigma of disgrace marked on your brows: '당신 이마에 수치(disgrace)라는 오명(stigma)이 붙은 채'; 동생 아벨(Abel)을 살해 한 후 신에 의해서 이마에 낙인이 찍힌 카인(Cain)의 이야기를 연상시킨다.

5 Return as heroes … turn their backs on the foe: turn their backs on the foe은 '적(foe)에게 등을 돌리다'. 즉 적에게서 도망친다는 의미; 이 구절은 단테의 「신곡」(Divine Comedy) 중 「지옥」(Inferno)편에서 그리스의 영웅 율리시즈(Ulysses)가 자신의 동료에게 새로운 모험의 길을 떠나자고 촉구하면서 하는 말을 연상시킨다. 또한 이 말은 「실낙원」에서 신에 의해 패배해 지옥에 떨어진 루시퍼(후에 사탄)가 자신의 동료에게 하는 말과도 유사하다.

6 modulated to: …에 맞추어 조절된.

7 strenuously: 격렬하게.

8 with reflection: 돌이켜 생각해 보고는.

They retired, and I turned towards my friend; but he was sunk in languor and almost deprived of life.

How all this will terminate I know not; but I had rather die than return shamefully — my purpose unfulfilled. Yet I fear such will be my fate; the men, unsupported by ideas of glory and honour, can never willingly continue to endure their present hardships.

September 7th.

The die is cast[1]; I have consented to return if we are not destroyed. Thus are my hopes blasted[2] by cowardice and indecision; I come back ignorant and disappointed. It requires more philosophy than I possess to bear this injustice[3] with patience.

September 12th.

It is past; I am returning to England. I have lost my hopes of utility and glory; — I have lost my friend. But I will endeavour to detail[4] these bitter circumstances to you, my dear sister; and while I am wafted[5] towards England and towards you, I will not despond[6].

September 9th[7], the ice began to move, and roarings like thunder were heard at a distance as the islands split and cracked in every direction[8]. We were in the most imminent peril; but as we could only remain passive, my chief attention was occupied by my unfortunate guest,

---

1 The die is cast: die는 '주사위'; '주사위는 던져졌다'는 이 말은 폼페이(Pompey)와의 일전을 치르기 위해 루비콘 강(Rubicon river)을 건너기 전 줄리우스 시저(Julius Caesar)가 한 것으로 이미 결정된 것은 더 이상의 논의 없이 따라야 한다는 뜻이다.

2 blasted: (희망이) 좌절된.

3 injustice: 잘못된 일.

4 detail: 상술하다.

5 wafted: 가볍게 실려 오다.

6 despond: 실망하다. 낙담하다.

7 September 9th: 매리 셸리의 모친인 매리 울스톤크라프트(Mary Wollstonecraft)는 매리를 낳은 후 얼마 되지 않은 1797년 9월 10일에 임종한다.

8 in every direction: 사방으로.

whose illness increased in such a degree that he was entirely confined to his bed. The ice cracked behind us and was driven with force[1] towards the north; a breeze sprung from the west, and on the 11th the passage towards the south became perfectly free. When the sailors saw this, and that their return to their native country was apparently assured, a shout of tumultuous joy broke[2] from them, loud and long-continued. Frankenstein, who was dozing, awoke and asked the cause of the tumult. "They shout," I said, "because they will soon return to England."

"Do you then really return?"

"Alas! yes; I cannot withstand[3] their demands. I cannot lead them unwillingly to danger, and I must return."

"Do so, if you will; but I will not. You may give up your purpose, but mine is assigned to me by Heaven, and I dare not. I am weak; but surely the spirits who assist my vengeance will endow me with sufficient strength." Saying this, he endeavoured to spring from the bed, but the exertion was too great for him; he fell back and fainted.

It was long before he was restored; and I often thought that life was entirely extinct[4]. At length he opened his eyes; he breathed with difficulty, and was unable to speak. The surgeon gave him a composing draught[5] and ordered us to leave him undisturbed. In the meantime he told me that my friend had certainly not many hours to live.

His sentence was pronounced[6], and I could only grieve and be patient. I sat by his bed watching him; his eyes were closed, and I thought he slept; but presently he called to me in a feeble[7] voice, and, bidding me come near, said — "Alas! the strength I relied on is gone; I feel that

---

1 with force: 세차게.

2 broke: (함성이) 터져 나오다.

3 withstand: 거부하다.

4 extinct: (생명이) 다한.

5 composing draught: (액체로 된) 진정제.

6 His sentence was pronounced: 그의 (사)형이 선고되었다.

7 feeble: 약한. 힘없는.

I shall soon die, and he, my enemy and persecutor, may still be in being. Think not, Walton, that in the last moments of my existence I feel that burning hatred and ardent desire of revenge I once expressed; but I feel myself justified in desiring the death of my adversary. During these last days I have been occupied in examining my past conduct; nor do I find it blamable. In a fit of enthusiastic madness I created a rational[1] creature, and was bound[2] towards him, to assure, as far as was in my power, his happiness and well-being. This was my duty; but there was another still paramount[3] to that. My duties towards the beings of my own species had greater claims to[4] my attention, because they included a greater proportion of happiness or misery. Urged by this view, I refused, and I did right in refusing, to create a companion for the first creature. He showed unparalleled malignity and selfishness, in evil: he destroyed my friends; he devoted to destruction[5] beings who possessed exquisite sensations, happiness, and wisdom; nor do I know where this thirst for vengeance may end. Miserable himself, that he may render no other wretched he ought to die. The task of his destruction was mine, but I have failed. When actuated[6] by selfish and vicious motives I asked you to undertake my unfinished work; and I renew this request now when I am only induced by reason and virtue.

"Yet I cannot ask you to renounce your country and friends to fulfil this task; and now that you are returning to England you will have little chance of meeting with him. But the consideration of these points, and the well balancing[7] of what you may esteem[8] your duties,

---

1 rational: 이성을 지닌.
2 bound: 의무를 지닌.
3 paramount: 가장 중요한.
4 had greater claims to: …을 누릴(받을) 더 많은 자격(claim)이 있다.
5 devoted to destruction: 파멸로 몰아넣다(파멸시키다).
6 actuated: 이끌려.
7 balancing: 여러 측면에서 고려함.
8 esteem: 간주하다.

I leave to you; my judgment and ideas are already disturbed by the near approach of death. I dare not ask you to do what I think right, for I may still be misled by passion.

"That he should live to be an instrument of mischief[1] disturbs me; in other respects, this hour, when I momentarily expect my release[2], is the only happy one which I have enjoyed for several years. The forms of the beloved dead flit before me and I hasten to their arms. Farewell, Walton! Seek happiness in tranquillity and avoid ambition, even if it be only the apparently innocent one of distinguishing yourself in science and discoveries. Yet why do I say this? I have myself been blasted in these hopes, yet another may succeed."

His voice became fainter as he spoke; and at length, exhausted by his effort, he sunk into silence. About half an hour afterwards he attempted again to speak, but was unable; he pressed my hand feebly, and his eyes closed for ever, while the irradiation[3] of a gentle smile passed away from his lips.

Margaret, what comment can I make on the untimely extinction[4] of this glorious spirit? What can I say that will enable you to understand the depth of my sorrow? All that I should express would be inadequate and feeble. My tears flow; my mind is overshadowed by a cloud of disappointment. But I journey towards England, and I may there find consolation.

I am interrupted. What do these sounds portend[5]? It is midnight; the breeze blows fairly, and the watch on deck[6] scarcely stir. Again; there is a sound as of a human voice, but hoarser; it comes from the

---

1 instrument of mischief: 악행을 일삼는 존재.
2 release: 여기서 '해방'(release)의 의미는 프랑켄스타인을 정신적 고통에서 해방시켜줄 죽음을 지칭한다.
3 irradiation: 광채. 광휘.
4 untimely extinction: untimely는 '시기상조의'. '때 이른'; extinction은 '죽음'.
5 portend: 미리 알리다.
6 watch on deck: 갑판위에서 대기하며 주변상황을 살피는 사람.

cabin where the remains[1] of Frankenstein still lie. I must arise and examine. Good night, my sister.

Great God! what a scene has just taken place! I am yet dizzy[2] with the remembrance of it. I hardly know whether I shall have the power to detail it; yet the tale which I have recorded would be incomplete without this final and wonderful[3] catastrophe.

I entered the cabin where lay the remains of my ill-fated[4] and admirable friend. Over him hung a form which I cannot find words to describe; gigantic in stature, yet uncouth[5] and distorted in its proportions. As he hung over the coffin his face was concealed by long locks[6] of ragged[7] hair; but one vast hand was extended, in colour and apparent texture like that of a mummy[8]. When he heard the sound of my approach he ceased to utter exclamations of grief and horror and sprung towards the window. Never did I behold a vision so horrible as his face, of such loathsome yet appalling hideousness. I shut my eyes involuntarily[9] and endeavoured to recollect what were my duties with regard to this destroyer. I called on him to stay.

He paused, looking on me with wonder; and, again turning towards the lifeless form of his creator, he seemed to forget my presence, and every feature and gesture seemed instigated by the wildest rage[10] of some uncontrollable passion.

"That is also my victim!" he exclaimed: "in his murder my crimes are consummated; the miserable series of my being is wound to its

---

1   remains: 시신.
2   dizzy: 아찔한.
3   wonderful: 놀라운. 믿기 어려운.
4   ill-fated: 불운한(불행한).
5   uncouth: 야릇한. 기괴한.
6   locks: 머리타래.
7   ragged: 텁수룩한.
8   mummy: 미라.
9   involuntarily: 무의식적으로.
10   rage: (통제할 수 없는) 격렬한 감정.

close[1]! Oh, Frankenstein! generous and self-devoted[2] being! what does it avail that[3] I now ask thee to pardon me? I, who irretrievably[4] destroyed thee by destroying all thou lovedst. Alas! he is cold, he cannot answer me."

His voice seemed suffocated; and my first impulses, which had suggested to me the duty of obeying the dying request of my friend, in destroying his enemy, were now suspended by a mixture of curiosity and compassion. I approached this tremendous[5] being; I dared not again raise my eyes to his face, there was something so scaring and unearthly in his ugliness. I attempted to speak, but the words died away on my lips. The monster continued to utter wild and incoherent self-reproaches. At length I gathered resolution to address him in a pause of the tempest of his passion[6]: "Your repentance," I said, "is now superfluous[7]. If you had listened to the voice of conscience, and heeded the stings of remorse[8], before you had urged your diabolical vengeance to this extremity[9], Frankenstein would yet have lived.

"And do you dream?" said the daemon; "do you think that I was then dead to[10] agony and remorse? — He," he continued, pointing to the corpse, "he suffered not in the consummation of the deed — Oh! not the ten-thousandth portion of the anguish that was mine during the lingering[11] detail of its execution. A frightful selfishness hurried me

---

1 close: 종결. 결말.
2 self-devoted: 자기희생적인. 헌신적인.
3 what does it avail that: …한다고 무슨 소용이 있겠는가?
4 irretrievably: 돌이킬 수 없게.
5 tremendous: 무시무시한.
6 in a pause of the tempest of his passion: 자신의 (괴로운) 감정을 폭풍이 몰아치듯 드러내던 것을 괴물이 멈춘 사이.
7 superfluous: 의미 없는.
8 stings of remorse: 양심의 가책.
9 to this extremity: 이처럼 극단적으로.
10 dead to: …을 느끼지 못하는.
11 lingering: 망설이는.

on, while my heart was poisoned with remorse. Think you that the groans of Clerval were music to my ears? My heart was fashioned to be susceptible of[1] love and sympathy; and when wrenched by misery to vice and hatred it did not endure the violence of the change without torture such as you cannot even imagine.

"After the murder of Clerval I returned to Switzerland heartbroken and overcome. I pitied Frankenstein; my pity amounted to[2] horror: I abhorred myself. But when I discovered that he, the author at once[3] of my existence and of its unspeakable torments, dared to hope for happiness; that while he accumulated wretchedness and despair upon me he sought his own enjoyment in feelings and passions from the indulgence of which I was for ever barred, then impotent[4] envy and bitter indignation filled me with an insatiable[5] thirst for vengeance. I recollected my threat and resolved that it should be accomplished. I knew that I was preparing for myself a deadly torture; but I was the slave, not the master, of an impulse which I detested, yet could not disobey. Yet when she died! — nay, then I was not miserable. I had cast off all feeling, subdued[6] all anguish, to riot in[7] the excess of my despair. Evil thenceforth became my good[8]. Urged thus far, I had no choice but to adapt my nature to an element which I had willingly chosen. The completion of my demoniacal design became an insatiable passion. And now it is ended; there is my last victim!"

I was at first touched by the expressions of his misery; yet, when I

---

1 susceptible of: …을 느낄 수 있는(할 수 있는).
2 amounted to: …정도에 이르다.
3 at once: 일찍이. 과거에.
4 impotent: 무기력한.
5 insatiable: 충족되지 않는.
6 subdued: 억제하다. 억누르다.
7 riot in: …에 빠져들다(마음껏 즐기다).
8 Evil thenceforth became my good:『실낙원』의 사탄이 자신의 행동원칙에 대한 말과 유사하다.

called to mind[1] what Frankenstein had said of his powers of eloquence and persuasion, and when I again cast my eyes on the lifeless form of my friend, indignation was rekindled within me. "Wretch!" I said, "it is well that you come here to whine over[2] the desolation that you have made. You throw a torch into a pile[3] of buildings; and when they are consumed[4] you sit among the ruins and lament the fall. Hypocritical fiend! if he whom you mourn still lived, still would he be the object, again would he become the prey, of your accursed vengeance. It is not pity that you feel; you lament only because the victim of your malignity is withdrawn from your power."

"Oh, it is not thus — not thus," interrupted the being; "yet such must be the impression conveyed to you by what appears to be the purport[5] of my actions. Yet I seek not a fellow-feeling in my misery. No sympathy may I ever find. When I first sought it, it was the love of virtue, the feelings of happiness and affection with which my whole being overflowed, that I wished to be participated. But now that virtue has become to me a shadow and that happiness and affection are turned into bitter and loathing despair, in what should I seek for sympathy? I am content to suffer alone while my sufferings shall endure: when I die, I am well satisfied that abhorrence and opprobrium[6] should load my memory. Once my fancy was soothed with dreams of virtue, of fame, and of enjoyment. Once I falsely hoped to meet with beings who, pardoning my outward form, would love me for the excellent qualities which I was capable of unfolding. I was nourished with high thoughts[7] of honour and devotion. But now crime has

---

1 called to mind: 상기하다.
2 whine over: …에 대해 애처로이 울다(흐느껴 울다).
3 pile: 대건축물(군(群)).
4 consumed: 다 타버린.
5 purport: 목적. 취지.
6 opprobrium: 불명예. 오명.
7 high thoughts: 고결한 생각들.

degraded me beneath the meanest animal. No guilt, no mischief, no malignity, no misery, can be found comparable to[1] mine. When I run over[2] the frightful catalogue of my sins, I cannot believe that I am the same creature whose thoughts were once filled with sublime and transcendent visions of the beauty and the majesty of goodness. But it is even so; the fallen angel becomes a malignant devil[3]. Yet even that enemy of God and man had friends and associates[4] in his desolation; I am alone.

"You, who call Frankenstein your friend, seem to have a knowledge of my crimes and his misfortunes. But in the detail which he gave you of them he could not sum up[5] the hours and months of misery which I endured, wasting in impotent passions. For while I destroyed his hopes, I did not satisfy my own desires. They were for ever ardent and craving; still I desired love and fellowship, and I was still spurned. Was there no injustice in this? Am I to be thought the only criminal, when all human kind sinned against me? Why do you not hate Felix who drove his friend from his door with contumely[6]? Why do you not execrate[7] the rustic who sought to destroy the saviour of his child? Nay, these are virtuous and immaculate[8] beings! I, the miserable and the abandoned[9], am an abortion[10], to be spurned at[11], and kicked, and trampled on. Even now my blood boils at the recol-

---

1 comparable to: …에 견줄만한.

2 run over: 대충 훑어보다.

3 fallen angel becomes a malignant devil: 『실낙원』에서 대천사였던 루시퍼(Lucifer)는 신에게 패배해 지옥으로 떨어진 후 사탄이 된다. 지옥으로 '떨어진'(fallen) 천사는 곧 '타락한'(fallen) 천사, 즉 '사악한 악마'(malignant devil)가 된 것이다.

4 associates: 동료. 한패.

5 sum up: 모두 알다(간파하다).

6 contumely: 오만무례. 모욕적 언동.

7 execrate: 통렬히 비난하다.

8 immaculate: 오점 없는.

9 abandoned: 자포자기한.

10 abortion: 기형적인 존재.

11 spurned at: 경멸되다.

lection of this injustice.

"But it is true that I am a wretch. I have murdered the lovely and the helpless; I have strangled the innocent as they slept, and grasped to death his throat who never injured me or any other living thing. I have devoted my creator, the select specimen of all that is worthy of love and admiration among men, to misery; I have pursued him even to that irremediable¹ ruin. There he lies, white and cold in death. You hate me; but your abhorrence cannot equal that with which I regard² myself. I look on the hands which executed the deed; I think on the heart in which the imagination of it was conceived, and long for the moment when these hands will meet my eyes, when that imagination will haunt my thoughts no more.

"Fear not that I shall be the instrument of future mischief. My work is nearly complete. Neither yours nor any man's death is needed to consummate the series of my being, and accomplish that which must be done; but it requires my own. Do not think that I shall be slow to perform this sacrifice. I shall quit your vessel on the ice-raft which brought me thither, and shall seek the most northern extremity³ of the globe; I shall collect my funeral pile⁴ and consume to ashes this miserable frame, that its remains may afford no light⁵ to any curious and unhallowed wretch who would create such another as I have been. I shall die. I shall no longer feel the agonies which now consume⁶ me, or be the prey of feelings unsatisfied, yet unquenched. He is dead who called me into being⁷; and when I shall be no more the very remembrance of us both will speedily vanish. I shall no longer

---

1 irremediable: 돌이킬 수 없는.
2 regard: 주시하다.
3 extremity: 끝.
4 funeral pile: 화장할 때 사용하는 장작더미.
5 afford no light: 어떤 '정보'(light)도 제공하지 않는다.
6 consume: 괴롭히다.
7 called me into being: 나를 존재하게 하다.

see the sun or stars, or feel the winds play on my cheeks. Light, feeling, and sense will pass away; and in this condition must I find my
happiness. Some years ago, when the images which this world affords
first opened upon[1] me, when I felt the cheering warmth of summer,
and heard the rustling[2] of the leaves and the warbling[3] of the birds,
and these were all to me, I should have wept to die; now it is my only
consolation. Polluted by crimes, and torn by the bitterest remorse,
where can I find rest but in death?

"Farewell! I leave you, and in you the last of human kind whom
these eyes will ever behold. Farewell, Frankenstein! If thou wert yet
alive, and yet cherished a desire of revenge against me, it would be
better satiated in my life than in my destruction. But it was not so;
thou didst seek my extinction that I might not cause greater wretchedness; and if yet, in some mode unknown to me, thou hadst not
ceased to think and feel, thou wouldst not desire against me a vengeance greater than that which I feel. Blasted as thou wert, my agony
was still superior to thine; for the bitter sting of remorse will not cease
to rankle[4] in my wounds until death shall close them for ever.

"But soon," he cried with sad and solemn enthusiasm, "I shall die,
and what I now feel be no longer felt. Soon these burning miseries
will be extinct. I shall ascend my funeral pile triumphantly[5], and exult
in the agony of the torturing flames. The light of that conflagration[6]
will fade away[7]; my ashes will be swept into the sea by the winds. My

---

1 opened upon: …에게 펼쳐지다.

2 rustling: 바스락거리는 소리.

3 warbling: 새의 지저귀는 소리.

4 rankle: 끊임없이 괴롭히다.

5 I shall ascend my funeral pile triumphantly: 고대 그리스나 로마의 영웅들은 죽으
면 장작위에 올려 화장을 한다. 『플루타크 영웅전』을 읽어 고대 그리스 로마의 영웅들
에 관한 이야기를 잘 알고 있던 괴물은 이들과 유사한 방식으로 자신의 죽음을 맞이
하려 하는 것이다.

6 conflagration: (큰) 불.

7 fade away: 사라지다.

spirit will sleep in peace, or if it thinks, it will not surely think thus. Farewell."

He sprung from the cabin-window as he said this, upon the ice-raft which lay close to the vessel. He was soon borne away by the waves and lost[1] in darkness and distance.

---

1 lost: 보이지 않다.

Essays in Criticism

Monstrosity, Suffering, Subjectivity, and Sympathetic Community in *Frankenstein* and "The Structure of Torture"

Josh Bernatchez*

Mary Shelley's 1818 version of *Frankenstein* displays a deep interest in how individual subjectivity arises out of a negotiated relationship with a broader social world. This interest is manifest in the Creature's physical construction by Victor and is also mirrored in the failed attempts by the Creature to achieve sympathetic relationships. The exact structure of these failed attempts and the subsequent monstrousness of the Creature can be analyzed through the model provided by Elaine Scarry in *The Body in Pain*, in which Scarry argues that an individual's perceptual world can be recoded by pain, which annihilates subjective identity by its systematic interruption and reversal of efforts at self-extension — -i.e., the individual's attempts at connection with others. In her chapter "The Structure of Torture," Scarry dissects a fully formed and established subjectivity. Shelley's *Frankenstein* offers an early science-fiction creation myth that describes a creature who comes into being in an attempt to assert himself despite a social world that is as structurally antagonistic to his efforts as Scarry's torture chamber is to a victim's consciousness.

Initially, Scarry's interest in what is ultimately a very physical process may seem unrelated to the Creature's succession of failed attempts at social communion. Nonetheless, the basis of comparison between *The Body in Pain* and *Frankenstein* is a compellingly similar conception of individual identity as being ontologically contingent on sympathetic social interaction. The development of the Creature

* 이 글은 2009년도에 출판된 *Science Fiction Studies* 36권 205-216쪽에 실린 것임.

in *Frankenstein* is informed by the theories about the relationship between individuals and their societies that were prevalent in Shelley'
s era. In *The Theory of Moral Sentiments* (1759), for example, Adam
Smith argued that the greatest hindrance to being a "good" person is
any withdrawal of sympathy by the human community:

> Human virtue is superior to pain, to poverty, to danger, and to death;
> nor does it even require its utmost efforts to despise them. But to
> have its misery exposed to insult and derision, to be led in triumph,
> to be set up for the hand of scorn to point at, is a situation in which
> its constancy is much more apt to fail. (83)

In the "Theatricality of Moral Sentiments," David Marshall draws
on the underlying imaginative function described by Smith, casting
it in terms of theatrical performance and writing that Smith "is concerned with the inherent theatricality of both presenting a character
before the eyes of the world and acting as a beholder to people who
perform acts of solitude" (594). For Marshall, physical and psychological suffering and annihilation exist in a continuum; denying individuals the refuge of community can be destructive to their sense of self.

The relationship between the physical and psychological compo-
nents of a conscious being is, however, better articulated in the structural model provided by Scarry. Indeed, these concepts form the locus
of interaction between Scarry's ideas and those contemporary to, and
rendered in, Shelley's *Frankenstein*. Scarry's model rests on the idea
that there is a structural interdependence between physical comfort
and the psychological well-being necessary to actualize human consciousness. She describes human consciousness as a product of civilization, in that civilization represents the large-scale consideration of
physical needs that precipitates human consciousness:

> There is nothing contradictory about the fact that the shelter is at
> once so graphic an image of the body and so emphatic an instance

of civilisation: only because it is the first can it be the second···. In the details of its outer structure and in its furniture (from "furnir," meaning "to further" or "to forward," to project oneself outward), the room accommodates and thereby eliminates from human attention the human body: the simple triad of floor, chair and bed ··· makes spatially and therefore steadily visible the collection of postures and positions the body moves in and out of, objectifies the three locations within the body that most frequently hold the body's weight, objectifies, finally, its need to become wholly forgetful of its weight, to move weightlessly into a larger mindfulness. As the elemental room is multiplied into a house of rooms and the house into a city of houses, the body is carried forward into each successive intensification of civilisation. (39)

Torture reverses this outward, creative progression, because all the self-extending markers of civilization are re-coded, becoming sources of pain and forcing people back into their own bodily sensations.

In conformity with Scarry's model, Mary Shelley's abandoned Creature relates his early experiences as arduous. He is is driven to fulfill basic bodily needs and to save himself from suffering: "oppressed by cold," for instance, he is forced to seek shelter in a shepherd's hut (130). He describes the hut as being "as exquisite and divine a retreat as Pandemonium appeared to the daemons of hell after their sufferings" (132), comparing himself to Milton's Satan, another outcast (who is, however, surrounded by a community, his army, even in exile). The Creature's respite in the hut is very brief, however: he is rejected from potential fellowship and treated as a transgressor, long before any malevolent action on his part, as the panic-stricken shepherd flees the hut, running across the countryside on a maimed leg.

The Creature, continuing his progression of expanding self-extension as set out by Scarry, moves outward toward successively larger emblems of civilization, from a hut of one room to a town of many houses. He describes his hopefulness at sighting a village: "How miraculous did this appear! The huts, the neater cottages, and stately

houses, engaged my admiration by turns" (132). Yet his attempt to enter a civilized space is again met with a forceful exclusion: "the whole
village was roused; some fled, some attacked [him], until, grievously
bruised [he] escaped" (132). In the Creature's narrative, representations
of civilization are recoded as sources of anguish. The village attacks
him, just as Scarry writes of the torture process in which "civilization
is brought to the prisoner and in his presence annihilated in the very
process by which it is being made to annihilate him" (44). Artifacts
that embody civilization (tables, chairs, walls) are re-coded as implements of pain: things to be beaten with or against, like "the conver-
sion of a refrigerator into a bludgeon" (41).

To understand both how these physical assaults on the Creature
translate into assaults on his identity, and to examine Scarry's arguments that support this idea, it is necessary to recognize that torture is
ostensibly a recourse necessitated by an impasse in a verbal interrogation. This verbal component structures torture because it demands that
the victims be complicit in their own self-annihilation by "betraying
themselves." Scarry asks why we commonly use the word "betrayal"
when describing the forced confession resulting from torture. Ostensibly, the word is appropriate because it implies that the elicited response typically requires that victims undermine their sense of self by
"betraying" their secrets, their families, or their organizations. Scarry
argues, however, that in such a context the term becomes absurd:

> One cannot betray or be false to something that has ceased to exist
> and, in the most literal way possible, the created world of thought and
> feeling, all the psychological and mental content that constitutes both
> one"s self and one"s world, and that gives rise to and is in turn made
> possible by language, ceases to exist. (30)

Scarry asserts that the content of the question or answer is often ir-
relevant, since the regime does not need the information, already possesses it, or the victim does not have it. What is crucial is "the form of

the answer, the fact of ⋯ answering" (29). The torture scenario is the performance of "the fiction of power" (27). It is empty, because all the act really exhibits is cruelty. "The question," writes Scarry, "whatever its content, is an act of wounding; the answer, whatever its content, is a scream" (46).

The narrative trajectory of the Creature's life can be interpreted as an implicit response to the implicit question: "what are you?" The interrogation demands of the Creature that he betray himself— -confess, against his aspirations for selfcreation, virtue, and recognition, that "I am a monster." This verbal component of torture played out in *Frankenstein* is, effectively, a naming contest. At the moment of his first sympathetic interaction, the Creature refers to old De Lacey's family as "your fellow-Creatures" (159), placing them all in a common category that excludes himself. He uses the phrase "thy Creature" (125) when speaking of himself to Victor, always in opposition to the designation of "monster" and always implying a shared culpability in his "misdeeds."[1] Conversely, Victor calls him a "devil," a "daemon," or a "monster" (125). Victor refuses to use a name that would link his creation to any shared community or category. The conflict between the two can be interpreted as a semiotic battle between Victor, representative of human community in general, and the Creature, in search of identity and social niche.

This naming contest and its structure extend beyond interactions with Victor. The human versus monster binary is also mirrored in the tension between the physical and the verbal or mental. In Scarry' s model, victims are forced into the suffering of their physical bodies, capable only of animal responses; their voices, the ultimate sign of human self-extension and community, are appropriated by their torturers. This process plays out repeatedly in *Frankenstein* as the Creature is

---

1   The exception that proves the rule is the Creature's association with the word "wretch,"which according to the OED, once specifically denoted "an exile" ("Wretch").

entrapped and isolated in his own body. When he is caught by young
Felix De Lacey in a potentially successful and classical gesture of supplication, touching the knees of Felix"'s blind father and reaching up-
ward, the Creature recounts the moment as one of anguish:

> Who can describe their horror and consternation on beholding me?
> … Felix darted forward, and with supernatural force tore me from his
> father, to whose knees I clung: in a transport of fury, he dashed me
> to the ground, and struck me with a stick.… I saw him on the point
> of repeating his blow, when, overcome by pain and anguish, I quitted
> the cottage. (160)

The Creature, in the verbal forum, begins to be successful in achieving
a sympathetic response, but is ultimately denied it because of young
De Lacey's rejection of the ugliness of his body. Over the course of
events, Frankenstein's Creature explicitly describes a sense of his body
as the root of his isolation:

> Once I falsely hoped to meet with beings, who, *pardoning my outward
> form*, would love me for the excellent qualities which I was capable
> of bringing forth. I was nourished with high thoughts of honour and
> devotion. But now vice has degraded me beneath the meanest animal.
> (242; emphasis added)

The passage identifies the contrast between the Creature's "excellent
qualities" (human), which would endear him to social beings, and his
degraded (animalistic) state.

Scarry's text emphasizes "the opposition of body and voice" (45).
She discusses a story by Jean-Paul Sartre in which a condemned character "perceives the body as an 'enormous vermin' to which he is
tied, a colossus to which he is bound but with which he feels no kin-
ship" (31). This is one of the opening anecdotes in "The Structure of
Torture" and defines the bodily estrangement fostered by torture, in
which the physical aspect of a condemned man"'s consciousness is sys-

tematically turned against him.

Once the victim's voice has been set against the victim himself, the next stage in Scarry's model is the appropriation of the victim's suffering and right to sympathy. As a victim's consciousness is pushed far from his communally-conferred identity and far back into painful bodily sensations, a parallel distancing occurs between torturer and victim. It is true that the Creature is not subject to the premeditated plan of a single torturer, yet this role is nonetheless filled at critical junctures, often by Victor, who always insists on his categorical moral distance from his creation. Victor responds to the Creature's civil first attempts to communicate with him by saying, "Begone! I will not hear you. There can be no community between you and me" (126).

The Creature, meanwhile, insists that he is of the same essential nature as humans, that his "soul" glows "with love and humanity" (126), and that he is capable of virtue. At the end of the novel he recounts that "when [he] first sought [sympathy], it was the love of virtue, the feelings of happiness and affection with which [his] whole being overflowed, that [he] wished to be participated" (242). The word "participated" exemplifies the idea that virtue is a capacity that must be exercised in conjunction with others and is stifled in isolation. Victor denies his Creature's needs when he insists that "there can be no community" between them because the Creature is fiendish and undeserving of compassion. Victor compounds the problem when he destroys the female companion, denying his creation an alternate community. He initially agrees to create her, conceding that "there was some justice in his [the Creature's] argument" (170) and that "his tale, and the feelings he ⋯ expressed, proved him to be a creature of fine sensation" (170). Yet the Creature's categorical monstrosity is finally cited as justification for Victor's destruction of the female.

Aside from the psychological pain inflicted on victims by denying their claims to community and therefore any claims to sympathy or rescue, the process of distancing also has a psychological effect on the torturer. A major concern of Scarry's text is the question of how "one person can be in the presence of another person in pain and not know it ⋯ to the point where he himself ⋯ goes on inflicting it" (12). Her answer is that a radical act of distancing interrupts natural sympathetic responses in the torturer: "it prevents the mind from ever getting to a place where it would have to make" a comparison between torturer and victim (59). Suggesting a parallel between the distancing of torturer from victim and consciousness from body, Scarry writes that "all those ways in which the torturer dramatizes his opposition to and distance from the prisoner are ways of dramatizing his distance from the body" and that "the most radical act of distancing resides in his disclaiming of the other's hurt" (57). Taken to this extreme, the act of distancing becomes the torturer's own act of appropriating the right to suffer. To illustrate, Scarry relates a victim's description of German concentration camp guards who testified that they would shoot prisoners were it not for the expense of the bullets. This would produce no intelligible effect on the victims, but rather indicated that the guards were being forced to pay for every expended bullet. Describing Himmler's strategy for conditioning guards, Scarry quotes Hanna Arendt, who writes that "instead of saying: What horrible things I did to people, the murderers would be able to say: What horrible things I had to watch in the pursuance of my duties, how heavily the task weighed upon my shoulders" (Arendt 106). So indoctrinated, individuals can perpetrate inhuman crimes, because torture reinforces in the individual the aggressor-state's assumption of justification and superiority.

That Victor has appropriated suffering as a means and justification for the continued infliction of pain on the Creature is evident in this speech: "you have made me wretched beyond expression. You have left me no power to consider whether I am just to you, or not" (Shelley 127). Even though Victor has been integral to the creation of the situation he bemoans, he insists that he alone is the innocent sufferer; he denies the Creature's right to sympathy or justice. It is worth noting that an analysis based on Scarry's model does not allow the Creature to be characterized as innocent; any such argument is eroded by the text. For the Creature in his turn often tortures Victor: "slave···. Remember that I have power; you believe yourself miserable, but I can make you so wretched that the light of day will be hateful to you" (192). Scarry's morally unambiguous model is not fully co-extensive with Shelley's protean fiction.

Yet even though the evil perpetrated by the Creature complicates the full application of Scarry's ideas, the framework she provides does offer two distinct but related avenues for reconciling Shelley's ambiguity, although we are still missing analogues for two elements of Scarry's model. First, we have not seen the actual "confession," which Scarry says that "whatever its content, is a scream." Second, we have yet to see any means of escape or rehabilitation for the victim. Both of these are accounted for in Scarry, and both have curiously linked analogues in *Frankenstein.*

To see how Scarry's confession-scream is played out, it is useful to turn to a question asked by Chris Baldick: why is Frankenstein's creature, given that Victor "selected his features as beautiful" (Shelley 85) and assembled them to create a beautiful form, so ugly that Victor, at first sight, reports that "horror and disgust filled [his] heart" (85)? Baldick bases his answer tentatively on a problem in aesthetic and social theory contemporary with the writing of *Frankenstein* — a conceptual gap between a whole and the sum of its parts. He draws on Samuel Taylor Coleridge's distinction between the assembling function of Fancy and the unifying, harmonizing Imagination, which makes something whole and beautiful:

> [T]he beauty of the whole can arise only from a pure vital principle within, to which all subordinate parts and limbs will then conform. The parts, in a living being, can only be as beautiful as the animating

principle which organizes them, and if this "spark of life" proceeds, as it does in Victor's creation, from tormented isolation and guilty secrecy, the resulting assembly will only animate and body forth that condition and display its moral ugliness. (Baldick 35)

Baldick relates the moral crisis that generates the Creature's ugliness to Johann Christof Friedrich Schiller's notion of the fractured human subject. Quoting Schiller, Baldick writes:

Modern society is but "an ingenious mechanism" made from "the piecing together of innumerable but lifeless parts." In Schiller's diagnosis, an advanced division of labour has dismembered the human personality so completely into distinct faculties that "one has to go the rounds from one individual to another in order to piece together a complete image of the species." Now that the individual has become just a stunted fragment, society can be little more than a monstrous aggregation of incomplete parts. (34-35)

Schiller describes in contemporary life a reciprocal degradation of the individual and also of society at large. The problem is more clearly (if perhaps reductively) articulated by Mary Shelley's father, William Godwin, in *Political Justice*: "Man is a social animal. How far he is necessarily so, will appear, if we consider the sum of advantages resulting from the social, and to which he would be deprived in the solitary state" (386). The tentative answer to Baldick's question about the root of the Creature's ugliness (physical and moral) is, we begin to see, an anxiety contemporary with Mary Shelley about the absence of social cohesion. The Creature adamantly refuses to be treated as an absence. As Denise Gigante writes:

This *via negativa* of aesthetic theory ⋯ will not suffice as a hermeneutic mode to account for the positive ugliness of Mary Shelley's creature. If the ugly object lacks beauty, the Creature, as the aesthetic object of Frankenstein's "unhallowed arts" ⋯ functions more actively than lack. He not only fails to please, he emphatically displeases···. Contrary to the ··· argument that conceives ugliness as the defective mode of beauty, as its distortion, one should assert the *ontological primacy of ugliness*: it is beauty that is a kind of defence against the Ugly in its repulsive existence — or, rather, against existence *tout court*, since ··· what is ugly is ultimately the brutal fact of existence (of the real) as such. (566)

Gigante goes on to state that the conception of the ugly as a lack is a failure of aesthetic theory, a sort of willful ignorance in which "aesthetic theory itself turns away, shrinking back, rejecting, and (in Kant's terms) setting its face against" (579) that which is called ugly. A thing becomes "ugly" because its positive existence is denied due to its conflict with accepted patterns.

If we understand the creature's moral ugliness to have been produced by a community's refusal to grant positive recognition, and yet reject that ugliness is the manifestation of a lack, we must conclude that the ugliness signifies something beyond itself: pain. The Creature never offers a literal confession in the text, but he does seem to concede the point that he is a monster implicitly through his crimes. If we take Scarry's formulation to heart, this confession of monstrosity, like any other such confession, is a scream. And what is a scream? In this framework, a scream is the instinctual attempt to extend the experience of pain into the world, to force its common recognition. Adjectives traditionally used to describe a scream, such as "blood-curdling," "heart-wrenching," and "bone-chilling," remind us that a scream recreates in anyone who hears it some of the pain felt by the screamer. The sound itself is disturbing, irrespective of any abstract compassion or sympathy one might feel (or fail to feel) for the screamer.

The Creature's more heinous actions, for all intents and purposes, may make him a true monster, but it is important to note that he is not irretrievably so. He consistently displays the capacity and drive to be something else. As he says, "[he] had feelings of affection, and they were requited by detestation and scorn" (192), and there is something compelling about his complaint. Throughout the Creature's development we see him work toward achieving his noble aspirations. Scarry's model identifies separate patterns for rehabilitating a person's identity as well as its dissection. In *Frankenstein*, however, we see these two processes superimposed. The Creature is constantly beaten back into his body, but this happens precisely at junctures where he has contrived opportunities for outward self-extension. He attempts to communicate, to participate in community, to find recognition, and to escape the isolation of his own frame, actions that can be mapped onto Scarry's model for the rehabilitation of a victim:

> As torture consists of acts that magnify the way in which pain destroys a person's world, self, and voice, so these other acts that restore the voice become not only a denunciation of the pain but almost a diminution of the pain, a partial reversal of the process of torture itself. An act of human contact and concern ··· provides the hurt person with worldly self-extension: in acknowledging and expressing another person's pain, or in articulating one of his nonbodily concerns while he is unable to, one human being who is well and free willingly turns himself into an image of the other's psychic or sentient claims, an image existing in the space outside the sufferer's body ··· until the sufferer himself regains his own powers of self-extension. By ··· giving the pain a place in the world, sympathy lessens the power of sickness and pain, counteracts the force with which a person in great pain or sickness can be swallowed alive by the body. (50)

All the Creature's actions constitute an attempt to achieve what in Scarry's model would lead towards rehabilitation and a return to human consciousness.

That the Creature relates his development in such vivid detail suggests that he is endowed from "birth" with a fully formed rational consciousness. His tale begins: "It is with considerable difficulty that I remember the original aera of my being: all the events of that period appear confused and indistinct" (128). While the Creature relates the sense of confusion, he also describes that confusion with detail usually only available to a fully functioning, analytic mind. He even describes the confusion itself: "a strange multiplicity of sensation seized me ⋯ and it was ⋯ a long time before I learned to distinguish between the operations of my various senses" (128). He displays, for a being who is in effect an infant, an excellent understanding of the world: "Before [he] had quitted [Victor's] apartment, on a sensation of cold, [he] had covered [him]self with some clothes" (129). The newly sentient Creature recognizes cold and then, by dressing, applies a typically learned response to the problem. Finally, prior to acquiring language, the Creature knows what language is and understands its function. He recounts that "thoughts [of interacting with the cottagers] exhilarated [him], and led [him] to apply with fresh ardour to the acquiring of the art of language" (141). Though he has been denied the benefits of social interaction, innate abilities lead the Creature outward in a quest for community and self-extension.

The creature is initially composed out of other human beings; as a created object, he is a metaphor for the dependence of the individual on a community, for he is an individual composed of many other individuals. Likewise, the Creature's preternatural consciousness, which suggests that his mental being is already composed of the faculties of others, drives him towards a moment the Creature himself identifies as one of creation:

> The old man paused, and then continued, "If you will unreservedly confide to me the particulars of your tale, I perhaps may be of use in undeceiving them [⋯]."
> "Excellent man! I thank you, and accept your generous offer. *You raise me from the dust* by this kindness; and I trust that, by your aid, I shall not be driven from the society and sympathy of your fellow-Creatures. (159; emphasis added)

As noted in Macdonald and Scherf's edition, the phrase "you raise me from the dust" is an allusion to the moment in Milton's *Paradise Lost* when Adam is giving their creation as a reason why he and Eve are indebted to God.

This second (verbal) instance of creation in Shelley's text is the only interaction in which the Creature is not perceived as ugly. This can be attributed to the blindness of his interlocutor, but it is telling that the Creature's ugliness is invisible at the precise moment when he is offered tentative admission into a community. This is chronologically the first instance in his narrative where the Creature uses his voice to convey his thoughts to another being. In referring to the "society and sympathy of [De Lacey's] fellow-Creatures," this conversation also marks the Creature's first attempt to imply that he and humans are "creatures" all — -the same in kind. Finally, this scene marks the moment when the Creature begins to consider himself categorically alienated from the human community; after Felix's beating he reports that "[his] protectors had departed, and had broken the only link that held [him] to the world" (162). Once this link is severed, the Creature sets out to track down and persecute Victor.

The Creature's actions to this point were accompanied by sincere attempts at a positive engagement with society. He first tried to help the De Lacey family anonymously, hoping that by "gentle demeanour and conciliating words, [he] should first win their favour, and afterwards their love" (140). Even after his disappointment, there were still moments of altruism, such as his efforts to save a child, that were requited with gunshots. After his failure with the De Laceys, however, the Creature moves towards more violent actions. Yet at first his purpose remains the same: to form a community. He tries to force Victor to create for him a being that, in parallel with Scarry's model, can acknowledge "the other's psychic or sentient claims" and act like an "image existing in the space outside the sufferer's body" (50). To this end, the Creature demands of Victor a mate "with whom [he] can live in the interchange of those sympathies necessary for [his] being" (Shelley 168). Denied, the Creature begs, "Let me see that I excite the sympathy of some existing thing" (170). At this point, the request for sympathy constitutes a plea for life.

Denied any opportunity to communicate, defeated by his own body, the Creature is driven to self-hatred. Scarry writes that "if self-hatred, self-alienation and self-betrayal ⋯ were translated out of the psychological realm where it has content and is accessible to language into the unspeakable and contentless realm of physical sensation it would be intense pain" (47). The Creature reveals just such a painful consciousness to Walton: "You hate me; but your abhorrence cannot equal that with which I regard myself" (243). All the Creature's crimes serve to attest to the monstrosity attributed to him. The violence of his suffering, exceeding Scarry's model of the torture chamber, culminates in his taking charge of his own annihilation. The Creature, who in his last words reveals his intent to immolate himself, says that "when the images which the world affords first opened upon me ⋯ and these were all to me, I should have wept to die; now it is my only consolation. Polluted by crimes, and torn by the bitterest remorse, where can I find rest but in death?" (244). Beginning with his first crime, the Creature moves simultaneously toward achieving both his and Victor's annihilation. Upon Victor's death, the Creature says that "in his murder my crimes are consummated; the miserable series of my being is wound to its close" (240), suggesting a coextensive relationship between his creator and himself that is only actualized in death.

The main difficulty in applying Scarry's model to *Frankenstein* is the perpetration by the Creature of premeditated crimes against the innocent. One example is the misery he forces on Justine, yet even in this crime there is an attempt at self-extension. Justine's fate, sealed by "circumstantial evidence" (112) — and in which a clear case of coerced confession and annihilation is played out in conformity to Scarry' s model — provides a reprise of the Creature's plight orchestrated by the Creature himself. Baldick suggests that Justine, accused of murdering the Creature's first victim, becomes a stand-in for the Creature:

> The Genevese court ⋯ is tricked into doing what Victor finally refuses to do for his Creature: it makes a female 'monster' of Justine, and the priest even comes close to convincing Justine of her monstrous nature ⋯ forcing her to confess falsely to the murder. Only by staging parodies of the injustice he suffers can the monster reproduce his outcast kind; so long as there are victims, he is not altogether alone. (53)

Justine, named a monster and condemned by the "popular voice" (Shelley 111) of her community, is "threatened and menaced" into confessing, on pain of "excommunication" (113), to being the child-killing monster. In one of her final acts she reports: "I did confess; but I confessed a lie. I confessed that I might obtain absolution; but now that falsehood lies heavier at my heart than all my other sins" (113). Scarry writes that during the torture process, "the torturers are producing a mime in which the one annihilated shifts to being the agent of his own annihilation" (47); Justine, falsely admitting her guilt, justifies her own execution.

While Justine participates, it is only to acquiesce to a prejudgment made by the judges over which she has no other control. She is no willing stand-in for the Creature. In fact, she serves to highlight the Creature's categorically irredeemable nature in contrast to her own access to contrition and absolution. This practice reintegrates even "the most depraved of human creatures" (120) into the Christian community in their last moments, a right to which the creature has no recourse.[1] Of course, Justine is innocent, and the only guilt in the events is shared by the judges and the Creature who has orchestrated the

---

1   It is interesting to note that the theme recurs later in the text: the Creature, apostrophising the deceased Victor, asks, "what does it avail that I now ask thee to pardon me?"(Shelley 240).

events. If we accept that the creature himself is the victim of torture, however, then we can also implicate his torturers by extension. Victor, notably, feels guilt and responsibility for Justine's plight and understands himself as having caused her death. He expresses compassion for her, which, she says, "removes more than half [her] misfortune" (114) and "consoles" her even though she is to "suffer ignominy and death" (113). Victor also decides that his contempt for the "monsters" of the convicting court is "unjust" (120) given the circumstances. But in spite of his complicity, he can extend no sympathy to the Creature or acknowledge responsibility for *his* suffering.

The one aspect of Scarry's model that is still lacking an analogue in *Frankenstein* is a containing torture chamber, apart, that is, from the world itself. This fact, in conjunction with the superimposed attempts at rehabilitation and torture, accounts for many of the text's moral ambiguities. The untapped possibilities hinted at in *Frankenstein* are signalled in the structure of the text, a matter emphasized in Elanor Salotto's examination of overlapping multiple narratives in *Frankenstein*.

> The text is involved in a dialectic between presenting the self and the subsequent absenting of the self. The artificial assemblage of the body parts of the creature signifies that body and narrative parts are productions to be put on. And Shelley rearranges those parts to suggest a new assemblage of fictional selves continually wandering away from origins···. (200)

The multiplicity of narrative voices ensures each speaker"s liberty and versatility.[1] Pertinent to this discussion is the idea of the self as some-

---

1 Salotto is concerned with developing a feminist reading of Frankenstein in which the multiplicity of narrative voice is cast as a means for a female writer to resist restrictive classifications. While the political implications of the argument cannot be dealt with here, this idea of a decentralized identity that resists categorization is clearly pertinent.

thing that can be inserted, hidden, and expressed through other voices.

The difference between Scarry's torture chamber and the experience of the Creature is the inevitability of the outcome. As Walton recounts, "I shut my eyes involuntarily, and endeavoured to recollect what were my duties⋯. I called on him [the creature] to stay" (240). Walton, even though indoctrinated against the creature by Victor, is able to restrain his visceral response and to converse with the Creature. The only difference between Walton and any other interlocutor is that he has access to Victor's narrative, which serves to prepare him against shock. And yet the resulting interaction is not undercut by rejection or violence. The scene suggests that the exiled Creature of *Frankenstein* has simply been in constant need of an introduction.

The subtitle of Scarry"s book is "The Making and Unmaking of the World," significantly not "the unmaking and remaking"; Scarry's model teaches us something general about our relationship with our world and the communities through which it is formed. In Shelley's open-ended novel, the Creature does not die *in* the text; his annihilation is only suggested as his form is "lost in darkness and distance" (Shelley 244), and the problem he represents continues beyond the text. The question we are left with: if we find the Creature to be sympathetic in his noble aspirations, pitiable in his loneliness, coerced by the terrible pain inflicted on him, and yet "monstrous" for his premeditated actions, what does that mean for our understanding of the boundaries of individual identity? The difficulty in assigning any unilateral culpability in *Frankenstein*, in spite of the usefulness of Scarry's model in the text"s structural tensions, suggests that all members (and would-be members) of a community bear responsibility for the world they collectively create.

WORKS CITED

Arendt, Hanna. *Eichmann in Jerusalem: A Report on the Banality of Evil.* 1963. 2nd ed. Harmondsworth: Penguin, 1977.

Baldick, Chris. *In Frankenstein's Shadow: Myth, Monstosity, and Nineteenth-Century Writing.* Oxford: Clarendon, 1987.

Gigante, Denise. "Facing the Ugly: The Case of Frankenstein." *ELH* 67:2 (Summer 2000): 565-87.

Godwin, William. *Enquiry Concerning Political Justice and its Influence on Morals and Happiness.* 1793. 3rd ed. 1978. Ed. F. E. L. Priestly. Vol. 2. Toronto: University of Toronto P, 1946.

Marshall, David. "Adam Smith and the Theatricality of Moral Sentiments." *Critical Inquiry* 10:4 (Summer 1984): 592-613.

Macdonald, D.L. and Kathleen Scherf. Introduction. *Frankenstein. By Mary Shelley.* Peterborough, Canada: Broadview, 2003. 11-38.

Milton, John. *Paradise Lost.* 1667. Ed. John Leonard. *John Milton: The Complete Poems.* Harmondsworth: Penguin, 1998.

Salotto, Elanor. "*Frankenstein* and Dis(re)membered Identity." *Journal of Narrative Technique* 23 (Fall 1994): 190-211.

Scarry, Elaine. *The Body in Pain: The Making and Unmaking of the World.* New York: Oxford UP, 1985.

Shelley, Mary. *Frankenstein.* 1818. Ed. D.L. Macdonald and Kathleen Scherf. Peterborough, Canada: Broadview, 2003.

Smith, Adam. *The Theory of Moral Sentiments.* 1759. Amherst: Prometheus, 2000.

Technology and Impotence in Mary Shelley's *Frankenstein*

Thomas Vargish*

AT THE MIDPOINT OF ALBERT CAMUS' EAMOUS PHILO-SOPHICAL novel *The Stranger* (*L'Étranger,* 1942), the protagonist, Meursault, kills an Arab. He appears to shoot involuntarily, overcome with the heat, the sun, the sweat in his eyes, the blinding reflection from the Arab's knife, the wine at lunch, fatigue, thirst. When he realizes what he has done, how he has "shattered the balance of the day, the spacious calm of this beach on which I had been happy," he deliberately chooses to fire four more shots into the "inert body."[1] The meaning of these additional shots has become a legendary crux of twentieth-century philosophy and literary criticism in numerous debates concerning the existential nature of human freedom and the nature of human freedom in Existentialism. But there exists another approach to the act, one that bypasses the familiar philosophical and psychological centers of the debate. This other, apparently philistine, approach I learned from a friend, a professor of engineering. He pointed out that Meursault shoots the Arab because the Arab has only a knife and he has a gun. The gun makes the catastrophe possible, "because," as my friend observed, "when you have the technology you use it."

The effect of technology on human action, its influence on individual choice and institutional change, is the knotty center of its relation to our freedom, to our autonomy. Camus' novel suggests that Meursault's initial shot was largely determined by the protagonist's sur-

---

* 이 글은 2009년에 출판된 *An International Journal of the Humanities*의 36권 321-337쪽에 수록된 것임.

1 Albert Camus, *The Stranger*, trans. Stuart Gilbert (New York: Vintage, 1954), 76.

roundings and by the gun in his hand, that the influence of his own will was minimized by the forces of the environment and the technology, and that firing the gun was effectively involuntary. Then, perhaps in order to reassert the primacy of his own will and choice, Meursault fires the additional, "undetermined" shots in an act that can be seen as "free," the *acte gratuit* explored by earlier writers (like André Gide) interested in the problematic of choice and causality. Meursault yields to external influences in firing the first round, but then regains command by choosing to fire the next four. The potential cost to his own interests (to say nothing of those of the Arab) suggests the importance he attaches to his power of choice. We can see that the ethical difficulties involved in the analysis of such choice can compound rapidly, as my engineer friend knew. His point was not that these questions involving choice and freedom and morality have no practical content but that the technology at hand influences the content by altering the possibilities of action, changing its range and timing and radically enlarging its consequences. Or, to put the matter more simply, the technology can usurp power traditionally reserved to human will.

Technology usurps and empowers simultaneously. It usurps authority at precisely the moment of empowerment, and this paradoxical effect means that all serious discussion of technology must involve a discussion of values. Technology appears to usurp the value-function, substituting its own imperatives at moments of choice, moments when we would desire and expect the application of values we think of as "human." Technological developments have a way of intersecting or ambushing the traditional values or at least of radically altering the contexts in which they operate, a fact of immense political consequence. We can see, for example, that the absolute political dictatorships of the preceding century relied heavily on techniques of surveillance and oppression unavailable to their predecessors. Such reliance has also been explored in numerous novels and films that deal with the perversions of technology in dystopias. Among the most influential of these are Yevgeny Zamyatin's *We* (1920), Aldous Huxley's *Brave New World* (1932), and George Orwell's *1984* (1949). These novels make the point that certain kinds of moral or ethical choice (and certain kinds of repression of ethical choice) would be impossible without certain technological achievements. This strongly indicates that our values never exist independent of the means of empowerment — our tools, our technology — but operate in a kind of intimate duality of alliance and conflict with them. It is the potential for conflict between the technology and the values that gives rise to the fear of usurpation, the fear of technology's influence on our freedom and autonomy.

Technology and Usurpation

Over the past two centuries this fear has been embodied in a narrative, now raised by its universally felt significance to the status of myth, the myth of Frankenstein. From its archetypal expression in Mary Shelley's novel (*Frankenstein, or The Modern Prometheus*, 1818; revised by the author 1831) the myth of a technological abortion or "monster" ranging out of ethical control has continued to grow. The story formed the basis of numerous nineteenth-century stage productions, such as Richard Brinsley Peake's significantly titled *Presumption; or The Fate of Frankenstein* (1823). The narrative's immense success in all its multiple permutations testifies to its continuing cultural relevance and it is not surprising that its perpetuation in the twentieth and twenty-first centuries was largely the work the most technologically advanced medium, film. From the beginnings of cinema as a popular art, Frankenstein's monster has repeatedly come to life on the screen — and usually as the creation that threatens its creator. Even before James Whale's *Frankenstein* (1931) and his equally admired *Bride of Frankenstein* (1935), both with Boris Karloff, there was a one-reel *Frankenstein* in 1910 and a five-reel *Life Without a Soul* in 1915.[1]

1　Albert J. LaValley, "The Stage and Film Children of Frankenstein: A Survey";

Many more could be added, varying in quality from the silliest heavy-handed contemporary production of *Mary Shelley's Frankenstein* (Kenneth Branagh, 1994) to such loving and lovable spoofs as *Young Frankenstein* (Mel Brooks, 1974).

Nor does the myth require containment exclusively in Dr. Frankenstein's own laboratory. There were versions of it in Robert Wiene's *The Cabinet of Dr. Caligari* (1919) and Paul Wegener's *The Golem* (1920). It has never gone out of fashion and in recent years the movies have offered numerous versions of a creation usurping the space, the freedom, the power, even the time of its creator. Among the most successful of these have been Stanley Kubrick's *2001: A Space Odyssey* (1968) in which the ship's computer tries to take over the mission; Michael Crichton's *Westworld* (1973) where a renegade robot, the nearly perfect Yul Brynner, starts shooting the resort's guests; and Ridley Scott's superb *Blade Runner* (1982, director's cut 1991) which represents the doomed rebellion of a small group of "replicants." It is almost unnecessary to cite the immensely successful *The Terminator* (1984) and *Terminator 2: Judgment Day* (1991), both directed by James Cameron, in which the ethical character of the robots, like their appearance, shifts ground and in which "the war against the machines" leads to human hands-on destruction of the most advanced technology — demonstrating that while technology is about what we can do it is also always leads to questions of what we will agree to do and not to do, what we will accept and what we will refuse. There is even a scene in *Terminator 2* where the brilliant scientist tries to destroy the world-threatening microchip with an ordinary axe.

To those who are not science fiction or film enthusiasts it will seem as if I'm offering more detail than necessary to make this point. In fact, I've cited a very small proportion of the films pertinent to

William Nestrick, "Frankenstein and the Nature of Film Narrative"; both articles in *The Endurance of Frankenstein: Essays on Mary Sheiiey's Novel*, ed. George Levine and U. C. Knoepflmacher (Berkeley: University of California Press, 1982).

this discussion, and if I were to include the relevant novels since the original *Frankenstein* my case would drown in its own evidence. Probably the major preoccupation of popular culture over the past century has been the tendency of technological developments to invade and disempower traditional values. This is evidence not just of our interest in the problems posed by technology; this is evidence of a cultural obsession. We can't seem to get enough of this narrative. It's our chief story, a myth comparable to that of the loss of paradise and the fall of man in Genesis. It is in fact our version of that myth, expressed as the fall of humanity from a projected technological paradise into an actual technological crisis. All of the films mentioned here deal with the same subject: *what it means to he human.* In terms of the Frankenstein myth, the myth of our technology, this philosophical problem can be broken down into two decisive ethical questions: What are the limits of legitimate power, of authority that can claim to be ethical? And how are these limits related to our freedom to choose — given that in our culture this freedom and power have been bound up since the Book of Genesis with our vision of our identity as special beings, as chosen, as human?

Such questions indicate the deep implications of technology, its persistent tendency to lead us far beyond considerations of material progress or manipulations of our physical environment. I will be exploring them in more concrete and specific terms when I turn to an analysis of Mary Shelley's *Frankenstein,* the one remarkable primary version of the myth that still touches on everything. But as a preface to that I want to propose a working definition of technology that will locate it strictly in relation to our discussion of values.

Technology is not a value in the same fundamental sense that antiquity, humility, freedom, or power are values. It serves to express, aid, and extend values. Values tend to be ends in themselves rather than means, though they often function as empowering motives. Technology derives from the Greek word *techne,* meaning art, craft, skill, and it carries connotations of organized, systematic activity. In ancient Greek and Roman culture, and to a lesser degree in European culture generally up through the eighteenth century, *technology* tended to be the realm of the "mechanical," meaning the province of those who labored with their hands, and therefore of slaves and other craftspeople. Their social status can be deduced from the words of the Tribune Flavius at the beginning of Shakespeare's *Julius Caesar:*

> What, know you not.
> Being mechanical, you ought not walk
> Upon a laboring day without the sign
> Of your profession? Speak, what trade art thou?[1]

The skill or trade lay in the hands and the hands provide the link between the person and the tool, the nexus of the human with the nonhuman.

This central significance of the human hand as the connection between the brain and the environment, between the mind and the world perhaps inherits its force from the long process of our evolution and the aboriginal reciprocity between our nature and our culture. From the pebble axe to the laurel leaf blade our brains as well as our minds grew with our technology. And this intimate connection between what we do and what we are often finds an emblem in the human hand. This appears to be well understood or at least intuited by the latter day manipulators of the Frankenstein myth. It is still exciting to watch Boris Karloff reach out toward the light in his great interpretation of the monster and then to notice how his huge and awkward hands, hanging from his wrists like unfamiliar tools, seem to change their character from pathetic and imploring to menacing. In *Westworld* the easiest way to tell a robot from a guest is to look

---

1 William Shakespeare, Mus Caesar, ed. S. F. Johnson (Harmondsworth: Penguin Books, 1987), 27 (1.1.2-5).

at its hands, because, as one guest puts it, "Supposedly you can't tell, except by looking at the hands. They haven't perfected the hand yet."[1] In *Blade Runner* the revealing organ is the eye (though this requires a careful screening and verbal test to determine the origin of the being), but the hand is not forgotten. The chief replicant, played by Rutger Hauer, finds as he begins to die that his hand starts to go first. He breaks two of the blade runner's fingers in revenge for the loss of his friends (fellow replicants) and drives a nail into his own palm in a twisted bit of Christ symbolism — but also to keep his hand functioning. In *Terminator 2*, the surviving pieces of the previous terminator are a microchip (to represent its brain) and an exquisite metal forearm and hand. When the "good" terminator needs to prove his identity to the prospective inventor of the lethal chip, he strips the skin from his arm and displays the working of his bright metal hand — a duplicate of the surviving part.

Dr. Frankenstein's Disease

Mechanisms like pebble axes and computers and robots are tools, extensions of the hand of the being that devises them. A question thus arises almost naturally of at what point the tool assumes an identity separate from its creator or owner, at what point it acquires autonomy. At what point does the creature have the right to assert independence, to exercise choice, to create in its own right? The Frankenstein myth thus raises rich and complex possibilities for those who see themselves as creations, as God's creatures or as Nature's, and also as potential creators (even if "only" as parents). Are human beings unique in their prerogative to think of themselves both as creatures and as creators? Are we the only creations with authority to create? Or, to question the

---

1 Westworld (1973), dir. Michael Crichton, perf. Richard Benjamin, Yul Brynner, James Brolin.

dark side of the parable that rises from our technology, in what sense are we ourselves tools of the universe, employed or discarded without consultation, without freedom? It was the fear aroused by these resonant speculations, a kind of echoing awe, that Mary Shelley sought in her story of Dr. Frankenstein.

We can enter further into the source of this fear by asking whether it is simple ignorance that leads people who have not read the novel to assume that the name Frankenstein refers to the monster rather than the scientist. The confusion is rich in implication. It suggests a merging of identity that implicates the creator in his creation: there exists a sense in which the creation images the creator and perhaps there is even a sense in which the monster (the technological achievement ranging out of control) represents an extension of the human scientist (the technologist who ought to be in control). The confusion of the creation with the creator also suggests a familial, hereditary lineage in which the offspring carries the name of the father and so becomes his link with the future, his representative through time. It is this ancient assertion of parent-child identification that I want to pursue at the beginning of my analysis of the novel

We first notice that Mary Shelley took pains to give Victor Frankenstein a happy childhood under the care of devoted parents. His description of their attitude toward their parental duties is striking:

> I was their plaything and their idol, and something better — their child, the innocent and helpless creature bestowed on them by Heaven, whom to bring up to good, and whose future lot it was in their hands to direct to happiness or misery, according as they fulfilled their duties toward me.[1]

The idea that the parents have duties toward their children is of

---

1 Mary Shelley, *Frankenstein, or The Modern Prometheus*, ed. Maurice Hindle (New York: Penguin Books, 2003), 35. This text is based on the third edition (1831) and contains Shelley's final revisions.

course a familiar one to parents, but in view of Victor Frankenstein's future abandonment of his creation (a kind of child, as the monster sees himself) this emphasis on his own parents' feelings of duty toward him seems very carefully planted:

> With this deep consciousness of what they owed toward the being to which they had given life, added to the active spirit of tenderness that animated both, it may be imagined that while during every hour of my infant life I received a lesson of patience, of charity, and of self-control, I was so guided by a silken cord that all seemed but one train of enjoyment to me. (35)

What Mary Shelley stresses here is the sacred duty of parenthood rooted in religious belief and practice, the obligation of parents to act as providential agents toward their children, to act as stewards for divine benevolence in relation to their offspring:

> No human being could have passed a happier childhood than myself. My parents were possessed by the very spirit of kindness and indulgence. We felt they were not the tyrants to rule our lot according to their caprice, but the agents and creators of all the many delights which we enjoyed. (39)

With these lessons behind him it seems strange that Dr. Frankenstein can extend no such care to his own creation.

He fails because he misconceives his primary relationship with the monster. When he discovers the secret of life ("animation") Frankenstein sees himself as a kind of surrogate providence. Having penetrated "the deepest mysteries of creation" (49), he imagines his creatures' gratitude flowing his way rather than recognizing his obligations toward them:

> A new species would bless me as its creator and source; many happy and excellent natures would owe their being to me. No father could

claim the gratitude of his child so completely as I should deserve
theirs. (55)

He will not only be a parent; he will be a god to his creatures. They
will worship him and this arrangement he presents as a kind of paradise.

As Mary Shelley's early nineteenth-century readers would have understood without effort, Frankenstein is bent on usurpation. He plans
to employ his new technology to create a race of dependents who
will worship and praise *him*, usurping what was almost universally
regarded as a divine prerogative. In what must certainly have seemed
to Mary Shelley a distinctly masculine attitude toward generation
(she wrote the novel amid extreme trials of maternity and loss), Frankenstein views his scientific paternity as the legitimate gratification
of vanity and the extension of his authority. But in fact he violates a
primal contract, the universal contract between creator and created,
which specifies that the father owes his children the means to live,
that creation mandates nurture.

Frankenstein can create but he cannot nourish. His instant, self-
indulgent, petulant rejection of the monster confirms the catastrophe.
After two years of work putting the creature together he finally gives
it life. Exhausted, he has a dream in which his fiancée turns into his
dead mother in her shroud (a precious moment for psychoanalytic
dispositions as suggesting the incestuous interaction between desire
and death) and awakes to find his creature staring at him:

> I beheld the wretch — the miserable monster whom I had created.
> He held up the curtain of the bed; and his eyes, if eyes they may be
> called, were fixed on me. His jaws opened, and he muttered some
> inarticulate sounds, while a grin wrinkled his cheeks···. one hand was
> stretched out, seemingly to detain me, but I escaped···. Oh! no mortal
> could support the horror of that countenance. (59)

Ignoring the near miracle of his own achievement and the infantile plea of his creature (it resembles a grotesque infant). Dr. Frankenstein rejects it on strictly aesthetic grounds. Why? The passages in which he tries to explain this rejection are painful to read, profoundly troubling in their hysterical rationale of paternal abandonment. And that rejection of providential stewardship carries with it troubling suggestions of cosmic abandonment, of creatures destitute of provision because their creator cannot or will not nourish. In the specific case of Dr. Frankenstein we can conclude that he rejects his creation because it does him no credit, because it is hideous, because it images something about himself that he cannot bear to acknowledge. It suggests that *he* is a monster. The story of Dr. Frankenstein is the story of a man with a breakthrough and it is even more the story of his breakdown. After he rejects the monster, denies his paternity, the monster roams loose on the world, creating suffering and havoc, especially for its creator.

Dr. Frankenstein had a choice. In fact he had a number of choices. He chose to usurp the prerogatives of God, of the Creator of living things. This the novel treats as a mistake, and Frankenstein himself comes to see it that way, especially when in a characteristic fit of disgust he destroys the mate he has promised the monster. Human knowledge, as Faustus learned before Frankenstein, should not extend into the prerogatives of the divine. And yet there is a sense in which this argument remains unconvincing, verging toward mere conventional moral pap. Mary Shelley's initial intended audience was her radical poet husband and the man who gave nihilism its romance. Lord Byron. The Shelleyan free spirit and the Byronic hero were not to be constrained or even limited by such pieties. In fact, the real usurpation, betrayal, ultimate failure lies not in the heroic act of creation but in the more pedestrian act of denial, of withdrawing when confronted with dire need. The problem is not at this point with power in itself; the problem is with the consequences of creative power, of potency. The problem lies not with the science or the tools themselves but with where they have taken us.

One way to see how prophetically Mary Shelley caught this direction in her representation of Frankenstein's failure is to cover the structure of the novel with a specific psychological grid, itself a technological achievement. The grid I propose to use is Freud's dramatic early twentieth-century reconstruction of the self as composed of ego, superego, and id. This emblematic pattern fits the novel's psychological structure almost perfectly, with Frankenstein as the narratingsentient ego or "I"; the idealized, selfless, virtuous Elizabeth (the narrator's betrothed) as superego; and the monster as denied id. Why this fit seems almost watertight may amount to little more than a serendipity of cultural history, but more probably derives from the function of psychoanalysis to sum up so much of those nineteenth century quandaries and aspirations of duty and fulfillment, the internal warfare of desire with morality, that Mary Shelley's novel suggestively illuminates. Freud's theories would in this context embody a *fin de siècle* attempt to come to terms with the elemental psychological forces celebrated in European Romanticism from the French Revolution through the first decades of the nineteenth century, the period of *Frankenstein's* composition.

Psychoanalysis may be seen as a method for making a voyage of discovery, an internal expedition into the unknown, and it was sometimes regarded as a kind of irresponsible adventuring into the monstrous that might awaken destabilizing passions difficult to put back in order. Sigmund Freud was ambivalently regarded — and has sometimes been celebrated — as a kind of Faust figure going beyond the boundaries established by morality and religion, the boundaries Frankenstein comes to regret transgressing. Freud's discovery, psychoanalysis, the "talking cure," seemed for a time to promise imperial governance of a region that had been beyond rational control because it was beyond scientific knowledge, the region of the unconscious. Freud proposed an inward voyage of discovery and devised the technology to take it.

It may be because of these affinities that a dynamic application of psychoanalytic terminology applies so neatly to *Frankenstein*. We have, first of all, the speaking ego — two of them in fact. The first narrator, Walton, foreshadows the narrator Frankenstein, for whom he feels an intense admiration and sympathy. Walton is engaged in a literal voyage of discovery to "the pole" — which he incredibly imagines as a kind of paradise. For our purposes of psychoanalytic application his self-justification must be quoted at some length:

> I try in vain to be persuaded that the pole is the seat of frost and desolation; it ever presents itself to my imagination as the region of beauty and delight. There, Margaret, the sun is for ever visible, its broad disk just skirting the horizon, and diffusing a perpetual splendor⋯. there snow and frost are banished; and, sailing over a calm sea, we may be wafted to a land surpassing in wonders and in beauty every region hitherto discovered on the habitable globe⋯. What may not be expected in a country of eternal light?⋯ I shall satiate my ardent curiosity with the sight of a part of the world never before visited, and may tread a land never before imprinted by the foot of man. These are my enticements, and they are sufficient to conquer all fear of danger or death, and to induce me to commence this laborious voyage with the joy a child feels when he embarks in a little boat, with his holiday mates, on an expedition of discovery up his native river. (15-16)

If we compare this rationale with Frankenstein's own self-indulgent wish to play providence to the creatures he expects to create, we can see that it contains — as an introductory parallel — the same psychological elements. It reveals a childish, narcissistic self-preoccupation in which all events and all animate beings become relevant only as they contribute to the gratification of the perceiving ego. The fantasized untrodden, virgin country exists concentrically for the happiness of the discoverer. But as the novel demonstrates, Walton is not on a child's "expedition of discovery" with his "holiday mates," but on a dangerous excursion over the broad, mysterious, treacherous sea of unexplored knowledge; and his "mates," when they find themselves seriously threatened, challenge his authority with mutiny.

In the same letter to his sister, Walton adds that before he became an explorer he "became a poet, and for one year lived in a Paradise of my own creation." The idea of a paradise of one's own creation is itself regressive and narcissistic, implying as it does that the self is all-in-all and ignoring as it must the outcome of the original mythic experience of paradise. We could see it as an expression of the Romantic ego — representatives of which Mary Shelley had closely in view in Byron and her husband, perhaps the type of poets "whose effusions," according to Walton, "entranced my soul" (16). In any case, this egocentric impulse toward infantile gratification of primitive impulses at all costs, when isolated from those social contexts that contain, integrate, and contextualize desire, produces the monstrous. And the penalty for this, as Frankenstein (still showing ambivalence toward his creation) tells Walton, is to be condemned to pursue and eradicate one's product. This parable is the parable of technology: as the tool extends its power, the ego that directs it becomes more dangerous and more liable to self-destruction.

When Frankenstein realizes that his technology rather than producing "excellent beings" actually leads to the monstrous, he rejects it. He tries to treat the monster as merely a failed experiment, not as an intimate extension of himself. With a self-absorbed masculine gesture of denial he tries to walk away. But this doesn't work. It doesn't work because the monster is Frankenstein more fully and more intimately than any natural child could be. Mary Shelley shows this in many ingenious ways, all of them subject to astonishingly straight-forward psychoanalytic explanation.

In the first place, when his younger brother William is killed, Frankenstein realizes immediately and intuitively that the monster must be responsible: "Nothing in human shape could have destroyed that fair child. *He* was the murderer! I could not doubt it. The mere presence of the idea was an irresistible proof of the fact." This equation between the speculation and the confirmation suggests — with one of those preternatural insights that romantic writers sought — an internal fusing between imagination and evidence, conception and explanation. Frankenstein knows what his monster does because the monster is his own:

> I considered the being whom I had cast among mankind, and endowed with the will and power to effect purposes of horror, such as the deed which he had now done, nearly in the light of my own vampire, my own spirit let loose from the grave, and forced to destroy all that was dear to me. (78)

As Freud was to conclude, the id contains two primal forces, eros (sexual desire or love) and thanatos (aggression or death). Only eros can be socialized, redirected and diffused (and in cases of extreme achievement, sublimated) toward a consideration of the well-being of others. Thanatos, the destructive power, retains its original direction and cannot be socialized. Bit by bit the monster loses its capacity to love because the social impulse, eros, is perpetually blocked. The monster turns to evil because it has nowhere else to go, and it has nowhere else to go because Frankenstein, its origin and source, has *denied* it. And as in psychoanalytic theory, the denial, the repression, cannot last: the monster returns.

This repeated act of denial has consequences for the ego, the narrating "I," just as Freud said it would. After he denies the monster, Frankenstein becomes less and less effectual, less potent. When duty clearly calls on him to testify as to his creation and save the falsely condemned Justine Marie from execution for little William's murder (the monster has framed her), Frankenstein cannot act: "my purpose of avowal died away on my lips" (90). When confronted with another being in dire need he again freezes. The paralysis derives directly from repression: unless the ego acknowledges the forces of the id, the id will rule—and so the monster does.

From a psychoanalytic standpoint, the most interesting consequences of the denial have to do with Frankenstein's relation to his betrothed, the sublimely virtuous Elizabeth. She represents all goodness and appears to be without longings for herself. She grew up alongside Frankenstein, like a sister, like a possession (as he first regards her), and he demonstrates a pronounced lack of passion for her. After all, she is already eternally his own. Rather than erotic fulfillment, she comes to stand for the obligations of social normalcy; marriage to her represents the life the narrator *ought* to enjoy but for which he shows little active inclination. In Mary Shelley's novel, as often in psycho-analysis, when a man denies his monster he goes limp. Frankenstein puts Elizabeth off so often that she offers to release him from his engagement; he rejects this idea and then continues to put her off. He treats her as she treats herself, as devoid of erotic inclination and as infinitely patient and virtuous. In fact she *embodies* patience and virtue, the distillation of altruism, and so almost beyond earthly accommodation, a Christian superego of devotion and selflessness.

This psychological / ethical allegory is not hidden in the novel, but insisted upon (though not, of course, in Freudian terms). Mary Shelley's achievement lies not in disguising it (as it might be disguised in a patient under psychoanalysis) but in fleshing it out in credible character, in making it believable. It is in fact so bold as to run to the grotesque. When Frankenstein destroys the monster's uncompleted mate in violation of their agreement, the monster tells him: "remember, I shall be with you on your wedding-night." The simple and straight-forward interpretation here seems perfectly obvious to the reader: as you destroyed my mate I will destroy yours. Even the makers of the crassest Frankenstein films can see this. But in the novel, Frankenstein himself bedded in his internal negotiations, lost in his solipsistic nar-

cissism, thinks that the threat refers to his *own* safety. In his characteristic inactive lethargy he muses:

> Why had I not followed him and closed with him in mortal strife?
> But I had suffered him to depart, and he had directed his course
> towards the mainland. I shuddered to think who might be the next
> victim sacrificed to his insatiate revenge. And then I thought again
> of his words — *"I will be with you on your wedding-night"* That then
> was the period fixed for the fulfillment of my destiny. In that hour I
> should die, and at once satisfy and extinguish his malice. The prospect
> did not move me to fear; yet when I thought of my beloved Eliza-
> beth, — of her tears and endless sorrow, when she should find her
> lover so barbarously snatched from her, — tears, the first I had shed
> for many months, streamed from my eyes, and I resolved not to fall
> before my enemy without a bitter struggle. (173)

What finally makes him weep is the image of Elizabeth's potential
grief for the loss of himself — clearly in his view the ultimate de-
pravation — and again the emotion is self-referential, self-recreating.
It will do *her* no good. In fact, like a patient with a deeply repressed
secret, the secret of the monster, the narrating ego will ignore the obvious. The sane reader finds it grotesque that Frankenstein cannot see
the sane monster's evident intention to kill the sublimated Elizabeth: it
is the *superego* that the id is after! And the thought is not far off that
if anything at all is to happen on the wedding night the monster had
better be there. The ego will be impotent.

Technology and Freedom

How, in this discussion of technology, did we get from power to
impotence? What is it about technological power that seems to lead
to weakness? Or, to put the question in terms of our discussion of Dr.
Frankenstein and his succeeding permutations in our cultural history,
do his weaknesses reappear in our current technological advances? To

what extent are his liabilities general to our contemporary technology? Do we still self-indulgently create and consume our creations without forethought? Do we lose ourselves in self-congratulation? Do we evade the full consequences of our advances: denying the ugly while claiming the beautiful, forgetting the new sickness while celebrating the new cure, ignoring the impoverishment while squandering the wealth? All thoughtful people know the answer to these questions — though some might add that we show a few late signs of improvement. But this is not the place, and I am not the writer to enter on a polemic against our technology (I love it too). My point is that to exercise true authority the liabilities of the vast technological extensions of power must be recognized. And by this I do not mean the acknowledged damage to the physical and cultural environment. I mean the inner liabilities. Dr. Frankenstein's liabilities, that such extensions of power bring so vividly to light and make so dangerous.

Technology brings into sharp relief the implications for authority of a relatively new conception of freedom, the conception of radical individual self-determination. This conception may be the dominant one today, and so familiar to most Americans and many Europeans that it goes almost unquestioned, especially after its development in anti-totalitarian, anti-deterministic movements such as Existentialism (Meursault's costly freedom) and especially as it functions as a premise: that the right of the individual to self-determination is primary. We forget that this idea has achieved respectability only very recently and that its numerous problems are still in process of resolution.

Traditional, socially contextual conceptions of freedom were questioned and revised during the European Enlightenment (the seventeenth and eighteenth centuries) and the American and French revolutions. They were radically challenged or abandoned during the Romantic period (approximately the period from the French Revolution through the first third of the nineteenth century), the period of Mary Shelley's *Frankenstein*. There had of course been earlier representations of individuals who denied their social or religious obligations, immoralists and nihilists like Edmund in Shakespeare's *King Lear* or like Marlowe's Dr. Faustus. But such characters were conscious of their alienation and of their war to the death with the moral world around them. Dr. Frankenstein must be among the first characters to feel socially justified in his unlimited pursuit of knowledge. He manages to ignore established boundaries and obligations without seeing himself as a social outcast — at least at first. In showing the consequences for him and his community, Mary Shelley follows and continues an intense speculation on the nature of human beings and their social obligations. As we have seen, her conclusions are not optimistic. Her protagonist ends up in a riddle of escape and pursuit, pursued by and pursuing his monster.

What brings the question of such radical freedom to our immediate attention is its association with technological advance. *Because* he conceives of himself as ethically unfettered, Frankenstein develops the science to create, or at least to recreate, life. He masters the technology to create a monster. The mastery, the power, appears to be inseparable from the freedom to achieve it and this freedom depends upon the ability to conceive of oneself as socially unfettered, a free creative spirit, someone paradoxically licensed to transgress ethical boundaries in the name of social progress. In this regard Dr. Frankenstein is a twisted predecessor of Raskolnikov as a failed *Übermensch*. The concept and the practice of technological advance take on a new and unpredictable character, the character of the free creator, a godlike character, the character of usurpation. The achievement of this character is potentially costly: in the case of Frankenstein and his many cultural descendants the cost appears to be the denial of those values that seemed for most of our history to constitute our humanity. Radical self-determination can lead us out of the realm of the human, at least out of the traditionally human. Paradoxically, the consequent psychological crisis can be expressed in terms of impotence; the power lures us to a social, ethical, emotional desert, to death rather than life.

Finally, this crisis leads to a general realization about our technology: that it is *us*. Frankenstein's monster is Frankenstein; the creation expresses the creator. The bomb, pollution, land-mines, poison gas, the stealth bomber are us. And so are motion pictures, relativity theory, vaccines, foreign aid, language, the symphony orchestra, durable pigments. It enriches our conception and our exercise of authority to know this, to acknowledge it. Our tools, far from being alien and inhuman, richly express human aspirations. Only we can use them: they are fitted to our hands. I am typing on the keyboard of my computer and I might be at the controls of an F-22 or holding a lariat or a violin. I can't deny that these tools express me, are made in my image. The Frankenstein myth tells me what will happen if I deny the resemblance. As Emerson summed it up in his essay on self-reliance, "My giant goes with me wherever I go."[1]

1 Ralph Waldo Emerson, Ralph Waldo Emerson: A Critical Edition of the Major Works, ed. Richard Poirier (New York: Oxford University Press, 1990), 46.

김일영

Univ. of Georgia (영문학 석사)
Univ. of South Carolina (영문학 박사)
한국 18세기 영문학회 고문
한국 근대영미소설학회 회장
성균관대학교 영문학과 교수

저서
「18세기 영국소설 강의」, 「영미소설해설총서: 트리스트람섄디」

역서
「업둥이 톰 존스 이야기 I」, 「업둥이 톰 존스 이야기 II」

논문
「로렌스 스턴과 포스트모더니즘」, 「The Nature of Game in Laurence Sterne」
「필딩의 "새로운 글쓰기"와 이중적 재현」, 「선정소설에 나타난 여성의 광기」
「불확실성과 "중간자"에 대한 공포: 전환기 시대의 고딕 「드라큘라」」 외 다수

MARY WOLLSTONECRAFT SHELLEY

Frankenstein or The Modern Prometheus
WITH ESSAYS IN CRITICISM

프랑켄스타인 – 주석과 비평

1판 1쇄 발행 _ 2013년 8월 25일
1판 3쇄 발행 _ 2021년 2월 25일

편 주 자 · 김 일 영
발 행 인 · 정 현 걸
발   행 · 신 아 사
인   쇄 · 대명프린팅
주   소 · 서울특별시 은평구 녹번동28–36 2층(122–826)
전   화 · (02) 382-6411 팩 스 · (02) 382-6401
홈페이지 · www.shinasa.co.kr
E-mail · shinasa@daum.net
출판등록 · 1956년 1월 5일(제9-52호)

ISBN: 978-89-8396-821-0(93840)

정가 15,000원